‖‖‖‖‖‖‖‖‖‖‖‖‖‖‖‖‖‖‖

◁ **W9-APV-356**

THE DARK VISITOR

A roaring sound rose outside the hall. It appeared like a whirlwind of black clouds, dropping in a corkscrewing pillar toward the floor. The pillar's base landed near by the fire, just before Finn's platform. As it did, the upper portion of it sank instantly down, the winds dying, the darkness fading away, disclosing an ominous form.

It was cloaked from head to foot in a black robe and seemed at first a slender column of dark stone. But then arms slowly lifted, raising out wide sleeves like raven's wings. The head came up, shaking back a hood to reveal the lean and lined face of the Dark Druid.

"So, these are the mortals who dare to oppose my will," he sneered. "A sorry lot, like all their kind."

"The Dark Druid!" Sabd cried in a despairing voice.

"Ah, there you are, my little fawn," he crowed triumphantly. "You didn't really believe you could escape me, did you?"

He stepped toward her and she cowered back. But Finn moved to draw her behind him, facing the druid with a look of defiance.

"Get back from her," he warned. "She has been given sanctuary here."

The druid stopped. His gaze flickered over the fair young man. "You would be well advised not to trouble me, boy," he said in a commanding tone. His right arm lifted higher, bringing into view from the robe's folds the long staff he gripped. "Stand away now, and I'll not harm you." The druid stepped forward, swinging up his staff to point its silver tip at Finn...

Bantam Spectra Books by Kenneth C. Flint
Ask your bookseller for the titles you have missed

A STORM UPON ULSTER
THE RIDERS OF THE SIDHE
CHAMPIONS OF THE SIDHE
MASTER OF THE SIDHE
CHALLENGE OF THE CLANS
STORM SHIELD
DARK DRUID

T ◦ H ◦ E
Dark Druid

K E N N E T H
C. F L I N T

◇

BANTAM BOOKS

TORONTO • NEW YORK • LONDON • SYDNEY • AUCKLAND

THE DARK DRUID
A Bantam Spectra Book / August 1987

All rights reserved.
Copyright © 1987 by Kenneth C. Flint.
Cover art copyright © 1987 by Steve Assel.
This book may not be reproduced in whole or in part, by
mimeograph or any other means, without permission.
For information address: Bantam Books, Inc.

ISBN 0-553-26715-9

Published simultaneously in the United States and Canada

Bantam Books are published by Bantam Books, Inc. Its trademark, consisting of the words "Bantam Books" and the por-
trayal of a rooster, is Registered in U.S. Patent and Trademark
Office and in other countries. Marca Registrada. Bantam
Books, Inc., 666 Fifth Avenue, New York, New York 10103.

PRINTED IN THE UNITED STATES OF AMERICA

KR   0 9 8 7 6 5 4 3 2 1

To my colleagues in the faculty of Plattsmouth
High School who, through my years of
writing these books, have put up with me,
humored me, helped me, and become my friends.

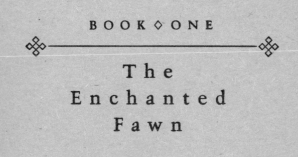

BOOK ◇ ONE

The Enchanted Fawn

◇

CHAPTER◦1

The
Fawn

THE FOREST CLEARING SLUMBERED PEACEFULLY IN THE quiet of a warm, bright afternoon.

Shafts of the purest sunlight from a cloudless sky slanted down through the high branches of the surrounding oaks and cast brilliant spots, like glowing emeralds, upon the open ground. Fine motes of dust, not rushed by any breeze, drifted lazily in the shining columns. There was little other movement in the clearing. A gray squirrel boldly browsed far from the safety of his trees. A few birds flitted in the treetops, their occasional calls sounding hushed beneath the vast cloak of silence that enwrapped the wood.

A magnificent stag pushed out from the underbrush into the clearing. It stood for a moment, head proudly erect, great spread of antlers lifted high in a display of exalted rank. Then it strode slowly, grandly, fearlessly across the empty ground to the center of the open space. Here it stopped, looked austerely around, and finally deigned to lower its head and nibble on the lush grass that could not grow within the shadows of the wood.

Then came the sound of the horn.

It was a low, sustained note, carrying clearly through the quiet forest. The stag's head jerked up, turning toward the sound. The squirrel froze, listening, bushy tail jerking nervously. The birds in the treetops about the clearing fell abruptly silent.

The sound came again, from much closer this time. And with it came new sounds, continuous sounds that grew louder rapidly: the baying of many hounds and the shrill, wailing cries of men!

The stag bolted away, vanishing into the trees. The squirrel scuttled for the safety of the nearest trunk. The birds, as if a single being, flashed upward just as a heavy body crashed through the last screen of underbrush into the open.

It was an enormous boar that had now charged into the clearing. Its size was closer to that of a small bull than of a pig. The massive, muscled shoulders reached as high as a man's chest. The body was sinewy and hard, moving lithely and with tremendous power. The head was im- mense, its bristled snout sporting long, curved tusks. Above the snout, tiny eyes glowed redly, like hot coals.

It didn't pause as it burst into the open area. The sounds of dogs and men gave evidence that they were close behind it. It started across the clearing at a run.

It was less than halfway across when a pack of hounds began to pour from the woods in close pursuit. At least fifty animals formed the energetic group, all in full cry. Most of them were sleek, slender, long-limbed animals with small heads and pointed muzzles. But leading them were two wolfhounds—great, shaggy-coated beasts nearly as large as ponies.

Close on the flying heels of the pack, a band of men leaped into the open. There were some twoscore of them, their tall, lean, wiry bodies clad in short tunics, their bared, fair-skinned arms and legs flashing as they ran. Their hair was long and mostly of light hues, either clasped at the nape of the neck or loosely plaited to keep it out of the way. They wore no adornment and carried no weapons save for short thrusting spears with broad points of gleaming black iron.

At their head ran a young man of striking looks, clean and boldly featured, with a thick plait of hair so blond as to shine nearly silver in the sun. His smoothly muscled body moved effortlessly, tirelessly as he flew across the ground. Close beside him ran another man of a like age, quite handsome too, but swarthier of complexion and dark of hair.

By the time these men were all into the clearing, the boar was nearing its far side. Before the beast could reach the cover of the trees again, however, the two wolfhounds were upon it. One nipped at a heel. The other made a tremendous leap, fastening its jaws upon a bristled ear.

The boar squealed with pain and swung with amazing agility. Its ear ripped and the hound was thrown aside, rolling to the ground. Further enraged by this wounding, the boar wheeled, brought to bay by the full pack who now encircled it, barking and snarling, but keeping a wary distance as they awaited the approaching men.

But the boar did not wait. As if knowing itself to be caught in a fatal trap, its desperate gaze fell upon the men. Focusing upon them as the source of its torments, it gave out a frenzied screech and charged, clearly bent upon revenge.

It clove through the pack of dogs like a scythe through ripe wheat, sweeping them aside. Head down, deadly tusks thrust forward, it was like a blasting gale, a raging torrent, that it now descended upon the hunters.

Most of them were nimble enough to leap from the path of its first rush. Only one hapless fellow, seeing the move just too late, was unable to get himself clear. A tusk point caught him at the back of one thigh as he turned away, tearing a ragged line deep into the flesh. He jerked and staggered, toppling to the earth, bright blood gushing from the wound.

The boar, carried past him by its momentum, pivoted with a speed equal to that of the long-limbed hounds and started back toward him, bent on finishing its work. But, as it did so, the dark-haired man bounded in. He came up close beside the charging animal, thrusting out with his spear, striking for the heart.

The point struck home, but just too high, penetrating the thick hide only to imbed itself in the knotted muscles of the shoulder. The boar gave a loud grunt, but more of anger than of pain, pivoting again to face him. He had saved the downed man only to find himself looking into the flaring eyes of the maddened beast—less than a spear's length away—and without a weapon in his hands.

He ducked to one side. The boar moved as swiftly, swinging its head up to catch him with those rending tusks. The tusks, however, never reached their mark. For the fair-haired young hunter, using the other's diversion as a chance to move up behind the animal, now leaped boldly onto it.

He mounted it as easily as if he were vaulting onto a tamed pony's back. The boar squealed in both astonishment and rage. It twisted its head about to get at him. Quickly realizing the futility of this, it began to buck and writhe with a most incredible vigor, as if seized by some fit. The convulsions of its powerful body seemed to take it in all directions at once.

But the man upon it stayed firmly seated there. His muscled legs were locked against its sides, strained taut with the pressure. This left both his hands free to raise the short thrusting spear high above the boar's head and take careful aim. Then, in a blow backed by all the weight and strength of his arms, he drove the weapon down. The spear head slammed into the corded neck at the base of the massive skull. The sharp point went deep, its keen edge severing the spine.

The boar died instantly. Its frenzied movements ceased and its heavy body crashed to the earth, rolling sideways. The fair-haired man, in a simple, almost casual move, hopped clear. The boar rolled down, its legs kicking up, splayed and jerking in a last death spasm. Then it settled limply and was still.

The other hunters moved in to stand around the beast, examining it with looks of keen interest mixed with awe. The pack joined them as well, the two great hounds venturing forward to sniff at the carcass.

"By the Dagda, Finn, that was a near thing," the dark-haired man remarked to the fair one. "He was more savage than any boar we've ever hunted."

"He was that," agreed the one called Finn.

He turned from the beast and strode to where the wounded man lay. Two of his fellows were already attending him, binding the gash with strips torn from their own tunic hems. The man looked a bit pale from his shock and loss of blood, but seemed in good spirits.

"How is it with you, Lughaid?" Finn asked.

"Well enough. I thank you for the saving of me. That animal would have made tatters of me, surely."

"It's Caoilte you should be thanking," Finn said modestly. "It was his risk that turned the boar from you."

"Think no more of it," the dark-haired man told the wounded one. "It was no more risk than you would have taken for me."

"None of you took as much risk as my brave hounds!" complained a broadly built, ruddy-faced man with flame-red hair. "That beast might have done them some real damage, tearing through them that way!"

"Ah, you think more of your hounds than you do of us, Comhrag," a lanky young man reproved good-naturedly. "That boar gave them good sport, the same as it did us."

"Bran. Sceolan. Come here," Finn called out.

The two wolfhounds left the carcass at once and came to him. He squatted between them, examining each one carefully.

"You seem all right," he said at last, giving each broad head a loving pat. "Brave work, lads."

He stood, turning his gaze about him at the company.

"Well, that ends our hunting for this day," he announced. "Still, we've a fine prize to take back. Let's make ready to start toward Almhuin."

Preparations were swiftly carried out. The boar was gutted and fastened to a stout pole to be carried by several of the men. A crude but efficient litter was constructed of saplings laced with pliant twigs to carry the wounded man. Soon the hunting party was starting on again, taking a new direction, moving at a slower but still rapid pace.

Instead of racing ahead, the pack of small-headed dogs now followed close on the heels of the ruddy man called Comhrag. The two great wolfhounds flanked the one named Finn, who strode at the head of the group with his dark-haired comrade.

As they made their way through the sun-streaked

wood, Finn noted that his friend was eyeing him in a way that could only be called quizzical.

"And what is it that's troubling you, Caoilte?" he finally inquired.

"Since you're asking," Caoilte responded frankly, "that was a large risk you were taking back there, don't you think?"

Finn shrugged.

"I had to stop the boar," he said in an offhand manner. "Otherwise, it would have had you as well."

"Maybe," the other replied, sounding unconvinced. "Still, you might have distracted it, instead of flinging yourself upon it like some madman."

Finn laughed at that.

"And what would be the sport in our hunting a beast like that if there weren't a bit of danger in it?"

"A bit of danger is one thing," Caoilte said tersely. "Being reckless is something else."

His voice had the tone of a scolding parent in it, and Finn looked at him with some astonishment.

"Reckless was I? Can this be Caoilte MacRonan speaking? The very same warrior who can never have enough of fighting or adventuring?"

"I'll not deny I like a hard fight or a good hunt as much as any man in Ireland," he admitted, "and even more than most. But I've been watching you lately, my good lad. And it's not the same Finn MacCumhal I've been seeing. The Finn I used to know loved the peace of a summer's morning as much as the thrill of a hunt. And he loved the feel of a fine harp's strings as much as the weight of a good spear."

"I was a boy then," Finn countered, lightly putting aside his friend's concern. "I've grown older. I've learned that it's the fighting and the hunt that truly make a Fian warrior feel alive."

"And that's the truth, is it?" Caoilte said, still sounding dubious.

Finn gave him an even more searching, puzzled look.

"And why are you so gloomy at that, I'd like to know," he demanded. "I'd expect you'd be happy to finally have me thinking as yourself."

"Well, and I suppose I am," Caoilte agreed. "Still," he added in a musing way, "I'm growing older myself, and maybe a bit more cautious with my age. You are the leader of all the Fianna now. And you've become the most important man to Ireland. You can't be taking such needless risks always. Even you, with the blood of the Others in you, aren't invulnerable, you know."

"Don't think of that!" Finn told him heartily, grinning and clapping him on the shoulder in a gesture of cheerful camaraderie. "I've a feeling we were meant to live forever, my old friend. We'll be fighting back-to-back and hunting these golden woods until the last sun sets behind the ridge of the world!"

His carefree manner seemed to sweep away the foreboding mood of his comrade like a warm spring breeze banishing a last winter's chill. Caoilte laughed too, returning Finn's gesture with a like one.

"That's the very wish I'd ask of Danu myself," he said earnestly. "I—"

But he broke off abruptly as, with no warning at all, something shot from the trees close beside them.

All the hunting party pulled up short in surprise as it streaked by them and then paused close ahead of them, turning its head to look back at the group. They could see then that it was a fawn of soft, golden hue. A beautiful and willowy creature, it stood poised there for a long moment on its slender, frail-seeming legs, regarding them with large, lustrous brown eyes. Then, with a flick of the tail, it was off again, bounding away ahead of them with an astonishing speed.

All of the hounds went uncontrollably wild. Bran and Sceolan were off like arrows fired after it. The pack was quick to follow, in full cry, looking like a single gray blur with scores of flickering legs.

"Look at it run," Finn said in awe. "Let's be after it!"

"Call back the hounds," Caoilte urged. "It's only a fawn. Not worth hunting."

"But well worth the chase!" Finn countered eagerly. "I've seen no deer—not even a great stag—with such a speed. Come on!"

He started ahead, but Caoilte grabbed his arm, restraining him. Finn looked to him in perplexity.

"Don't do this, Finn," the dark-haired one said, his face drawn by a frown of worry.

"Caoilte, what's become of your sporting blood?" Finn asked with disbelief. "Come on, my lads!" he shouted to the whole party. "A new spear for the one who catches it!"

And with that, he was off after the pack. The others—including a still-frowning Caoilte—joined him with elated hunting cries. Only those burdened with the boar and the wounded man kept on a course for home, muttering dark oaths at their ill luck in being thus left out.

Through the sun-streaked woods the hunters chased the fawn, splashing across brooks, scrambling up hills, forcing their way through brush, pressing on with all their speed and strength in an effort to close with it.

Despite their best efforts, however, the fawn stayed easily ahead, slipping through the trees like the shadow of a soaring hawk, moving effortlessly, tirelessly, until even the tremendous stamina of the Fian men and their fine hounds began to ebb.

Still the hunters persisted, even when the animals and men began to drop out from overwhelming exhaustion. Little by little their numbers thinned, the strongest stubbornly pushing ahead, fired now by a growing frustration at this frail animal who taunted them with the white flash of its flicking tail.

At last it was only the two great wolfhounds and the one pair of young hunters—dark and fair—who still kept up pursuit. And Caoilte, realizing this, appealed once more to his companion.

"Let's leave it, Finn," he gasped out. "It's no use."

There was no response from Finn.

"Well, I'm quitting!" Caoilte announced in an annoyed tone, pulling to a halt.

This too had no effect. Finn went on, not slackening his pace or even looking around.

"Finn!" Caoilte called after his swiftly dwindling form. "Finn, please give it up!"

His voice echoed after the speeding man, but Finn would not relent. He was too totally caught up in the challenge now, his face aglow and tensed with concentration, his muscles pumping rhythmically, steadily to carry him on, his eyes riveted on the way before him.

Bran and Sceolan could be seen some distance ahead, pounding on as strongly, as stubbornly as himself. They were keeping within sight of the racing fawn, but barely.

They ran on through the silent, glowing forest, leaving the others farther and farther behind. Time seemed suspended. It was as if they were alone now in a mystical wildwood that went on forever, where pursuer and pursued were intent only on this contest and there was nothing else in the world for them.

Then, abruptly, the fawn stopped.

It pulled up, turned, and faced the enormous wolfhounds who still charged upon it at a full run. Finn, seeing this, tried to put on yet more speed, crying out, "Bran! Sceolan! Don't harm the fawn!"

But there was no need at all for his warning. As he came closer to them, a look of astonishment overspread his face. For the two wolfhounds had made no move that might harm or even frighten the slender fawn.

They had stopped some way from it and were now approaching it with great care. The fawn watched them with some signs of timidity, its liquid eyes apprehensive, its frail body trembling slightly. But the hounds only thrust forward their broad muzzles cautiously to have a sniff at it. They then exchanged a look that bespoke a most human puzzlement, their heads cocked to one side, their thick brows lifted.

"Bran, Sceolan, what's wrong?" Finn asked, striding toward them.

Instantly the hounds whirled toward him, taking up flanking positions by the fawn that could only be called defensive. Finn stopped, staring at them in surprise.

"Well, by all the gods," he said, "what are you two about?"

He took another step closer, but Bran lifted his head and bared his teeth, growling in a deep, warning tone.

"Be easy, Bran," Finn told him soothingly. "I don't know what's happened to you, but I promise you that I'll not harm the fawn."

This seemed to reassure both the hounds. They nodded and stepped slightly aside, allowing him to move between them. The deer, still trembling, still with fear glistening in its dark eyes, nevertheless kept its place, letting him approach.

Very slowly he lifted a hand. Even more slowly he put it out. Finally and most gently he caressed the smooth, soft head. At his touch the fawn voiced a small sound, like a sigh, and lifted its head to rub against his hand. It was a clear gesture of returned friendship, of acceptance, as might be given by a cat. Finn's look of amazement grew.

"Well, you're a friendly enough creature," he said. "But why did you stop?"

As if in an attempt to answer, the fawn stepped forward, resting its head against his side. It stared up at him with an expression in its eyes that seemed to implore. From its throat there came a low whimpering.

Finn shook his head.

"I don't know what it is you're wanting, fawn, but our own game is ended. We'll not harm you and we'll not pursue you any longer. You're free to go." He looked to the hounds. "Come on, lads. It's time to be starting back to find the others."

He stepped away from the fawn, turned, and started off, heading back the way they had come. But after a few strides, he glanced around, only to stop and stare again in an uncomprehending way. The two dogs were following, but the fawn was prancing right along between them!

"Fawn, I told you to be off!" Finn said more forcefully. "You can't be following us!"

This made no impression on the creature. It remained between the hounds.

"I said, be off!" Finn said sharply, stepping toward it as if to shoo it away.

The hounds crouched, snarling. Finn backed away, lifting his hands in capitulation.

"All right! All right!" he told them in a humoring way. "I understand you, lads. If your new friend wishes to come with us, I'll make no more objection."

Once again he turned and started off. But as he led the way back along the faint passage their chase had created, he glanced behind him often. Always the fawn was with them, shepherded closely by the pair of hounds.

They traveled back for only a short way before they came upon the rest of the company, now recovered, rejoined, and following Finn's trail with Caoilte at their head. Upon seeing the fawn, the pack of small-headed dogs went wild once more, swarming forward, barking excitedly.

Bran and Sceolan dealt swiftly and quite sharply with them. They both leaped before the fawn, hair bristling, ears laid back, great jaws snapping out. With yelps of terror the leaders of the pack quickly retreated into their fellows, throwing the pack into confusion. Then they were all withdrawing before the savage threat of the wolf-hounds, falling into a cowering, chastened mass far from the fawn.

"What in all the great world . . ." Caoilte exclaimed, moving forward.

"Easy, Caoilte," Finn warned, stepping toward him and away from the fawn with its two guardians. "Not too close just yet. The lads are being very . . . protective."

"So I can see. You'd think the thing was their own pup!"

"They have struck up quite a friendship," Finn agreed.

"But why?" Caoilte said in a perplexed way, looking from the dogs to the frail, innocent-seeming creature. "Why would they act that way? And why would this creature be wanting to join us?"

"Perhaps it was raised by men," Finn suggested. Then he shrugged. "I don't know. It is a strange thing."

"It's more than strange," Caoilte said darkly. "I don't like the feeling of this, Finn. I don't like it at all."

Finn laughed.

"Maybe you are getting too cautious, old friend," he said in a cheerfully scoffing tone. "Leave off your worrying. It's just a fawn."

"It's madness!" Caoilte retorted in exasperation. "That fawn can't stay with us!"

"And would you like to explain that to the lads?" Finn asked him quizzically.

Caoilte looked at the two huge animals who were

watching him closely, warily, challengingly, as if they well understood what he was saying. He sighed and shook his head.

"No," he admitted. "That I would not."

The mouths of both wolfhounds stretched widely in what could only be called triumphant grins.

CHAPTER ◊ 2

The
Druid's
Lair

THE FANGS OF THE TWO BEARS SHOWED IN THREATEN-
ing snarls as they forced the man out of the woods into the
open.

He was lanky of build, very youthful of look, but with
rather wolfish features—long nose and pointed chin—-and
with a crafty slant to his small eyes. He looked to be much
the worse for some long wear: his tunic ragged, his face
and body bruised, his knobby elbows and knees scraped to
bleeding. Just now he was looking behind him at the two
pursuing beasts with an expression of great apprehension.

There was obvious good reason for this. The bears
were of an enormous size, more than waist-high to him
and well over twice his bulk. Broad of shoulder, thick of
body, and short of limb, they lumbered forward, driving
the man ahead.

With his attention directed upon them as he moved
on, he missed his footing, staggering and falling heavily to
the rocky ground. The raw flesh was badly scraped again.
He groaned and lay still, as if too weary to rise.

But the bears would allow him no respite. They crowded up close on either side, growling menacingly.

With agonized movements the man levered himself up
on his arms, drew in his long legs, and finally clambered
upright once more. As he did, his eyes lifted to fix on what
now lay before him.

A round-crested, craggy-sided mount of blue-gray stone

rose abruptly, starkly, to loom ominously, like a thunder-storm rising on the curved rim of a calm sea.

A look of abject terror filled the young man's face at the sight of it. He stood frozen, staring. One of the bears moved in, nudging him in the back with its broad nose. He wrenched his gaze from the mount and looked to it, his expression pleading.

"You can't really mean to take me there," he said in a whimpering voice. "You've got to believe me. I didn't do anything! Please let me go!"

The bear's response was to take another step forward, roughly shouldering him ahead. He stumbled, nearly fell again, but caught himself, drawing up, his body tense, his eyes searching around him desperately.

The bears appeared to anticipate his move. With a swiftness extraordinary for the seemingly hulking beasts, they bounded up on either side of him, trapping him close between them. He looked from one to another, and his body sagged in defeat.

"All right," he told them, nearly in tears. "I'll not try to escape again.

They went on. The young man moved slowly, limping now, but the beasts had no mercy. They kept very close, one or another constantly shouldering him in the side to urge him along.

Soon they reached the base of the rocky mount and turned to follow along its base. When they reached a cliff face of gray, smooth, slatelike stone, they stopped.

Here one of the bears reared upward on its hind legs. It towered nearly a head above the man as it walked forward to plant a massive paw against a faint circle inscribed in the wall of stone. Then the beast dropped again to all fours and shuffled back several steps.

The cliff face began to vibrate. From within came a low rumbling sound, growing swiftly louder. A crack appeared at the foot of the wall, running upward, as if an earthquake were fissuring the cliff. It widened rapidly, the halves of smooth stone pulling apart like great portals opening, revealing a broad, high tunnel.

As the hapless young man stared along this shadowed passageway, his strength seemed to abandon him. He looked incapable of movement, rooted to the spot, white-faced and trembling. But his guardians quickly took care of this. They pressed in close on either side again, and one started him on with a hard swat to his behind.

The corridor ran straight into the mount's depths, angling slightly downward. As soon as they had entered, the opening in the cliff face rumbled closed again, shutting off the view of the world outside, sealing itself up as if it had never been. The young man looked back and watched as this happened, his face a mask of despair as he saw this only avenue of escape disappear.

With the sunlight shut off, it was now apparent that other light was filtering up from the tunnel's farther end. It was faint at first, reflecting softly from the smooth stone of the corridor walls. But it grew steadily as the trio moved along, and accompanying it came the growing sound of music: a lively air being played on pipes and tiompan and harp.

Then the corridor widened and abruptly opened into a chamber which contained the source of both music and light.

It was a single space of enormous size. Not a room so much as what appeared to be the interior of the entire mountain hollowed out. Its walls were formed of the rough, living stone. They slanted slightly inward as they rose, forming a cone enclosing an area in which an eagle might soar and wheel without brushing a wingtip against a side.

Scores of openings to what seemed chambers or other tunnels pierced the walls at many places. They were reached and connected by stairways hewn into the rock, corkscrewing up the cone level after level, crisscrossing at many points to form a complex interlace design. Figures dwarfed by the immensity of the place moved upon them, toiling up and down, many carrying burdens that looked nearly too great to bear but still struggling gamely on.

The stairs climbed, dwindling with the distance, to the very peak, disappearing into the glow of a great globe suspended there. This object acted as a sun for the underground world. It seemed to be incandescent, like iron heated red-hot in the forge. Its blaze illuminated all the vast space, casting everything in a lurid, blood-red sunset hue.

It was an appropriate light to fall upon the scene that occupied the center of the chamber's floor.

This area was many acres of smooth and level stone. It was broken only by bizarre rock formations thrusting up here and there, looking like grotesquely sculpted statues of beasts or birds or even human forms distorted to make them not comical, but obscene. They were widely scattered about the floor for the most part, but at the center a dozen of them formed an evenly spaced ring. A great fire burned within it, sending high twisting tongues of its flame, as if to lick hungrily at the radiant globe above it. Its light cast long, sinuously writhing shadows far out from the ring of monstrous stones, making the floor seem to undulate and crawl as if alive.

Around the fire, just within the stones, several scores of long tables formed another ring. They were crowded by a large company engaged in a great revelry, their shouts and laughter echoing in the room, nearly drowning out the music at times. In the open space between them and the fire, other figures capered in a lively jig.

The lanky man had come to a halt once more at the sight of this most eerie spectacle, but the bears pressed in on both sides of him again, forcing him reluctantly forward. As he stepped out, something large and sluglike slid from his path, heaving its slime-covered softness into the deeper shadows of a serpentine pillar of stone. The man looked at it, shuddered, and went on.

The cavern was alive with a myriad of other creatures. Many of them were not recognizable as anything natural. Things crawled or fluttered or oozed about the room. A ball of fluff, like a headless, limbless sheep, even rolled along.

A larger number of the cavern's denizens seemed to be combinations of several animals, mismatched by some diseased mind as a kind of perverse joke. The worst of these had portions clearly recognizable as human. Bats with men's faces soared in the updrafts above the fire. A crab skittered along on human limbs. A long-necked crane had a woman's busty torso absurdly propped on its skinny legs.

With others, the mixture of man and animal parts was less grotesque. A whole company of warriors—standing guard at the tunnel's mouth, upon the stairways, and about the central ring of stones—were largely human in form, but sported heads of various creatures of an appropriately savage type. Wolf and weasel, fox and cat, bull and boar, were all represented here.

About the central fire and the ring of tables bustled another group who appeared to be largely servants. Cooks labored at spit and cauldron while stewards rushed food and drink to the seated company of revelers. Here the heads were of a more domestic and herbivorous type: cow, goat, deer, and—not surprisingly—a great many sheep.

Only at the tables were there beings that seemed to be of wholly human form. But even over them there was a strong aura of the bizarre, of the unnatural.

The dress of most was rich and quite exotic, the cloth of wonderful textures and bright colors embroidered heavily with threads of silver and gold, but all too gaudy, and all oddly mismatched, as if they had been gleaned haphazardly from widely varied sources and matched with not even the faintest sense of taste. Many of these beings were also laden with glinting jewelry, arms sometimes all but hidden by rings and bracelets, each piece beautiful and tasteful by itself, but in such numbers creating a vulgar and ostentatious show.

The faces about the ring formed a gallery of human degeneracies: bloated and flushed by dissipation, twisted by strange passions, etched deep with cruelty, lit by maniacal glee. Some animal faces were amongst them, too. A horselike beast stood at one table, a hawk of nearly man-size perched at either side of it. All three dipped often and avidly into a great vat set before them.

In fact, all the company at the tables were drinking heavily from an assortment of goblets, tankards, and mugs. Each was the product of fine craftsmanship, worked in precious metals and set with jewels, though some were cracked or badly dented from rough and careless use.

Their present use had apparently been going on for some time, helping to create the raucous, festive mood.

That mood was being presently enhanced by the dancers cavorting in the space about the fire. The entertainment seemed quite innocent at a casual glance. A group of musicians—wearing the heads of goat and sheep—played a merry jig on their pipes and harps and drums. Three young men and as many young women danced in a lively manner to their tune. But a close look at them was awful proof that they took no joy from their dancing.

All were panting, red-faced from exhaustion, their bodies soaked with sweat from their labors and from the proximity of the intense fire. Though their legs were pumping madly, their upper bodies sagged with weariness. Their shoes were nearly worn from them by the rubbing upon the stone, and the leather soles of one young man's shoes, already worn through, were stained dark by the blood from his raw scraped feet.

They groaned in torment, but they went on dancing to the music as if they had no will of their own, but had to follow the mad dictates of their lower halves. The sadistic crowd roared with obscene laughter at their antics and at their grimaces of pain, yelling for them to dance on and on while the musicians, seemingly possessed themselves, maintained a frenzied pace.

The two bears and their prisoner finally reached the company. They pushed their charge past the circle of stones and through a gap in the ring of tables. A hard shove from one sent the man staggering forward into the open space.

The attention of those at the tables went from the dancers toward him. At once, their cheering died. Directly across the fires from him, a figure stood at one of the tables and gave a curt command for silence.

The musicians ceased to play, dropping their instruments as if their arms had become in the instant boneless. The dancers collapsed to the floor like rag puppets cut suddenly from their strings. Some cried in their relief. Some moaned in agony from the pain of their tortured feet.

But none of the awful company at the tables now paid

any mind to them. All their attention was fixed intently on
the wolf-faced young man and on the one who now came
around the tables and moved toward him.

He was a dramatic figure, tall and slender and proudly
erect, clad in a long, full, sweeping robe of black. He
moved with slow, grand, haughty step, head up, chin
thrust forward. His face was shaped like a long wedge, very
wide at the brow, narrowing to a boldly jutting point at his
chin. He might have been handsome but for a skin that
looked as if it had been badly burned, creased and blackened
like crumpled parchment, mottled with dark stains. His
nose was a thrusting, bony beak, his cheekbones high and
sharply prominent. A thin, neatly plaited mustache drooped
at either side of a wide mouth, partly hiding the scarred
lips.

In such a dark face, the eyes were startling: the bright
blue of a still pond reflecting a clear sky, glowing with an
almost piercing light.

He strode around the fire toward the lanky man. One
lean, long-fingered hand clutched a rod of polished black
wood that reached as high as his shoulder. He used it as a
staff, putting down its silver-tipped end with a sharp click
at each step

As the other saw him approach, his final strength
seemed to desert him. He dropped to his knees, hunched
and shaking, head down, eyes lowered in total subservience.

The tall man stopped close before him, gazing down on
the bowed head. A look of hatred glimmered in the eyes
and drew taut the thin line of mouth.

"So," he said in a low, ominous tone, "you have
returned to me—" he glanced up at the two bears who
had stopped close behind him—"with a bit of help."

"Please," the man said pitifully, "I've done nothing."

"Nothing!" the man repeated, his voice rising suddenly to a shout. "THEN . . . WHERE . . . IS . . . MY . . . FAWN?"

"I . . . I don't know," the other responded faintly.

"You don't know?" said the one looming over him.
"Well, I know that it was you who helped it escape from
my domains. I know it was you who led it far from here.
And now you return alone." He stepped closer, leaning
down, the tip of his staff lifting up beneath the young

man's chin, forcing his head up until his panicked eyes met the blazing ones. "Where is it? You have one chance."

A look of stubbornness came into the young man's face. "No," he said. "I won't tell you."

The tall man shook his head.

"I am deeply disappointed. I let you come and join me when your own people cast you out. I gave you a place to stay. I gave you my trust. I made you my forester and gave you the responsibility for my outside domains. And for that you betray me. Why!"

"I . . . I felt pity for the creature," the other said. "I could not stand to see it suffering—"

"So, the spell worked upon you, too," the tall man said. "Was it the eyes? Well, no matter. No matter. Perhaps I can understand why you did this. Perhaps I can let you keep your life at least. But you must tell me, boy!" The tip of the staff pressed deeper into his throat. "Tell me!"

The young man hesitated. Fear blanched his face, his head vibrated with the strain. But then a spirit of courage, of defiance, seemed to well up from some source within him.

"No!" he said fiercely. "I will not tell. I've seen your cruelty. I'll stand no more of it. At least one poor creature will escape this awful place alive."

"Don't let your love or your pity destroy you," the man replied warningly. He pulled back the rod and lifted the silver tip to point at the boy's forehead. "Speak now!"

"I will not tell," the boy said, pulling himself up proudly.

A rage suffused the tall man's face with blood, making it darker. The eyes took on an icy chillness and the voice cut sharply like a well-honed blade. "Fool! Then you will die—and painfully!"

The staff shot forward. The silver tip touched the young man's forehead.

Instantly an aura of silver light appeared about him, growing swiftly brighter. The audience sat forward, gazes fixed avidly on the spectacle, smiling with malicious delight.

The aura strengthened to a surrounding glow so bright it obscured the figure of the lad. Then the shadow of him within it began to convulse. He gave a scream that blended pain and fear, and toppled sideways, thudding to the floor. His glow-wrapped form lay stretched upon the stone, its movements growing more frenzied. It seemed as if he had gone liquid within the translucent pod, bubbling, writhing, like a thick stew on the boil, spreading and sinking.

Then the elastic form began to shrink, to contract, to dwindle down, down from the size of a man, until there seemed nothing left within the bright mass.

The light itself faded then, waning like the dying glow after a sunset, dissolving into nothing.

The audience craned forward, staring at the spot, searching for the remains of the hapless lad. And there was something left. The aura had not destroyed him. It had transformed him. Where he had lain there now crawled a black, round-bellied spider no larger than a thumbnail.

The tall man stepped forward, looking down at it, a gleam of satisfaction in his eyes. Then, in a slow and deliberate gesture, he lifted the stick and drove it down. The tip slammed crushingly upon the small insect. With a chill little smile of cruelty the druid twisted the stick, grinding the spider thoroughly into the stone.

He lifted the stick and peered down at the result. His look of satisfaction turned to one of disgust. He stepped away from the spot toward the two bears.

"And just where was our poor insect coming from when he was found?" he demanded.

One bear turned to point with his muzzle.

"From the south and west," the man interpreted. "Very well."

He turned in a swirl of his robe and started away, but paused to address a spindly, goat-headed man in a leather apron.

"Oh, and clean up that mess, quickly!" he brusquely ordered.

As the being moved hastily to obey, the man strode on, out of the circle, past the ring of stones and toward one of the staircases in the outer wall. At his departure, the revelry began again, laughter echoing out, music striking up, and the poor dancers forced to their torture once more.

The man in black reached the base of the stairs and started upward, moving swiftly, his robes swirling behind, his dark face set in grim and purposeful lines.

His climb took him far up, curving around the cone of walls as he rose. He passed by many creatures, most starved and weary and badly used, struggling with burdens or on their way for more. He passed by openings to smaller caverns where various occupations were underway. More dispirited creatures quarried ores or labored at massive looms. In an armory, sparks flew under the hammers of brawny, bull-like smiths. And in a warren of small chambers, a host of red-capped men little bigger than hares painstakingly shaped intricate jewelry.

Finally, nearly halfway up the wall of the great cavern, he came onto a broad landing. From there a tunnel led back some way into the rock. Two guards with heavy spears and round iron shields flanked its opening. They were both massively built men with bulging muscles, a fact not difficult to judge as both were clothed only in short leather skirts. Highly developed specimens of manhood they were, save for one thing: both sported the horned heads of rams.

He moved between them and strode up the corridor. It was lit by torches that gleamed from walls damp with moisture and studded heavily with translucent white rocks. As he traveled down the corridor, his passage fluttered the torch flames, making the walls shimmer. But ahead, a steady, rose-white glow grew stronger as he approached it, pushing back the paler light.

He stepped at last into a chamber of unusual form. It was not a crude, rough-walled cave scratched from the dark rock. Instead it was a sphere of perfect proportions, its smooth walls curved and polished with what must have been either a most delicate human skill or some astounding artistry of nature. The surface was of a substance like purest quartz, milky white with the faintest blush of pink, and giving off a pale luminescence that evenly lit the room.

A great mound of cushions filled the bottom of this sphere, creating a level floor and a bed at once. Upon this there reclined a woman.

Her long, slender, but still voluptuous form was revealed by a sleek gown of white silk edged with silver, which clung to the smooth curve of breast and hip and leg. She lay stretched out in a languorous pose—a knee slightly raised, an arm thrown back—that in its subtleties of position managed to suggest great sensuality.

She seemed to be sleeping, her head laid back, eyes closed, her thick black hair spread out over the cushions in a great, shining wave. But as he entered the room, she spoke in a voice as golden and rich as the purest honey.

"So you came to me," she said, the caressing voice giving even that simple statement a suggestive connotation. "I knew you would."

"That fool would tell me nothing," he said irritably. "But I do know for certain that he helped the fawn escape."

"Of course," she crooned dreamily. "He couldn't help himself. He is another fool . . . like you."

"Take care, Miluchradh," he answered sharply. "Your skills make you useful to me, but even you are not beyond my wrath."

She sat up and looked to him. Her features were beautiful in an emphatic way, with wide forehead, cleanly sculpted chin and nose, and high cheekbones. There was a smooth, tawny color to her skin, complemented by the deep red of her full lips and the hot brown of her eyes. The eyes gazed at him now with no look of concern, and the lips smiled with amusement. Clearly she was not moved by his threat.

"If you wish my help," she told him, "you know that you only have to ask. Come, join me."

"Very well," he said. He made his way out across the floor of cushions and dropped down beside her. "I believe he took the fawn away to the southeast. Search there."

"If I must," she said with a sigh of reluctant acceptance.

She drew herself up stiffly. She looked about her at the softly glowing curve of wall. Then she held her arms straight out before her and dropped her head back. For a moment she was quite still, not even seeming to breathe. Then she spoke a soft, coaxing incantation, as if even the spirits she invoked must be seduced to her will.

"Forces of the Sphere of Knowledge, Powers of the Realms of seeing, give me the means to find the truth I wish. Carry me on your winds!"

She moved her arms about her in sweeping gestures to include the whole interior of the globe. The curving walls began to glow more brightly, and as they did, they also seemed to grow more translucent. Shadows of vague forms seemed to be moving beyond them. These grew swiftly clearer, clearer, as if the polished surface were becoming transparent. The images resolved slowly, colors appearing, blue above and green below, until finally it could be seen that they were the sky and earth.

The view surrounded the man and woman, out of sight only when it curved beneath the floor of cushions. The effect was as if the cave had become a sphere of glass, an enormous bubble encasing the two and floating across the open countryside.

She looked around her and nodded in satisfaction. In one direction was visible a line of mountains and the grim peak in which they still actually sat. She shifted position slightly, gazing off across the meadows and forests that spread out in the opposite direction. Then she pointed. At once they began to move away from the mount. The scene began to sweep past, faster and faster, the ground turning to a green blur as they seemed to fly along, reaching a nearly breathtaking speed.

"Must you move so swiftly?" the man complained. "The sensation always makes me feel quite giddy."

"You are the one so anxious to find your precious fawn, are you not?" she asked pointedly.

This silenced him. He dropped his gaze to the cushions and sat unmoving as the view sped by.

"You know," she said in a casual way after a time, "I don't understand why you're wasting time on this. You're well rid of the creature."

"What do you mean?" he asked, looking at her suspiciously.

"I mean, why must I do this?" she asked. She swayed her body toward him, her face moving close. "Must you waste time on this creature when you have . . . so much here to satisfy you?"

He gazed down at the eyes bright with invitation, at the parted, waiting lips. His own lifted in a sneer.

"You mean yourself?" he said contemptuously.

Not daunted by this, she lifted slender, elegant fingers to caress his face, running the tips down the long line of his chin. Her voice was throaty with its seductive tone, beckoning, promising and sensuous.

"And why not?" she said. "Would I not be enough?"

"Enough for any man, or men, or beasts, or those creatures of pure brawn you call your guards," he shot back, pushing her hand away. "What I want, I feel certain you could never understand."

She sat back, her expression of chagrin at his rough denial giving way to anger.

"Is it your great love of purity you mean?" she said, and gave a scornful laugh. "It is a waste. A weakness and a living death. And your obsession with it has flawed you and sapped your powers." She leaned forward again, her voice taking on a pleading tone. "Please let it go. Don't throw away—"

"No more!" he snapped. "Just do as I ask, Seer, and quickly!"

Defeated, she turned away and indicated a section of the sphere with a sweeping, irritated gesture.

"It is already done," she said.

The rushing movement of the country had begun to slow. The image beyond the curved walls was steadying upon a panorama of meadows and glades.

"There," she said, and indicated a dark moving patch upon the green. It was just discernible at the distance as a company of men and dogs.

"And what is this?" he demanded impatiently.

"You wished to find your fawn," she said simply. "It is there."

"Closer," he ordered.

She waved a hand toward the group and they swept closer, gliding down and in, then stopping to hang seemingly suspended above their heads, drifting along with them.

Now individual men and animals could be seen. The warriors moved at the front, the sleek, sharp-headed dogs trotted behind, and, at the rear, a bit separate from the rest, two huge hounds flanked a small, golden fawn.

"So, he said, "it is there." He looked to her in puzzlement. "But why? Why with them? They are clearly mortals. What is it doing?"

"Following them, it would seem," the woman said.

"But where are they going?" he asked exasperatedly.

"There, I imagine," she said, pointing ahead with one hand and waving upward with the other.

At her gesture of command the bubble lifted higher, showing the countryside far ahead of the company. There, upon a rounded, grassy hill, were visible the walls and buildings of a large fortress, glowing golden in the slanting rays of afternoon sun, like a crown upon a brow.

"Perhaps the creature thinks it can find sanctuary there," she said.

"Then it will soon discover that it is wrong," he said, grating out the words. "Can you tell me how to find this place?"

"Of course," she said.

"Then I will prepare to leave at once. And Queen Danu herself hasn't the power to protect those idiot mortals if they try to stand in my way!"

He rose and stalked purposefully from the chamber. But the woman called Miluchradh paid no attention. It was all upon the hunters.

She waved again, and the bubble swept in closer, closer upon the company. It stopped and seemed to hang now above one man: a stalwart, muscular young man with silver hair who marched at the front.

This man she watched closely with those smoldering eyes, and a small admiring and licentious smile played across her lips.

CHAPTER ◇ 3

Sanctuary

THE HUNTING PARTY HAD NOW REACHED THE HILL AND started up the slope toward the fortress upon its crest.

Its outer wall was twice the height of a man and constructed of thick logs set upright in a ring of piled earth and stone. Outside this wall there lay a broad, deep foss, itself encircled by yet another rampart of earth. Crossing these defenses to come against the wall would place any would-be attacker in a very perilous position indeed.

There was only one place where the fortress might be entered. A bridge of planks spanned the ditch to a wide gateway with stout doors of heavy timber. These doors stood open now, giving the approaching party a view of the courtyard beyond. In the center of it could be glimpsed a portion of an imposing structure. It was circular and well over two stories in height. Its peaked roof was thatched and its curved walls were smooth-daubed and washed with lime to a startling whiteness, as were the outer palisades. It was this that was causing the fortress to glow in the red-gold tingeing of the evening sun.

Finn's group reached the outer embankment and circled it to the bridge. They clattered across the planking and passed through the gateway into the yard.

There were a number of people busy at a variety of domestic tasks. Two women were drawing water from a well just within the gates and pouring it from their buckets into a long basin of white stone. Within a lean-to structure set against the inside of the stockade, a carpenter repaired the shattered spoke of a cartwheel while keeping a watchful eye on the progress of a young apprentice who most delicately smoothed the slender bole of a casting spear. Nearby them, in the open, a smith labored beside his glowing forge, hammering out a slim, graceful, tulip-bladed sword on his anvil.

Close beside the large, central building, the boar killed by the hunting party was already laid out upon a chopping block, which had once been thick but now was carved to a deep valley in the center by long use. A pair of men in trousers and leather aprons were at the butchering of it while two of the hunters who had strained to carry it back watched with a naturally proprietary air. Not far from them, on a square field of beaten earth, a number of boys were playing a most furious game of hurley, bashing the wooden ball about with their curved sticks, taking swings at one another as much as at the ball. The sounds of clacking sticks and the grunts of pain were a continuous accompaniment to the play.

While many of these people glanced around to note the entrance of Finn's party, there was no show of excitement. The return of the hunters was evidently accepted as a quite ordinary event. The ruddy man took his pack of hounds on across the yard toward a line of wooden stable sheds. Finn's other men made directly for the stone basin and began to thoroughly wash the grime and sweat of their day's labors from them.

But Finn himself, in company with Caoilte, did not follow them. Those two had stopped upon the threshold and were staring back across the bridge.

At its far end, still closely flanked by its two guarding hounds, stood the little fawn. The creature was gazing into the yard of the fortress with what could only be called uncertainty in its dark eyes.

"I can't believe it followed us all the way here," Caoilte said in a wondering tone. "Do you think it's meaning to come in?"

"I don't know," said Finn. "It seems a bit afraid now."

"Then chase it off!" Caoilte said with sudden sharpness. "It won't take but a shout and a hop toward it to make it bolt."

"Why so savage?" Finn asked, giving his friend a puzzled look. "You've been strange about it from the first."

"There's just something wrong in it," the other said in a vague way, shaking his head irritably. "I don't know. I just feel a great trouble in this fawn."

"Trouble?" Finn repeated, smiling. "In this fierce beast?"

"Come along now, Finn," Caoilte shot back. "Don't be trying that again. You know as well as I there could be magic working here, and danger too, for all its innocent look. We've met such things before. Be wary!"

"All right then," Finn agreed. "I'll grant there may be magic here. I may even have a feeling of it myself. But when has fear of that ever made us turn away? If there is magic, why, it only gives some adventure to this. And, magic or not, the fawn has followed us here for some reason of its own. If I don't soon discover what it is, I'll go mad from wondering about it."

He stepped back through the gateway onto the bridge, leaving Caoilte to look after him misgivingly. The fawn retreated a step, as if expecting that he might be planning an attack. As before, the hounds moved forward protectively.

"Easy, lads," Finn told them. "I said I meant no harm. I only mean to welcome your charge to our dun." He met the glistening gaze of the nervous animal. His voice took on a gentle and reassuring tone. "Little fawn, if it's my own permission that you wish to enter Almhuin, then I grant it to you. Enter here safely if you will."

He stepped aside, sweeping back a hand in a gracious gesture of welcome. The fawn hesitated a moment longer, looking from Finn to the open gateway. Then, slowly, it began to walk across, flanked closely by the watching, wary hounds.

Within the yard, Finn's men had taken note of this peculiar little scene and had given over their washing to observe it more closely. This had caused the others about in the yard to cease their own activities and become curious onlookers as well. For some unaccountable reason, a strange air of expectation descended upon the now hushed yard as the fawn's tiny hooves tapped lightly across the planks.

Just outside the gateway it paused once again, head

thrust forward, eyes scanning the interior searchingly. Its frail body was tense and trembling. But finally it moved on, taking a first, tentative step across the threshold.

When the tip of its outthrust forefoot penetrated the invisible boundary that separated inside from outside, a shimmering, silver glow appeared around it. As the fawn stepped on, drawing the rest of its form across, it was slowly enveloped by the light, as if it were passing through a screen that was charging it with energy, or diving through a surface into some liquid that engulfed it, until, once within the gates, it was totally encased in a shimmering aura.

It stopped, standing stiffly on the spindly legs, body trembling quite violently now. As the fascinated watchers stared, the glow began slowly to intensify, swelling outward, forming a brilliant, translucent chrysalis within which only the dim outline of the creature could be seen.

"There is magic in this, Caoilte!" Finn said excitedly. "Look there! It's shape-shifting!"

"Careful," warned Caoilte, stepping back and lifting his spear defensively. "It could become anything!"

Within the pod, there was clearly something unusual happening. The shadowy form was growing, stretching in a most grotesque way, as if great forces were jerking it, twisting it, distorting it in ways that would have to cause immense pain to anything shaped like the little fawn. But these forces were not destructive. They seemed, instead, to be succeeding in altering the creature's shape. As the form grew larger, it also rose upright, appearing to stand upon its hind legs.

The glow about it now began to fade. The concealing shell of silver began to melt away from about the encased form, as ice would melt before an intense heat. In moments the chrysalis was gone, revealing what had been newly formed within it.

It was a young woman who stood before the astonished gathering. She was very young and fair, with a wealth of unbound golden hair cascading about her shoulders. Her slender, willowy form was clad in a simple gown of white linen.

But there was no time for the watchers to form more

detailed an impression of her, for as the glow faded it seemed to release some supporting hold from her. Her body sagged as if drained of all its strength. She swayed, clearly ready to collapse. Her eyes fell upon Finn and she weakly raised an arm in supplication to him.

He leaped forward at once, sweeping an arm about her just as she sank down.

"You . . . you've saved me," she breathed out, and then fell back limply, eyes dropping closed.

Finn looked up from her to Caoilte.

"By the Dagda," the dark warrior began, "what—"

"She's fainted," Finn answered tersely. "Let's get her inside."

He slipped his other arm under her legs and lifted her easily, as if she were a child. Cradling her gently, he carried her toward the central building. The rest of his men, joined by the others in the yard, trooped after him, drawn by the curiosity that shone in their captivated gazes.

Finn passed through a large doorway into an interior that seemed very cool and dim after the late-afternoon glare in the yard. The central portion of the structure consisted of one large room of a circular shape. It was open to the peak of the thatched roof, nearly three stories above. The roof beams were supported by a number of thick wooden pillars deeply carved with intricate designs of curling, interlacing vines and elongated, stylized birds and animals, all polished and inset with gleaming bronze. These pillars surrounded a wide fire pit with a circular stone hearth, where a cheery fire now blazed.

The decor of the room was simple. Woven reed mats covered a floor of beaten earth. Plank tables and benches formed their own circle about the fire pit. Outside these was a second ring of pillars. Wooden walls ran from them to the outer wall, like spokes, dividing the space into wedge-shaped compartments, while movable wickerwork partitions separated each room from the large central space. On the walls above hung shields with a variety of brilliantly painted devices and weapons whose polished iron glinted redly in the firelight.

A number of men and women in small caps and aprons

of white cloth were busily engaged about the fire, tending game cooking on long spits or slipping ingredients into immense, steaming cauldrons suspended from the roof beams on iron chains. Around the room other servants, clad in tunics and trousers of dark wool, were hard at work cleaning, laying out the plates and tankards for a meal, and setting new tapers in the many wall sconces in preparation for the coming night.

All of these folk quickly gave over their labors to stare agape as Finn entered with his burden, followed by the crowd.

"Garbhcronan!" Finn called loudly as he strode across the floor.

A gray-haired man wearing a leather apron and carrying a short, thick staff left a group of cooks he had been haranguing and rushed to meet the fair-haired man.

"Yes, my captain?" he asked crisply, drawing his angular form stiffly up. Though his sharp features were as expressionless as stone, a flicker of puzzlement did show in his eyes as they swept over the unconscious girl.

"Have my quarters opened and my bed made ready," Finn ordered. "I'll put her there."

Without a word of question the man went swiftly into action. He signaled to a pair of nearby serving men and led the way across the room at a jog.

They reached the far side of the central space, stopping before the wickerwork partition that set off the outer segment there. At the direction of Garbhcronan, the two servants lifted the moveable wall easily and shifted it aside, creating a wide entrance to the chamber beyond. The three then moved inside. The gray-haired man threw open the shutters of a window in the outer wall, flooding the room with the golden evening light. His helpers quickly smoothed the covering of furs and blankets upon a low pallet.

They drew respectfully back as Finn entered with the girl. He crossed to the bed, bent down, and eased her slowly onto the soft mound of covers. For a moment he lingered there, his arms still beneath the slender form, his face very close to hers. His eyes were minutely searching that young face, something there seeming to hold him, keeping him from releasing her.

"Finn," Caoilte said from the doorway.

As if the voice had awakened him from some dream, Finn started, shaking his head. Then, but with clear reluctance, he slid his arms gently out, stood up, and drew away from her.

Caoilte and the others from the yard, their ranks now much swelled by those from the hall, had crowded in behind Finn, jamming the opening to the chamber, to stare wide-eyed at the figure. Save for Caoilte, they all appeared to be as totally captivated by her as was Finn.

There was good reason for that. She was of a most rare beauty indeed. Her looks were fine, fair, and fragile as a spring blossom in its first flush of blooming. Her skin was smooth and white and seemed almost luminescent in the beam of sunlight that fell upon her and sparked her streaming hair to golden flame.

"Get out of my way now, you great herd of oafs!" came a voice high, clear, but edged with irritation. "Let me through! What's happening?"

The people of the crowd shifted suddenly, and from the dense forest of their legs emerged a small figure. It was of the size and light build of a boy of ten, but its face was that of a man of mature years. The features were small and sharp, tapering from a wide forehead topped with bushy brown hair to a neatly pointed chin.

He stopped when he had gotten free of the crowd and had a clear view. A shrewd, carefully calculating gaze took in Finn and the young woman on the bed, and his expression of irritation changed to one of keen interest.

"Ah, well," he said, "I see what all the great rushing here is about now! And who is this, then?"

"I don't know, my Little Nut," Finn told him. "She followed us back here from the hunt in the shape of a fawn. When she came inside the walls of Almhuin, she transformed into this."

"A fawn, you say?" said the little man. "And she transformed!" He moved closer to the bed to peer at her, his eyes bright with an even greater fascination. "So, the Sidhe are in this somehow, are they not?"

"They must be," Finn said. "But I don't know how."

"She is a lovely one, so she is that!" the other exclaimed in open admiration. "She's fairly shining with it. A very dangerous beauty, so she has."

"Dangerous?" Finn repeated, clearly surprised by this odd choice of terms. "What do you—"

But he was interrupted. The girl stirred, moaning softly. Her eyes fluttered and then slowly opened. Green eyes, intense and deep as the summer meadows they were now, not the dark eyes of the fawn. They stared upward a moment as if focusing, then shifted, falling upon Finn. Her smooth brow furrowed in a worried frown.

Finn swiftly moved forward again, kneeling beside her.

"There's nothing to fear," he assured her gently. "You're safe here."

She lifted a small, slim hand and ran her fingers along the firm line of his jaw. Her troubled look vanished, replaced by one of joy.

"Oh, you are real!" she said in a tone of relief. "I—I was afraid that I had dreamed."

"Who are you?" Finn asked, taking the hand and holding it in his own. "Why was the appearance of a fawn on you?"

"It was a curse," she answered. "It was put upon me for refusing the love of a druid of the Sidhe. An evil man he is, called Fear Doirche."

Finn exchanged a quick glance with the little man standing beside him, whose pursed lips and cocked eyebrow announced that the name was both a familiar and an impressive one.

"My own name is Sabd," she went on. "It is three years now that I have lived the life of a wild deer in a far part of Ireland. But finally, a man who served the druid took pity on me. He helped me to escape and showed me the way here."

"Why here?" asked Finn.

"He told me that if I could come within the fortress upon dun Almhuin, the druid would have no more power over me. My enchantment would be broken. He showed me to where you hunted and told me I must lead the hunt until no one but you and those two great hounds were still with me. He said the hounds had human wits and would not harm me, for they would know my nature to be like their own."

Making this long speech was obviously wearing for her. At its conclusion her head sank back and she breathed heavily, in an exhausted way.

"No more now," Finn told her. "You just rest. Your long run and your transformation must have used much of your strength. Sleep. Later, if you feel stronger, you can join us at our feast."

She smiled a grateful but sleepy smile at him for that and snuggled down into the covers like a small child. Voicing a soft sigh of contentment, she closed her eyes, relaxed, and was asleep almost instantly.

Finn rose and went to the window, quietly easing closed the shutters to darken the room. Then he turned to the crowd.

"Be off now, the lot of you," he told them in a hushed voice. "She needs rest."

He moved toward them, lifting his arms in a shooing gesture. As they dispersed, he moved out of the room, shifting the partition back to narrow the opening to a crack.

"Have one of the women come to keep a watch on her," he told Garbhcronan. "When she awakes, supply any of her needs and see that she's given some proper clothes to wear."

"I will, my captain," the man assured him crisply and set off about his task.

The crowd had vanished by this time, and the people of the fortress had gone back to their activities. Finn looked about to find himself left with only Caoilte, Bran, and Sceolan, and the one he had called the Little Nut.

The two great hounds, overlooked in the excitement about the girl, had continued to stay as close to her as possible. They had planted themselves on either side of the narrowed opening to Finn's chamber, clearly on guard once again.

"Well, lads, you've done well," he told them. "But your task is ended. She's safely here. You can go off now. Rest yourselves."

Neither budged. They only sat all the straighter, lifting their heads higher in a gesture of stubbornness.

"All right, then," he said with a grin. "Protect her if you still feel the need." He glanced through the opening at the shadowed figure on the bed and his voice took on a more introspective tone. "She's surely a prize worth the protecting."

"So she has something to do with the Others, as I guessed," Caoilte said tersely.

Finn, with an effort, tore his gaze from the girl and turned it to his friend. The dark-haired man was standing with arms folded on his chest, chin out, and face set in stern lines.

"I don't much like the idea of her being here," he went on in a disapproving tone. "She'll bring trouble."

"We can't turn down her plea for help, Caoilte," Finn told him reasonably. "She came here for sanctuary."

"The Sidhe do not interfere in our affairs or give help to us freely," the other returned obstinately. "I say we should act in the same way toward them."

"I don't believe that this girl is of the Sidhe herself," the little man put in. "I don't feel any of their aura about her."

"And how many times have you been wrong before, small one?" Caoilte said derisively. "And nearly gotten us all killed because of it?"

"Not so often as yourself, you great, arrogant lout," the Little Nut fired back.

"Quiet, both of you," Finn said. "Sidhe or not, she will not be turned away from here." He fixed a meaningful gaze on Caoilte. "She will be welcomed here, and there'll be no more said of it."

To this the dark-haired man gave no reply, but the look he returned to his comrade was still smoldering with unhidden discontent.

CHAPTER ◊ 4

A
Visitation

THE GREAT HALL OF ALMHUIN WAS FILLED WITH LIGHT
and life. The fire blazed high and, with the many tapers,
gave the white-walled room a pleasant glow. The lively
tunes of a dozen musicians filled the air, mingling with the
talk and laughter of the feasting assembly.

It was a colorful company now gathered at the circle of
plank tables. The men of the hunt had given over their
simple garb for brighter trappings whose varied colors and
textures reflected the quite individual tastes of the wearers.
Tunics were often of satin or silk, but even the woolen and
linen ones were richly embroidered with colored threads
and edged with fringes of silver or gold. Over these were
flamboyantly draped cloaks skillfully woven in patterns of
brilliant hues.

Large brooches fastened these cloaks at the throat or
shoulder, and they were as unique and striking as the
garments they adorned. Circles of precious metal glinted
with jewels and enameling forming intricate, coiling designs.

These brooches were far from the only ornament for
the men. All wore bracelets about wrists and upper arms,
and golden torcs of pipe or twisted strands about their
necks. But an even grander display of their vanity was
seen in the elaborate styling of their hair. The simple,
loose plaits they had worn on the hunt had been replaced
by coiffures that only loving attention and much time
could have created. Most wore their long hair in several
small, neat braids. Upon these braids were strung beads of

colored glass or precious metal, and through these were twined strands of silver and gold, while the ends were fastened in large bangles, also of gold or glass.

Seated with this nearly dazzling array of men were others in a somewhat different garb—different, but no less impressive. At one table were several men in long robes of a deep red trimmed in gold, at another were men clad in gleaming white edged in silver, while at a third sat men wearing fur-fringed green. The members of each group wore matching torcs of complex design, clearly designations of their class and rank.

One table was set upon a low platform to lift it just slightly above the throng. At the center of it sat young Finn, himself much transformed from his former simple look and making a show of resplendency that easily rivaled the rest. His tunic was white silk all stitched in silver. His cloak was a fine blue wool edged in rich sable. And although he had left his hair in a single, unadorned plait, its glowing silver-whiteness was still enough to distinguish it above the others.

At his right hand sat the girl, now elegantly dressed in a soft, brocaded gown of rich green. She was gazing about her with wide-eyed fascination as Finn most enthusiastically—and a bit boastfully—pointed out personages in the company to her.

"And over there," he was saying, gesturing toward the table of red-gowned men, "are my own physicians. Four are from Ireland, and one is from the far east, over the sea!"

She made a little sound of amazement at that, and Finn went on to indicate the white-cloaked men.

"And there are my druids. Five of the best such that ever came into the west they are, and led by Cainnelscaith of the Shining Shield, who can bring down any knowledge from the sky and foretell battles!"

She stared in awe at them as if they were fabulous beings. Finn, clearly much gratified at her response, proudly pointed out the green-clad men.

"Those others are my five bards. Full Ollamhs they all are, and among them Daighre, son of Morna. And—see that red-haired one?—that's Suanach, son of Senshenn, he that was my own father's teller of the old stories! Never has there been a man in Ireland with sweeter voice than Senshenn, except his son."

"The music of your players is sweet as well," said Sabd in her soft but earnest voice. "Even the birds of the forests I wandered as a fawn could make no finer sounds."

"That is a compliment indeed," Finn said. "But you should be giving it to the man who sits at my other side: Cnu Deireoil—our own Little Nut."

Beaming with pleasure, the little man responded both speedily and enthusiastically.

"I thank you, Finn MacCumhal," he said, and then leaned across the young man to address Sabd. "And I thank you with even greater heart, beautiful lady. For, you see, it was myself alone who chose these musicians, and they are indeed better than any in the whole length and breadth of Ireland." He paused, then added with a broad grin, "Save for myself, of course."

"Though he has no modesty at all," Finn said, laughing, pushing the man back, "he does speak the truth. With harp or pipe, he can coax clouds from the sky and draw waves onto the shore to dance for him."

"The ones who serve us are the finest in Ireland as well!" This came from the young man named Lughaid, seated beyond Cnu Deireoil, and clearly also most eager to join in the conversation with the lovely Sabd. "Even the High-King himself has none better. Not cupbearers, or cooks, or serving men, or—"

"Or stewards . . ." Finn cut in, smoothly reclaiming her attention, much to the obvious disappointment of the other. "Our whole great troop of servants is led by Garbhcronan of the Rough Buzzing. Look, there he is." He pointed out the spare, austere, gray-haired man with the staff. He was now engaged in soundly reprimanding a serving boy—red-faced with shame—who had spilled a cup in the filling of it.

"You can see where he comes by his name," Cnu Deireoil said with a grin. "Quite ruthless with them all he is. You'd think he was a chieftain of the clans."

"And who is that large man?" she asked. "I seem to remember him from the woods."

She was indicating the ruddy-faced one called Comhrag, who was at the moment engaged in downing a near cauldron-size goblet of ale in what seemed a single gulp.

"Ah, well that's one of our most prized fellows, that is," Finn told her. "He's Comhrag, my chief huntsman. Master of near to five hundred hounds he is when all the Fian clans of Munster are on the hunt."

"Oh, this place is too wonderful," the girl said, looking about her in an enraptured way. "I've not the eyes or the mind to take it all in at once. It has too many riches. Too much finery. I've never seen a company so grandly dressed as yours."

"Our warriors are not usually quite so grand," came the voice of Caoilte.

The dark warrior had been relegated to a seat on the far side of the girl. And, though he had a place surely envied by every other man in the hall, he had up to now taken no part in the talk or even paid any apparent notice to Sabd. His expression was stony. His own clothing was a simple white linen tunic and a plain dark blue wool cloak fastened by an iron pin. His black hair was twisted into its same single plait, unadorned by bangles.

"The Fian warrior is quite a simple sort of man," he went on, his voice dry but still managing to convey just a hint of sarcasm. "But all our lads have chosen to don their finest tonight, for some reason."

On these last words, he fixed a penetrating look on Sabd that caused her to drop her eyes and brought a blush to her white cheeks.

"She's well deserving of our showing her our best," Finn put in defensively. "You might do with a bit of sprucing up yourself, Caoilte. You look like a gray-necked crow after a great storm."

This drew a good deal of laughter from the men at the table. Caoilte scowled and turned away, lifting his cup sharply for a deep draught.

"Well, if all of this fine show really is for me, I am too much honored," the girl said earnestly, looking to Finn. "I thank you for it, as I thank you for this gown." She lifted the material of the garment's skirt. The elaborate embroidery scintillated in the light.

"Your thanks for that should also rightly go to others," Finn said modestly. "There are fifty of the best sewing women in Ireland brought together in a rath on Magh Feman, and they make the clothing for the Fianna through the whole of the year. It was they who made that gown."

"It's a wonderful thing to see them working," Cnu Deireoil put in. "For three of them play on little silver harps to entertain the others. And there's a great candlestick of stone in the center of the room to give them light, for they're not willing to kindle a fire more than three times in a year, fearing that the smoke and ash of it might harm the needlework."

"It is the finest clothing in the wide world they make," Finn said, "and not really deserved by such coarse men as the likes of us." His eye met and held hers while he added with great sincerity, "But it is surely fitting for you. I've never seen your like for putting its beauty to shame, or green eyes that would make its own green seem so pale."

At this she blushed again and, clearly flustered, turned her gaze away.

"It is most welcome to have such a gown," she said, "and especially after so long under the curse, without any human comforts at all. But it is still more than I deserve. It was only a simple, tiny rath I came from. We had no such things as these; no harpers, no bards, no powerful druids or bright warriors. It was a plain and peaceful life I lived there with my . . . my family."

Her voice had become more uneven, more choked with emotion as she had gone on. Now she faltered to a stop, her face a mask of sadness.

"Be easy," Finn said, putting a comforting hand lightly upon her slender shoulder. "Could you tell us what happened to you? How you came under this curse? Or is it too painful?"

"No," she said, bravely drawing herself up and speaking with determination. "No, I have had three years of mourning for my lost home and family. I can control the sorrow. But the image . . . the image is undimmed."

She stared straight ahead, her bright gaze fixed on empty space as if she could see the image before her

there. Her soft voice took on a sharp edge honed by
bitterness.

"Our rath was attacked, taken, ravaged by those...
creatures. Not beasts. Not men. His creatures, led by
him. They killed my family and left them unburied and
unmourned, cloaked black by the carrion crows. But
me... me he wished alive. He wanted my love. When I
refused, he changed me to a fawn."

For all her courage in the telling of it, the terrible fears
recalled by the tale had clearly been a strain upon her,
draining her emotionally. Pale now, she dropped her head
forward, her shoulders shaking with her grief. Finn slipped
his arm about her protectively.

"I have heard of this Fear Doirche," Cnu Deireoil said,
"It was his own people, the Tuatha de Danaan, who put
the name Dark Druid upon him. He is an evil man,
shunned by the others. An exile by his own choice. It's
said that many years ago he went off to find some hidden
place of his own. Many other outcast scum of the Sidhe
have joined him since."

"They are horrible," the girl said with force, looking up
again. "Monstrous and cruel."

"Well, my girl, there're bad amongst every people,
even the Others," the Little Nut responded in a reasoning, somewhat defensive way. "But you can't be condemning
the whole of the Tuatha de Danaan for that lot."

"That's true enough," Finn put in supportively. "Cnu
Deireoil is the proof of that. He's of the de Danaan blood
himself."

"He is?" the girl said in surprise, staring at the little
man as if uncertain whether to be fascinated or alarmed.

"Well, it's more truthful to say I was," he assured her,
grinning. "But, you see, I left them. There's more freedom and excitement in the mortal world. So I've nothing
at all to do with them now, nor they with me. They don't
think much of one of their own leaving the Hidden Places
for the great Outside."

"And what about you, Finn MacCumhal?" she asked,
turning a speculative eye upon him. "On our wild coast,
we knew little of the rest of Ireland. I've heard nothing of
you. You called your people the Fianna. What are they?"

"We're simply fighting men of Ireland," he briefly explained, "banded together in the service of the High-King. It's our sworn duty to see the laws of Ireland upheld and to defend her from her enemies." He smiled at her. "And now, our duty is to defend you."

She smiled in return. Their gazes locked, their faces now close together. Both seemed to become oblivious to the rest of the room, as if held by some spell.

Caoilte, glancing around to see the reason for this sudden fall of silence, noted the mutual rapture with a jaundiced eye. The musicians' last tune was just coming to an end, and he wasted no time seizing the chance to interrupt this tryst.

"Cnu Deireoil," he called loudly, "why don't you favor us with a tune? Surely you can't disappoint our guest."

This did manage to catch Finn's attention, breaking his contact with Sabd. He enthusiastically endorsed the suggestion.

"Aye! The finest harper should play for the most lovely woman. Something bright, my Little Nut. To give her cheering."

"I would never let such a chance pass me by," Cnu Deireoil readily agreed

He took up a case of soft leather from beside him and most gently opened it. From within he removed a wonderfully crafted harp, its gracefully curving bow of red yew wood intricately carved and set with jewels. Taking it up, he moved around the table, hopped down from the low platform, and strode out to near the fire pit, where all in the room might best hear.

On seeing him about to play, the whole company fell silent. He bowed graciously toward the young woman and then his long, slender fingers lightly touched the strings.

The silvery strands shimmered, giving out a fresh, bright, airy sound that, though soft, still filled the enormous space. It was like a spring afternoon captured and brought within the hall. It was an atmosphere as much as a sound that wrapped itself about the company, holding them spellbound, hanging on each note, gazes turned inward to their own, separate reveries.

The girl too was clearly enchanted by the tune. A look

of pleasure filled her young face, made her eyes sparkle and brought a flush of warmth into her cheeks as she relaxed to listen.

Finn MacCumhal, however, seemed to have found a captivating force much stronger than the musical web spun by the little man's harp. His own gaze was still fixed on the profile of Sabd, his eyes seeming to drink her in like a long-parched man would drink at a cool pond, his whole attention, his whole being caught up, and his body leaning toward her as if drawn by some irresistible power.

Then, with the suddenness of a lightning stroke, a roaring sound rose outside the hall.

It sounded as if a great wind had risen from nowhere to boom about the roof, rattling the thatch. But, not content to stay without, the force quickly focused at the peak and shot down through the wide smoke hole of the fireplace.

It appeared like a whirlwind of black clouds, dropping in a corkscrewing pillar toward the floor of the hall. It created a windstorm within the room, fluttering the hair and clothes of the astonished gathering, spinning away the smoke of the central fire while fanning the flames to a crackling height.

Cnu Deireoil, closest to the descending spiral of darkness, was nearly thrown backward by the blast, but stood his ground stubbornly, leaning into the force, clutching his precious harp tightly to him while his cloak stood straight out behind him.

The pillar's base touched the floor near the fire, just before Finn's platform. As it did, the upper portion of it sank instantly down, the winds dying, the darkness fading away, disclosing an ominous form.

It was cloaked from head to foot in a black robe, and seemed at first a slender column of dark stone. But then arms slowly lifted, raising wide sleeves like raven's wings. The head came up, shaking back a hood to reveal the lean and lined face of the Dark Druid. He turned, looking about him with a haughtiness at the staring crowd, his lips curled in a smile of contempt.

"So, these are the mortals who dare to oppose my will," he said with a sneer. "A sorry lot, like all their kind."

Finn had jumped to his feet at the first appearance of

the dark whirlwind. Now the girl rose too, her face ashen, her body trembling as violently as had the fawn's.

"The Dark Druid!" she cried in a despairing voice.

At the sound of her voice, the man whirled to fix his gaze on her.

"Ah, there you are, my little fawn," he crowed triumphantly. "You didn't really believe you could escape me, did you?"

He stepped toward her and she cowered back. But Finn moved to draw her behind him, facing the druid with a look of defiance.

"Get back from her," he warned. "She has been given sanctuary here, and you've no power over her any more."

The druid stopped. His gaze flickered over the fair young man, but his expression showed only a faint interest, as if he were considering a pestering fly.

"You would be well advised not to trouble me, boy," he said in a commanding tone. His right arm lifted higher, bringing into view from the robe's folds the long staff he gripped. "Stand away now, and I'll not harm you or your people. I give you one chance, mortal."

"Don't fight him, please," the girl whispered urgently to Finn, clutching his elbow in a tight grip. "He'll only destroy you. Please. I'll go with him."

Finn leaned back to whisper in return: "That you will not. Don't fear him. You're safe here."

He patted her clutching hand in a reassuring way, then straightened and looked back to Fear Doirche, giving him a broad smile of real amusement.

"Don't be making a greater fool of yourself than you have already, man," he said. "You've no power here. Don't you know that? You can do no harm to anyone within the walls of this fortress. The hill on which you're standing is of the Tuatha de Danaan. It was passed to me from Nuada Silver Hand himself—he that was High-King of all the de Danaans. You've surely heard of him."

"Nuada?" said the Dark Druid, a hint of uncertainty showing in his eyes.

"Ah, so you do know of him!" Finn said. "Then you understand that the hill protects those upon it from the magic of the Sidhe. You'll be casting none of your enchantments on those within this hall!"

"You lie!" the druid snapped. He stepped forward, swinging up his staff to point its silver tip at Finn.

Nothing happened, save that Finn laughed outright.

Fear Doirche's face grew yet darker with a flush of rage. He swept the staff around him to point at the others in the crowd. It had no more effect.

Now it was Finn's turn to move. In a sudden, single vault he was over the table. A second leap from the platform put him close before the druid.

Startled by the young warrior's move, Fear struck out with the staff, meaning this time to use it as a club.

Finn raised an arm in a swift countermove and easily knocked the weapon aside. At the same time his other arm shot forward, his open palm slamming against the druid's chest. Fear staggered backward, legs striking the hearth. He sat down hard upon the stones.

This raised a chorus of derisive laughter and catcalls from the crowd at the druid's expense. But the humiliation only seemed to goad the man to another effort. Snarling with rage, he rose up, swinging out again.

This time Finn stepped forward, moving inside the blow. One hand seized the druid's wrist in a viselike grip, halting the staff in mid-swing. The other hand swept down to grip the handle of a long iron cooking spit laid in the fire. Finn lifted it, bringing the sizzling, red-hot point up toward the druid's face.

The man ceased to struggle, his eyes fixing on the glowing tip so close before him.

"You would not kill me," Fear said, but with a shade of doubt just tingeing his words. Though he was still trying to maintain his haughty manner, he was having little success under the circumstances.

"Don't make any mistakes about me, druid," Finn told him coldly. "You're not a man of honor, to be treated with the rights due an honest man. You've enslaved this woman and killed her family. For that I should kill you now. But I will free you, if you'll pledge before us that Sabd will be forever free of you." He brought the heated point a bit closer as an inducement, saying threateningly, "Pledge now, druid, or this spit will burn through your eye socket to the center of your brain and Sabd will be free of you anyway!"

The man's face convulsed in fury.

"Never!" he spat out, and, with that word, his form dissolved from the young warrior's grip. In an instant he had faded into a plume of gray smoke and was shooting upward like a geyser to spout through the chimney hole.

Finn, taken off guard by the suddenness of the transformation, thrust forward with the spit, but too late. He missed the rising column, and looked upward in frustration as it slid through the opening.

But as the tail of the serpentine plume of smoke vanished from sight, a voice charged with rage and venom floated back to echo within the hall.

"She will never be free of me, proud warrior! I will have her yet, and I will see you destroyed!"

CHAPTER ◊ 5

Promises

THE ONLY ILLUMINATION WAS FROM THE WINDOWS OF
Almhuin's great hall. The squares of gold evenly spaced
about its walls made it look a giant, jewel-set crown in the
night. And with the light, the sounds of music and of
voices came also from the hall where the feasters sat late
over their drinking and telling of tales. The rest of the
fortress yard was dark and quiet and nearly empty.

But not quite. There was one pair of figures strolling
along the parapet walk that circled the yard high on the
inside of the palisade. From here the view of the countryside was impressive, spreading away in all directions about
the hill.

A sweet, soft darkness lay upon the nighttime countryside. The air was fresh, not chill, and scented with the
invigorating tang of spring's new growth. A full moon
silvered the clouds that sailed beneath it and made the
meadows seem a billowing cloak of deep green wool. It
also shone upon the young faces of the couple on the
parapet: Finn and Sabd.

The sounds of the hall drifted to the strolling pair, but
they seemed oblivious to them, detached somehow, as if
they had a little world of their own together there. Sabd
was listening raptly again as Finn spoke, her gaze shifting
to follow his pointing arm as he proudly told her of the
construction of his fortress.

"And that trough of marble was created by our master
sculptor for us," he said, indicating the white basin just
within the gates. "At the end of each day it's the custom of

the Fian warrior to first have his bath and see to his grooming, so the trough may be the best used thing within Almhuin." He paused and then added with a grin, "After our weapons and our ale tankards, of course."

"It's most fascinating," she said, but the last word was mingled with a small yawn.

He looked at her with sudden concern.

"I'm sorry!" he told her contritely. "You've had a wearing day and so many shocks, and here I am keeping you up through half the night with my bragging. Like a child showing off his newest toys."

"No, no!" she protested quickly. "I've been most interested. Really! And it is amazing that one so young as yourself has built up all of this."

"Well, I had just a bit of help with it," he said, smiling again. "And the idea for building it came from my clansmen. You'll soon find that modesty is not a trait of anyone in my family. The old stronghold of my father was long abandoned and decayed. They felt a captain of the Fianna needed a grander place, and one that would remind all that the Clan na Baiscne was once more the most powerful in Ireland."

"Once more?" she repeated. "What do you mean?"

"It's a very long tale," he told her. "Someday, when you're wanting another chance at being bored, I'll tell it to you."

"Oh, I'm certain that nothing about you could bore me," she said with great enthusiasm, looking up at him and then, suddenly abashed, turning away to look out across the countryside.

"And these lands," she asked, swiftly changing subjects, "are they yours as well?"

"All Ireland is ours," he said in a grand way, moving up beside her and sweeping a hand around at the horizon. "The Fianna are not bound to duns and tuaths and provinces as are the other folk. We're free. We rove where we will and fight where we must. In the cold half of the year we find quarters in our own homes or the homes of those we serve. But in the warm half . . . ah, then the wild woods and the rough mountains and the wide plains of Ireland are our home. Then is our real living time."

"You say you're free," she said, looking to him with a small frown of puzzlement, "yet you tell me that you serve the people of Ireland, that you're bound to them by oaths of loyalty and by payments made to you."

"We're loyal, yes," he said, "but that's by our own choice now, not as tribute forced from us by Ireland's lords, the way it was with our fathers. There's no power in Ireland that can make the Fianna do what they've no wish to do. Not even that of the High-King."

"And you, Finn MacCumhal," she said, regarding him with curiosity, "who are you?"

"I don't know what you mean," he said, smiling disarmingly. "I'm nothing more than a fighting man of the Fians, like my comrades."

"No. You are more," she said with certainty. "To lead such a wondrous company, to have so grand a fortress, to face Fear Doirche as you did; those things make you something more."

She leaned toward him, her eyes searching his. Her face grew serious, and her tone turned gravely earnest as she asked, "And are you happy?"

"Happy?" he echoed. The unexpected question seemed to nonplus him. He drew back a little, looking at her with surprise. "Why . . ." he began, then halted, as if suddenly aware that an answer did not come so readily. He considered a moment, then began again.

"Of course!" he said with enormous certainty. "And why wouldn't I be? There's no grander life. I have my comrades, my adventuring, my hunts. They're what I was meant for. They're what my whole life has been."

"And yet," she said slowly, thoughtfully, continuing to probe the depths of his eyes with her own, "I see something in you. I hear it in your voice. I feel it. Some . . . yearning maybe? Some . . . regret?"

He clearly didn't know how to respond to this, only looking puzzled and uncomfortable. Finally she shook her head as if irritated by herself.

"I'm sorry," she told him. "I've no right to be prying into your feelings. I'm only grateful for the help you've given me, and regret the danger you've taken upon yourself."

"Danger?" said Finn. "But I've told you, there's no danger."

"There is," she insisted. "The Dark Druid won't rest until he takes me and has revenge on you. You don't know how powerful he is."

"He can still be destroyed," Finn assured her most boldly, striking a gallant pose. "And if you tell me where he is, I promise you I'll go to him and either force him to release you, or see his treacherous life ended."

"I wish it could be," she said truthfully, "but I've no idea where he is. His home is far away and it's well hidden. That's all I know. I went and left there in the fawn's shape. Even what memory I have is clouded by my transformation." She paused and considered, then went on more philosophically. "But perhaps that's best. For even if I were to know, I couldn't have you risking yourself more for me. He would be far too deadly on his own ground."

"Nothing is too great a risk to see you free," Finn said fervently, taking her small hand and enveloping it tightly in his.

"I am content enough with my new fate," she replied with a matching ardor of her own, lifting her other hand to clasp his. "To be here, with you, as a woman once again, is great freedom to me after my years as a fawn."

"Then, my lady, there's no greater pleasure I can think of than to have you here," he said. "And I promise you that I'll make your life as happy a one as it can be."

In their absorption with each other, neither took note of the figure standing silhouetted in the light streaming from the hall's doorway. The golden light glowed behind the profile of Caoilte MacRonan and struck a hard gleam from his eyes as he stared up toward the pair upon the wall.

Sword swept against sword, clanging as the blades met.

Finn stepped back as Caoilte drove in, parrying a savage cut, striking back with his round shield in a blow that knocked the dark warrior sideways a step.

In the warmth of the open, sunny yards, the two were stripped to only their simple tunics, which clung to their sweat-soaked, straining bodies as they battled back and forth across the hard-packed earth.

Both men were truly laboring; their fight, though practice, was of little less intensity than the real thing. Their moves were broad, powerful, and very swift. Their tactics were shrewd, loose, and brutal, both combatants using legs, knees, shoulders, and whole bodies as weapons along with swords and shields. They were in constant motion, whirling about one another, lunging in, often swinging about locked in close embrace, their battle appearing a grotesque parody of a dance. Their grace, energy, and skill had even afforded them an audience: a few other warriors who had quit their own exercises to watch, the two wolfhounds, a few idle servants, and some admiring women of the fortress. And nearby, two small boys copied the fighters with wooden staffs, at a play that also had a practical, if grim, purpose to it.

Finally both men drove in together, weapons locked against each other's shields, arms thrown wide, grunting with the strain, their taut and streaming faces pressed close together. For a long, tense moment they were frozen this way. Then Caoilte lowered his head and shot straight forward, butting Finn hard in the breastbone. The fair-haired man gave an *oof* of pain and staggered back, bent forward, barely maintaining his feet. He lowered his weapons and looked at his companion in surprise.

"We're being a bit rougher than usual today, aren't we?" he asked.

"With no enemy to hone our skills upon since the summer past, we've both gotten very dull," Caoilte tersely replied. "Especially . . . YOU!"

The last word was a shout and he attacked again upon it, clearly seeking to take the young captain off his guard. He did manage to drive his opponent back with a swift series of blows, but Finn soon recovered and they fell to it evenly once more.

But this time Finn wheeled right, feinted as if to come at his comrade's side, then darted back in and up under Caoilte's guard, fetching him a blow under the chin with his shield boss that snapped the dark man's head back.

Now it was his turn to retreat, recover, and stare in surprise.

"Dull, am I?" Finn told him with a grin. Then he tossed down the battered practice sword and shield. "Enough now. There's a great thirst on me."

He went to the stone basin and leaned over. After drinking from his cupped hands, he stuck his head right in the cool water, swooshing it up over his head and neck, then rising to let it run down over his sweating body. As he rose up, his gaze lit on a figure upon the parapet. It was Sabd, standing alone where he and she had stood before, looking out over the countryside.

He continued to gaze thoughtfully up at her while Caoilte moved in beside him to wash his own face.

"She's up there again," Finn commented to his friend.

"Is she?" the other replied without interest, splashing more water down his tunic front and then standing up.

"She's been on that parapet walk every day, just staring out," Finn added in a pitying tone.

"Let's get back to it," said Caoilte brusquely, taking up his weapons again.

Finn made no move for his own.

"There's little enough in this dun to cheer her," he went on. "She's not complained, but I know she's pining for her freedom."

Caoilte picked up Finn's sword and stepped close, his voice stern and almost lecturing: "Now, you listen to me, Finn. You can't do anything else for her. You've freed her from the spell and given her a place here. You owe her nothing more." He thrust the weapon into his friend's hand. "Now, come on. Let's just have another good fight."

"You're wrong, Caoilte," Finn replied, turning his gaze to the dark warrior. "I've promised to make her as happy here as I could. And that I will do."

Caoilte looked at the determination in his comrade's face. He gave a weary sort of sigh and shook his head.

"And what was that for?" Finn demanded.

"It was nothing," said Caoilte. "Nothing at all."

"It was something, all right," Finn insisted. "I know that sound well enough."

"I suppose you do," the other agreed. "And then you

also know what it means. Another smiling face, beguiling
gaze, lissome figure—"

"It's not like that at all," Finn protested. "It's that she's
so frail, so helpless, so—"

"Beautiful," Caoilte finished.

"Forlorn, I meant to say," Finn corrected in a testy
way. "And if I can't give her the whole world again, at least
I can give her a bit of it beyond these walls." He tossed
down the sword. "I'll take her outside myself," he said
decisively. He started toward her, but paused, looking
down at the old, stained tunic that he wore. "First, though,"
he added, "I think I'll change."

He turned about and headed for the hall. Caoilte
watched him go, his expression one of frustration. But
then an anger took him.

"The Morrigan curse it!" he spat out savagely and
heaved his own sword far across the yard.

The stick spun in the air as it arched high and then fell
back, thumping softly into the thick grass.

Bran and Sceolan were upon it together, rolling over
one another in their eagerness to be the one to possess it.
After some scuffling, snapping, and growling, Bran got the
stick firmly clenched in his massive jaws and went tearing
away, up the hillside, Sceolan close behind.

Above them, halfway up the slope to the fortress walls, sat
Finn and Sabd. She was applauding and laughing delightedly
as the hounds bounded to her. Bran dropped the stick before
her like some prize of gold and then offered his broad head
for her to pet. Then Sceolan arrived, crowding in beside
his brother and whining for like treatment.

"It's like puppies you two are," she said with vast
amusement, stroking the heads of both.

Their tails wagged furiously in their ecstasy.

"Easy, lads," Finn cautioned, grinning. "You'll be knocking
her down pressing in at her that way."

The solicitous pair quickly backed away, and Finn
stood up. He was now wearing a clean white tunic and his
green wool cloak. At his side hung a long sword in a
sheath of bronze etched with figures of beasts and warri-

ors. He picked up a plain, oval shield of gray metal and fitted it on his left arm, then offered his right hand to her.

"Shall we walk?" he said. "The brook below us is a most lovely place—especially in the spring."

She put out her hand and he drew her lightly to her feet. He pulled up a long, broad-bladed casting spear he had grounded beside him and they started down the slope. The two dogs frisked along with a most unseemly abandon at her either hand.

"Ah, it's good to be out here," she said as they swished through the meadow's lush, knee-high grass. "It's like coming into the light from a darkened room."

"And I'm certain the day's that much the brighter for your coming into it," he said.

"Get away with you," she said in embarrassment. "It's a teller of very pretty lies you are, Finn MacCumhal."

"Ask any man in Ireland and he will say that Finn MacCumhal has never told a lie," he protested. "It's a thing I'm most proud of. And I don't lie now in what I say. The lads know it." He pointed at the hounds. "Look at them. With you they forget all their dignity."

"That's as it may be," she responded laughingly, watching them cavort. Then her expression grew more thoughtful. "They are rather strange hounds," she went on. "They seem quite human in many ways."

"That they are," said Finn. "It's why the servant of the Dark Druid who sent you here told you they wouldn't harm you. You see, they were born of a woman—my own aunt it was—who had been transformed by a spell as you were, but into a hound."

"Transformed?" she said, looking at the pair with new interest. "Why?"

"It was for reasons much like your own—love and revenge. The lads were born when she had the hound's form upon her. She was restored, but they remained this way. Still, they have very human wits, and they sense in you a spirit kindred to theirs."

"Poor creatures," she said in a tone of deep compassion. "Doomed forever to wear those shapes. And I felt myself trapped!"

They reached the bottom of the slope. Here flowed a

small but exuberant brook, its banks lined with trees whose luxuriant foliage created a cool, shadowed haven from the bright, warm day. The four entered, moving down to the water's edge.

An ancient oak arched over the water at one point, its exposed roots making natural chairs at the bankside. Finn helped the girl settle herself comfortably into a cozy spot. The hounds, their manner sobering, took up positions on either side of the tree, sitting with heads up, alert and watching, clearly on guard.

"It's good that the lads still see themselves as your guardians," Finn said. "You couldn't have more clever, more ferocious, or more loyal friends." He grinned and added, "Besides myself, of course. They're very comforting to have along outside the dun."

"And is that the reason for your weapons, too?" she asked.

"It is," he admitted. "Do they trouble you?"

"I can make no complaint of anything that gives me a chance to walk the countryside," she said. "If only they weren't a reminder..."

"That the threat of this black druid hangs on you still," he finished. "Yes, I understand. Look, I'll put them away, out of sight. At least for a while you can try to forget and feel truly free."

He propped the spear behind the trunk and set down his shield beside it. He unstrapped his sword and put it out of sight between two roots.

"Are you certain it's safe to do that?" she asked him.

"Of course," he assured her as he sat down next to her. Still, he had been careful to lay his sword so that its hilt was very convenient to his right hand.

For a while, then, both just sat there quietly, listening to the pleasant, natural music of the flowing brook and the songs of birds. They seemed to need nothing else, not speaking but looking quite content, as if just being here, together, was enough.

But after a time, the girl gave a little sigh and said: "I am enjoying myself too much. I feel quite guilty, making you come here just for me. You must have so many other things to do."

"I haven't," he quickly protested. "I'm enjoying this myself." He gazed around him in a thoughtful way. "It's as if... well, as if I haven't really seen any of this in a very long time."

"Why not?" she asked.

"I suppose I've just not taken the time. I've been... busy."

"So I've heard," she said. "Some of the ladies told me you've spent all your days since the beginning of spring in the hunting. But they say you were a fine bard once."

"When I was young, maybe," he said dismissingly.

"But you're young now!" she said. She leaned toward him, her face flushed with excitement, her voice coaxing. "Please, could you do a poem—for me?"

He hesitated, looking into that glowing, earnest face. Then, as if there were a power there he could not deny, he nodded.

"Very well, then," he said with a smile. "But I'll not guarantee the worth of it."

He stood up, striking a formal pose. He began to speak, his words flowing from him, bright like the flow of the sprightly brook, rich like the grass in the summer glens, vividly colored like the spring flowers blooming on the hills.

The girl listened, raptly, and for that moment they formed an idyllic picture there, on the banks of the sparkling river in the peace of the golden, dreamlike afternoon.

CHAPTER◇6

Proposals

THE GOLDEN SCENE WAS SPREAD OUT BELOW THE watching Dark Druid and the seer Miluchradh.

The magic bubble that enclosed them seemed suspended close above the trees beside the brook. Peering down through the foliage of the upper branches like two curious crows, they spied unabashedly upon the young pair. The expression of the druidess was one of sardonic amusement. But the expression on Fear Doirche's face was one of nearly apoplectic rage.

"Look at them there!" he stormed, his fist clenching about his staff. "They defy me! They humiliate me again! They flaunt my power! That arrogant mortal—how dare he?" He started to climb up from his seat on the bed of cushions. "I will destroy him. I must destroy him!"

"Don't be too quick to act," she advised, placing a restraining hand upon his arm. "You may be risking yourself if you confront this warrior again."

"What do you mean?" he demanded impatiently. "He has no protection outside his fortress. I can use my powers upon him. He'll be helpless."

"That he will not," she said. "Sit down, and listen to me or you may find yourself more than humiliated the next time you meet that young man."

"What do you mean?" he asked brusquely, dropping back down beside her.

"Only that since you rushed blindly off on your quest to retrieve your precious fawn, I used my own powers to find out more about this Finn MacCumhal. He is a most formidable enemy."

"And how so?" Fear prompted irritably. "Quickly, woman!"

"Well," she began, in a deliberately slow and teasing way, "he is captain of the Fianna. They are mercenary batallions made up of the fiercest warriors in all Ireland. To be their leader alone speaks of great prowess, for a mortal. But this Finn is more. He is of the Sidhe blood, daughter of Muirne and great-grandson to Nuada Silver Hand. He has none of the Sidhe skills, but he does possess some magic of his own."

"Magic?" the druid said, his impatience tempered with interest now. "What magic?"

"He gained the power of the legendary Salmon of Knowledge, so long sought by learned men—mortal and Sidhe alike. It lies within his thumb, which he burned in cooking the fish."

"His thumb?" the druid repeated, his tone skeptical.

"He has only to thrust it into his mouth when his life is threatened, and it will grant him the knowledge to help himself," she assured him. "And he has used it to defeat even the Sidhe before, killing Aillen, son of Nidhna, who had come out of Sid Finnachaidh to burn Tara of the High-Kings at Samhain time. He has some other magic help as well. He has won the weapons forged from Balor's head—the sword named Son of the Waves and the Storm Shield. He used them to destroy Daire Donn, the one who called himself King of the Great World. It is those same weapons he has with him now."

"Does he?" Fear said, peering down through the fluttering screen of leaves at Finn in an attempt to catch a glimpse of them. His voice had taken on a definite note of concern now. "But no champion of the Sidhe in a thousand years has been able to bring them from the Country of the Fair Men or even survive the tests of its king."

"Well, this champion did," she needled. "He survived the tests, he won the weapons, and he destroyed the king."

"An amazing task indeed," the druid said thoughtfully.

"Now you begin to see what I mean by my warning,"

she said. "And even without these powers to help him, Finn seems impossible to defeat. He is a warrior without equal who has destroyed giant and serpent and water monster with like ease. With only his wits and his daring he has outfoxed the High-King of Ireland and his own grandfather Tadg, one of the most powerful sorcerers of the Sidhe. Finn even caused Tadg to be stripped of all his powers and left a broken and isolated old man."

"And why was it that you knew nothing of these things before I went off to confront this Finn?" the Dark Druid complained.

"We have been here too long," she explained defensively, "isolated from the rest of Ireland, separated from our own people. All this has happened within the last few years. Your young forester who helped the fawn escape joined us only a year ago. He had heard the tales of this new champion and his powers. That's how he knew she could go to Finn for help. Do you understand, Fear? To face Finn is a most dangerous thing. He has destroyed those with powers as great as yours."

"No one has powers as great as mine," he shot back indignantly. "Even the great leaders of the Tuatha de Danaan do not dare to challenge them."

"But no one who has challenged Finn has survived," she pointed out emphatically. "You would be a fool to risk it."

This seemed to have an impact on the druid. He stared down at the two figures beside the brook for a time, brooding and silent.

"Yes," he said finally, his tone one of reluctant concession, "I suppose that you are right. To face him myself would seem an unnecessary risk. But there must be some way to destroy him. Some way!"

"You would do best to let it go," she said soothingly. She lifted a hand to lightly stroke his temple. "It is only for this one, frail, mortal girl. Forget her. There are pleasures enough here." She leaned closer, her body pressing against his, her voice caressing, her eyes inviting. "I can give you happiness. You have no need—"

"No!" he said savagely, shoving her away. "I want nothing from you. It's only that one I want . . . and even more now. No half-mortal boy will defy me! I'm not like the others he has met. I will find a way to have what I desire."

He stood and leaned over her threateningly.

"You, woman, have only one service you can perform for me, and that you had best do well. You keep watch upon them. Watch day and night if you must, but watch their every move. Someday my chance to act will come and I will know of it at once."

He turned and stalked to the door. There he paused and turned back, raising his stick to point at the seer in a meaningful way.

"Make no mistake, my dear Miluchradh, or you'll find yourself a rooting sow for all your endless, immortal days."

He went out, leaving her to glare hatefully after him.

The eyes of Caoilte MacRonan were glaring as they lifted to the open gateway of the fortress.

No figures were visible there, and after staring a moment, he dropped his gaze and went back to his work. He was sitting on a stool beside the smithy, honing his sword with a whetstone. He worked with sharp, rhythmic, angry strokes, his obvious mood of irritation reinforced by the shrill scraping sound of the stone along the blade. Again and again he would pause to glance up at the gateway, only to take up the honing at an even more furious tempo each time.

Out from the hall came the little musician called Cnu Deireoil. Glancing about the yard, his eyes fell upon Caoilte and he strolled across to the dark warrior.

He stopped beside him, watching the, by this time, vehement honing with interest. Then he remarked casually, "You're putting a bit too much of your arm into that, don't you think?"

"And what business would that be of yours?" Caoilte answered curtly, honing on.

"Only that you'll have that fine weapon down to a needle soon."

Caoilte made a harsh noise of disgust and threw down

both sword and stone, then looked toward the little man.

"There," he said. "I hope that's to your liking. Now, what is it you want here, bothering me?"

"There's no call for such belligerence, lad," Cnu told him soothingly. "I only meant to ask if you'd seen Finn."

"That I have not!" snapped Caoilte, turning away in a dismissing gesture.

"It's not myself seeking him," the harper persisted. "But some tuath folk are here to have Finn judge a land dispute, some chieftains of the province want to speak of their summer allotment of calves and whelps to the Fians, and Rough Buzzing is complaining with great volume of how bare the larder has become."

"Well, why ask me!" the warrior retorted angrily. "Haven't I been waiting here myself for half the morning because I thought we were to go on the hunt today? And hasn't he spent every moment of these past days with that woman? Find her if you want to find Finn!"

Caoilte was right. As he spoke, Finn and Sabd, flanked as usual by the wary hounds, were climbing a nearby hill and picking the wild flowers as they went.

He carried a harp, and when they reached the top, she sat, laying out the flowers and gathering them in bright bundles while he stood nearby and played a lilting tune that matched the flowers' bright colors in its notes. The dogs sat down and seemed to smile in appreciation as they listened, while Sabd's body swayed easily with the tune.

When he had finished, she clapped in delight.

"You play very well," she said. "I didn't know you could do that, too. Another talent you've kept hidden?"

"Cnu Deireoil taught me," he said. "I've not played in some time." He smiled and moved over to sit down close beside her. "But then, there are many things I've not done in some time, thanks to you."

"Please," she said in embarrassment, "I don't want to feel I've taken you away from other things. From what you know . . . and love."

"But you haven't!" he said earnestly, taking her hands. "You've given me more! You've given me back what I'd lost. These past days I've realized that what you said was true. There was a regret in me. I'd told myself that I was rushing about, keeping busy because it was what I was meant to do, that it was all a Fian warrior needed to make his life happy. Now I see that I was only trying to fill up my days, to keep myself from thinking, from facing the loneliness, the desire for . . . something else."

"Why?" she asked, her eyes searching his with compassion. "What would make you that way?"

"There was another woman," he said frankly. "She told me that there was no room in our lives for anything but our duty to our destinies. Mine was to be captain of the Fians, as my father was. That has led me, driven me, directed me, all of my life. I thought that she was right. But she wasn't, Sabd. I was as trapped by that life as you were trapped within the fawn's shape, doomed to live as others felt I should, cursed to never be free."

"This other woman," she said in a careful, almost reluctant way, "did you love her?"

"In a way, very much," he said. "But not in the way that I do you."

"Me?" she said in surprise.

"Yes, you!" he said, exuberantly bringing her hands to his lips and kissing them. He spat out a mouthful of blossoms from the flowers she still held before going on with undiminished passion. "You've freed me, Sabd, as I freed you. We can continue to have that freedom together. But I want to know that it will go on always the same!"

"I . . . I don't know what to say!" she said, completely flustered.

"Just say that you feel as I do, Sabd. Say that you accept my love and return it."

"Without you, I'd have nothing," she said. "Now you have become my life. What else can I say, Finn? Of course I love you."

He pulled her toward him and her lips met his, her body pliant, willing, her arms encircling him.

The dogs, clearly embarrassed by this emotional display, politely looked away.

* * *

Caoilte stood in the yard just inside the main gates, tapping his foot in an impatient way as Finn, Sabd, and the two dogs entered the fortress, the young man and woman laughing together. It was late afternoon, the lowering sun already growing red within a band of horizon-lining clouds.

"Well," Caoilte said in a pettish way, "you've taken your sweet time in getting home."

They looked up at him, but his grim expression had little effect on their buoyant mood.

"Caoilte!" Finn greeted cheerily, slapping his comrade on the shoulder. "It's the one person I'm most glad to see!"

"Is it?" the other replied testily. "And do you even know how late it is?"

Finn glanced around at the sun as if realizing the lateness of the day for the first time.

"Well, it is late, isn't it?" he said, grinning. "We lost track of the time. We were picking wild flowers."

Caoilte lifted a hand and plucked a stray violet blossom from Sabd's unbound and flowing hair.

"So I see," he said without amusement, handing it to her.

She took it, looking down, her lashes hiding her eyes, a flush of embarrassment coloring her white cheeks.

Finn only laughed boyishly and threw an arm about her.

"It's a fine sport, Caoilte," he said. "Better than hunting boar. You should try it."

"I need to talk with you, Finn," Caoilte said.

The voice was chill, the expression hard. Sabd looked at him with some concern, and then at Finn.

"I'll just go inside and prepare for the evening," she said.

"If you must leave," said Finn, giving her a warm parting hug.

She went off toward the hall, carrying the bouquet, his eyes following the lightly swaying figure of her. Then he turned, still smiling, to his friend.

"Now, Caoilte," he said with excitement, "I've something to tell you."

"First, Finn MacCumhal, you'll listen to me," the

other replied heatedly. "No one else has been able to talk to you for days, except your little fawn."

"What do you mean?" said Finn, his smile changing to a puzzled frown. "What's wrong with you?"

"I've had as much of your behavior as I can endure. So have the others in this fortress. You've ignored us, and what's worse, you've neglected your duties. All to play nursemaid to that girl!"

"That girl needs me!" he retorted.

"So do the Fianna."

"There's no war. There've been no troubles for a year! What do they need me for so desperately as that?"

"There are other things."

"You're my right hand. You take care of them!"

"And haven't I been? It was I who took out the hunt today, or we'd have had no food tonight. I settled the disputes and bartered with the lords for you."

"And I'm sure you did it as well as I would have done," Finn told him. "Now, let me be about washing for dinner."

He started away, toward the basin. Caoilte, aghast at his cavalier response, let him get away a step before going after him, grabbing an arm and swinging him around.

"What are you saying?" he cried. "Those things aren't for me to do."

His angry gesture and his rising voice had called the attention of those about in the yard to them. Now many ceased their activities to eavesdrop openly on this unusual confrontation of the two friends.

"They are now," Finn blithely announced. "Am I not the captain of the Fians? Why shouldn't I have things as I wish? And for once I wish to have some time for myself!"

"For the girl, you mean," Caoilte argued. "She's bewitched you! She's using you. She needs you to go outside these walls. She's brought you to deny your own duty for her!"

At this, Finn finally grew angry.

"You've gone too far now, Caoilte, old friend or not. It's not true what you say. Sabd loves me and I love her."

"Love?" said Caoilte. "No, Finn, you don't mean that."

"I do. And you're forcing me now to tell you in anger

what I meant to tell you in great joy, thinking you'd join in my celebration. I mean to wed Sabd as soon as the arrangements can be made. I will build a new house for her here, with a great sunroom high upon it where she can go and see the countryside, and the two of us will dwell there as husband and wife from that time on!"

With these words, he wheeled and stalked off across the yard, leaving Caoilte to stare after him in dismay, and the others in the yard to exchange wondering looks.

CHAPTER ◇ 7

VOWS

THE MATERIAL FANNED OUT AS THE GOWN FELL OPEN, displaying its richness. The wealth of deep blue silk in its many gatherings shimmered in the sunlight. The elaborate, exquisitely stitched embroidery of golden thread that bordered neckline, sleeves, and hem was radiant, like strands of flame against the cool, billowing waves of the material.

Sabd gave a soft exclamation of delight and ran a hand slowly, sensually over the garment before looking up at the beaming, round-faced woman who displayed it for her.

"It's a most wonderful gown," the girl said in a voice touched with awe. She had to all but shout this, however, to be heard over the sound of banging and thumping that seemed to fill the room, echoing as if they were within a drum. "I've never seen its like for grandness."

"It's only what's deserving for the woman who'll be marrying our fine captain," brusquely observed a dour, black-haired older woman standing beside the first.

"Finn must see it," Sabd told them excitedly. They were within Finn's chamber of the great hall, and she crossed to the large outer window, whose shutters were thrown fully open, letting in the daylight and giving a view of the yard.

It was from there all the noise was coming. For, not far from the hall, a new structure was being erected.

It was much the same in construction, but smaller in girth and with a full second story that had a granian—a broad sunroom with a balcony—upon its western side.

The plank framework of its outer wall was fully up, and the long posts of its roof supports set within. Now some workers were busy at weaving and attaching the wattle panels that would form the building's skin; others were daubing with thick, mucky plaster the sections already in place; while yet more climbed precariously about atop the structure to set the roof beams and the ribs of supporting joist needed for the thatching.

Altogether, several scores of men were hard at these various tasks, and the combined sounds of their hammerings raised quite a din.

Sabd leaned out the window and looked about the construction site. She soon picked Finn out of the confusion, standing near the new building, deep in conversation with a short, broad-set man while gesturing emphatically at parts of the construction.

"Finn!" she called out, waving energetically. "Finn!"

Hearing his name, he turned to see her at the window.

"Come here, please, if you can," she cried, gesturing him to her. "I have to show you this!"

The words did not carry to him through the noise, but the gesture was enough. He smiled and waved in quick acquiescence, then spoke briefly to the beefy man.

"Just keep them at it, Cronan. I want this all completed before the wedding day. And everything must be right."

"Aye, Captain," the man assured him with a grin. "It will be."

Across the yard, far removed from the work, Caoilte and some other warriors idled, watching the construction. Like most people, these men largely seemed to be entertained by the intriguing spectacle of a building going up. All but Caoilte. He stood moping, his gaze sullen. And when he saw Finn leave the site and go bounding across to Sabd at her call, he remarked bitterly upon it to the young warrior called Lughaid: "See that now, will you? The boy sails to her as if he were her banded falcon, coming at her whistle."

"He's in love, Caoilte," the other said in smiling defense. "And who of us hasn't acted so when the same illness was upon us? Be easy with him. It'll pass."

"Will it?" the dark warrior said doubtfully.

Meantime, Finn was leaning in through the window while Sabd had the women hold up the gown for him to see.

"Isn't it wonderful?" she gushed. "The sewing women of Magh Feman have made it for me."

"It truly is their finest work," Finn agreed. He looked to the two women. "I thank you for it, sisters."

The round-faced woman giggled at the compliment, but the stern one shot an elbow to her ribs that sobered her, and the two made a low curtsy together, chorusing, "We thank you, Captain."

"I can't wait until I see you in it," Finn told Sabd. "But we haven't long now. The guests are beginning to arrive."

"I know," she said. "I'm feeling the anticipation of it tingling within me. The other ladies are coming to help with the gown's fitting this very afternoon."

"Ah! And could I come and help as well?" Finn asked playfully.

"Oh, Finn," she replied, coyly dropping her gaze and blushing prettily.

"Sorry," he said, but not contritely, adding in a still teasing way, "I'll have all our lives for seeing you, won't I?"

The round-faced woman tittered again, and Sabd's blush became all the more glowing.

"Enough of that now," the dour woman said severely, taking charge. She moved toward the window, shooing him back. "Be away with you, Finn MacCumhal. It's ashamed you should be, saying such things to this lamb." He stepped back as the woman grabbed the shutters. "You're not needed more here," she told him, "so good-bye!" And with that she slammed the shutters closed in his face.

Grinning broadly, Finn turned and started back toward the construction site. But he paused as he noted a group of warriors riding in through the fortress gates.

They were a somberly dressed and stolid-looking lot, all in similar green and black patterned cloaks denoting their clan. As they came into the yard, Finn strode up to them, raising a hand in greeting.

They reined in before him, raising hands in response.

At their head were two men whose similarity in looks marked them as brothers. One was a large, square-shouldered man of rugged looks, one eye covered by a leather patch. The warrior beside him was much softer in shape, with a great belly, full and flamboyantly mustached face, and balding head.

"Goll!" Finn addressed the one-eyed man heartily. "I'm glad that you could come." He looked to the stout warrior, adding, "You as well, Conan."

Conan's reply was an unintelligible grumble.

"I'm certain my brother said he's pleased to come," Goll said with dry sarcasm. "He knows how much food and drink you'll be having."

"That we will," Finn said, laughing. "Dismount, now, and I'll have the grooms see to your horses. You and the Clan na Morna are welcome to Almhuin."

The men climbed down and several of the leather-liveried grooms rushed from the stables to take the horses' reins. As the mounts were led away, Finn escorted the men toward the main hall.

"I've quarters readied for you," he told Goll. "Rough Buzzing will see that you have refreshments and a place to rest. Tonight we'll feast and talk about old times. You must meet Sabd."

At this, Conan gave a grunt of laughter and said gruffly, "Can't imagine a woman getting you to marry her. Wouldn't have a bit of games with you otherwise, eh?"

"I see that you've lost none of your coarseness with age, Conan," Finn answered affably, "nor any of your weight."

They reached the hall's main doors and Finn stepped aside to usher the clansmen inside. But as Goll started in, he paused, pulling back to let a woman emerge.

"Mother, hello!" Finn said with pleasure.

She seemed more a girl than a woman old enough to be mother to Finn MacCumhal. Her looks were beautiful, she was small and fair, her hair a silver-blond like Finn's own.

"Lady Muirne," Goll said, bowing graciously. "A great pleasure it is to see you once again."

"And you, Chieftain," she responded with like courtesy, smiling at him. "We've not met since your clan came to fight at the White Strand. I hope you are well."

"As well as any man can expect," he said in a practical way.

"And Conan!" she went on. "You still seem as healthy as ever you were."

"That fact your son has already pointed out," he growled and went on into the hall.

"Excuse my brother," Goll told Muirne. "He's hungry from the trip. My own good health to you and to your husband, Mogh Nuadat."

He bowed again and entered the hall, the rest of his clansmen following. Finn lingered behind to speak to his mother.

"Have you been settled?" he asked solicitously.

"Yes, my dear," she assured him. "Everything is fine. And I've been to see your Sabd. I'm to help her with her gown this afternoon."

"What did you think of her, Mother?" he asked with an air of pride. "She's a beautiful woman, isn't she?"

"She's lovely," Muirne said, but with a note of care in her voice. "Very intelligent, quite sweet, but..."

She hesitated, and Finn, clearly expecting an unqualified endorsement of his choice from her, frowned in puzzlement.

"But what, Mother? What's wrong?"

"Well," she went on with a certain reluctance, "I've spoken to the other women here. I've learned the story of this poor girl. I wish that I could help you to find this terrible Fear Doirche and remove the curse of him from her forever, but I can't. I've been too long separated from the Sidhe to get any help from them. And even if I could, it might not help. When he left so many centuries ago, it was said that his magic was so strong that not even the greatest druids of the Sidhe could find his hiding place."

"It is all right, Mother," he assured her. "I've resigned myself to the fact that I might never find the Dark Druid, as has Sabd. We are content that she stay here, with me."

"Still, it is a hard thing," she went on, still with that odd tone of concern. "I feel very sorry for the girl. And I...well, I hope that sorrow is not all you feel."

"I don't understand," he said.

She hesitated again, then faced him squarely, steeling herself and speaking in a frank, parental way.

"My Finn, you know I'd not ask this if I weren't your own mother, concerned for your welfare: you're not marrying her out of pity, are you? Out of some feeling that she needs your help, your comfort, the freedom only you can give her?"

"Of course not," he protested, looking shocked. "Mother, you know me. It's much of your own spirit that's in me! You can sense my true feelings, can't you? I do love her. She's become more my life than I have hers, and she's given me much more than I've given her, things you've wished for me yourself—freedom from what my destiny has done to me. Can't you feel that?"

She looked deep into his eyes and then she smiled with pleasure and relief.

"I can, my son. I hope your marriage will be a happy one. The blessing of Danu be upon you both."

She took his hand in her own and clasped it tightly.

The hands were clasped above the basin of beaten silver. They were tied loosely by a string of mistletoe twined about them and up the arms of man and woman, literally binding them.

Another pair of hands moved in and began to unwind the vine.

Finn and Sabd—she in the blue gown, he in white tunic and crimson cloak—stood patiently upon the dais, looking at one another with beaming smiles as the gray-haired druid named Cainnelscaith, clad in gleaming white robes, proceeded with the slow untwining of the prickly leaves. A second druid stood beside him, holding the silver chalice below the couple's hands by its gracefully curved, swan-shaped handles. Around them in the hall a hushed company crowded the vast floor, watching the sacred ritual with great solemnity.

The mistletoe was unwound and handed to another young druid hovering behind the chief one. Then Cainnelscaith took from a third acolyte a crystal carafe.

"With the ivy, you are bound," he said, and slowly

poured water over the clasped hands. "With the water of life you are washed, cleansed, and made pure in each other." The water sparkled over their hands, running down to be caught in the bowl. When the carafe was empty, the druid handed it back to his attendant and placed one of his hands upon those of the pair.

"The wedding is ended," he announced in a resounding voice. "Before these witnesses who all give surety to see its vows are kept, Finn and Sabd are from this day man and wife!"

The solemn crowd instantly went mad with elation. Men hooted, bellowed, shouted out their joy. There was one general rush forward to give best wishes to the couple, and another toward the tables loaded with food and immense tankards of ale.

Through the laughter, congratulations, and general confusion of celebration, Finn and Sabd made their way to the door. Here Finn gave a great hug to his mother, passed final good-byes to his guests, and led his bride from the hall. Some of Finn's friends, clansmen, and chieftains followed them out, stopping just outside the door to watch the young couple cross the yard toward the new house.

It was quite finished now, its upper sunroom catching the afternoon sun that glowed against the fresh white coat of lime. Waiting on either side of its doorway, sitting proudly on guard, were Bran and Sceolan.

The newlyweds paused upon the threshold, where Finn threw a final grin and a jaunty wave to the watchers, while Sabd smiled too, but in a more bashful way. Then they were gone inside.

"I hope that young girl will be all right," said his mother. "She seems so frail."

"With Finn to care for her, she'll be fine," Goll MacMorna assured her. "I wish a good marriage to them. And now, Lady, would you give me the honor of joining the wedding feast in my company?"

"It would be my own pleasure," she responded graciously.

She took his proffered arm and they returned inside with the others. The festivities were already well underway, with a great deal of eating, but a great deal more drinking, as people milled around, and musicians played. Some danced in the open space about the fire, capering to jigs of great liveliness, helped along by the ale that made them seem to glow.

Conan was already well on his way to demolishing the contents of an entire table of food alone. Cnu Deireoil circulated, joking and greeting and playing here and there when coaxed. He'd traveled about nearly all the room when he paused, catching a glimpse of something through the shifting crowd.

Curious, he tried jumping up to see more clearly through the forms that towered over him. Frustrated, he clambered onto a table to peer above the heads. From this vantage point he was finally able to see clearly across the gathering to the outer edge of the hall.

There, at a table as removed as possible from the milling throng, sat Caoilte MacRonan, alone save for a cup and a very large pitcher.

He looked quite forlorn, and the Little Nut, climbing down from his vantage point, forced his way to him through the crowd.

"Well, it's a time for real merriment!" the harper said, addressing him in boisterous tones.

There was no response from Caoilte. He lifted his mug and took a deep draught, still staring ahead morosely. Cnu Deireoil tried again.

"There'll be a fine time tonight. Feasting, drinking, dancing through till dawn. Yes, a fine time!"

Still no answer, not even flicker of notice from the dark warrior.

"It would seem that you're not so happy as you might be," the harper commented.

At last this elicited a response, but a far from amiable one: "And why should I be?" Caoilte barked, turning a hard gaze upon the little man. "Why should you, for all of that?" he added challengingly. "Can you watch him doing this and not feel something, man?"

"What I feel is a happiness for Finn," Cnu Deireoil told him. "You should be feeling the same. I only want what's best for him."

Caoilte gave a snort of derisive laughter.

"Best for him? Is it mad you are? How can this be best for him? It'll be his ruin!"

"His ruin?" the Little Nut echoed in disbelief. "And how is that?"

"Can't you see it?" the other nearly shouted in a heat of frustration fueled by the drink. His outburst caused others around to look toward them in alarm. "Haven't you watched? She's made our proud wolfhound into a nursing puppy. She's taken his spirit! She's managed to do what all the creatures and the magic and the warriors and the kings of Eire and of the Great World couldn't do."

"It's nonsense you're speaking," Cnu Deireoil retorted. "No one can challenge Finn now. Ireland is at peace, and the Fianna have the respect of the world. It's Finn who's done all that. Now it's time for him. He's earned this for himself. Let him live his life a while—and in his own way!"

"But his way is to give up everything," Caoilte bellowed despairingly. "Everything that makes him a warrior. Everything that's worth being. Not to be hunting, fighting, seeking some new adventure . . ." His voice trailed off in overwhelming exasperation and he drank again.

"I see it now!" the little man proclaimed with a dawning understanding. "It's jealous that you are! You think that you've lost him to her. Lost your closest comrade."

"That's not it at all, you wretched dwarf!" Caoilte scathingly protested. "It's not just Finn and myself. It's something more. I can feel it! Why can't you?"

"Are you certain?" the harper replied, keeping his voice calm, patient, and reasonable, as if only a slow hammering could drive his points into a brain made thick with ale. "Think, Caoilte: you've protected him as a brother—as a father even—since he was an untrained boy. You've been always at his side, fought back-to-back with him, saved him a score of times; as he has you. Couldn't it just be that your sorrow comes from knowing things have changed?"

Caoilte eyed him searchingly, his dark eyes smoldering. Then he took another drink, draining the cup. But this last draught, instead of adding to his belligerence, seemed instead to drown it. The fire faded in him and he sagged, sinking down defeatedly.

"Maybe you're right, my old friend," he said in a dispirited voice. He looked around the room at the rejoicing throng. "Maybe things have changed. Maybe I'm not needed here anymore. It could be time to move on to someplace where a fighting man is still of some value."

"You've said that a hundred times before," said Cnu Deireoil, smiling, but with worry showing in his eyes.

"This time I might just mean it," Caoilte darkly replied.

The firelight flickered along the edge of the mirror as Finn held it out to Sabd.

She exclaimed in delight as she looked at it, turning it over in her hands. It was a most exquisitely worked piece of bronze, shaped in a circle with an open basketwork handle of interlacing curlicue design. The mirror face was carefully polished to give a smooth, perfect reflection of the young woman's face. The back was intricately decorated in scrollwork of most minute detail, curving pattern within pattern, and inset with gold, silver, and bright enameling.

"It's wonderful," she said.

"I have brushes and combs to go with it," he said. "The finest work of the best metal artists in Ireland."

He gestured toward a glowing array laid out atop a table near the bed upon which they sat. The room, sumptuously appointed, plush with rugs and tapestries, already glowed with other textures—golds and bronzes and woods and rich materials.

"And I have more for you," he said eagerly. "The glories of the world I've brought to you. The finest gowns, the richest cloaks, and jewelry that will make you shine like no queen has ever done. And—"

She put up a hand, her fingers to his lips, stopping him. She smiled.

"I thank you," she said, "but you have already given me the greatest gift you ever could."

She leaned toward him, her lips softly meeting his. Then they were embracing, falling back upon the bed in a passionate kiss. The mirror slipped from her fingers to fall into the coverlets, forgotten in this newer and more absorbing interest.

After a moment, she pulled back, looking at him. There was a certain speculation in her eyes, touched with concern. That smooth brow was marred by the crease of a frown.

"What . . . is it?" Finn managed after a deep breath.

"Are you really certain about this?" she asked him gravely.

"I am," he replied without hesitation. His hand came up to cup her chin while he looked into those emerald eyes. "I've not wanted anything more or been so sure. For the first time in my life, I know I'm doing something only for myself. I love you, my wife."

"Then I give you freely what you desire—no less than I desire it myself," she said in a soft, throaty way.

She sat up, and in a single, lithe move, slipped off the simple shift that she now wore. Her smooth, fair body gleamed white-gold in the firelight. She pulled the combs from her long hair and shook it free, letting it billow about her slim shoulders. Then she lay back again, close to him, smiling at him expectantly and a bit timidly.

His sun-bronzed hand moved out and stroked gently, slowly, caressingly, down her shoulder, across the firm roundness of her breast, over the smooth swell of her hip. She gave a small sigh of pleasure at the touch, raising her own hand to stroke the strong line of his jaw and trace the cleft of his firm chin.

"I no longer feel afraid—of anything," she said. "It's my strength you are now, my husband, as you are my freedom. I give my full will, my full heart and being into your care."

"Then from here, we will be one," he said, pulling her to him. "You'll have nothing ever to fear again."

They embraced, their bodies pressing together. The light of the fire cast a warming glow upon them. A log fell, and the flames flared, crackling high.

The flames leaped higher, crackling greedily as they ate through the thatch and snapped at the wood rafters of the hut. The rising plume of firelight cast a ruddy glare upon the chaos below.

There were rushing people and shrill cries of terror. From the smoking interior of the hut a woman ran, a wailing infant clutched protectively in her arms.

She ran into a man in chain-mail vest and peaked iron helmet and tried to back away, screaming, her face twisted by fear.

He grabbed her and held her easily with one hand, his broad face split by a yellow-toothed grin. The broad-bladed sword he clutched in the other hand lifted and slashed down.

Beyond the blazing hut were a number of other buildings, huddled together like frightened hares caught in a storm. Several of them were afire too, illuminating the whole village, the wide beach and the white surf of the black sea beyond. The light fell too on the sleek, serpentine forms of carved figureheads glaring balefully from the bows of the dragonboats grounded on the shore.

A great slaughter was just concluding, the blood and carnage of it spreading from the water's edge, across the silver strand to the stricken village.

More fearsome warriors in mail and elaborately spiked caps stalked like the ruthless predators they were amongst the ruins, seeking more prey. Others collected the heads of the victims, piling the trophies in great cairns whose draining blood formed rivers across the white sands to the sea.

A broad, bearded man in a shirt of mail, his head covered by a helmet sporting elk horns of gleaming bronze, strode through the stricken village to its inland side. There he joined several others and stood peering about him in a triumphant way.

"They are all dead," one of the warriors said scornfully. "They put up a poor enough fight."

Another warrior held up a golden locket, intricately worked and set with jewels, but badly dented and splattered with wet blood.

"Look, my chieftain," he said, eyes bright with greed. "They have much wealth."

The broad man snatched it away, chuckling in satisfaction. He held it aloft in the ruddy firelight, the blood looking black against the glowing brightness of the gold.

"Easy riches," he said, examining the prize. "If the rest of the Irish have no more stomach for the fight than these, we'll take this whole coast."

He tossed the trinket back and strode away, followed by his men. But once they were gone, a figure rose in the shadows of a thicket not far from where they had stood.

He was a grotesque sight, his face cut from temple to chin, his clothing torn and streaked with gore. He looked pale and weak, his body shivered violently. Still he was able to stagger away, leaving the horrid, flame-lit scene behind, disappearing into the cloaking night.

CHAPTER ◇ 8

A
Parting

THE FACE LOOMED OUT OF THE DARKNESS OF THE YARD,
into the light spilling from the wide doorway.

Two warriors supported the drooping figure, helping it
to move stumblingly forward, across the threshold, into
the hall of Almhuin. There, in a bright array, in jocular
fellowship, in cheering warmth and glowing firelight, the
company of Finn's household were met in their evening's
feast.

At first none of them noted the arrival of the grim and
ominous intruder. The gaiety was at its height, the chief
bard regaling Finn, Sabd, and the gathering with a most
colorful tale.

"So, the Dagda took up the ladle," he was saying, "and
it big enough that a man and a woman could lie down
within the bowl. He scooped up the broth with it, taking
out bits as large as half a pig each time, and putting the
full ladle in his mouth until the great hole was empty, and
he left scraping through the earth and gravel from more."

The audience roared in laughter at this image of the
famous Sidhe champion. The bard waited for it to subside
just enough to continue, keeping the roll of the crowd
expertly to build another swell.

"When he was finished, sleep came on him. The
Fomor laughed at him lying there with his belly swollen
like a great cauldron. So he rose up angrily, bloated as he
was, and started home, dragging a wheeled fork it would

take eight men to carry, and it making a track after him deep enough to be the boundary ditch for a whole province."

This brought more laughter. But it was interrupted by a loud cry of alarm from Sabd.

Her joy had in that instant vanished from her. She stood up, lifting a hand to point across the room, horror in her eyes as if it were her curse come upon her once again.

"By all the gods!" she cried out. "Finn, look!"

Heads turned. There were more sounds of consternation, spreading rapidly through the crowd like ripples from a stone dropped in a pond. Eyes followed the gazes of others, focusing all attention toward one spot. Finn, along with many others, now rose too, his body tensing, his cheerful expression turning abruptly grim as his own gaze fell upon the man.

He was indeed a doleful sight in his ragged clothes all streaked with the rust of dried blood, and the long gash from forehead to throat vivid against the dead-white of his pale skin. So thin and worn was he that he seemed a wraith, an apparition of the dead of some forgotten war, fluttering in on the night winds as a dark omen.

But he was no wraith, and he had not yet lost the last of his strength. He now pulled himself away from the supporting men, straightened himself, and, with an obvious effort that seemed a proud display of fortitude, took a few more faltering steps into the center of the room.

"My captain . . ." he gasped out. "We were . . . attacked! It was Lochlanners!"

There was a collective gasp of shock from the crowd. Many of the warriors leaped to their feet. But the man's effort had drained the strength he had mustered and he swayed. He would have collapsed had not the guards moved up to support him once again.

While his words had naturally raised a storm of emotion in the hall, Finn continued just to stare at the man, his face stony.

Caoilte looked toward him expectantly, as did many others, clearly awaiting his response. But when nothing came, when Finn continued to stand as if frozen there, Caoilte's expression turned to one of puzzlement. To cover

Finn's unaccountable lapse, he himself then stood, moving around the table to address the refugee.

"Where was this attack?" he demanded. "How long ago? How large? Give us more details, man."

"It . . . it was on the coast," the other forced out between labored, weary pants. "The ships are in the bay below Beinn Edair. The warriors have landed there . . . many hundreds of them. They mean to raid inland."

"They'll do great damage if they're not stopped," said Caoilte grimly.

"They destroyed my village, slaughtered my clansmen," the man said, voice choking with rising sorrow. "My own wife . . . my child . . ." Overcome with emotion, he sagged between the men, head hanging, and began to weep.

Caoilte turned toward Finn, again obviously awaiting some response. Still there was none. His gaze met a shuttered stare. Finn was like a man struck blind and deaf by some nearby lightning stroke.

"Well, Captain?" Caoilte finally demanded, his voice taking on a prodding note, as if he were trying to awaken his comrade. "What are we going to do?" And then, more impatiently, "Finn! What will we do?"

This last seemed to reach Finn. He wrenched his gaze from the man to Caoilte, then swept it over the others in the room, who were all staring at him now. Their puzzled looks indicated that they too were sensing something wrong. So did the frown of Sabd as she lifted her eyes toward her husband's face.

There was a long silence as he looked about him, his expression one of discomfort and uncertainly. His eyes swept the crowd, returned to Caoilte, then dropped to meet those of his wife. He stared at her a moment fixedly, then looked about the room again.

"I . . . must consider this," he said hesitantly, vaguely.

There was a muttering of astonishment at that. But Caoilte's response was more explosive.

"Consider?" he cried. "What is there to consider, Finn? This man's village has been destroyed! Irishmen have died! Our country has been invaded! What else is there to do but fight!"

To this fiercely stated proclamation there were loud, eager cries of support.

"I said I must consider!" Finn said in a voice now angry and so keen of edge that it cut across the voices, silencing them all. "See to the man," he ordered curtly. "We will retire now."

He held out a hand to his wife. She looked around her at the stunned gathering, then up to him again, somewhat fearfully. But finally, obediently, she took his hand. He led her down from the dais and across the silent room at a brisk stride, not pausing, sweeping out the doors, leaving those behind staring after him in disbelief.

Then Caoilte, momentarily nonplussed like the others, came to life.

"Well, I'll not accept that!" he bellowed and started after them.

He stalked out of the hall, the gathering exploding into excited talk behind him. He charged across the yard toward Finn's new private residence, reaching its door only moments after the couple had passed inside.

As Caoilte stormed across the threshold, Finn swung around, his expression first surprised, then darkening with indignation.

"What do you mean, following us here, bulling into my quarters uninvited?"

Caoilte was taken aback by this scathing rebuke.

"What are you saying, Finn?" he said, aghast. "Can you be hearing yourself? I'm your best friend, come to talk. Before, there were no private places. Has she taken even that?"

The girl colored and moved away from them, crossing the room.

Finn grew more angry, striding up to Caoilte, facing him challengingly.

"No more of that!" he warned. "She's taken nothing from me. I'm not a part of you, MacRonan."

Caoilte was clearly stung more greatly by this. Pain swept across his face. Then a determination hardened it again.

"But you are still captain of the Fianna!" he retorted. "You are still bound by your oath!"

Finn turned on his heel and stalked away to stand by Sabd, one hand upon her shoulder, his face turned from the dark warrior.

"Finn, you can't ignore what's happened!" Caoilte said, his tone almost pleading. "There must be an answer, and it must be given now!"

"I'm not ignoring it," Finn responded coldly. "I said I would consider. There may be ways to deal with this without a hosting."

"Deal with it?" Caoilte repeated in disbelief. "Is it madness you're speaking? This is an invasion, and within our own province. It is for our Fians to meet it, and it's for you to lead them as you always have."

"Things are different," Finn said tersely. "I've other considerations now."

"You mean her, don't you?" the dark warrior cried, pointing to her in an accusing way. "Is that what's happened? Has she so enchanted you that you can't pry yourself from her side even for this?"

"She must be protected," Finn said stubbornly.

"The fortress protects her. It's Ireland that you should be thinking of."

"Ireland. Ireland!" Finn chanted angrily, turning back toward Caoilte again. "Why is it always her? I give to her and I have nothing for myself. Why?"

"Because it was what you were meant to do," Caoilte told him. "Because it's what you've given your oath to do."

"Is it?" Finn shot back. "Not by my own choice!"

"You can't really mean this," his friend argued. "You've given up hunting and all your other duties to the Fians for her. But you cannot give up this. It's your honor you're meaning to destroy."

"You told me once that honor only kills men foolish enough to follow it," Finn reminded him.

"And maybe I did," Caoilte admitted. "But Goll MacMorna said once that a man lives after his life, but not after his honor. Remember that as well."

This seemed to have some impact upon Finn. His look grew less adamant. And Sabd, listening to Caoilte's speech, seeing the expression on her husband's face, now put a hand upon his arm, and spoke imploringly.

"Don't do this, my love. He is right. You can't betray what you're sworn to out of fear for me. I would never rest with the thought of it. That poor man," she said in pity. "His family was killed just as my own. You can't let that remain unanswered. You have to go!"

"But what about you?" he asked, looking down at her.

"As Caoilte said, the fortress protects me, so long as I stay within its walls. You can leave me safely."

He put his hand upon hers.

"All right," he agreed reluctantly. "If it's what you wish." He looked to Caoilte. "Go and tell our warriors. Send Fergus True-Lips to call our clans. And fetch the Dord Fionn. We will host."

Caoilte smiled with relief.

"I will, Captain!" he answered elatedly and then rushed out.

Finn turned and took his wife's arms, his eyes searching hers.

"My dearest Sabd, is it certain you are of this?"

"I am," she assured him. "Though I will fear for you and miss the warmth of you beside me, it is right that you should go. Were you not the great captain that you are, you'd not have saved me, and I'd not have so great a love for you."

She left him, crossing to a wall hung with weapons. From its hooks she lifted down the glowing, gray-iron sword called the Mac an Luin—the Son of the Waves. It was a heavy weapon for the frail girl, and it was with some effort that she carried it back, holding it out, hilt first, to Finn.

"I put your sword into your hands myself," she said. "Use it to answer the wrongs done that man and all other helpless people of Ireland."

He looked at the proffered weapon, then at her. Finally, slowly, his hand came up and gripped it.

"I hoped that I might never have use for this again," he said wistfully, and held it up.

Light gleamed along its smooth, slender, lethal blade.

The sword slipped into the silver-banded sheath. Finn MacCumhal then took up the great oval of metal called the

Storm Shield and slipped his left arm into its grips, settling it firmly. He nodded with satisfaction and turned to examine the company of his fighting men.

It was a more grim and businesslike company of warriors who now filled the yard. The romantic firelight and surroundings of the grand hall were gone. The sharp, hard light of the chill dawn etched them clearly, starkly, as simple, hardened men preparing for the one occupation that was their real life and their real love: fighting other men. Their rich ornaments had been put aside, their fine clothes changed for the warrior's simple tunic and the dark blue cloaks of the Baiscne clan. The only things about them that glittered now were the keenly honed points of their spears and the cutting edges of their blades. The air had no music, no laughing, no sweet sounds of birds to it, but only the talk of battle and the harsh clattering of arms.

Finn ran a scrutinizing eye over the assembly. They seemed nearly ready to move. He turned to where Caoilte stood, a score of other clan chieftains, each in a cloak of his own identifying colors, grouped behind him.

"Our clan is ready," Finn said to Caoilte, and then looked to the chieftains.

"All our fighting men are prepared as well, Captain," one said. "With the other clans that mean to join us on the way, we will reach the coast with the full battalion strength of the Meath Fians."

"Very well," Finn said briskly. "Go to your clans, chieftains. We will leave at once."

As the chiefs departed and Caoilte passed the word to the Baiscne men to be ready to march, Finn strode to the hall. There the families of the warriors were gathered, making their good-byes. Sabd stood there too, with Cnu Deireoil at her side and the two hounds flanking them.

"Remember now," Finn admonished the little man, "all but the servants and the families of the clan and a handful of our older fighting men will be gone. I give the charge of my wife's safety to you, my oldest friend." He clapped a hand to the shoulder of the Little Nut. "Keep her within the fortress's walls until our return. You better than any of us here should be able to guard against any of that druid's trickery."

"And don't I know that better than my own name?" the
harper said with a smile. "It must be a hundred times now
you've said these things to me." He gripped Finn's arm
and said gravely, reassuringly, "I will take care of her.
Have no fear of that!"

Finn nodded, gave the man's shoulder a final, affec-
tionate pat, and turned to Sabd.

"You listen to him, now, and keep safe," he told her,
smiling, but with a serious tone behind it.

"You sound like my father used to," she said, laughing.
She leaned forward and gave him a final kiss upon his
cheek. "Go on, now, my captain. Your men are waiting.
And you," she told the dogs, "you go as well. Stay with
him and protect him for me."

"I'll come back to you as soon as I can," Finn said
earnestly. "I promise you."

He and the hounds joined the warriors and they
moved in a body out through the gates. Sabd, Cnu Deireoil,
and the families of the warriors moved out after them.

Outside the fortress, the warriors of a dozen other
clans made the hillside of Almhuin a bright patchwork
with their massed cloaks. They fell in behind the Baiscne
men as Finn led them down the slope at a brisk pace.

The families stopped just outside the gateway, solemnly
watching the men move away. Cnu Deireoil glanced up at
the girl and noted that her own look of cheerfulness—put
on so bravely for Finn—had now been replaced by a
worried frown.

"What's wrong, girl?" he asked. "You're not worrying
about his going off, are you? After that brave show?"

"I dreamed of him in battle," she said. "He looked wan
and badly hurt and in great pain."

"Ah, have no fear of that," the little man assured her
heartily. "No man born, mortal or Sidhe, can defeat that
one."

The warriors were heading away from the dun now at a
ground-eating pace, their individual forms joined by distance into a single, moving thing, glints from the sun on
their spear points like silver threads in a tapestry.

"I've just a feeling..." she said vaguely, as if trying to
grasp it. "A feeling that I'll not see him again."

"Nonsense," Cnu Deireoil scoffed. "Come in, now, and I'll play you a tune that'll be sure to give cheer to you. Come on along."

Most of the others had already returned inside the fortress. He led her across the bridge while she cast many a backward glance after Finn. Once within the gates, he gestured to a pair of gray-headed warriors.

They pulled the heavy portals slowly closed, and Sabd watched with uncertainty as they came together with a final-sounding boom.

When the gates closed, shutting off the view of the yard, the glowing bubble seemed to lift and turn in a sweeping move as the seer provided Fear Doirche with a panorama of the countryside and a clear view of the army moving away.

"You see?" Miluchradh said triumphantly, pointing. "They have left the fortress." The bubble abruptly soared forward and down in a stomach-lifting drop that ended just before the moving force. "And there is Finn himself, leading them."

Fear Doirche leaned forward, staring intently at the image of the fair-haired warrior, striding toward him at full life-size.

"You are right," he said.

"I told you that they were gathering to act, somehow," she said. "When I saw them starting out this morning, I called for you. They are off on a campaign! Finn has finally left your precious fawn alone!"

"Alone," he repeated thoughtfully. "Of course, the dun itself still protects her."

"It does," she agreed. "And I'm certain this so-clever Finn would not leave her without guardians. To enter without your own powers to help you would still be too dangerous."

"Yes," he said, "I suppose it would." But then his thin mouth lifted in a smile of cunning. "But I may have a way of getting to her. Yes. A safe way." He turned to the seer, galvanized by a rising excitement. "First I must be certain that Finn will be safely out of the way for some time. That must be for you to discover for me. Keep watch upon this army and tell me how far they go. Then I will visit this Almhuin once again."

He gave a low chuckle of pleasure and stepped toward the image, standing face-to-face with it.

"Then, my proud Finn MacCumhal," he said, gloating, "I will have what is mine, and take my revenge on you in the same brilliant act." He lifted his staff, poking the silver tip toward the unaware young warrior's face. "For it's yourself who will give me the means to take Sabd back from you!"

"But what?" Caoilte asked in alarm. "Why were you and Joe've got those that linear.

"I said between and What" cried running to their Caoilte

CHAPTER ◇ 9

Deception

FINN'S SWORD SLASHED THE MAILED WARRIOR FROM HIS path. He winnowed the attacking host like a fall wind sweeping through dry leaves thickly covering the ground.

There was no finesse in him now, no heroic posturing, no championlike challenges to single combat, only a grim determination to slash his way ahead as swiftly as his fighting skills could take him.

The invading Lochlanners reeled backward toward the sea under the fierce onslaught. Finn led the Fian warriors in pressing them, forcing them to retreat until their feet were trampling in the surf and their blood was tingeing the white foam to rose. Relentlessly, the young captain went on slaughtering with great strokes of the Mac an Luin, slamming away thrusts and counterstrokes with the impenetrable Storm Shield that seemed to thunder its defiance. The Lochlanners began to panic, realizing they were trapped, overwhelmed by the determined Irish fighting men, whose numbers were less than half their own. In a growing rout they began to leave the fight, splashing out to clamber into their boats.

Caoilte, fighting close beside Finn, shouted to his comrade: "Finn, they're running! They're beaten! We can make a truce!"

"No!" Finn said savagely, a hard cut neatly beheading yet another foe. "No! No truce with them. We kill them. Destroy them all. Let none escape. Chase them into the sea!"

"But why?" Caoilte asked in shock. "Why waste good men? You've not done that before."

"I said to press on!" Finn cried, turning to face Caoilte. His sword ran with hot blood that reddened his arm to its elbow and was splattered across all his body. His face glowed and his eye blazed with battle light. "Kill them, Caoilte. We must finish them . . . finish them!"

His gaze swept around, over the melee. And then he pointed with his sword.

"There! There is their chieftain!" he proclaimed exultantly. "That's the one I must have!"

He was indicating the broadly built warrior with flowing beard and elaborately horned helmet who now stood before the dragon-headed prow of a long boat and tried to muster his dissolving force. Finn at once dove into the press of struggling men and began to cleave a bloody path for himself through the hapless Lochlanners, straight for the chief.

That individual was in desperate straits. His exhortations to his men to keep on the fight were useless. The air of cruel arrogance that had been on him when his host had crushed the village was gone, replaced by an expression both fearful and amazed as he watched his men so easily overcome.

Finn slashed through a last, intervening barrier of men and leaped before the startled chief.

"You were a fool to come to Ireland," Finn snarled.

The chieftain was older and heavier than the fair warrior who now confronted him so challengingly, but he was a veteran fighting man. Though surprised by the suddenness of Finn's appearance, he reacted with speed, striking out with a massive, double-bladed ax.

But not twice his speed would have been enough to counter Finn this day. The young captain easily ducked away from the blow and then charged in. Their battle was hard, brief, and one-sided. Finn beat down the chieftain's guard with a few massive strokes, smashed away his shield, hacked through the thick haft of his war axe, and sent the man staggering back with a sweeping blow of the Storm Shield.

The chieftain dropped heavily to his knees. A hopelessness overspread his face as he looked up to the young captain standing over him, glaring down so sternly.

"My warriors are beaten," he said in a broken voice. "We are lost. We will yield to you. We will pay whatever tribute you ask if you will let those remaining live."

"I will not," Finn said without pity. "I have no more patience. There'll be no more invasions of Ireland. The world will know that to do it will mean death!"

With that he stepped forward, making a sharp thrust with the Mac an Luin that slammed through the chieftain's chest and pierced his heart.

The man grunted once, his eyes registering his surprise. Finn yanked back on the sword, pulling it free. The lifeblood gushed from the wound, and the chieftain toppled forward, burying his face in the trampled sand, already dead.

The rest of his once-proud force was finished as well. Many fleeing men were cut down in the surf or as they scrambled for the boats. A handful escaped, leaving hundreds of their fellows strewn upon the crimson-stained beach.

Caoilte, witnessing this massacre and Finn's own ruthless act, moved to his side to speak in protest.

"Why are you doing this?" he said angrily. "Where is your justice, Finn?"

"Justice?" Finn said irritably, swinging his bloody sword sharply sideways in a gesture that seemed to sweep the concept contemptuously away. "There'll be no more of that. No. I've made my last mistake in the name of justice! No one who dares invade my land will live to come again. They'll learn. They'll all learn! I will have peace. Nothing will happen to make me leave Almhuin again."

He turned to his friend, fixing him with a commanding gaze.

"Let all men know what making war in Ireland will bring." He pointed to the dead chieftain. "His head I want, to show as a trophy and example to the lords of Ireland. Have the heads of the rest piled in a great cairn here, as a warning to other raiders. The bodies can be sent to their homes in their own boats."

He turned away from a dumbfounded Caoilte and

stared off toward the west, his tone at once softening with yearning.

"Then we start home," he said, as if to himself. "Home—to Sabd."

There was a look of yearning on the face of Sabd also as she stood at the rail of the sunroom, looking out across the country toward the east. The day was overcast, with a softening haze of mistiness that gave a gauzelike texture to the scene and made the meadows somehow a more intense green beneath the gray-white. Against the dampness, Sabd's head was covered by a knitted shawl.

Below, Cnu Deireoil stepped from the doorway of the main hall and looked up toward her. One of the old warriors, serving as a guard beside the door, followed his gaze, then shook his head in a pitying way.

"That poor, poor lass," he said. "It's every day now since himself went away that she's been up there, sunshine or driving rain, looking out after him."

"Ah, well, you can understand her doing that," the harper replied. "Finn is nearly all her life now. There's little for her here with him gone and only the sorry few of us to cheer her. I've done everything I can think of. But still the sorrow comes more upon her each day, like these clouds creeping upon the sun. Only Finn's return can bring the brightness back into that child's face."

"Well, he'll be coming back soon enough, I'm certain," the old warrior said. "The bloody Morrigan herself couldn't keep Finn away."

"True enough," the Little Nut agreed. Then he shivered. "Well, she can do as she likes, but I'm going back in. It's too chill for me." He looked at the warrior, who appeared quite cold and miserable himself, though stoically standing at his post, wrapped tightly in his wet cloak, his damp, graying hair plastered about his head. "And why don't you come in, as well? At least have a bit of hot broth to warm your bones."

"If you say it's all right," the man said with a grin, "then it wouldn't take a club about my head to make me accept."

"Maybe a little game of fidchell, as well?" the little

man suggested as he ushered the guard inside. "There's no one else about who can play. How are you?"

With them gone, the yard was empty, save for the figure of the lonely girl upon her balcony. She continued to stand there, seemingly indifferent to the damp and cold as she gazed intently out.

For a time she saw nothing but the empty, mist-shrouded countryside. Nothing moved there except a few soggy birds, fluttering like wet scraps of cloth in the wind, their cries plaintive and distant in the muting heaviness of the air.

And then, within a little copse of trees just below the hill, there was movement. It caught her eye. She looked toward it at first casually, then more intently, her eyes growing wide in disbelief.

From the trees moved three figures. One was Finn MacCumhal, while on his either hand trotted the faithful hounds, Bran and Sceolan.

The surprise in her face changed to elation. She opened her mouth to cry out in joy. But the cry was cut off as yet another emotion swept over her—this time, great alarm. For as the three reached the hill's base and started up the slope, she could see that Finn was moving haltingly, supporting his body on what looked to be a shattered spear pole, and that there was a great scarlet streak of blood staining his tunic at one side. Finn was wounded, and very gravely it appeared.

In fact, as she watched, he staggered badly, dropped to one knee, and rolled down onto his back. The hounds moved up quickly on either side to nose at him in a manner of great concern.

Sabd gasped in fear for him. Without hesitation she turned from the balcony, all but flying down the stairs to the lower level of the house and out its front door. She paused just outside, glancing desperately around the yard for help, but it seemed deserted still. Not taking any precious time to seek someone, she instead ran across the yard to the unattended gates. With a strength clearly enhanced by the power of her need, the frail girl wrested the heavy locking bar aside and shoved a gate outward far enough to squeeze her slender body through.

But her departure did not go unnoticed.

Cnu Deireoil and the old warrior—he holding a steaming mug of broth—stepped out into the hall's doorway in time to catch just a fleeting glimpse of the gowned figure as it slipped through the crack. But that was enough. The Little Nut stared in shock for an instant. Then he was running forward, shouting back over his shoulder to the warrior: "Get help! Quickly, man! And follow me!"

He reached the gates and pushed his small body through the opening. Behind him, the warrior had begun raising the alarm. Below him he could see Sabd already far down the slope, and he took in the little tableau of the fallen man and the two hounds at the hill's base.

He watched with growing horror as she reached this trio and dropped down beside the figure of Finn, lifting his head to cradle in her lap.

"No, Sabd!" he screamed in desperate warning as he charged down toward her. "Get away from him! That can't be Finn!"

The cry reached her. She looked up to see the little man rushing down the slope. Bewildered, she dropped her gaze back to the face of the man she held.

It was the scarred, blackened face of the Dark Druid that now looked up at her, its mouth stretched wide in a cruel and gloating smile.

She shrieked and jumped to her feet, dropping him back as if he were white-hot iron searing her flesh. She whirled about to flee from him but where the two hounds had been, two bears now stood, blocking her other avenues of retreat.

She wheeled back about to see that Fear Doirche had now arisen and was stalking toward her, arm extending what before had seemed a spear but had now become his magic druid rod. Its silver tip pointed toward her, threatening.

She tried to back away, but her legs thudded against the shaggy side of one bear who had moved up close behind her. She tried to turn and leap past it, but she was too late. The druid moved swiftly in, striking forward with his rod.

The tip touched her arm.

From it streamed a silver light, more like a liquid as it poured across her, encasing, trapping her, holding her as if she'd been suddenly frozen in a cocoon of ice. Only one low moan of agony escaped her before her head dropped back and she stood completely enveloped by the light. It grew brighter, shrouding her body in the translucent glow. Then, as before, the shadowy form within that glow began to shift. It writhed and shrank, the erect form dropping down, as if she were falling to her hands and knees.

But this time the transformation came more quickly. It was only seconds before the glow was fading, leaving revealed the form of a trembling fawn.

By now Cnu Deireoil had reached the group. Fearlessly the little man hurled himself upon the Dark Druid, crying out in rage.

He grappled with the larger man, tearing at his clothes, butting at him with his head.

"You'll not take her!" he shouted. "I'll kill you first!"

Fear Doirche's response to this was a cool one. He seemed more amused than disconcerted by the little man's attack. He shoved Cnu Deireoil away with one arm and swung his rod sideways with the other in a hard blow that smacked the harper sharply across the temple. He was knocked sideways and tumbled to the ground, stunned.

Fear stepped over him, looking down at the still form with a sneer.

"So you dared to interfere with me, little man?" he said. He gave a sadistic laugh and extended the deadly rod. "Well, I'll show you what kind of horror I can make of those who do."

The rod moved closer to the helpless Cnu Deireoil. The silver tip hovered just above his face.

A warning growl from one of the bears drew the Dark Druid's attention. He glanced around to see the animal pointing uphill with its muzzle. His gaze lifted to the fortress. A score of men brandishing swords, tools, and cooking utensils were pouring from the gates and charging down the slope.

He looked down at the harper again.

"No time for you now," he said with regret, drawing back the rod. Then he looked to the bears, brusquely ordering, "We must be away. Direct our prize back into the trees. Hurry!"

The bears moved to flank the fawn and herd her toward the wood. She moved with great reluctance, casting despairing glances back toward the fortress and her would-be rescuers. But they were still some distance up the slope when the bears forced her into the shadow of the trees. They were closely followed by the Dark Druid, who paused to cast a last, triumphant leer toward the Fianna men before he too slipped away into the cloaking wood and vanished from their sight.

Most of the men charged into the trees after him, looking around. But now there were no signs of movement in the deep shadows, or even any sounds. They split up, spreading quickly through the wood, searching the tree-tops and beating the underbrush.

Meanwhile, the old warrior and another of their number were seeing to Cnu Deireoil. The little man recovered consciousness quickly. He jumped up, looked frantically around him, and then turned to the two men.

"Sabd!" he cried. "The druid has her! Where are they?"

"They went into the wood," the old warrior replied. "It's small. They can't escape."

"Escape?" the harper said in despair. "He's a druid of the Sidhe, you fool!"

And even as he spoke, some men were emerging from the trees, looking defeated and angry, shaking their heads in bewilderment.

"It can't be," said the grim-faced steward called Rough Buzzing. "It can't be so, but we've searched all the wood. There's no sign of them. They've vanished as if they were never there!"

The host of the Fianna—bloodied, worn, but proudly triumphant—sped swiftly toward the fortress of Almhuin, following the pace set by their anxious captain.

Finn looked eagerly ahead to the white-walled dun as they neared, eyes searching most hungrily to catch a first glimpse of his wife. But no familiar, slender figure showed upon the palisades or in the balcony of her granian. There was only the form of a warrior who turned to shout to those inside the news of the host's return.

When the Fianna reached the bottom of the slope, Finn's eagerness seemed to overcome him. He sprinted ahead of the others, the great hounds running at either hand, crossed the bridge, and pushed through the gates as they were being opened to him.

He ran into the yard, noting that the inhabitants of the fortress were gathered about it as if to give greeting. He started toward the hall, smiling broadly, his eyes scanning the faces for that of Sabd.

But the faces held no answering smiles of joy. The people gathered were not cheering the returning men. Instead, their looks were solemn, their manner subdued, as if it were a mourning time.

Finn faltered to a stop in the middle of the yard, looking about him.

"What's wrong?" he said. "What's happened?"

Eyes were averted. People shuffled nervously or wrung their hands. Some women wept. An uncomfortable, ominous silence hung upon the yard.

"Tell me what's wrong," Finn asked with growing alarm. He scanned the crowd again, more anxiously. "Where is Sabd?"

"Finn," said the voice of the Little Nut as he moved out from the hall and through the gathered folk to confront the young captain.

"Cnu Deireoil, what's happening here?" Finn demanded in a desperate way. "Tell me what's happened! Where is Sabd?"

The harper's small face was drawn into a mask of agony. He hesitated, and then he spoke it out in one terse, unpleasant phrase: "She's gone."

The other Fian warriors were moving in through the gates now, but Finn paid no attention. His stupefied gaze was on the Little Nut, blank, uncomprehending, as if his mind refused to accept what he must have suspected since first sensing the atmosphere in the yard.

"Gone!" he repeated hollowly, this word of such terrible import seeming to have no meaning. "What . . . what is it you're saying?"

"I'm sorry, lad," the harper told him, his voice hoarse with sorrow. "The druid came. He took her."

Finn took a step back, as if he'd been struck a physical blow. The Fian warriors still moving into the yard fell instantly silent and motionless with their own shock.

"Took her?" Finn echoed again, still dazed. "How?"

"He came here disguised as yourself," Cnu Deireoil said in a weary, doleful tone, his body sagging, "and with what looked to be Bran and Sceolan. Before anyone could stop her, she ran out to him." The little man seemed close to tears. He had to force himself to go on with the awful tale.

"He . . . he struck her with his druid rod. He transformed her to a fawn and was away with her on the instant. There was nothing anyone could do."

Finn listened, staring dumbfounded through all of this. But then he gave an animal growl of rage, suddenly released. He rushed forward, face twisted, eyes flaring with madness. He seized the little man by the throat of his tunic and hauled him up, off his feet, shaking him like a pup, shouting into his face.

"You let her go! You were her protector! Her protector! And you let her go!"

"It . . . it was druid trickery," Cnu Deireoil managed to gasp out. He was being choked by Finn, his face growing crimson from suffocation.

Caoilte ran to them, grabbing Finn's hands, trying to pull them from the harper's throat. But Finn hung on, fingers clamped with the strength of his mad rage.

"Let him go, Finn," Caoilte pleaded. "You're killing him. Please let him go."

This had an effect. Finn released his hold abruptly and the little man dropped to his knees, coughing, pulling the tunic away from his bruised throat.

"I will not kill you," Finn said through clenched teeth, glaring down on Cnu Deireoil with hatred. "But I'll have no more ever to do with you. I left in your care the thing most precious to me. I trusted you, my oldest friend. And you betrayed me. It's a curse I put upon you for that. And it's no part of my life that you'll be from this day on."

He turned on his heel and stalked away, back toward the fortress gates.

The Little Nut watched him go silently, saying no more word in his defense. Then he sagged down in a crumpled pile, sobbing brokenly.

But Caoilte followed after his comrade who strode so purposefully from the yard.

"Finn, where are you going?" he said.

Finn seemed not to hear, his fierce gaze fixed on the way ahead, striding on, forcing Caoilte to grab his arm and swing him around.

"Where do you mean to go?" the dark warrior repeated.

"To find her," Finn told him stolidly.

"But where?" Caoilte asked. "You don't know where to seek her. She could be anywhere."

"Then we'll search the whole of Ireland if we must," he shot back. "From the point of Corca Dhuibhne to the Mountains of Mourne."

"Wait, Captain," said one of the clan chieftains, moving forward. "Our warriors are wearied from this campaign. They've not had rest or proper food for days following you back here at the killing pace you set, and there're many wounded among them from the fight—"

"You are Fian men, not children to be complaining of your aches and your empty bellies," Finn interrupted scathingly.

"What are you saying, Finn?" Caoilte asked in shock. "You can't ask these men to follow you now. At least give them a chance to rest for a few days and gather new supplies. What difference can it make?"

"No!" Finn nearly shouted in reply. "There is no time! The thought of every moment more she spends in that monster's clutches is like another knife plunged in my heart. Nothing can delay us! Until she is found, there can't be a moment's rest!" He glared about him at the warriors. "But I want the help of no man who has neither the stomach for it, nor the loyalty to me."

This raised looks of anger and mutterings of outrage amongst the assembled men.

"There's no call for you insulting us, Captain " the outspoken chieftain said indignantly. "It's not a matter of loyalty to you. This has nothing to do with the welfare of Ireland, or with the Fian laws, or any of the clans. This is your own loss, and, although we're sorry for it, it is only a woman."

"A woman?" Finn echoed in rage, stepping toward the man in a threatening way. "This is my life! Don't you see? Don't you understand?" He looked around him at the grim faces. "Don't any of you understand?"

There was no response.

"No, you don't!" he spat out. "You've no care for me at all. I ask your help and you deny me. You are treacherous hounds, and I'll have nothing to do with you. Slink back to your homes and whine and lick your wounds. I've no more need of the likes of you."

With that, he wheeled about and stalked from the fortress yard, the hounds following. The warriors and chieftains of the other clans stared after him with expressions of hurt pride. The warriors of the Baiscne clan looked to Caoilte.

"What should we do?" asked Lughaid in a dumbfounded way.

"We have to follow him," Caoilte said simply. "He is our chieftain and our friend. It's only the sorrow on him that's making him this way. We'll go with him and help him with his hunting until the madness of it dies out."

And so the Baiscne warriors, still carrying the same battered weapons of their last fight, still wearing the same torn and bloodied clothing of their hard campaign, weary and wounded, stoically turned again and marched out of the yard they had just entered.

Behind them, still kneeling, still sobbing brokenly, they left the forlorn figure of the little harper, surrounded by the solemn, silent crowd.

CHAPTER◊10

The
Search

FALL WINDS SCOURED THE COUNTRYSIDE. THEIR CRISP, chill dampness was tangy with the foretaste of the coming winter. The emerald meadows had faded to the dull gray-brown of a weathered thatch roof, and the sky was a sodden cloak of rumpled gray wool. Only the trees added any note of warmth to the scene with their leaves in the last death flame of autumn colors. But the winds had already stripped much of this glory and were moaning in the naked branches like Ban-Sidhe keening for the coming death of a loved one.

Across this desolate landscape moved a forlorn company of men: the Fian warriors of the Baiscne clan, following a Finn MacCumhal who pressed on doggedly.

They were beginning to look a somewhat worn lot now—a bit leaner and· a bit threadbare. And the expressions of all, save the determined Finn, were uniformly glum.

They crossed a ridge, reaching a place where the land dropped off more sharply, providing a view of a broad, rolling countryside that stretched far away. It looked rather bleak, with only scattered patches of bare woods and no rising plume of smoke or cattle herd or circle of rath walls to give sign of any human habitation.

Finn stopped there, his eyes moving slowly, searchingly over the scene ahead. His young face was set in a frown of concentration that had furrowed his brow, drawn down curving lines about his tightly drawn mouth, and crinkled the corners of his narrowed eyes.

The dogs, as always, were close at either hand. But the others of the band, including Caoilte, had stopped some way behind. As he examined the countryside, they huddled together in what seemed an intense discussion in muted tones, accompanied by much sharp gesticulation and by occasional glances toward the back of the young captain from one or another of the warriors.

Caoilte was apparently the focus of this group, much of the talk being directed toward him, while his response was largely the shaking of his head. But finally, after giving one more troubled glance toward the lonely figure of his comrade, he sighed in an unhappy way and nodded.

He moved away from the group and started toward Finn, then hesitated, looking back at the rest. They all stood watching him, their attitudes tense and expectant, their expressions hopeful. Caoilte sighed heavily again and went on, stopping at Finn's side.

"Finn," he began, in an uncharacteristically hesitant way.

"What?" Finn asked tersely, not turning his gaze from its intense perusal of the distance.

"It's the other lads. They've been talking, Finn. And . . . and they wanted me to speak to you."

"What about?" Finn said flatly, his attention still elsewhere.

"Well, it's how fast the weather's changing that they're thinking of. The fall is well on us now. Winter's coming. You can smell it heavy in the air."

"I suppose you can," Finn agreed, appearing finally to register the words and the ominous tone of his comrade. He turned to regard him with a piercing look. "Tell me your meaning, Caoilte. Say it out plain."

"All right then," the dark warrior said more stoutly. "They're thinking that it's time we gave this up."

"Gave it up?" Finn said with shock. "But we can't give it up! We've only begun the searching."

"We've searched the summer through, Finn, and through the fall. The men have to think of their winter quarters now, and of their families—"

"Their families?" Finn cut in in outrage. "Is that what they're thinking of? Their warmth? Their comfort?"

Caoilte stepped closer, his voice dropping to become hard, intense, and scolding. "Now you listen to me, Finn MacCumhal. What you've said is unfair, and you know it as well as I. It's a long, hard way they've come with you, searching across the most rugged and barren parts of Ireland. They've gone without food and even drink sometimes. They've gone without rest or even a warming fire to follow this mad quest on and on. And never a complaint have you heard."

This argument had no effect on Finn other than to fuel his rage.

"How dare you talk that way to me?" he said. "It's Fian men you're speaking of. No labor is too much. It's only their loyalty to me they should be thinking of. But they betray me like the rest!"

Before Caoilte could stop him, he wheeled and stalked to the waiting group.

"So you'd abandon me!" he shouted at them bitterly. "You who think yourselves men of the Fian. My own clansmen who I thought, at least, would support me. Now, when I've most need of your help, you act in treachery!"

The exchanged bewildered looks at this scathing outburst.

"We don't mean to abandon you," Lughaid tried to explain earnestly. "We think it's yourself who should give over this search. Finn, it's useless. You'll not find one fawn in all the wild places of Ireland, for a lifetime of hunting! Likely she's been hidden by the druid's power, and no mortal can find the dwelling of the Sidhe without their allowing it. Why, we may have already passed the place where Sabd's been taken and not known it! You've got to give it up, or you'll destroy yourself."

"I'll not give up," he said. "There is no life for me without her, don't you see? I'll search every slieve and every glen until I find her. Or I'll die in the searching."

Lughaid looked around at his fellows, all grim-faced as he was, shaking their heads in doubt. Then he met Finn's eye again with resolve.

"My captain, if you persist in this, then it's truly a madness that's on you. If you don't quit and come with us, if you don't take up your life again, then we'll not follow, for it's as man possessed and not as our leader that you want this. Now, we mean to go back to Almhuin. Will you go with us?"

"I will not. You are cowards, and traitors to me, not ones fit to call yourself Fian fighting men. I'll have no more to do with you. I will go on, with only my two hounds to search through Ireland. Go back then, to the safety of Almhuin, and the Bloody Morrigan take the lot of you!"

He wheeled and strode away, brushing past Caoilte and returning to the waiting hounds.

"Well, lads," he told them, "if you still have loyalty to myself and to Sabd, follow me."

He stalked on, starting down the slope, and the hounds followed without hesitation.

"Were he any other man," said Lughaid, angrily, stepping to Caoilte, "I would have given him challenge for those insults."

"If you had, you would have died," Caoilte told him bluntly, looking after the figure striding so determinedly away. "He is a troubled and a desperate man."

"He is a man unhinged," Lughaid harshly replied, "and not the Finn MacCumhal who was our captain. We'll not follow him. We'll turn back to Almhuin. Will you join us?"

"No," said Caoilte with a resigned look. "No. Much as I may agree with you, I can't abandon him. I don't blame you for what you're doing. But if he's mad, he needs help more than ever, and a guardian as well."

"Your loyalty is commendable," Lughaid said, "but it may kill you along with him."

"Then I'll meet you next time in Blessed Lands," Caoilte told him with a game smile, and, turning, he started after Finn.

So the company parted. The band of warriors watched their departing captain for a time. Finally, with an air of reluctance and sorrow, they turned and made their way slowly back in the direction they had come. But the trio of man and dogs, soon joined by the second man, went on

into the new, empty lands, moving purposefully ahead and
not looking back.

The four figures seemed very tiny and very lost in the
midst of the vast, white wasteland.

Snow raggedly blanketed the ground, and more blew
down from a gray-white sky. A sharp wind drove the ice
particles along the ground, scouring the surface, sweeping
it bare in some spots and piling it with drifts in others.

The two hounds went ahead, breaking a path, wallowing
ahead through the deepest parts, at times using their
broad chests to plow a way. Behind them, the men fought
their way along, bodies wrapped tightly in their cloaks,
faces burnished to glowing redness by the stinging blasts,
in the storm undistinguishable save for the fair and dark
hair streaming out around their heads.

Finn staggered and dropped to one knee. Caoilte
moved up quickly to help him rise. But Finn shook him off
in an irritated gesture and rose alone, starting right on
again. Caoilte fell in close beside him.

"Why do you keep going on?" he said, shouting to be
heard over the wind, his voice hoarse, creaking with the
cold. "We've had no food in two days now. No rest. This
cold will kill us soon. We have to stop."

The other seemed not to hear, just pushing stubbornly,
mechanically on. Caoilte caught his arm and swung him
around. He looked into a face much like death already,
gaunt and hollow-eyed, darkened with stubble, chapped
by wind, lips cracked and blackened with dried blood. A
face that was almost a mirror of his own.

"All you'll achieve is to die here!" Caoilte reasoned
brutally. "We'll all die here."

"Every moment we rest is another moment she is in
his power," Finn said in a rasping drone, like a man
repeating an incantation in his sleep.

"Dying won't help her!" shouted the dark warrior. "We
don't' even know where we are! I can't see, and neither
can you. We've got to find a place to rest!"

Some sanity seemed to return to Finn's bleary eyes at
that. He shook his head dazedly.

"Maybe you are right," he said, looking around at the white wasteland. "But where?"

"We passed that abandoned rath not too far back," Caoilte told him. "We could find shelter there, at least for tonight. Maybe this snow will stop."

"All right," Finn agreed. He looked to the hounds and gestured back in the direction they had come. "That way, lads!" he shouted to them.

They understood, turning about to start back along the path they had just plowed, the two men falling in behind.

None was aware that their plight was being observed by a gloating Fear Doirche.

He stood beside the lounging Miluchradh in the snug quiet of the Seer's crystal globe, which seemed to hover just above the four as they struggled on through the waist-high drifts.

"That stubborn fool. He'll never survive," he said with a chuckle of sadistic pleasure. "He's nearly alone, wandering aimlessly, and half-frozen now. Oh, this is too great a treat! To have him torture himself so willingly for me, and to be able to watch him do it as well!"

"I thought you might be interested in seeing this," she said, her head back, not watching the painful scene. "Still," she went on more guardedly, "he's not an easy man to destroy. It would be a grave mistake to underestimate his powers."

"Your constant warnings tire me, woman," he shot back. "And they interrupt my entertainment." He moved close to the curving surface, his gaze fixed avidly upon the struggling four. "Could we move in nearer?" he asked. "I want to see every mark of suffering on his face."

"If you wish," she said, without any enthusiasm of her own. She waved a hand carelessly toward the images and the bubble seemed to drop lower to drift just above and before the young captain.

"Oh," she said, in a most careless way, her voice neutral, but her full lips parting in a malicious smile. "I do have another bit of information. It's about your little fawn."

"Yes? What about her?" he asked impatiently, not really paying attention in his absorption.

Her head lifted and her eyes fixed on his back, clearly eager to observe his reaction.

"Well," she said slowly, savoring each word, "I've been watching her at times, as you ordered. I'm afraid there's a small problem."

This caught his attention. He whirled toward her, his expression now one of concern.

"Problem?" he repeated. "What do you mean? Isn't she well? Isn't she looked to? I said she was to be kept safe!"

"Oh, she's quite safe," Miluchradh assured him. "And quite secure. She has a snug little den in a sheltered vale she can't escape. She's supplied with food. No. It's not that." She smiled more widely. "It's that your lovely, precious, perfect Sabd is not quite what you think anymore."

"Explain, woman!" he thundered, stepping up to loom over her threateningly.

"I've discovered what you have not," she answered smugly. "I have sensed and seen the life growing in her; sensed the warmth in her, seen the soft belly of that slender body begin the first swelling. Your Sabd, my druid, is going to have a child."

"What!" he said, stunned by the revelation.

"A child," she repeated, driving it home hard. "And my seer's powers tell me that it is the child of Finn MacCumhal." She laughed openly, callously, and delightedly. "Your Sabd has given herself to his charms, it seems. You have truly and completely lost her now."

"No!" he raged. He swung out at the grinning face, the back of his hand catching her cheek, knocking her back. He thrust the silver tip of his rod against her throat, pressing her back against the cushions, the metal denting her flesh at the hollow of her throat. "You treacherous hag! I should turn you to the she-wolf that you are!"

"You won't change the truth," she said, still smiling as she rubbed her bruised cheek. "And it's worth this pain to see the look on you. The Great Druid, made a fool by this little girl. You wanted yourself to win her, and now the flower is despoiled. Destroy her. Be rid of her."

"I will not!" he said impatiently, jerking the rod from her neck and turning away. With the first shock of this

discovery past he was now considering it, clearly rational-
izing. "It . . . it makes no difference. It's her love I want,
and that this creature MacCumhal forced himself upon her
will not change my feelings. It only gives me the greater
reason to see him dead."

"You can't mean that!" she said, her gloating look
slipping to one of dismay. "What about his child?"

"Yes, his child," the druid said musingly. "Much as I
loathe the idea of the thing, to harm it would only turn
her more against me." Then his face brightened with an
evil glow. "But maybe MacCumhal has given me another
way to revenge myself upon him while winning her as
well! Yes!"

He paced around her on the cushioned floor of the
sphere, deeply engrossed in this new idea. Miluchradh's
concerned gaze followed him.

"What do you mean?" she asked. "What will you do?"

He stopped and looked down at her with an exultant
smile.

"Why, I'll let the child live!" he proclaimed. "More,
I'll nurture it, give it a place of comfort in my Sid! That
will show her my love. Perhaps it will change her!"

"It will change nothing!" she spat out contemptuously.
"You're a fool to think otherwise. How blind this love has
made you. How dangerously weak."

"What do you know about it, you poor, loveless creature?" he said with scorn. Then he went on in a voice now
soft with cunning: "Besides, even if my kindness does not
move her, think of the weapon I will have. How can she
deny me with the fate of her own child at stake?"

He chuckled in a slow, deep, greedy way and began to
pace again, going over the details of his plan in careful,
loving detail.

"I will have her this time. I'll see her brought here for
the winter. She'll have fine quarters and I'll put her own
form upon her again until the child is born. Then it will be
human. Yes. That will make her agony all the greater. For
it to be human, and her not . . . why, that notion would be
intolerable!" He stopped and fixed his triumphant gaze on
the scowling druidess. "Do you see? Then she will be

most anxious to accept my love, to save herself and her child."

He wheeled toward the image of Finn struggling in the snow. His face grew hard with cruelty once again.

"But you, MacCumhal, you have earned my greatest wrath. I'll not be content now to see you suffer there, or to tolerate any possibility of your surviving. No, I want to be certain that you die, and I want a part in killing you myself."

"How can that be?" she asked in alarm. "You can't risk facing him."

"I won't face him," he told her. "No, I won't need to. The storm will do it for me, with only a little of my power to twist it to my end. Watch, my Miluchradh."

He lifted his druid rod, pointing the silver-tipped end upward toward the gray clouds arching across the top of the sphere.

"Powers of the sky," he intoned solemnly, "great spirits of the winds and snows, I command you to obey my will!"

The silver tip began to glow, the hard, white light growing swiftly to an almost blinding intensity. The clouds began to coil and writhe as if new, shifting winds were tugging at them.

"Concentrate your storm upon this spot," he called to the skies. "Bring all your force to bear here, upon these four."

The clouds grew darker, heavier, their bellies swelling downward toward the ground. They churned, they boiled, as if vast energies were stirring within them. They descended upon the men and hounds like a herd of enormous, monstrous beasts leaping upon some very small and very helpless prey

Finn and his companions found themselves suddenly at the heart of a blizzard of most overwhelming proportions. The winds slammed at them from what seemed all directions at once, striking with all the power of a great club. They tore at the men as if to rip their clothing away. The snows came so thickly that the countryside was lost to view behind a solid screen of white.

"Where did this come from?" Caoilte shouted to be

heard above the shrieking wind. "I've seen no storm like this ever before!"

"I don't know," Finn called back. "But we've got to keep going. Reaching that rath may be our only chance!"

"Where is it?" Caoilte asked, trying to look around him. "I don't even know our direction anymore."

"The lads will have to find it," Finn said. "Bran, Sceolan," he called to them, "it's up to you. Find the rath!"

Obediently, the hounds pressed on, Finn and Caoilte following, holding fast to the animals' long tails. In the blinding snow, even a separation of a spear's length was enough to cause one to be lost.

They staggered ahead, moving ever more slowly against the punishing wind and the drifting snow. It was piling around them, growing deeper almost by the instant. The white clung to them, coating them, encasing them in ice.

Soon they were barely moving, the snow rising like great sea waves, flowing over them and covering them as they tried to flounder on.

The last view Miluchradh and Fear Doirche had of them was a glimpse of Bran's head, struggling valiantly to rise above the crest of a great drift before sinking out of sight. Then the curtain of snow fell across the scene, the swirling white hiding all from their view.

"There, woman," the Dark Druid crowed triumphantly, looking to her. "Do you see? Not so difficult a task as you have thought. A little of my powers, and the long quest of your young captain is finally at its end!"

BOOK TWO

The Wandering of Finn

◊

CHAPTER · 11

More
Treachery

THE TROOP OF HORSEMEN SPLASHED ALONG THE MUDDY roadway. The riders, wrapped closely in their cloaks against a sharp, chilling rain, pressed forward on mounts plastered chest-high in the rich, black ooze. They guided their horses upon the grass verges at the worst spots to save them the labor of slogging through deep mire, but the animals were clearly much worn already.

"I don't see why we can't be stopping for a bit—just to rest the horses," grumbled a thickset rider bundled and hooded in a cloak so voluminous that it made him seem a round bundle perched upon the saddle.

The man at the head of the troop, himself hoodless, turned toward the speaker and revealed the face and leather patch of Goll MacMorna, chieftain of the Fian clans of Connacht.

"You know, Conan," he answered tersely. "The High-King has summoned us."

"The High-King has summoned us," the other repeated in a mocking way. He pulled back his hood in an angry gesture. His broad, sullen face was running with water, despite the covering. The few curling wisps of his remaining hair were plastered like wet rattails to his forehead.

"Brother," he went on argumentatively, "I don't see why we've still got to be rushing out in any sort of weather, riding bone-weary and empty-bellied, like hounds called to their master, anytime old Conn whistles. He's not the power in Ireland anymore."

"He's still our High-King, Conan," Goll told him, more warningly this time, "and we're still sworn to serve him and to obey his will. No true fighting man of the Fians would deny that. Not even Finn. So no more of that treasonous talk from you."

"That doesn't explain why we can't have a bit of rest and maybe a little fire," Conan muttered, subdued but still complaining.

"You'll have your fire quick enough, brother," Goll said, pointing ahead. "There's Tara."

Ahead of them, a broad, rounded hill had come into view. Through the slanting screen of fine, hard rain, the outlines of structures upon it could be dimly seen.

Conan's sullen expression at first lifted to one of hopeful spirits at the sight. But as they drew closer and the intervening screen of rain thinned to reveal the fortress more clearly, his look altered again, this time to a puzzled frown.

"The dun's looking just a bit shabby, don't you think?" he asked.

The reason for his comment was quite evident. The great fortress called Tara of the Kings, center of the political and spiritual soul of all Ireland, should have been its most imposing sight as well. Indeed, it was a grand place in size, a complex of many structures that sprawled across the top of the rounded hill and other, smaller hills about it. But the look of it all now was threadbare and sorry, like the look of a once-proud chieftain worn by the battering of a hard life.

This impression grew even stronger as the riders mounted the slope of the main hill toward the palisade which circled its crest. It could be seen now that the thick logs of the high defensive wall were rotting at their bases, some already sagging from their positions in a badly eroded earthen rampart.

Goll's troop rattled over a shaking bridge that spanned the fosse and rode through a gate where a miserable-seeming pair of sodden guards huddled by a pitiful, smoking fire in a rusty iron brazier. They dismounted by a disintegrating stable building where a bent-backed ancient took their horses.

"Stay here and see that they're properly looked to," Goll ordered one of his warriors, casting a dubious eye around at the decrepit surroundings and the wheezing old man. Then he led the rest of his company across the rain-soaked yard toward the immense, circular structure in its center.

"Even the teach mi-cuarta has a neglected air," Goll commented, sidestepping a wide pool.

The great hall of Tara certainly did show signs of deterioration. The daub was crumbling from its walls and the thatched roof was worn thin from weathering and sagging forlornly under the beating rain.

"Neglected air?" said Conan with a scornful laugh, hopping over a rivulet that had carved a deep channel across the soggy ground. "That's the rot of it you smell. The whole, bloody place is ready to topple about us!"

They reached the hall's main doors. Goll thumped upon the panels with a fist, causing them to rattle loosely upon their hinges.

After a lengthy interval, a shuffling was heard within. It grew louder until, at last, there was the clanking of a latch undone and the door creaked shrilly open.

A face was thrust out on a long, scrawny neck. It was wrinkled and wreathed by an unruly tangle of white hair and beard. It peered at the men with clouded, red-rimmed eyes and then spoke in a voice that rasped as rustily as the door hinges.

"And who are you dripping vagabonds to be coming to the door of Tara's hall to bother us?"

"I am Goll MacMorna," the chieftain announced, "of the Clan na Morna. I have come to see the High-King."

"Who's that, you say?" the man asked, cocking his head and directing an ear at the warrior. "Goll . . . what?"

"MacMorna," Goll said again, a little testily. "Of the Fianna of Connacht. I've come to see the High-King."

"Ah, I don't care who you are," the man cawed sharply. "The king's resting now. You can't be disturbing him. Go away!"

He started to push the door to. But the hand of Goll shot out, gripping it, holding it open. Startled, the old man looked up as the one-eyed chieftain leaned forward, bringing his face close. Goll's expression was hard now, and his voice was uncompromising.

"We have come a great way in a cold rain to see the High-King at his own request, Steward," he rapped out. "You will let us in, and you will tell him we are here... now!"

The old man, clearly frightened, released the door and scuttled off into the shadows within. Goll shoved both portals fully open and gestured to his warriors to follow him. They stepped through into the interior of the hall.

The vast, desolate space that opened before them was like the gloomy depths of a dank cavern. A few guttering candles feebly, flutteringly, lit the dingy walls and the scores of empty, dust-cloaked tables. The air was thick with humidity and the odor of mildew. Water dripped from uncountable places in the battered thatch, making stagnant pools on the floor and the plank tabletops, sizzling and spitting as it fell upon the few glowing coals in the central fire pit.

The company of warriors moved forward into the room and stopped, looking around them with expressions of open dismay at what they saw. Then, from within deep shadows at the back of the room, there came a rustling, drawing the attention of everyone to it.

Two figures emerged into the faint light. One was the wild-haired old steward, fixing an indignant glare upon the intruders. The other was a man so stooped and wasted that he caused Goll to exchange a glance with his brother, the brow of his good eye arching in what was for the stolid chieftain a show of great astonishment.

For Conn, winner of a hundred battles, High-King of all Ireland, had become a shockingly decrepit being.

His body was nearly skeletal, his cloak of faded red silk hanging loosely about him, his arms and legs withered sticks with knobby joints. His lean, long-featured head was gaunt, with cheeks hollow and eyes sunk deep into their sockets, giving him a ghastly, cadaverous look.

He advanced across the floor slowly, his movements very stiff. When he reached the low platform which elevated the table of state, the old steward had to help him climb, with considerable difficulty, onto it. He tottered to an elaborately carved armchair at the center of the table and lowered himself creakingly into it. He fixed his eyes—glowing points of ice-blue light within the shadowed sockets—upon the Fian chief.

"So, MacMorna," he said in a hollow voice, "you still obey me. I had wondered if you would abandon me as those parasites who were my court have done."

"You are my king," Goll told him flatly. "I am sworn to you and to the laws of Ireland for so long as you . . ." He paused, clearly realizing the unpleasant connotation of the next word.

"Live?" Conn finished. His mouth stretched upward in a death's-head grin and he chuckled—a dry sound like the rustling of fall leaves. "Well, that may be long enough. Long enough."

"Why did you call me here, my king?" Goll asked. "Is there some danger?"

The smiling mouth drew into a thin line. The voice grew chill.

"Yes. A great danger. And a great opportunity, my old friend. I have heard that Finn MacCumhal has abandoned the Fianna to quest after some woman."

"I . . ." Goll began. He hesitated as if considering, then went on in a somewhat reluctant tone. "I have heard something of it, my High-King."

"So, you did know!" Conn said accusingly. "And you did not tell me?"

"I saw no need—" Goll began in a defensive tone.

Conn interrupted curtly.

"No need to tell your king that the Fianna—the defenders of Ireland! the keepers of its laws!—have no leader?"

"The trouble was Finn's and for Finn to deal with," Goll said firmly. "I had no right to interfere."

"We are talking about more than Finn here," Conn said with greater power. "It is the captaincy of the Fianna that concerns me."

"Finn will surely return," Goll told him.

"It's said that he is mad," Conn shot back. "The tale is that the woman had bewitched him, had stolen his will to lead you. And now he wanders, obsessed with finding her, broken and spiritless."

There was a note of cruel glee in his voice, and his eyes glittered with satisfaction.

"I'll not believe any of that," the chieftain countered. "I know the strength of Finn. I know his honor."

"Do you?" Conn said derisively. "Still, you cannot deny that he has chosen to break his oath, disregard his duty, and abandon his fighting men for some selfish quest. That is treason. It means that someone else must take control. You must assume the Fian leadership again!"

"No!" Goll snapped. "I will not."

"But you must," Conn insisted, his tone ever more heated, his eyes glowing with an ever more angry light. "He has given me the chance I've sought. And he's given it to you as well. Think of it, my friend: a chance to assume the captaincy again."

"I don't want it," Goll said, sweeping out his hand in a gesture of vehement denial. "You took it wrongly from his father once before, and I was fool enough to help you. I'll not help you again."

The old king's face grimaced in sudden fury. He leaned forward, his wasted body rigid, shaking with tension. His bony hands gripped the arms of his throne like claws upon their prey.

"He deserves this!" he snarled at Goll. "Look what he has done to me! Since his victory on the White Strand, he is the most feared warrior, the greatest leader in the world. He has given your Fianna all the esteem, all the power and wealth that should be mine. Do you hear that? Mine! I am abandoned by my lords, by my servants, even by my own son who dares to call me weak. I am left here, in this moldering ruin, alone." He lifted a hand and shook a clenched fist in triumph. "But now I will have my power back. Now I will have respect again. Finn will be gone, and you"—he pointed a talon and grinned—"my loyal and faithful Goll MacMorna, will return it all to me."

"It's only the venom in you that's keeping you alive, my king," Goll told him. "It hisses in your words like a serpent's tongue. And if it's vengeance you're seeking, I'll do nothing for you. I'm loyal, yes, but only to the laws of Ireland, and to the good for her that you should represent."

"I see," the old man said bitterly, sinking back in his

chair. He contemplated his defiant chieftain for a time, and then a look of shrewdness came into the glinting eyes.

"Well, then, if that's your feeling," he said in more reasoning tones, "then you must still act for me, and to Ireland's good. The Fianna cannot be left leaderless. Why, Finn may not even be alive. He left in the fall, and has been seen by no one since. Now it is spring, and the winter was harder than any I've ever known."

This appeared to perplex Goll. He considered, exchanging a look with Conan who only shrugged in a noncommital way. Finally Goll responded.

"Very well," he agreed reluctantly. "I will go to Almhuin and see what the situation is. Should there come a need, I'll be forced to take the leadership of the Fians. But otherwise, I'll only wait and watch. I'll not assume the captaincy of the Fianna unless I know that Finn has either truly abandoned them or is dead. Do you understand?"

"I do," the king told him, his skull-like face beaming with a victorious light. "It is enough. For I know that he is finished."

"And I am certain he is not," Goll answered. He nodded curtly, turned, and led his men back out of the great hall at a brisk stride.

But as they left it, its vast silence was filled with a peculiar sound.

It came from Conn. His head was back, his mouth open in a shrill, staccato laugh of triumph that echoed eerily in the empty room.

Finn and Caoilte followed the two dogs across a broad meadow. A bright sun shone down from a clear sky, warming them. The day was invigorating, fresh, fragrant with the blossoming of new growth, brilliant with that jewellike clarity of spring.

But the little group was itself far from fresh. The spring sun shone on forms decidedly the worse for the brutal honing of a hard winter's traveling. All were much gaunter now. Their muscular forms were lean and sinewy, though without making them seem less strong or less dangerous, but somehow more so, both hounds and men were now much like half-starved, prowling wolves.

The clothes of Finn and Caoilte were badly worn, their cloaks nearly in shreds, their tunics stained and torn. The hair of the two was long uncombed and gone wild. Finn's fair, fine stream of hair was now a stringy tangle caught up in a knot behind his neck. Caoilte's thick hair was carelessly twisted into a thick plait from which wiry strands had escaped to form a bush about it. So too were the coats of the dogs long ungroomed, the thick, curling fur matted close to the hide by dirt to make them seem all the more gaunt.

In what was the most striking abandonment of the Fian warrior's normally fastidious look, both men were now bearded. Caoilte's thick beard and flamboyantly jutting mustaches of a startling red-brown gave him a rakish look. Finn's finer beard and drooping mustaches, more silver than his hair, added to an air of melancholy that seemed to hang upon him. The beards of both concealed their youth, their looks, and their identities, making them seem even more like savage and very desperate men.

And still the quest continued. As through the winter and the fall before that, they pressed on at that same steady, determined gait, eyes searching about them as if to spot some quarry. They moved on across the meadow, mounting a great soft swell of it through grass that switched knee-high about the men and stroked the bellies of the hounds.

At the top of the rise they finally paused. From here they had a view of more meadows that undulated away in sensuous waves richly furred with the intense green of the spring growth. Beyond them began a more hilly land covered with trees whose lace of branches, just starting to show the coloring of budding leaves, was like a fringe to the green cloak of meadows folded against the base of the sky.

Farther yet, just at the curving rim of the horizon to the west, the color changed more abruptly, rolling hills giving way to the steeper rises of a ridge of mountains. They formed a line that looked like a resting beast, its back running from a tail in the north to the south where it rose to create a large, rounded head. The mountains looked stark and rocky, their sides a grayish purple that grew darker as they rose to a sharp line against the light blue sky.

The men stood gazing across the wide lands to this line of mountains, the attention of both focusing on that highest, brooding peak as if drawn to it.

"What is that mountain?" Finn asked.

"In all my travelings in Ireland, I've not seen that before," Caoilte said, sounding surprised himself that he did not know. He looked at Finn. "We're very far, my friend, from the places that we know, and from our people."

Finn didn't seem to hear, his own eyes still fixed on the peak.

"Strange," he said musingly, "but it seems to pull at me. Since it's a place we've not seen before, I say that we go toward it."

"If we turn south, we'll find a fine bruidhean not two days' walk from here," Caoilte urged in a hopeful way. "A bit of hot food, a drink, and a night's rest there might do great, healing good for our spirits."

Finn turned his gaze upon his friend. The set look of determination seemed to have etched permanent lines about the eyes now. The voice spoke its words in a kind of toneless incantation, as if they'd been repeated many, many times before.

"The summer will be upon us soon, Caoilte. The summer. And that means it's almost a year gone since she was taken. A year in that monster's hands."

"A year," Caoilte repeated, sighing wearily. "And well enough I know it. And each day more that passes I see the pain of it wearing harder on you, stabbing deeper into you. That's why I'm asking you to rest. Just for a bit. That mountain won't be going anywhere."

In reply, Finn only shook his head morosely, turned his gaze back on the way ahead, and plodded on.

Caoilte looked after him, shook his own head sadly, gave another sigh that seemed to well up from his depths, and looked down at the two hounds.

"Well, lads, I tried. Let's be on, then. And good-bye, bed and ale." He patted his hollow stomach regretfully, then smiled and shrugged. "Ah, never mind. I was needing a bit more slimming anyway."

The three started after the fair-haired warrior, and the tiny company set its course like an arrow shot toward that purple-gray peak—a peak that seemed both foreboding and beckoning at once.

They couldn't know that inside it lay their goal, a vast chamber hewn from the living rock, or that, within that chamber, a strident cry was now loudly echoing.

CHAPTER◇12

The
Seer's
Plan

WITHIN THE VAST CAVERN, THE GROTESQUE BEINGS OF the Dark Druid's host ceased their activities to listen to the cry.

It was a blend of fear, discomfort, complaint, and even indignation, voiced in a thin but lusty tone. It issued from the mouth of a smaller cavern cut into the outer wall several levels above the floor.

There, the amazingly tiny source of this most impressive sound squirmed within swaddling covers, its face red and puckered with its wailing, while its mother cuddled it in her cradling arm, crooning soothingly.

The comforting sounds and movements soon calmed it, and it drifted off to sleep, face relaxing into smooth, soft lines, eyes dropping closed. Sabd peered down at it with great tenderness and fascination, her own young face glowing with joy over her newborn child. But there was worry showing in her expression as well.

The worry deepened to a frown as she finally, reluctantly, lifted her head and fixed her gaze upon the dark figure who stood nearby, seeming to loom threateningly above her even at a distance. The druid watched her closely, with what appeared great interest, a little smirk of triumph tugging the corners of his lips.

"And what do you mean to do with me now?" she demanded, the protective instincts of a mother seeming to give her greater courage.

"Why, nothing," he said reassuringly, but adding with more point, "if you wish! Your child will not be harmed by me. That I've already promised you. You may continue to live here as you have through the winter. You may raise your child here."

"Here?" she said, grimacing with horror. "Raise my child in this awful place?"

"Awful?" he said, irritation giving a harder edge to his soft tones. He lifted his hands to gesture about him at the chamber. "And can you call this awful?"

The room in which Sabd and her baby lay was, indeed, far from that. A cozy nest had been created there, completely disguising the fact that it was a cave hacked from the rock. Thickly woven rugs and sumptuous cushions covered the floor. The walls were hung with tapestries depicting scenes of glens and forests so vivid and detailed they might have been windows to the outside world.

"I've given you every comfort here," he told her. "Every luxury. And I've asked nothing in return."

"And what payment would you be asking to continue giving this to me?" she asked in a cynical way. "Would that be nothing as well?"

"You know what it would be," he answered with great earnestness, moving toward her, leaning down toward her, hands out in supplication. "I only ask your love for me. Even the semblance of it! Choose me, and all the rest can be."

"But I cannot!" she said emphatically. "Don't you understand? I wouldn't give my love to you before, and I'll surely not do it now. I've accepted another! I've given my full love to him! The child I'm holding is the proof of that. Look at it." She lifted the sleeping babe so he could see. "Look at it, and believe you cannot have me. Please, just let us go."

He looked at the innocent face, but his own was not softened. Instead it grew more hard. His chin lifted and he gazed down pridefully on her.

"The child I can accept. The knowledge that this . . . this crude warrior forced himself upon you I can overlook. But I will not let you go. Your tie with Finn MacCumhal is gone. He's no longer alive!"

"That I do not believe," she said fiercely. She put a hand to her breast. "I feel, here, that he is alive. I know that he is seeking me. Nothing would stop him from that. And one day, Fear Doirche, he will find you and destroy you. You will never have me."

"You say that now," he told her in a slow, ominous way, "but how long will you endure it when your child aches for a mother's arms or wails in the night for the comfort of a mother's voice?"

"What . . . what do you mean?" she said, her defiance giving way to fearfulness.

"You understand my meaning, Sabd. If you refuse me, you will leave my Sid, but it will be the form of the deer you wear upon you again."

"And my child?"

"I said I would do nothing to the child. You may keep him with you. You'll be taken to a sheltered valley, closed in by steep hillsides. You'll not be able to escape this time. Food will be brought to you. You'll have a burrow to shelter you from the chill and rains, but that is all." He shrugged, adding carelessly, "Who knows? You may survive. You can still nurture the infant, after a fashion. It will be a most amusing tale for the bards: 'The Fawn and Its Human Child.'"

Her look became one of despair. She looked down at the sleeping face—so small, so vulnerable.

The druid's expression softened as he watched. He dropped down beside her. An intense yearning filled his eyes. Dignity abandoned, he spoke to her in cajoling, nearly begging tones.

"Sabd, please think. I only wish to love you and to have your love. Don't refuse me. Think of the child if not yourself. Please . . ."

He put out a long hand, extending his fingers to gently caress the fine, softly glowing hair of her bent head.

At the first touch she shuddered, drawing away, turning toward him with an expression of revulsion.

"If you truly loved me, you'd not imprison me here," she told him angrily. "I would rather live my whole life as a fawn than suffer your touch, vile creature that you are. And I would rather raise this child as a beast of the woods, or see it die at least under the open sky, than ever have it breathing the air of this foul place."

His tender look was swept away as if she had struck him across the face. He jerked to his feet and stepped back, his mood of chill arrogance returning.

"You have made your choice, Sabd. Now you'll live with it. But I will visit you from time to time to see if your feelings have changed. And they will change, I know that. When you cry out to hold your baby in your arms again. When you realize that you have no escape. When you believe that your champion will never come to rescue you. Then you will accept me!"

With that, he wheeled and stalked out of the room.

She looked down at the baby, her eyes filling with tears.

"My son," she said in anguish, "you will be my only comfort. And I hate what I must do to you in return. But to live in this terrible place is worse than to die. My poor babe"—she hugged him to her, the tears running upon her fair cheeks now—"feel my warmth. Remember. It may be the last time my arms will ever be about you."

Fear Doirche, meantime, was striding up the winding stairs, about the interior of the main cavern, mounting level upon level until he reached the opening to the seer's lair.

He pushed between her muscled, ram's-headed guards and swept up the corridor to the threshold of the glowing, glass-walled sphere.

On his entrance, the surface of the bubblelike room was fully lit. He caught a quick glimpse of a wide vista seeming to sail slowly past below. Then Miluchradh—seated as usual upon her plush bed of cushions—caught sight of him. She started in what seemed a guilty way, fluttering her hands about. The images instantly faded to the blank, white glow.

"Oh, my druid," she exclaimed, sounding a bit breathless, "you quite surprised me! What is it you want?"

"It's the woman," he stormed, moving toward her. In his angry state he appeared not to have noticed her odd behavior. He strode back and forth, venting his wrath to her with great force as he waved his arms. "She is a stubborn fool. Even with the welfare of her child at stake. Even with the comforts I've lavished upon her, and the care I've given her. Still she spurns me. Ingrate! Ingrate! Ingrate!"

He stopped, hands clenched, head back, eyes closed, body tense in frustration.

"Now do you see?" she said. She rose and moved to him, raising a hand to soothingly caress his brow. "Poor, dear man. Do you see what she's done to you? She's driven you to near madness. But now maybe you understand. You'll never have her. Be rid of her." She leaned toward him, pressing herself against him. Her voice became low, sultry, and provocative. "Come to me, and I will heal you. I will make you forget her."

"No," he said with a new outburst of anger, pushing her away. "Don't seek to beguile me again. I will have her. Her need to have her child, to be a woman for it, will overcome her yet. It can only be the hope she sees in this wretched Finn that still sustains her." He fixed the Seer with a commanding eye. "That is the reason—the only reason!—I seek you. Give me some proof I can show her of his death. Find me his body!"

Her look grew troubled at that. She turned away and sank down on the cushions. When she finally replied, she did so with reluctance, not meeting his eye.

"I . . . ah . . . think that that might be somewhat difficult."

He looked at her in perplexity.

"Difficult? What do you mean? You said that you had last seen him lost in the winter's snows. You said he must have died and been buried. But it's spring now. The snows have been gone many days. And still you can't find him?"

"Well," she said carefully, "I have found him. I've just located him recently, to tell the truth. But I . . . I'm afraid that he's alive."

He stepped toward her, his voice threatening.

"Show me!"

She swiftly brought the sphere back to life. The image came into view, sharpening to reveal a countryside of open meadows spreading away in all directions below. They seemed to be drifting above four familiar figures trudging steadily along.

With a wave of the hand she brought the bubble swooping down closer to them while Fear glared at the images, face taut with anger.

"You see," she offered. "A bit more battered and shaggy, but still quite alive, and moving with no less energy." She looked at Finn and added, almost in an admiring tone, "His strength is really amazing!"

"The Bloody Raven take his strength," Fear said sharply. "Where is he now?"

His gaze went from the figures to their surroundings. He scanned the countryside once, and then again with more care. His eyes narrowed in suspicion.

"Wait!" he said. "This is the same countryside that you were watching when I first came in!" A light of suddenly dawning realization came into his face. He whirled upon her. "Just how long has it been since you found them again?" he demanded angrily.

"Well, I've actually known they were alive for some days," she admitted in a tone that made it sound trivial. "I came upon them after they escaped your blizzard's attack. I've been tracking them closely ever since."

"And you didn't tell me?" he bellowed, raising the staff as if he meant to strike her.

Clearly frightened, she lifted her hands in defense.

"There was no need, my druid," she earnestly explained. "They've been far away, and of no danger."

"Far away?" he raged, pointing to the horizon beyond the four. A quite familiar-looking line of purple mountains was visible there. "And isn't that my own Sid they're heading for? How close must they come?"

"I . . . I was going to tell you of their coming," she assured him. "This very day, in fact."

"Were you?" he said, understandably skeptical. But he lowered the stick. "Well, that we can speak of later." He turned toward Finn. "Right now our attention must go to dealing with this irritating man."

"Yes, Fear," she said, relaxing and sighing with relief.

"There must be a way of dealing with him for good," he said thoughtfully. "I want him dead for a certainty this time."

"Kill him?" she said. "Is that necessary?"

She said this in a somewhat regretful way, and he gave her a curious look.

"Are you having some . . . feeling about this warrior?" he asked. "Some closeness from having watched him for so long perhaps?"

"No, no!" she said quickly. "It's just the danger to you! He's escaped your magic more than once. Those creatures of yours would surely be no match for him. And to face him yourself would still be far too great a risk."

"I am growing immensely weary of these suggestions that I cannot take on this half-mortal boy myself," he said testily. "In our last encounter, he took me by surprise. That is all! I'd welcome another chance to face him!"

"Of course! Of course!" she told him soothingly. "But why should you take any risk when there's no need?"

"What do you mean?" he asked.

She waved the bubble closer. It seemed to hang before Finn. His shoulders and bearded face filled the view. She gazed at him thoughtfully, and then she gave a cunning smile.

"I have been watching him—very closely," she said. "And now I think perhaps I've learned how I might deal with him."

"You?" He gave a scornful laugh. "Why, you haven't a fraction of my powers. How could you deal with him?"

"I haven't your magic powers," she agreed. Then she struck a blatantly provocative pose, shoulders thrown back, hands upon hips, expression boldly wanton. "But I am a woman, am I not?"

"That you are," he readily agreed. "I would never argue it."

"Then that may give me a power over Finn greater than your own." She looked back at the image of the fair warrior. "It's said that women may be his weakest point, and your Sabd seems to have proven that. He is too much their champion, even to the risk of his own life. With that knowledge as a weapon, I think that I can make him harmless—quite, quite harmless."

"I want him more than harmless," he told her harshly. "He must be dead. Can you manage to do that?"

"Must he be dead?" she protested. "He would be a

fine slave. A magnificent slave. I thought you would wish that. What fine revenge! To humble him! To make him serve you!"

"And perhaps serve yourself as well, Miluchradh?" he asked in a shrewd way. "No. I'll take no more chances with him. I want to know that he is forever gone. His death, and Sabd's surrender, will be enough revenge."

"If you insist," she said sullenly. "But only if you will give your word to me that I may at least make my own use of him first."

He eyed her stubbornly for a moment. But then he shrugged.

"Very well," he agreed. "That I'll give to you. But, to see that there are no mistakes, take some help with you. Take the bears and some of the warriors. And take the pookas, too. They'll see that once he's helpless, he'll die."

"I need no help," she said indignantly. "Not from that sorry lot of misfits and exiles."

"You will take them," he ordered, "just in case your...desires shall we call them?...should somehow interfere with my command. I know how you can be."

"You're not one to speak of desires, my druid," she responded, coloring with rage. She turned her back upon him. "Leave me now. I have to prepare myself!"

"Just see that I have a body to show Sabd!" he said as a last warning and strode from the room.

As he went out, she cast a scalding glance after him. Then her eyes went back to the huge image of Finn and their gaze grew softer.

She stood, waving her hand slightly, and the image moved back. The globe seemed to float just above the ground before him. His image was life-size, close, so real it seemed it would stride through the curved surface.

She stepped toward him. Her hand lifted to the image, stroked across the muscles of his arm, ran caressingly across his chest, outlined the firm lines of his jaw.

"Dead," she said softly, shaking her head regretfully. "Ah, what a great, great waste that is!"

Finn and his companions now left the open lands, entering the more rugged and thickly forested area which lay between them and the druid's mountain. The grim peak was lost to sight as they moved into hills whose trees were growing thick with new foliage.

There was more game here, and they hunted as they traveled deeper into the cool greenness that was speckled with sunlight, like the coat of a new fawn. Many lakes were nestled into valleys amongst the hills. Serene, beautiful, isolated places they looked, like bright sapphires sparkling there.

As the afternoon came on, Finn and his companions made a camp upon some higher, open ground above one of the lakes, where they could not be come upon by surprise. Here they dug a broad, shallow pit, building their fire within it to heat the cooking stones, wrapping their dressed game in rushes and burying it with the stones to broil it.

While it cooked, the men made couches for the night by laying out a pallet of supple branches covered with a layer of moss and another of rushes. Caoilte then sat down to await the finishing of their evening meal, the two dogs stretching out nearby him for a doze.

"Well, it's a nice, warm, dry evening for a change," the dark warrior said with pleasure. "Time I had a moment to get some of the rust off my poor blade."

He pulled the weapon from its sheath and began to fish in the leather pouch upon his belt.

"In a spring as wet as this one's been, I could wish for that strange metal your own Mac an Luin is made of," he commented, pulling out a whetstone.

Finn wasn't listening. With the fire and beds prepared, he was looking about him restlessly.

"I'm going to stroll around a bit," he said, almost absently.

"It's a bad habit you've gotten into, going off like this each evening," Caoilte scolded. "You'll do nothing for yourself by being alone to brood."

"It's what I feel like doing," Finn responded testily. "Is that all right with you? I'll be back when the supper's done."

He took up the Storm Shield and strode off through

the trees, leaving his comrade staring after him, shaking his head.

"It's the poet in him," Caoilte muttered to himself. "I knew that one day it would come to curse him."

Finn moved downhill through the trees, toward the lake that was just visible as scattered sparkles through gaps in the boughs. Finally he came out on a more open hillside that sloped downward to the water's edge. He dropped down on a boulder there to look out over the water.

It was a beautiful but quiet and solitary spot. At this time of year, the sun remained up quite long. Its late afternoon rays were now slanting sharply in, flaming the tops of the surrounding trees, flashing against the smooth surface of the lake.

Finn seemed oblivious to his surroundings. He stared ahead of him with those haunted eyes. His young face was sullen, aged by the lines of his despair.

In the sparkling lights of the gently rippling lake other images seemed to dance before him. They were images of light dancing in unbound, golden hair, of a smiling face and bright green eyes meeting his. He saw Sabd, running in the meadows on a spring day such as this. He saw her in the bronze glow of firelight. And then he saw her as a fawn, cowering before the looming figure of the Dark Druid.

Tears filled his eyes and he squeezed them shut in his anguish. He dropped his head forward, shaking it from side to side as he cried tormentedly, "Sabd, my love, I am sorry. I am so sorry!"

He sat quietly after that, unmoving, head still hung forward in an attitude of complete despair. For a time there was no other sound, as if the land itself had hushed in sympathy with this unhappy man.

Then, there was another sound.

It was very faint, drifting to him from what seemed a great distance. But it was clear enough. It was the sound of a woman crying.

CHAPTER◇13

Finn's
Madness

AT ONCE FINN WAS ON HIS FEET, PEERING INTENTLY through the trees, turning slowly, head cocked, holding his breath, trying to establish the direction of the faint and plaintive sound.

His expression was eager, his eyes filled with a hopeful light. Clearly the unthinkable, the impossible possibility was in his mind. He listened, shifting fraction by fraction until his gaze was fixed upon the lake glittering below. He stared at it searchingly, as if to verify. Then he burst into motion, seizing up his shield and leaping down the slope.

He moved recklessly, bounding over rocks and sliding down gravel inclines, sweeping to the water's edge in moments. There he stopped, listening again.

The sound of crying came to him once more, and much louder this time. Distinctly a woman's voice, its tone was one of great distress.

He moved along the shore, but slower now, pausing often and constantly listening. He explored the way ahead carefully with his eyes. He passed a small copse of fir trees growing right at the water's edge. Beyond it a peninsula came into view. It was little more than a thin, curved line of boulders, like a crooked, skeletal finger, thrusting out into the lake. But as his eyes fell upon it, Finn stopped, staring ahead.

There she was! She sat upon a boulder at the tip of the rocky point. A dark crimson cloak was thrown back over one shoulder, revealing a gown of shimmering white that clung to a lithe figure. Her head was forward, her face hidden in her hands. A heavy screen of softly gleaming golden hair hung forward and about the slender shoulders which now shook with her sobs.

He moved toward her. His breath was coming rapidly. His body was tense. His eyes—hope-filled, wondering, afraid—were fixed unwaveringly upon her, as if the breaking of his gaze might cause this phantasm to vanish.

Cautiously he moved closer, stepping with care from rock to rock as he made his way out the peninsula. His gaze traveled over her form scrutinizingly. There could be no question of the thoughts that now had to be tumbling confusedly in his mind. The hair and the figure of her were so achingly familiar, so like those etched in his memories. But . . . it could not be! He couldn't dare to believe that it was, only to go finally and completely mad from a dashing of that hope.

The woman seemed to hear him, for she turned suddenly, ending his agony. She lifted her head and gazed at him, brushing back her hair.

She was young. She was fair. She was very beautiful. But she was not Sabd. He stopped short as if a fist had driven against his chest, knocking out his breath. His head jerked back. The frail hope flickering his eyes was in that instant swept away as if it were a feather on a stream, and he seemed to sag as the despair rushed in again.

"Who are you, grim warrior?" the woman asked.

Her expression was one of fear—the fear of a startled fawn. Tears shone in her large, intensely bright green eyes. Though she was not Sabd, the resemblance was still a haunting one. That fact coupled with her obvious fear had an effect on Finn. He seemed to take control of himself, banishing the despairing look and drawing himself up, becoming in a measure like the stalwart warrior of earlier days.

"You've nothing to fear from me," he assured her gently, lifting his sword hand palm out in a gesture of peace.

"I . . . I'm sorry," she told him. "I was surprised, your coming so suddenly from nowhere. And you seem . . . so . . ."

She paused, looking him up and down as if not certain how to continue.

"So ragged and wild?" Finn supplied. He managed a smile as he looked down at himself. "Well, I'll grant you that my look is none the better for some hard traveling. But I'm no ruffian, that I tell you truly. My name is Finn MacCumhal, and I'm a warrior of the Fianna."

"Are you?" she said, her face brightening with excitement. "I have heard of the Fianna, and of the great Finn MacCumhal who is their captain. Is that who you are?"

"I am," he acknowledged, giving a little bow.

"I have heard that Finn was a man of great handsomeness," she said musingly, giving him a most penetrating look. Then she nodded. "Yes, I suppose you are that, beneath that scruff of beard."

"I thank you, lady," he said, amused. "You're quite a comely young woman yourself."

There was more than slight truth in that. She was of a beauty rivaling that of Sabd, though somewhat less fragile in type. Her features were bold and cleanly sculpted. Her mouth was wider, with full, deep red lips. The gown she wore scooped low in front, revealing the fair, smooth skin of her breasts and of her slender throat, banded by a thin necklace of red-gold.

His gaze wandered down, over the gown, slipping along the curves of hips and legs it most enticingly revealed, then rose back to her face. She was watching him intently, and in a knowing way. Embarrassed by his own boldness, he said hastily, "Well, my lady, what is troubling you? From your crying you sounded to be in some distress."

"Ah, yes," she said dismally. "It's a great sorrow that has come upon me. I've lost something of such value that it means my life to me."

"Tell me," he urged. "For I'm bound by my oath as a Fian warrior to give you help."

"It's a ring of gold—red-gold like my necklace—that I'm fretting after," she said. "It was the dearest thing to me, and the only treasure of my poor, dead husband left to me. And the shame of losing it is entirely upon myself, for I was bathing in the lake when it slipped from my finger." She shook her head in despair. "Ah, I've searched there all the day, diving about. But I'm not a swimmer, and I had to give it up. There's nothing left now for me to do."

"Don't fret for your ring any longer, my lady," Finn told her stolidly. "For it's never that I'd leave a woman with such sorrow upon her. Especially a woman like..." He paused, unwilling to go on.

"Like what?" she asked in innocent curiosity.

"It's of no importance," he said quickly. "But I'll find that ring of yours if I have to sift all the bottom of this lake for it."

She grew ecstatic at this, jumping to her feet and sweeping upon him. Clutching his arm, she pulled herself to him, pressing her body to his, lifting up to plant a kiss fully on his lips. Taken by surprise, Finn let her prolong the kiss for a moment before he could react. Then, with some difficulty, he broke away.

"There's no need for that, my lady!" he told her a little breathlessly as he looked at her in surprise. "It's my own pleasure to help you."

"Oh, of course!" she said, blushing and dropping her eyes in a manner that was suddenly quite demure. But from beneath the long, screening lashes she cast a veiled look of wantonness upon him.

The unwary Finn busied himself in laying down his shield, taking off his sword harness, and unfastening his cloak. He laid them all out carefully on the rocks, then turned to examine the lake, his muscular body now clad only in the short tunic.

"All right, my lady," he said. "Where was it you think the ring was lost?"

"Out there," she said, pointing to a spot some distance from the rocks.

"So far?" he said in a puzzled way, glancing at her. "I thought you said you couldn't swim?"

"It's very shallow there," she assured him, giving him an engaging, girlish smile.

A touch of uncertainty entered his expression, as if a vagrant suspicion had flitted across his mind at the strangeness of all this. But then he shrugged it off, stepped to the end of the rocks, and made a neat dive out into the lake.

The woman gave a laugh of triumph as his lean form sliced through the surface, vanishing from sight. For what seemed a very long time he did not reappear, and only the widening ring of ripples showed where he had gone in. She leaned forward, her expression becoming more expectant and more tense, her eyes scanning the surface.

Like a bright, leaping salmon he suddenly exploded from the water not far away, surprising her. She stepped back, showered with spray, as his body shot upward and then dropped back. He shook his head to clear the water from his eyes and looked toward her. There was a faintly bewildered look in his eyes.

"You'll have to excuse me for asking this," he said in a hesitant way, "and I feel a fool for it, but—just what is it I'm looking for out here?"

"It's a ring," she told him. "A red-gold ring."

"A ring," he repeated as if some great light had dawned. "Of course! Well, don't worry. I'm certain I'll find it soon."

"I know you will," she said. "But it's the wrong place you're looking. I said I lost it over there"—she pointed to a spot a great way from where she had first indicated—"much farther along the shore."

"Did you?" he said in surprise. "Well, all right then."

He began to swim toward the new spot, moving with powerful strokes. She had to move with great sprightliness to keep up, leaving the point of rocks and running along the shore, keeping close watch on him. When he reached the area, he once more dived beneath the surface, vanishing for some moments. This time she eyed the spot with a little smile of satisfaction instead of concern.

When he finally popped to the surface again, it was to look about him searchingly, as if something had greatly bewildered him. As he turned slowly about, his gaze fell upon her. He stared, frowning deeply, clearly trying to concentrate.

"Lady, I . . . I seem to be confused," he said foggily. "Could you tell me who you are—and why I'm here?"

"I am Miluchradh," she said in a slow, definite way, "and you are under a bond to me not to come out of that lake until you have found my lost ring."

"Am I?" he said in the dull manner of one just awakened from a heavy sleep.

"You are," she said firmly. "And it is up there you must go to seek it." She pointed yet farther up the shoreline, another great distance away. "Fulfill your promise to me now. You must do it."

"I must do it," he echoed in a mechanical tone, and obediently began to swim on.

Once more she followed, moving along the shoreline parallel to him. It was easier this time, as he now swam slowly, heavily, as if something dragged upon him.

Finally they reached a spot nearly opposite where Finn had first entered the lake. A small break showed in the line of trees above the shore, and, upon seeing this, the woman called out to the laboring Finn.

"Here! Here is the spot! It's right below you now! Please, get the ring!"

Like a hound fetching a stick, Finn dived at once, disappearing beneath the surface for a third time. She watched now with a smile whose open cruelness and covetousness wiped away her look of innocence.

"This time you will be fully mine," she murmured.

She hadn't long to wait. He was gone only briefly, bobbing back to the surface with an expression of great consternation. He turned this way and that in a jerky manner looking about him at the surroundings like a man disoriented by a nightmare. Then he saw her and called out imploringly, "You there! Woman! Please, can you help me? Please!"

"Be calm now," she told him. "What's wrong?"

"I . . . I don't know!" he said. "I don't know why I'm here or where I am!"

"Do you know me?" she asked.

He stared fixedly at her, clearly searching his memory for some record of her.

"No!" he finally said in frustration. "I've not seen you before, have I?"

"And who are you?" she put to him.

"I'm—" he began, then stopped short, eyes widening in terror. "I don't know that!" he cried. "I don't know!"

He looked near panic, and she acted quickly, dropping

to her knees at the water's edge and extending a hand to him.

"Now, now," she said soothingly, "it's all right. Come to me, poor boy. I'll help you. Just come to me."

He hesitated, eyeing her warily at first like a lost and frightened child with a stranger. But her smile was warm, her voice was coaxing, and she seemed unthreatening. Indeed, she seemed the only comfort in a world that had suddenly become strange to Finn.

At last he swam to her, thrashing awkwardly through the water to the shallows, clambering up onto the rocks in a clumsy way, as if the power that had sapped his mind had drained his strength as well.

She helped him, taking his arms and pulling him upon the shore. There he dropped down in exhaustion and sat shivering uncontrollably.

She moved in close beside him, encircling him with her arms, drawing his head to her breast, cuddling him like a mother with a child.

"I don't know what happened," he gasped in anguish through his chattering teeth. "I feel lost! I feel . . . afraid!"

"There, there, poor lamb, you're safe now," she assured him softly, stroking his face. "It's only an illness that's come upon you. But I can help you. I can make you well."

She unfastened the pin of her crimson cloak and pulled it from her shoulders.

"Here, you're soaked and chilled through. Put this on." She drew the wool garment about him. "Then I'll take you somewhere warm and safe. I'll care for you there, and you'll feel better. Come now. Come with me."

She gently but firmly urged him to his feet. He stood head down, still shivering and weak, like an old man. She looked toward the woods above and gave a high, sharp whistle.

There was an immediate response. The underbrush rustled, and from its cover stepped a tall, gray, sleek-limbed horse.

It trotted down to her and stood waiting. Though it seemed at first glance to be no more than a horse, Finn was in no condition to note at closer hand the oddities that would otherwise have given him alarm: sharp, catlike ears, luminous yellow eyes, and feet that were not hooves but taloned paws.

With an effort she managed to get the stuporous Finn onto its back, climbing up behind him, clutching him about the waist to hold him upright. Then she ordered the animal forward. Even with the great weight upon it, the creature trotted effortlessly away, up from the rocky shore, into the trees, vanishing in the deep shadows of the darkening wood.

The sun had just vanished, dropping below the tree-lined ridges. Its last glow lit the sky, reflecting from a few drifting clouds to give the lake a parting glitter that was bright against the shadows filling up the woods.

In the twilight stillness the call was a forlorn sound, echoing across the waters.

"Finn!"

It died away. And then it came again, louder, with more urgency.

"Finn! Finn MacCumhal!"

There was no responding cry, no sound or movement save for a fish leaping far out in the lake, making spreading, shimmering ripples across the surface.

From the woods appeared Bran and Sceolan, spaced apart, moving warily. Close behind came Caoilte, shield up and sword in hand, looking about him with like carefulness, his expression revealing his concern.

The trio moved down onto the shore of the lake and stopped, gazing out across the waters. They were growing darker as the sunlight dimmed, rapidly becoming a fathomless, mysterious expanse. The trees around the lake loomed blackly, giving an even greater atmosphere of eeriness to the place.

"Finn!" he called out again, and again the sound of it reverberated across the waves, dying slowly away.

The two hounds began a scouring of the shoreline, one moving in each direction from where Caoilte stood. It was Sceolan who picked up a scent, barking to attract their attention and then taking off along the shore at a run. Bran and Caoilte swiftly followed.

The hound led them through a small copse of trees and onto a finger of rock thrusting into the lake. As Caoilte started out after him, he caught a faint gleam of light from metal. More anxious now, he put on greater speed.

Sceolan reached the tip of the peninsula and began nosing a folded garment. As the others approached, he raised his head to give a howl of dismay. Caoilte looked down at the familiar, ragged cloak, then shifted his gaze to the weapons neatly laid out beside it. He knelt, lifting the sheathed Mac an Luin tenderly in his hands.

From the sword he lifted eyes now filled with his agony to the blackening waters. A look of dreadful certainty came into his face as he stared into the concealing, ominous depths.

"No!" he cried suddenly, jumping to his feet. "It can't be!"

He lifted his head and shouted out with a power brought from the very depths of him.

"Finn!"

The name boomed back at him from the surrounding hills.

But there was no reply.

CHAPTER ◇ 14

Seduction

THE HORSELIKE BEING WITH ITS TWO RIDERS PULLED TO a stop in the dark woods.

A structure could be seen just ahead. Nestled deep in a hollow surrounded by a thick wall of trees, it had been quite invisible until they were all but upon it. It would be nearly so even now if it weren't for the light that poured from its open door and windows. There was enough to reveal that it appeared to be a small, rude bothie—a round-walled hut with walls of wattle and a roof of thatch.

Finn and the disguised druidess had come some distance from the lake to this spot. The strange creature they rode had great power and an amazing surefootedness in the night woods, carrying them swiftly along. Now it stood quietly, not even breathing hard, as she slid from its back and helped down the still dripping and still trembling warrior.

"Here is my little liss," she told him in that same soothing, warming tone. "Here you can rest and find comfort, my poor, handsome young man."

As she led him unprotestingly toward the door, the horse looked after them with its narrow, glowing eyes. The miserable Finn took no note of this, nor of the fact that from the woods about the hut other malevolent eyes were peering out at him.

The collection of grotesque creatures that owned these eyes were shifting around, shuffling for better viewing positions. One wretched, weasel-faced being gave a low snork of not fully repressed excitement and received the sharp elbow of a lean, wolf-headed warrior in his ribs as warning. But his odd little noise and the thud of the blow were enough to attract Finn's notice, even in his sorry state. Some deep-seated hunter's instinct, not wiped away with his memory, brought him alert, and he pulled up, looking sharply around, muscles tensing for action.

"What was that?" he demanded.

The things in the shadows sank far back.

"It was nothing, my poor, sick lad," she assured him quickly. "Just the night birds. Come inside."

He submitted and she led him in, but she cast a baleful look back at the trees as she did.

Though the liss seemed a most tiny and humble place from the outside, once across the threshold the difference was most startling.

The structure seemed somehow much bigger from within than from without, and very much grander. Its roof pillars were of polished red yew, carved in sinuous lines made up of what seemed many forms that intertwined in softly glowing curves. The walls were hung with tapestries of plush textures, patterned in warming reds and browns and yellows, while the floor was cushioned with a thick layer of sumptuous furs.

In a large, central fire pit, a fire already blazed in welcome, though there seemed to be no one else about to tend it. At the hearthside there was a mound of furs forming a couch, and beside it a low table holding a silver flagon and two chalices.

This time, however, Finn's muddled state kept him from noticing the hints of danger. Like a lost child he allowed his apparent rescuer to lead him across the room and ease him down upon the pile of furs.

"Now you sit here and rest," she said. She knelt beside him and poured from the flagon into a chalice a stream of rich, honeylike liquid that shone in the firelight as if it were molten gold. "And drink this," she added, handing the chalice to him. "It is fine mead. It will warm you and help you to relax."

He took the cup, but looked across the rim of it to her with an expression that now held some curiosity.

"Why are you doing this for me?" he asked. "Are you someone that I should know?"

"Of course I am," she told him in that calming, nearly hypnotizing voice. "I am your own true love. I am your comfort and your savior. I will take care of you. Now, drink."

He took a small, tentative draught, and then a large one.

"It is warming," he said. "It takes the chill."

His body lost its tenseness, the shivering fading away.

"Drink more," she urged and, while he complied, she pulled her cloak, now quite damp, from around his shoulders. "But to truly help you to get warm, you must take these wet things off and let the fire dry you."

She tossed the cloak aside. Her hands moved to the hem of his ragged tunic, taking hold.

He looked down, a faint uneasiness showing in his eyes.

"Wait . . ." he said. "Do you—"

"I must do this," she said firmly but reassuringly. "You are chilled through. This will help you. Just drink and be at ease."

He seemed to accept this, and took another drink. The liquor was clearly contributing to a growing ease in him, and giving his skin a warm tinge as well. She slowly and mostly gently pulled the garment up, letting her hands slide in a caressing way across his chest as she did so. She slipped it off over his head, leaning close, her lips near his ear as she crooned soothingly to him.

While thus engaged, neither she nor Finn were aware that the shadowy figures in the trees had crept from their hiding places to the hut. They now moved stealthily to the open windows and peeped into the interior. The light revealed what a monstrous lot they were, mixtures of men and beasts, the best like a twisted caricature of a human. They gazed into the room, fixing glinting eyes on the pair with lecherous interest, mouths stretched by leering smiles, elbowing each other for best vantage points.

Meantime, with her disrobing of the young warrior complete, Miluchradh took his nearly emptied cup and gently pushed him back.

"Now, you must lie down and rest," she told him.

He complied without resistance, stretching himself out on the furs. She lay beside him. Her hand lifted to stroke his temples lightly, rhythmically. He closed his eyes, relaxing further. His voice took on a dreamy, distant tone.

"It seems strange that I've no feelings of how I came to be in that lake, or where I've come from, or who I am. There are faint images, like wraiths of smoke, in the blackness of my mind. I see myself running through a forest, alone. I have a sense of having come a great way. I . . . I think there were others . . ." His eyes squeezed tightly shut as he concentrated.

"Think no more of it," she urged in a calming whisper, continuing to stroke. "You have been lost. You have been ill. You are worn and weary. But now you are safe. You can rest. You can be with me. That is all you want. All you want. . . . All . . . you . . . want."

The tension left his face. His chest began to rise and fall with a slow, regular rhythm, which she matched with her stroking hand. He seemed on the verge of sleep, totally at ease.

Her other hand lifted, sliding up his arm and then across the hard and smoothly muscled chest.

"You have a most wonderful body," she said, her voice caressing as softly, as sensually as her hand. "A strong, young, and virile body." Her elegant, slender fingers slipped down across his breast. Her long nails, carefully shaped and colored a deep red, traced his ribs, gently raking across the flesh. They paused at the ragged white line of a scar upon his side. "You have been through much. But now you can rest. Now you have me. Only me. I will give you strength. I will be your comfort and your warmth. Let me give my warmth to you."

The hand trailed on, down over his flat belly, moving slowly, lingeringly down . . . down . . .

One of the rapt creatures at the window—the same scrawny, weasellike one who had made a noise before—could not contain a lewd-sounding guffaw. Though Finn seemed not to hear, Miluchradh certainly did. She sat up, her gaze swinging toward the sound.

The creatures pulled back, but not before she glimpsed

the peering eyes. Her gaze swept around to the other windows, seeing more of the careless voyeurs, including the strange horse, whose head had been craned nearly through the window in its eagerness to see. It too withdrew hastily.

"What's wrong?" Finn asked, opening his eyes.

"Oh, nothing. Nothing," she said quickly, looking back to him. "I . . . just realized that the night's becoming chill. I must close the windows. Just rest. Rest."

She rose and crossed toward one of the windows, his eyes following her. With her back to him, her expression hardened instantly to one of rage. She leaned out the window to grasp the shutters, at the same time addressing the beings concealed outside.

"If I see anyone again, he'll be a slug," she hissed in a voice too soft for Finn to hear, but losing none of its venom for that. Then she pulled the shutters closed and dropped a latch.

Turning to cast a bright, loving smile at Finn, she went on to repeat her task at the next window. As she did, Finn's gaze strayed from her over the rich appointments of the room, finally stopping on one of the roof pillars. The elaborate carving of it caught his eye and he looked more closely.

The soft, glowing curves included the shapes of birds and beast and serpents, stretched and stylized into sinuous lines that twined, tangled, interlaced in never-ending patterns running up and down the columns. And amongst them, there were the forms of human beings as well, men and women both, their forms sleek and long, but still voluptuous, entwined in incredible and most imaginative convolutions.

Finn stared fixedly at these, his eyes widening in both wonder and fascination.

But now she had finished closing the shutters and was moving back toward him, drawing his gaze again to her. Her movements were slow, languorous, echoing the carvings in their sensuousness. Her look was sultry, like the atmosphere of the room, her gaze burning with an open wantonness.

"Now," she said in a low, torrid voice, "at last I will

truly make you well." She stopped at the foot of the pile of furs. "Now I will heal you with my own warmth."

She lifted her hands. His gaze, fully captured by her now, followed her movements. Her hands rose to the shoulders of her gown. Slowly, almost casually, she pulled its sleeves from her shoulders and shrugged. The gown fell from her, whispering to the floor about her feet. The full, lithe curves of her white body were burnished like the carvings to softly shining red-gold from the firelight. The light cast her in contrasting glowing light and intriguing shadows, accenting the voluptuous figure all the more.

She moved to his side, dropping down upon the cushions. She leaned forward, her breasts brushing against his chest as her lips came down to his.

He had watched all this with great interest, but with curiosity as well, as if not fully comprehending what it meant. But as her body came against him and the kiss began, he started very quickly to respond. One hand moved forward, sliding up the soft flesh of her bare leg to the warmth of her thigh. The other lifted, slipping around her back, pulling her forward to prolong the kiss.

After a moment she pulled back, catching her breath, looking at him with a little surprise.

"Well," she said, "it seems that you've not forgotten everything!"

"I . . . I'm not sure," he said, seeming surprised himself. "It just seemed a . . . a natural thing."

"Such things are," she said, and a look of even greater passion flamed in eyes that seemed much darker now. "Let me help you remember even more."

Her hands slid from his shoulders down across his chest. He pulled her to him again, this time with much greater fervor, both his arms sliding up around her. She rolled fully onto him, stretching out her legs, pressing the length of her body to his. The two sleek and lissome forms seemed to intertwine, like the carved figures on the pillars. The flickering light of the flames playing across their bodies tinted them and made their flesh seem to burn with the fire that now raged within them both.

* * *

Finn was unsure of where he was. A great meadow it seemed, green and cool and peaceful.

There were confused impressions, a jumble of images. Many faces flickered past him, wavery like reflections in a wind-ruffled pond. A dark-haired warrior waved to him from a distance, shouting something urgent that he couldn't understand. A great fortress, like a golden crown, glowed on the brow of a far hill. Then he was running on the plain, with two immense hounds bounding beside him. A fawn appeared, only to turn and run away. He pursued it, fighting his way through dense forests where lights and shadows twisted about him as if to entangle him. He saw the fawn close ahead. But suddenly, it was not a fawn but a woman that stood before him. She was fair and young and beautiful and she smiled at him with the brightness of a spring dawn. She moved to him and he lifted her, carrying her away.

They came to a sparkling brook, its music filling a sunny glade. He put her gently down beneath an arching tree and lay beside her. She leaned over him, ready to kiss him . . .

His eyes snapped open. There was a face above him. For an instant it was that same face, comely, fresh, and smiling. But then it blurred and seemed to alter before growing clear again. When it did, it was another face—darker, with a flood of black hair instead of gleaming gold, and smoldering deep brown eyes instead of bright green.

With a cry of shock, he rolled sideways, throwing the woman down onto the pile of furs with some violence, pulling back to stare uncomprehendingly at her features, still beautiful, but in such a different way.

Surprised by his abrupt move, she sat up to stare back at him.

"What . . . what's happening?" he demanded. "Who are you?"

"Be calm," she told him in an attempt to soothe him. "You are still confused by your illness. You know me. I am your savior, your comfort. I am your love."

These words seemed to jab Finn like a spear point, making him jerk back further.

"No!" he cried in denial, shaking his head. "No you are

not! I don't know you. I don't know you! There's something wrong!"

He clambered to his feet, casting his gaze around him anxiously. His eyes fell upon his tunic, lying crumpled beside the bed. He grabbed it up.

"I don't understand what's happening," he said in a hurried way, slipping the garment over his head, "but I'll not stay here."

"What's wrong?" she said, getting up and moving toward him, her hands out in a solicitous way. "Please don't be afraid. You're safe. Stay. Rest. Have more drink!"

She tried to put a hand upon him, but he avoided it, backing away, the apprehension growing.

"No!" he said again. "This is sorcery! This is something evil! I won't stay."

"Please!" she said with greater urgency, moving in and putting both hands against his chest to restrain him as he started toward the door. "Please, you must stay. You can't go! Not yet!"

He thrust her aside and surged past, reaching the door, grasping its handle.

"No!" she cried. "Don't do it! You are a fool!"

He swung the door open. The enormous figure of one of the druidess's ram-headed guards stood blocking it. As Finn looked up at him in surprise, he swept down the axe he held raised, aiming it in a blow at Finn's skull.

Even with his memory gone, the long-bred warrior instincts were still enough to save Finn. He leaped back as the blow swept past, fanning him with its breeze. He retreated into the room as the creature stalked forward, followed by a motley collection of others who crowded through the door, with two large and snarling bears entering last.

This lot separated as they came in, spreading out to come at Finn from front and sides. He backed up until his calves struck the stones of the hearth.

With the blazing fire behind him and the menacing beings closing in from the front, he seemed trapped. He looked about him at his foes and their glinting weapons. His expression was one of desperation—the savage desperation of the encircled prey.

The ram's-headed one came in again, swinging his great axe. The move seemed to spur Finn to action. He ducked beneath the blow as it whizzed overhead. His hand shot into the fire pit. He gripped the end of a stick of wood as long and as thick as his arm and swept it up. Though its other end was blazing, he used it as a club, bringing it around in a hard, quick blow that caught his attacker across both arms as they swept by.

The axe dropped from the being's hands and he staggered back, shrieking, the skin of his forearms badly scorched.

The other bizarre warriors moved in. But now Finn met their attack with a zeal and a fighting skill that clearly dismayed them. The spirit of battle was on him, and he glowed with the light of it, sweeping the log about him here and there with great speed and power, knocking back all their attempts to strike.

The two bears had at first stalked back and forth outside the area of combat, seeking an opening. When one of them finally lunged in at Finn, it was only to receive a thrust of the burning stick into its face. It pulled back yelping in pain, and the air was filled with the acrid scent of singed fur. Both animals became more wary after that.

Miluchradh stood by, her eyes fixed avidly upon the battle, lips parted, her breast heaving with her excited breathing, body agleam with perspiration. She seemed to be actually reveling in the violence, aroused by the sight of Finn fighting off the score of men and beasts, his body moving powerfully, muscles straining, limbs flashing against the backdrop of the fire. But her own warriors seemed to be wearing down, holding back, eyeing Finn and one another as if each waited for his fellow to make the next attack.

"What's wrong with you, you cowardly vermin!" she shouted at them. "At him! He's besting the lot of you!"

At her command, the weasel-faced being leaped bravely in, thrusting with a sword. Finn twisted away, slapping the creature across the back of the neck as it staggered by. The burning log touched fire to the collar of its clock and it was suddenly screaming, leaping around the room as if it had gone mad, trying to tear off the blazing garment. Finally it succeeded, casting the cloak away. But it fell to the floor beneath a tapestry, and soon that was ablaze as well, the flames crawling swiftly upward through the sumptuous material.

Meantime, both bears were trying to come in against Finn at once. He drove one back, but the other managed to swing a paw that slapped the stick from his hands. Now weaponless and with the creatures closing in from both sides, Finn had only one avenue of escape left. He turned and vaulted across the fire pit.

It was a prodigious leap, impossible for most men, and it caught the attackers by surprise. They were forced to rush around the circle of the pit before they could close in again.

But by this time the room was filling with billows of smoke. The room glowed luridly with the flames, and the figures of the fighters were lurching shadows within them.

The smoke aided Finn. It all but blinded his attackers. They struggled clumsily in the florid half-light, swinging wildly at anything they thought was Finn. He ducked under an axe swing from another ram's-headed giant, then used his body to knock the being away. When a bear lunged toward him through the clouds, he yanked another tapestry down over its head.

Flames now reached the thatching of the roof. It caught instantly and the fire spread swiftly. Sparks began to shower down into the room and the rafters were quickly set ablaze.

Miluchradh glanced upward. Clearly the house would soon be engulfed by flames. Near her on the floor lay her cloak. She grabbed it up and threw it about her to protect her naked body as she moved toward the door.

A burning rafter dropped before her, but she dodged around it, reaching the open door, stumbling out into the night. Behind her, the battle was continuing, but with little effect. The combatants were smoldering from the sparks showering heavily upon them. They coughed and their eyes streamed from the suffocating smoke.

The wolflike warrior finally managed to find and close in on Finn, a sword and short sword flicking out toward him. But a rafter fell between them, knocking the weapons down. At this the warrior panicked. With a yelp of fear he gave up the fight, stumbling toward the barely visible door.

Others caught his panic and quickly joined the exodus. The wolf-man and some few others made it out, but a rafter fell behind them, bringing down a large section of the roof upon a boar-headed creature just behind, smashing him to the floor, not dead but trapped, set afire by the burning thatch. He began to squeal in pain and terror.

The door was blocked. The raging conflagration in the closed room was now causing an updraft, the fire twisting and roaring up in a single column of flame, involving all the roof. The other creatures of the Dark Druid, realizing they were trapped within the house, now went mad with fear, abandoning the fight to rush aimlessly about.

But Finn, still retaining a calm and logic in the chaos, felt his way to one of the windows. He threw himself against its shutters, smashing them open. Then he dived through, rolling down onto the ground, rising at once to scamper away into the trees.

The others, seeing his move, wasted no time in copying it. They ripped open shutters of other windows to dive out or crashed right through them. The huge bears, least subtle of all, simply drove against the thin wattle walls, smashing their way out in a shower of splinters and plaster dust. All of them staggered away from the house as it went up, a great cone of flame now, the rest of the roof falling in with a loud *whoomp*. The screeching of the trapped man rose to a shrill, horrible crescendo, then died away in the engulfing roar of flames.

Miluchradh stood like some embodiment of fury itself, the crimson cloak blown about her naked body by the gale of heat, her hair streaming wildly behind, the red glare of the fire making her eyes blaze as she pointed toward the pale figure flitting away into the trees.

"He's escaped!" she screamed. "Get after him, you idiots! All of you!"

The scorched, battered, and still smoking company stumbled off in pursuit. The druidess turned to the horse-like being who stood nearby.

"You stay with me," she told it, then called toward the

woods, "but you other pookas, you get after him, too. I rely the most on you to find him. Don't fail me!"

In response, two large forms shifted in the branches of the trees. Great wings unfurled and began to flap out. A pair of eaglelike birds slowly lifted from the woods and sailed away. She watched them out of sight, then climbed onto the horse-pooka's back.

"All right then," she snarled, "let's be after the rest. That fool has refused me—me!—and he will pay. This time, when I find him, there'll be no help for him. This time he will die!"

Its mouth stretching in a broad and grotesque grin, the horselike beast turned and carried her off swiftly into the trees. Behind them, the walls of the house collapsed inward, sending a great billow of sparks up into the night sky.

CHAPTER ◇ 15

The
Hunt

THE GLADE LAY QUIET, ITS GREEN GRASS GLOWING UN-
der the afternoon sun, making it seem like an emerald in
the dark setting of the surrounding forest. Nothing moved
there save the dust motes dancing in the rays of light and a
few birds pecking over the ground around a rotted log.

Then, some sound seemed to alarm the birds. They
flew up together in a whirr of wings as a form leaped
through a last screen of underbrush into the clearing.

It was a wild figure that bounded out onto the open
ground, naked but for a tattered remnant of tunic, lean
muscles pumping, long, unbound hair flying behind. It
paused on the margin of the open space, crouching,
looking warily about it with the harried, desperate eyes of
the hunted beast. Then it went on, sweeping across the
ground with the fleetness of a great buck, slipping away
into the trees on the clearing's far side.

Not long after, a group of figures pushed out of the
brush into the clearing. Two bears led the nightmare
band, followed by several creatures more or less manlike
but all equally monstrous. They were clustered quite
close, as if for security, and moved very slowly.

They too stopped as they entered the glade, looking
around them searchingly. All seemed weary, and several
looked most disgruntled.

"The Bloody Raven eat his stinking flesh," the wolf-
headed one growled. "We're still no closer to him. All

night we've hunted him, never even getting him in sight. Now his track's lost altogether."

"It's the bears' fault," bleated one of the ram-headed warriors. "They've not the noses for following a trail."

One of the bears snarled angrily in reply.

"It's not them," the weasely one whined. "That man is like a wraith, so he is, flitting away through the woods."

"All I know is that my arms are giving me great pain," cried the other ram-headed man, looking upon his badly burned and swollen forearms. "I want to go back to the Sid and have them looked to."

"Aye," agreed the weasel, rubbing a blistered neck. "I know what you mean. That lad did fine for the lot of us back there, too."

"He did that," grunted a stocky, boar-headed man. "And I thought the old hag was to see to him. Make him harmless, she said. Harmless. Ha!"

"Well, she may have taken his memory with the spell she put on that lake," said the first ram's-head, "but there's still something driving him, that's certain."

"Careful," said wolf-head in a warning whisper. "Here comes Herself!"

The horselike beast moved out from the woods, Miluchradh astride it. It pulled up behind the gathering and she glared down upon them.

"Why have you stopped?" she demanded. "Keep on! Keep on! We've got to capture him."

"We're not going to capture him this way," grumbled the burned ram's-head. "He's too fast and he's too wily. We'll never catch up to him."

"The Dark Druid will give you something more terrible to wear upon you than that head if you fail," she threatened.

"And maybe he'll do the same to yourself as well," the other boldly returned.

"Begging your pardon, Miluchradh." The horselike being spoke up, his voice a throaty rumble. "But these poor creatures are right. They can't come up with that lad this way. But one of my fellows can. Now the sun's risen, they can find him, and they can come ahead of him."

"I hope so," she said to it, then directed a warning

glare upon the rest. "But none of *you* can afford to wait to see! Spread out! Keep searching for his track! Keep after him!"

"You want us to split up, Mistress?" the weasely one said uneasily, looking around him at the shadows between the trees. Several others followed suit.

"You cowards," she said scornfully. "I tell you he's no danger. He's confused and he's unarmed. He's harmless."

"He's giving a good imitation of the opposite," the wolf-head muttered, rubbing a bruised shoulder.

"Quiet," she ordered. "And get moving!"

They grumbled but they went, splitting up into several groups and moving out in different directions.

"It'll be plain luck if they happen on anything," the pooka muttered. "Only my lads will have a chance."

"Someone must," she said darkly. "For I'll not answer to Fear Doirche alone. Now, on with you."

The animal carried her off after one of the parties. When they left the clearing, it was again deserted. Miluchradh did not know that the eyes of the very one she sought had watched her from not so very far away.

Finn had observed and marked the direction each of the parties took. Now he set off in a way that would remove him from the vicinity of all the hunters.

Only his hunting instincts seemed to be sustaining him, to be carrying him forward even though his memory was gone. His eyes scanned the way ahead warily as he moved forward. His body was always taut and ready. He was truly little more than a wild beast now.

He made no noise. His leather-shod feet cracked no stray twig, rustled no dry thatch. He slipped through the underbrush and under the hanging tree branches, touching nothing, indeed seeming like a wraith gliding so rapidly through the wood.

But as he moved, his eyes fixed intently on the scene ahead, another vision came into his mind. It overlaid the image of lights and shadowed forest with another much like it, hazy and dreamlike at first, but clarifying to a scene more real than what was before him.

Slipping stealthily through this imagined forest was a boy he somehow knew to be himself, clad in a shirt of leather, clutching a rude spear, stalking a tall stag who moved before him. And this vivid picture slid quickly into others that flickered by like objects on a stream of shimmering light: of himself as a child, playing in glens and woods; of him sitting with a solemn, sharp-faced old woman who spoke to him of the lore of the woods, or with a cheery, round-faced woman who told him tales of great palaces and kings.

The bewildering flow of images brought him to a halt, his body swaying from the disorienting effects. His eyes squeezed closed and he frowned as if in deep concentration. But the images were gone. He shook his head, opening his eyes. Only the real forest, the strange forest filled with his unknown enemies, lay about him now. And he was still alone.

He moved on through the forest again, traveling some distance. He saw no signs of danger, no signs of other beings at all save for a few hares, some small birds, and one great hawk which soared overhead and past, swooping down into the treetops far ahead.

He made his way farther, soon coming onto the edge of another, but much broader glade. He paused within the shelter of the brush, gazing out. It was empty except for a single, black-sided cow who sat chewing in a lazy, rhythmic way upon the lush grass. Still, it could be a dangerous place to cross, leaving him in the open for a great time. He might have skirted it, but his gaze fell upon something and fixed there.

Not far from the feeding cow, in a hollow nearly in the center of the space, a small pool shimmered.

As he stared at the water, a longing filled his eyes. His tongue licked thirstily across his parched lips. He had been all night on the run without a drink.

The desire clearly overcame his caution. He moved from his cover and crept out toward the pool. The cow lifted its head and stared at him. It looked a rather rotund animal, sitting primly upon its knees. Its face was quite placid and it seemed little concerned by him. After a brief glance it dropped its head back and went on with its browsing. When Finn moved past it to the pool, it paid him no mind.

Once at the water's edge, he cast a careful, searching look about at the surrounding woods. There was no sign of movement. There were no suspicious sounds. Seeming satisfied, he knelt down by the water, leaned forward and drank.

He drank deeply, lifting up to let the water trickle down his chin and throat onto his chest. He splashed more into his blackened face and over his scorched arms. He leaned down for another long drink and then sat up, expelling a great sigh of pleasure.

There was a low, short huff of sound, and he glanced around. The cow had now gotten to its feet, rather agilely for such a hefty beast, and was striding toward him. It seemed to be moving toward the pool to drink, and Finn looked away, only to glance back again in surprise as the huffing came again, this time from far too close.

This time he looked into the face of a beast that was most certainly moving purposely toward him, and the eyes that were fixed with an undoubtable malevolence upon him were not a cow's liquid brown ones but the slitted, glinting yellow of a serpent.

Finn threw himself backward as the creature charged upon him. It wheeled, snapping out at him with a mouthful of teeth whose sharp points were clearly meant for more violent work than chewing cud. He rolled sideways. The cow moved too, leaping agilely to stay above him, snapping down at him again.

He rolled back the opposite way. With a savage and most uncowlike roar, it reared up, looming over him, then sweeping out at him with feet not hooved, but fitted with the long talons of a giant hawk. Desperately he rolled forward, this time right under the beast as it dropped down again, its feet thudding heavily to the earth.

He went on, under its belly and out behind it. But it wheeled around and lifted to drop atop him as he rose. Its foreclaws caught him in both shoulders, the keen points digging into his flesh. It dug in with its hind feet, trying to drag him back.

He couldn't move forward. He couldn't turn. He struggled to pull loose, but the effort only ripped his pierced flesh more. The powerful legs of the creature pulled him back, back, while the huge mouth opened, prepared to snap its rending teeth into his neck when he was within reach and finish him like a cat finishing a hare.

He couldn't move away from it, so he moved in. He thrust suddenly back against the forelegs, then dropped down and heaved the beast over one shoulder. It was taken off guard and rolled forward, but held on, carrying him with it. Locked together, they rolled down and into the pool.

They thrashed their way out into the water. Finn managed to twist about and hold its head away with straining arms while the beast began to strike at him with its hind feet, raking his legs with its claws. In the middle of the pond, the waters were deep enough to swallow them. They sank down, still struggling, and disappeared beneath the surface.

Now the whole pool boiled, its surface churned to a white froth by the furious activity beneath. For a time longer than it seemed possible for any air-breathing being to survive, it continued unabated. But at last it began to fade, the pond settling finally to calm again.

For several heartbeats more there was no movement. Then, suddenly, a great form whooshed to the surface. Like a whale surfacing, the wet, round-bodied form of the black cowlike being bobbed there. But then it rolled, the yellow eyes staring blindly upward for a last moment before it sank again under the water. And as it vanished, another form shot up.

Finn surfaced, giving a great gasp for air. Then, weakly, he splashed to the pool's edge, drawing himself out with agonizing slowness, dragging himself onto the verge. He collapsed there, panting with exhaustion, streams of blood from the wounds across his shoulders flowing down to tint the water that streamed from his body.

"He escaped you?" Fear Doirche shouted, jumping to his feet. He swept back a frail, goat-headed woman who had been washing his feet, scattering a bevy of other hybrid servants hovering about as he strode out into the center of his cavern to confront Miluchradh.

She stood before him within the circle of tables. The

scores of other degenerate de Danaans who sat about them had been stilled by his rage, giving over their carousing to watch in silence, their predatory gazes fixed on her.

"He escaped you!" he repeated, this time in outrage and disbelief, striding up to her, shaking the fist that gripped his druid rod close in her face. "You promised me you would destroy him, and you failed!"

She drew herself up, eyeing him fearlessly, defiantly, and indignantly.

"I did not fail. My scheme worked perfectly. I lured him into the lake. I took his memory with the spell I put upon its waters. I even used my cloak's magic to disguise his scent and separate him from his friend! I did what no one, not even the most powerful of druids"—she paused and gave him a sneer of superiority—"has ever done: to strip Finn MacCumhal of his powers and his weapons. I've made him harmless."

He swept out the knobbed end of the staff, flicking it beneath the cloak she wore, throwing it back to reveal her nakedness.

"It's clear you did more with him than that," he shot back. "No wonder you couldn't manage to destroy him. It was as I feared. Your own desire interfered. That's what allowed him to escape."

She jerked the cloak back around her.

"You're not one to be speaking of such a thing!" she told him hotly. "It was your own foolish desires which have caused all this!"

He brought the rod up, swinging the tip to press against her throat, forcing her head back.

"Watch your words, woman," he said, grating out the words. "I've little patience left."

This threat cooled much of the heat of her audacity. She stepped back, her voice placating now.

"Forgive me, my High-Druid. I may have erred. But please remember that I did this only to help you."

He considered, then seemed somewhat appeased.

"Yes," he said, lowering the stick. "I suppose you did."

"And what I have done truly has been successful," she went on. "Finn is no danger to you now. He has no memory of you or of the girl. He has no identity. He can use none of his powers. His weapons are lost. There's little he can do now but wander aimlessly."

"Not good enough," he said sharply. "He is still dangerous, as his escape proved. And what if he were to find help, or somehow to have his memory returned? He's overcome Sidhe magic before." He shook his head. "No, I'll take no more chances with this one. While he's without his memory, without friends or weapons, he is vulnerable. Now is the time to finish him, and I mean to see to it myself!"

"Yourself?" she said.

"Yes, woman. Go to your cavern of glass. Use your powers. Seek him. Find him again. And when you do, tell me. I will go to him this time. I mean to see him before me when he dies. I want to make him crawl before me like a slug and then I will slowly squash the life from him!"

This brought chortles of sadistic glee from the gathering.

"Yes," he said, smiling about at them. This time I'll take my own revenge!"

CHAPTER◊16

Caoilte

THE DARK WARRIOR TRUDGED TOWARD THE SLOPE OF the fortress of Almhuin wearily, the weapons of Finn MacCumhal upon his back, the two hounds of the young captain flanking him.

"It's Caoilte!" a watchman atop the wall called down into the yard. "Caoilte is back!"

The Fian warrior named Lughaid heard this and rushed up below the watchman to call back.

"Caoilte? And is he alone?"

"He has Bran and Sceolan with him," the man replied, "but there is no Finn."

Others in the yard, hearing this news, began to drop their work and congregate about the gates, murmuring in wondering tones. By the time Caoilte MacRonan stepped through the gates, he found himself accosted by an excited throng.

"Caoilte, what's happened?" they asked. "Where is Finn?"

"I don't know! I don't know!" he answered irritably, pushing through them. Then he saw Lughaid moving through the crowd toward him. He seized the warrior's arm in relief. "Lughaid! It's good to see you. Listen, we must host the clans at once. I need your help. It's Finn . . ."

"What happened to Finn?" the warrior asked.

"I don't know!" Caoilte said again. "But he needs our help. We've got to host the clans!"

"Come into the hall," the other urged him. He took

Caoilte's arm and directed him through the crowd to the hall's main door.

"What's wrong with you?" Caoilte asked him. "We've got no time to waste. Get the Dord Fionn. We've got to host at once!"

The other seemed not to take note of Caoilte's plea. His expression was neutral, his manner reserved.

"Just come into the hall," he said again. "You'll understand. There's a court there now. Some chieftains arguing a division of wages."

"A court?" Caoilte said in surprise as they crossed the threshold into the vast room. "But who can be presiding over a—"

He stopped, staring ahead of him. A hundred warriors filled the hall. The druids and justices of the Fianna sat at the table upon the dais, resplendent in their gowns and torcs of office. But his gaze was fixed only on the figure who sat in the seat of the captain, a figure who now rose on seeing Caoilte and fixed upon the dark warrior the gaze of his single eye.

"Goll MacMorna!" Caoilte exclaimed in shock. His eyes swept around the room, noting the rotund figure of Goll's brother Conan and the green plaid cloaks of many warriors of the Clan na Morna. Then he strode out into the center of the room toward Goll, calling to him in an accusing tone: "And what is the chieftain of the Morna clan doing in the stronghold of the Baiscne, and sitting in the place of Finn MacCumhal?"

Goll lifted a hand in a gesture of restraint.

"I understand what it is you're thinking, Caoilte," he said in a careful, placating way, "but there is no treachery here. I've come only at the order of the High-King."

"You mention no treachery and the High-King in one breath?" Caoilte shot back. "Ha! I should have known he'd not miss such a chance to act against Finn, nor would you!"

"That is close to insult, MacRonan," Goll replied indignantly. "We've had a rivalry in the past, but that's long ended. I am as loyal to Finn as yourself. But when he . . . disappeared, he left the Fianna leaderless. My loyalty to it is greater than to him. I agreed to come here to see to things, but only until his return." He leaned forward, adding pointedly, "If he does return. And that's for you to tell us. Where is Finn? What's happened to him?"

"I don't know," Caoilte answered again, this time with a tone of weariness.

"What's he saying?" one of the chieftains called out in disbelief. "Hasn't he the very weapons of Finn strapped upon his own back now?"

"Is that the Storm Shield and the Mac an Luin you're carrying?" Goll asked.

"They are," the dark warrior admitted. He pulled them from his shoulders, setting them down upon a nearby table.

There were gasps of surprise and mutters of consternation from the assembly as they craned forward to look at the fabled weapons. Then one warrior more loudly voiced the thought that had to be going through everyone's minds: "Finn is dead! By all the gods of Eire—Finn must be dead!"

"No!" Caoilte shouted, whirling toward the man. "You can't say that!"

"Yet there's little else but death that would separate Finn MacCumhal from his weapons and his two hounds," Goll said reasonably. "How else could it be?"

"I . . . I found the weapons," Caoilte said. "Finn left the hounds and myself for a time and didn't return. When we went seeking him, we found these"—he hesitated, then went on reluctantly—"on the shore of a lake."

"Finn's drowned then!" someone cried.

"I don't believe that," Caoilte retorted. "Finn was like an otter in the water. And there's no power that could have drowned him."

"Even Finn isn't immortal," Goll pointed out. "And did you find something to make you believe Finn was still alive?"

"No. No, I didn't," Caoilte said unhappily. "We searched about the lake for signs of him, and found nothing." Then, more aggressively, he added, "But I know Finn is alive! I'd feel it if it was otherwise. So would the hounds!"

"You've a loyalty for your friend that I admire," Goll

said. "But my mind makes me see this more practically. If Finn were alive, why wouldn't he come back to you? If he had left that lake, why couldn't the noses of Bran and Sceolan, the finest hunting dogs in Ireland, find scent of him?"

"I don't know! I don't know!" Caoilte said in exasperation. "It could be some magic—some sudden scheme of his own—"

"And it could be something else," put in the white-haired druid called Cainnelscaith. "We all know Finn had become . . . ah . . . most strange over his loss. Had your year of searching given him any hope?"

"No," Caoilte was forced to reply truthfully. "He'd become more lost in his sorrow, if anything. More defeated."

"Then maybe he had given up," the druid suggested. "The bards know many and many a sad tale of lovers giving up their lives for ones they've lost. If Finn had decided he'd never find her again, maybe it was a blessing for him to swim out and let himself sink quietly beneath the waves of that—"

"That could never be true!" Caoilte shouted at him. "None could think he'd do that!"

"And why not?" spoke up the ruddy-faced hound master called Comhrag. "Finn had gone ravin' mad over that woman! He didn't care about anything else. Not the Fianna, not the clan, not the fighting or the hunt, not even you, Caoilte. And you know it well! You said many times yourself he'd given up everything else for her. Why not his life?"

"But he's still your chieftain," he said to Comhrag, then swung his eyes back to Goll. "And he's still the captain of all the Fians! We can't just think him dead! We've got to look for him! That's why I came back here. We must host, and host every warrior in Ireland if it comes to that. We must look for Finn!"

Goll's look grew doubtful at that. There were murmurings of protest from about the room.

"I don't know, Caoilte," Goll said. "There is no reason to believe Finn is alive. There is no greater loss to us, and we must mourn him, but to host the entire Fianna to seek him seems unnecessary. And even if he is somehow alive, it would seem that it must be his choice to return, as it was his to leave. If he does not, maybe he truly is mad. In either case, someone must assume the leadership."

"And that would be you!" Caoilte said bitterly. "Well, there'll be no mourning for Finn until his body is seen. And no man will take his place until there's no question that he'll never return."

"Please understand, Caoilte," Goll said in a reasoning way. "I've no more liking for this than yourself, but there's nothing else to be done. It's the good of Ireland we must all be thinking of. The truth of it is that Finn is gone, dead or not. The logic is that someone must take command. Still, for your sake, I'll not take his place until he's been wanting to us for the length of three years, and till no person in Ireland has any hope of seeing him again. After that, I'll have no choice but to let the High-King put the captaincy upon me."

"That's what you say, is it?" Caoilte returned angrily. "That's your fairness?" He looked about at the other warriors. "Do all of you support this? Would you all abandon Finn and see Goll as your captain?"

Most of them stood silent, averting their gazes and shifting uneasily. But one chieftain spoke up in a defensive way.

"There's little enough we have to say about it. We need a leader, that's right enough. We're all bound to accept the Brehon Laws and the oaths we made in joining the Fians. They say it's right that Goll should take the leadership."

"And he is a fair man," said another chieftain. "We've had hearings in his court and justice too—something Finn had given over long ago."

To this there were mutterings of agreement.

"So that's the way of it," Caoilte said. His eyes moved more slowly over the crowd, picking out the Baiscne. "And what of Finn's clansmen? Will they help me?" He looked around to Lughaid, who had followed him in and stood close by. "Lughaid, what about you?"

"It was Finn's choice to leave us," the man said uncomfortably. "He said then he'd have no more to do with us. Now . . . well, there doesn't seem much to do."

"He left you?" Caoilte raged, his pent-up frustration giving way. He strode to Lughaid, seizing him by the tunic, dragging him close. "After the risks he's taken for you, for all Ireland? After his restoring the clan, making the Fianna a great force, defeating the king of the great world when his army would have destroyed you? After that, you can abandon him? Traitor. Treacherous, treacherous wolf—"

Comhrag rushed in, grabbing Caoilte about the waist, dragging him off Lughaid and throwing him back. Caoilte grabbed his sword hilts. The two hounds crouched, snarling.

"We want no fight with you," Comhrag said. "But you've no right to call us traitors. Finn went mad over a woman. We all know that. It was he who abandoned us. Now he's likely dead or gone for good, and that's an end to it. If your own friendship for him has blinded you to the truth—well then, you've become as mad as he was."

"Mad am I, you..." Caoilte stepped forward, his sword starting to come out of its sheath. Other warriors moved to draw.

"Hold on!" Goll shouted warningly.

All eyes went to him.

"Caoilte, if you draw your blade here, I'll not be responsible. You are welcome, but only if you've come in peace and can accept our will."

"I'll not do that," he retorted, shoving back the sword. "Maybe I am as mad as Finn now, but I'll not give up. He is my friend, no matter what he's become."

He picked up Finn's weapons and slung them again on his back. He looked at the two hounds.

"Well, lads, are you with me, or are you thinking as the rest of them now?"

They moved at once to him, tails wagging eagerly.

"I thought so," he said. He turned and started toward the door, the hounds trotting at either hand.

No one interfered. All watched in silence, some defiantly, some sullenly, some with the flush of shame. As he neared the door, Goll called out after him.

"Wait. What will you do?"

Caoilte paused on the threshold, looking back to him with the light of determination flaring in his dark eyes.

"That I don't know," he threw back. "But my friend's out there. And, somehow, I'm going to find him."

"I've found him," Miluchradh said as the Dark Druid came into the sphere of glass.

He stepped across the room, his eyes already fixed upon the screen.

"Where?" he said, staring, eyes narrowed. "It's so dark . . ."

The sphere's curved walls did seem almost black. But the glow from a nearly full moon and the stars of a clear night sky faintly illuminated the scene, revealing that they appeared to hang above a countryside of rolling meadows spotted with the darker clumps of woods.

"There," she said, dropping them closer and closer.

A dim figure had just come into view, moving out from the cover of a stand of trees.

"Are you certain that this is Finn?" the druid said skeptically, peering down. "He looks like some creature of the woods."

"That is Finn," she said with conviction. "I've been watching him for some time to be certain."

"So, Finn," he said, gloating, "you are reduced to this. What a sorry sight our captain has become. I'm almost reluctant to put you out of such exquisite misery."

"Must you do so?" she asked. "Are you certain that to leave him so, a poor wreck, wandering the woods, would not be a more fit punishment?"

"Perhaps. Perhaps it would," he agreed. "But as long as he lives, there is a chance he will recover, and Sabd will have some hope to cling to. No. This time I mean to show his ragged corpse to her. I'll make preparation with the pookas to leave at once. You make certain of where he is and which way he's moving. I don't want him becoming lost again."

He turned and strode toward the tunnel. She waved a hand and lifted the sphere higher, revealing the moonlit landscape for some distance around.

"Wait!" she said suddenly, staring intently into the distance. "What is that?"

He stopped and looked back, then wheeled about and returned to her, eyes fixed on the same spot.

Below the dark, tree-fringed line of the horizon was a large patch that seemed nearly circular and glowed more brightly than the rest of the open countryside.

"I'm not certain," he said. "Where did you say we were?"

"I've not figured it exactly yet," she said. "But near to Slieve nam Ban."

"Well, whatever it is, that Finn is making directly for it. Go closer!"

She gestured the sphere forward and it swooped toward the horizon. The patch grew larger, its shape more definitely circular.

"Slieve nam Ban," she said musingly, examining the spot. Then, with a look of dawning realization, she turned to him. "But I do know of that place! Isn't it—"

Ahead, some most peculiar objects had become visible within the circle's boundaries.

"Oh, no!" the druid said, staring with dismay. "Not there!"

The figure staggered between two trees, stumbled badly and fell, rolling into a beam of moonlight slanting down through the branches.

The pale light revealed a figure that seemed more some awful specter than a living man. Finn's hair was matted and dark, his clothing tattered, his body streaked with the blood from his shoulder wounds. He was wretchedly lean now, and the pale flesh of his sunken cheeks glowed brightly as if with fever.

With an effort he forced himself to his feet and moved on into another area of thick woods. Here, out of the glow of the bright moon, it was extremely dark, the blackness only accentuated by the occasional silver shafts of light shooting down through gaps in the treetops. There were shrill sounds of nightbirds and the distant cry of a wolf victorious in the hunt.

The eerie nature of the woods raised new images, a complex of terrible visions, in the worn and fevered brain of Finn. He saw scenes of savage battles, of terrible slaughters, of piles of grinning heads. All kinds of horrors—toothless hags, fire-spitting wraiths, snarling wolves, reptilian monsters, giant birds, men in gleaming armor—seemed to be rushing upon him at once, crowding in to engulf him, to rend and to devour him. So vivid did these hallucinations become that he glanced about him with alarm, as if these things were really rushing at him from the trees.

"No! No!" he cried in panic, waving his hands about him wildly to fend them off, running away through the woods at a reckless pace.

Heedless of direction, moving blindly in the darkness, he stumbled along some way, suddenly coming out of the trees onto the edge of a precipice. Unable to stop himself, he fell forward, rolling and tumbling down a slope, landing abruptly, heavily, in a crumpled heap at the bottom.

With a low moan for the new, additional pain, he managed to pull himself up to a sitting position and look around him. The shock of the fall had driven the nightmare images away. But the reality that his eyes now fell upon he stared at with almost as great a wonder.

Slowly, still staring, he got to his feet and walked forward. His fatigue seemed momentarily forgotten in his fascination. His look was puzzled as he gazed about. Was this real, or only another hallucination?

It was certainly a most bizarre and yet beautiful sight. The round white moon hung in a sky so clear that the stars were glinting pinpoints, like jewels set in a shield of smooth black iron. The light of stars and moon cast a hard, even blue-white light that illuminated the scene with a startling clarity. It revealed a broad field stretching away in a wide curve to either side. The light shone against its lush covering of grass, making the level surface glow sapphire. And it gleamed whitely against the scores of peculiar objects dotting the open ground.

Finn moved out onto the plain, examining the objects with great curiosity. They seemed to be of two distinct types.

One was a simple structure formed of two massive stones, almost as tall as himself, roofed over with a third, flatter stone. This piece was so large that it seemed no number of men could possibly lift it atop the other two, even though the things were clearly not natural formations. He stopped to examine one of these structures closely, peering beneath the stone roof at a hollow in the earth which it sheltered.

The objects of the second type were stone monoliths, mostly much taller than himself and all standing upright, thrusting toward the night sky. They were rectangular, some crudely hewn, some skillfully cut into obelisks with sharply mitered corners. He paused to examine one of these more closely as well. It had rows of deep groves, like ladder rungs, incised neatly into the stone of the corners. They showed as sharp black lines against the moonlit stone.

There was no order to the placement of these enormous pieces. Some were widely scattered across the open ground, separate and aloof. Some were grouped like sleeping herds of strange, massive beasts. Under the clear, hard light, the effect of the whole collection was both stark and mysterious.

Finn made his way farther out onto the plain, winding amongst the looming stones, a tiny, lonely figure there. He looked about him with an expression of reverential awe, as if he could sense some sacred nature to the place. But then his gaze fell upon something else.

Near the center of the circular plain of stones there rose a hill. It was wide and low and smoothly rounded, with a flattened crest. And atop this crest, there glowed squares of golden light.

They looked quite warm and pleasing in contrast to the chill light of the field. He drew closer, and it became clear that a single structure filled the whole hilltop. It was an enormous liss whose curved walls were pierced by many windows and an open door from which the light poured out like liquid gold. And from the smoke hole in its high-peaked roof, a plume of smoke, lit to silver by the moon, rose up into the night.

He hesitated, staring up toward it with a look of misgiving. He recalled a similar image of the liss of Miluchradh as he had first seen it. But from this house the aroma of cooking food came to him, and the silvery notes of a harp's strings drifted on the quiet air. These called up another, cheering image of a bright hall filled with feasting, laughing comrades, and a cunning little harper plucking out a lively tune. A light of hope appeared in the worn face of Finn, and he moved on toward the liss again.

As he plodded on, it became clear that the house was much larger and much farther away than it had first seemed. It grew in size very slowly as he approached it, and the hill gradually swelled upward. Still, he would soon reach it if he could just keep on.

And now, with the harp's tune, he could hear other sounds of human warmth and pleasantness—the occasional sound of a laugh, and the fair, high sound of a woman's voice lifted in song.

Like a starved wolf drawn by the scent of a cooking fire, the lean and wasted young man crept closer, closer. His face was now shining with his eagerness. Soon he would reach it. Soon!

Then, suddenly, he staggered as if he had been struck a blow. It spun him around and, dizzied, he almost fell. He caught himself, gazing about him warily. There was no sign of anyone or anything. But he did get a different and greater shock. For now, instead of the mound being just before him, it was far away, as if it somehow had shifted to another place!

He shook his head as if not believing this part of his general bewilderment or his fevered hallucinations. Then he started toward the mound again. Once more it grew closer . . . closer . . . closer. Without incident he approached the base of the slope.

Again there came the dizzying rush, the image before him blurring as if he had been violently spun away. And again he was now looking off across empty space, only to turn and find the hill far away in another direction.

His strength was clearly ebbing quickly now. He was stooping with fatigue, sagging with despair as this last hope grew so unattainable it could no longer sustain him. Still, with no other chance of salvation left to him, he could only stumb= house once more.

Step by painful step he dragged closer. As before, he heard the voices, smelled the food. He reached the mound's base. He had only to take one more step to be upon the slope.

He was wrenched about and tossed away with an even greater force, to find himself once again far from the house.

This time the disorienting effects knocked him down. And this time, his energy nearly gone, he could not rise. Still he crawled forward, face lifted to the light that was his only hope, tears of desperation and frustration streaking his dirty face. It took a great while for him to crawl up near the mound's base again, stopping just short of the place he had reached before. By dint of an enormous effort—more of will than strength—he pulled himself up and propped himself against a tall spire of stone.

He raised a hand imploringly toward the house and opened his mouth to call out. His voice caught, coming out a faint, hoarse croaking from his dry throat.

He coughed, and then he tried again. This time there issued a harsh, strangled animal cry of pain. And with this effort came the end of his strength. He sagged forward, crashing heavily to the ground.

CHAPTER◇17

The
Tail
of
Fire

THE MUSIC STOPPED.

After a moment, two figures appeared in the doorway, casting long shadows out into the wedge of light. They paused there a moment, then they detached themselves and moved down the slope.

The soft moonlight shone on the two, a man and woman: he tall and elegant in form, graceful in movement; she smaller and rounder of shape, moving with a great vitality.

They reached the bottom of the hill and moved outward onto the plain slowly, looking about them.

"You see, sister?" the man said after a time, his tone superior and scoffing. "I said there was nothing. Let's go back inside." He looked up, scanning the night sky. "The time is close."

"I know I heard something, Donn," she answered stubbornly. "It would be beyond the barrier anyway."

He stopped, standing in an impatient pose, but she went on, looking about in the dark.

"Moirrin!" he called testily. "Enough!"

"Quiet, brother," she told him. "I—" She stopped, her gaze falling upon the dark lump of Finn. "Oh, look! There's something!"

"Careful now!" he said. "You don't know what kind of thing it might be!"

She ignored him, rushing to the unconscious Finn. Her brother followed her, reluctantly.

"It's a man," she said. "I told you I heard a cry."

She knelt by him, gently rolling him over.

"A very scruffy one," her brother said austerely, looking down at Finn with open distaste.

"He is badly worn, and hurt," she told him in a severe tone. She lifted Finn's head gently to cradle it. "He is very thin, and wounded, too."

"Some kind of outcast or brigand no doubt," Donn sniffed. "We'll not have anything to do with the likes of that. I wouldn't even be touching it if I were you!"

"How can you be so cruel?" she asked him angrily. "You can't just leave him here!"

"Why not? It's only one of Them. Not worth our notice in any case."

"He is a living being," she said. She felt his face. "And he is very hot with fever. He may be dying. We must help him."

"You are a fool, sister," he told her, unmoved.

She looked up to him, her voice imploring.

"Please, brother. At least let us bring him in and give him warmth and rest. Just this one night!"

He looked at her for a long moment, his body stiff, his manner unbending. Then he sighed and shrugged.

"Very well," he said reluctantly. "But you'll be the end of us one day with your taking in of every stray creature you find."

"Thank you, brother," she said with triumphant glee, then turned her concerned gaze back to Finn's worn face.

Finn's head was lifted enough to put the cup to his mouth. The cup tilted slowly to pour its liquid against his lips. Most ran out the sides, but a small amount made its way through into his mouth.

He coughed a little, then shifted and gave a soft groan. Some of the hot color of his face receded, and some of the pain relaxed from his tensed features. His eyes fluttered and then slowly opened. He looked up, his gaze focusing. Then a look of surprise filled his expression.

He was lying upon a pallet, propped up against a

cushion. The first thing he could see was a young woman of pert and pleasant features and copper hair who leaned over him, one arm about his head. On seeing him awake she smiled in a warm, most assuring way.

"It's all right," she said soothingly. "You're safe here. Drink more of this."

She held the cup to his lips again, but he pulled back, suddenly alarmed.

"What's wrong?" she asked.

"I . . . I remember another woman," he gasped out in a weak voice. "She gave me drink. She . . . meant to kill me."

"Did she?" the girl said, her eyes widening. "Well, if you don't drink this, you may well die. Please, trust me."

He looked at the fresh, open face, and then he complied, letting her pour more into his mouth. This time he swallowed a deeper draught. It seemed visibly to strengthen him. His fevered look vanished. The pinched look of pain eased. Even some of the gaunt look of his face seemed to fill out, as if the liquid were restoring him.

"That drink is marvelous!" he said with a stronger voice. "I feel much better!"

He sat up, looking around him with more lively curiosity.

He was in a small chamber, wattle-walled and thatch-roofed, done neatly and simply with rush mats upon its floor and bright tapestries hung about for color. Behind the girl stood a tall, spare, austere young man in warrior's dress, adorned richly in white silk tunic and light green cloak. His features were long and lean and quite sharply cut, with straight nose and pointed chin. His rather close-set eyes stared down at Finn with an icy blue aloofness.

"What is this place?" Finn asked. "Who are you?"

"We'll answer all your questions later," she assured him gently. "First, are you feeling better?"

He considered, then nodded.

"I do!" he said in an astonished way. "I feel almost well now. What was that you gave me?"

"It's a potion of our own," she said. "It's meant to keep us healthy. Then, do you feel well enough to come and sit at our table and feast with us?"

"Oh, Moirrin," her brother said in an exasperated tone, "you're not bringing him to dine?"

"I am," she said, giving him a nasty look. "He looks as if he'd not had a meal in days."

"That I have not," Finn said, adding more vaguely, "At least I think that's so. My ... my thoughts have been a muddle recently."

"Well then, you just come with us," she said. "We'll see you made well. Eat and warm yourself by our fire."

She helped him up, and he arose with a nearly normal agility, stretching his limbs and smiling with delight. He lifted a hand to touch the wounds and declared in astonishment, "Why, they seem nearly healed!"

"I think you might give him something to cover him at least," the brother said, looking Finn over distastefully. "The man's nearly naked, and quite unpresentable."

This was no understatement. The few shreds of Finn's poor tunic covered little of his bruised and filthy body.

She quickly took up a thick cloak of fine blue wool knobbed with white tufts and gave it to Finn.

"Here," she said, sticking her tongue out at her disapproving brother. "You can wear my own cloak."

She slipped it around Finn's shoulders, and he smiled gratefully. Then she led him out through a narrow doorway into a larger room beyond.

This was a great hall, structured in the traditional round style of Finn's own forgotten Almhuin. Around its fire in a circle were ranged long tables, enough to hold many scores of diners. But those tables were now almost empty.

On one side of the room there sat some two dozen men, all clad in warrior garb much like Donn's, all with similar long, noble features and most lordly bearing. Across the room from them sat six young women, also with similar pale hair and handsome, if a bit less severe, features. The one exception was the red-haired and vivacious Moirrin, who seemed the only warmth countering the chilly atmosphere the others exuded.

As she led Finn across the room, the gazes of these others—all equally austere, all with one brow equally lifted—followed him. And as Donn came into the room behind his sister, he announced in a scandalized tone, "The . . . ah . . . person is going to dine with us."

This drew some expressions of dismay, which Moirrin ignored, showing Finn a place.

"You sit right here," she said, putting him at a table midway between the two groups. She moved quickly around the room, snatching platters of food from the others, returning their nasty looks with like ones, and running back to slide her prizes under Finn's nose. "Eat all you like. We have plenty. And I'll give you a tune."

She smiled winningly and trotted out to the center of the floor, near to the fire, where there was a chair. She picked up a gold-fitted harp from beside it, sat down, and looked to him.

"Go on," she ordered, good-naturedly. "Eat!"

She began to play. Her tune was lively and bright and of an uplifting mood. Finn listened a moment, clearly enjoying it. Then his attention was drawn to the food. His famished condition overcame him, and he began to eat with a certain abandon, picking up joints of mutton or whole chickens to bite from, tearing off bread in great chunks, grabbing up handfuls of fresh cresses, slurping steaming broth from bowls and downing ale right from the tankard in loud gulps.

Once his initial pangs of hunger had apparently been eased, he once more became aware of his surroundings, looking around the tables. The others had not begun their own dining again, but were staring with dismay at his uninhibited and rather unseemly exhibition. Only the girl appeared not to care, playing cheerfully on.

Finn became uncomfortable under the staring eyes. He put down a handful of fruit and a gnawed chicken and coughed nervously, lifting his gaze up to see Donn, who still stood near, looking down over his shoulder. This young man's glare was an especially disapproving one.

"I . . . thank you for helping me," Finn said awkwardly. He looked down at the piled remnants of his meal and flushed. "I . . . I've been long without food."

"That is evident," the man said with a sniff. "But you may thank my rather headstrong young sister, Moirrin, for your salvation."

The girl smiled at Finn and gave a small bow in acknowledgment.

"I've been lost," Finn told him. "I've wandered far . . . I think. Could you tell me where I am, and who you are?"

"It's of no importance to you," the man said haughtily. "I don't think you'll be here long enough to strike up any friendships."

He looked about at the company with a smug little smile at the wittiness of this remark, and there were some titters of superior laughter in response. Finn seemed hurt, and Moirrin ceased her playing to respond sharply.

"Don't play games with the poor man, brother, you awful priggish toad! He's clearly had enough hardship without having to endure your smirking arrogance. Tell him, or I will!"

Her brother sighed in a way which clearly said that this was far from the first time he had been forced to accommodate the aggressive young woman.

"Very well, Moirrin." He indicated those at the tables with a sweep of the hand, not deigning to address Finn directly, but rather intoning to the empty air above his head. "Those twenty-eight men and these women had the one father and mother as myself. We are children of Midhir of the Yellow Hair, and our mother was Fionnchaem, the daughter of the king of Sid Monaid. We came to Slieve nam Ban to dwell many years ago over our conflict with Bobd Derg. My own name is Donn, son of Midhir."

At this point, one of the other tall warriors arose.

"My brother," he said gravely, "it is nearly time."

"All right, Aedh," Donn acknowledged. "See to it."

Aedh gestured to the men on either side, and they rose as well. All three moved to the outer walls of the room and began to close heavy wooden shutters across the score of large windows, throwing iron bolts to secure them. The final-sounding clangs punctuated all the talk that followed.

Finn watched them begin this process, but then turned a questioning gaze back to the man beside him.

"I'm sorry," he said, "but I'm afraid your explanation does little to help me. I know of no place called Slieve nam Ban, nor of yourselves, nor of this Bobd Derg."

The man's disinterest changed to surprise at this. He looked at Finn with eyebrows raised.

"Indeed, ruffian, you are a strange one not to have heard of the High-King of all the Sidhe. I think the time has come for you to tell us just who you are."

The three brothers moved on from window to window, slamming each one shut and shooting its bolt.

"That I can't tell you," Finn said apologetically. "I remember nothing of myself, my own lands or people, or even where I've been. My last days are a confusion, filled with such things that I can't tell what was real and what my dreaming." He gazed around him at the room. "Even this seems more a dream to me"—his eyes fell on the girl and he smiled at her—"but one of the more pleasant I've had."

"Well, it is certainly a sad creature that you are," the tall man said, but with no tone of pity to his words. "Though my sister may feel sorry for you, there's nothing we can do. We've enough troubles of our own. We've no need of ragged wanderers complicating things."

These rather ominous words, coupled with the boom of more windows being sealed, brought a look of alarm into Finn's face. He glanced around him quickly.

"What's happening?" he demanded.

A last window bolt clanged to just behind him, causing him to start and jerk around toward it.

Donn ignored him, gesturing to the three men.

"Now the door," he said.

They went to the large portal, a massively constructed thing of thick oak planks, and pushed it closed. Half a dozen huge latches fastened it.

"What is that for?" Finn asked, half rising, body tense, voice edged with anxiety.

"You'll know that soon enough, ruffian," Donn answered brusquely. "I'll only warn you to see to yourself quickly when it comes."

"Comes?" Finn echoed. "What—"

There was a tremendous, splintering crash as the heavy shutters of a window exploded inward, spewing the splintered wood across the room.

All those in the company dove for shelter beneath the

plank tables. Finn too ducked down as something large shot through the gaping hole and swept close overhead, trailing what seemed to be a plume of flame.

As it sailed past, he peered up over the table edge to see it. It was a bird much larger than an eagle, and of a far more exotic type. Its body was gold feathered. Its long, viciously curving beak and sharply taloned claws seemed made of polished black iron. Most terribly, its great flare of tail was made of fire, in curling plumes that flicked about it as it swooped, threatening to scorch all it touched.

"What is that thing?" he cried to Donn who crouched beside him.

"It is the bird of Lir of Sid Fionnachaidh!" Donn replied. "It's for a year now he's sent it against us every night to plague us. Nothing can keep it out."

"Kill it!" Finn suggested forcefully.

"We might if we could reach it, but it never lands or comes within our reach."

"Then knock it from the air!" Finn said.

Donn ducked beneath a sweep of the fiery tail, then cast an indignant eye at Finn.

"That is a fine suggestion from a useless vagabond like yourself. Each of my brothers and I are champions, yet none has had a hand true or swift enough to strike that cursed bird."

Finn looked out again as the bird swooped low over the tables, its tail knocking down the candelabras and scattering goblets. He saw Moirrin cowering beneath a table, sheltering some of her sisters with her arms and trying to look brave. Finn's own face filled with anguish for her. Then his gaze lifted to the wall above her, hung with weaponry, and his look grew fierce with sudden determination.

"I'll do it!" he announced boldly, jumping up.

"Wait, you fool!" Donn cried, and made a grab for him. But before his grip could close, Finn had leaped across the table in an easy, single move, and was running across the open floor.

The bird saw him, and, with an elated squawk, dove right for him. It swooped in with incredible speed, iron jaws parted to rend him. He moved straight ahead, seeming to ignore its attack until it was nearly on him. Then he dove forward, letting it sweep by, its jaws snapping shut on air with a clang like sword striking sword.

Finn hit the floor rolling, and went on over, coming up agilely onto his feet and running on. All the others in the room were watching now, most with amazement, Moirrin with delight.

The bird turned and dove in again. This time Finn leaped aside as it descended upon him, rolling beneath some of the unoccupied tables. The beak slammed shut on wood, ripping through the thick planks like an axe, but missing Finn, who rolled under and out the other side.

The bird flew past, and Finn was up again, running around the room outside the ring of tables. He reached the tables below the hanging weapons and leaped atop one.

The bird shot in again. Finn ducked its snapping beak. The tail whooshed around as the bird wheeled. Finn leaped above the licking flames as they slipped across the tabletop, leaving a smoking swath of scorched wood and sweeping away the food platters with a clatter.

Finn ran along the tabletop as the bird turned for another attack. He reached the weapons just as the iron beak snapped out. He leaped up, grabbed a round shield, and, swinging it down, slapped the beak away.

The surprised bird turned aside, but took a parting swing with its tail that Finn dropped flat to avoid. The flames swished close over his back. Then the bird banked tightly around to attack again and he came up, flinging the shield out sideways, its edge catching the bird across the breast.

It screamed with pain and rage, sharply pulling up, rising almost straight toward the peak of the high ceiling only to turn and soar down upon him at full speed, talons and beak poised to finish Finn this time.

He crouched and jumped, reaching up, just managing to seize a casting spear hanging above. As the bird closed in, he coolly set himself, drew back his arm, and cast.

So rapid was the move that the creature had no time to turn aside from it. Rising projectile and diving bird darted together. The spearhead rammed into the golden breast, the power behind it sending it through the burst from the creature's back in a shower of gold feathers and sparks.

Its wings folded back as the bird rolled into a ball, plummeting down without control, smashing into the table below Finn's feet. Finn jumped back as the bird took the table to the floor with it in a tangle of shattered wood and bones.

The magnificent and deadly tail of flame flickered, faded, and was extinguished in a final puff of smoke, leaving nothing but a spindly, bent and blackened stalk.

Finn walked around the ruins to inspect the creature. The others of the company, a bit more cautiously, came out from beneath the tables, looking in wonder from the bird to Finn.

Moirrin was openly exuberant, running to Finn and unabashedly giving him a great hug.

"You did it!" she said. "You risked yourself for us!"

Donn came over to Finn, the haughty look gone from him for the first time as he gave Finn a new, carefully appraising look.

"Well, ragged stranger, there is a bit more to you than it would appear."

"Yes," Finn said, looking at the dead bird with a certain amazement of his own. Now that it was over, he seemed to be bewildered by what had happened. "I'm not certain how or why I did that myself."

"But you did it," Moirrin told him enthusiastically. "And you've earned the right to stay as long as you wish." She looked at Donn. "Isn't that right, brother?"

"You have," he admitted, without reservations this time. He plucked a golden feather from the wreckage of the creature and held it up, contemplating it. "Yes, that you surely have."

CHAPTER◦18

The Drunken Harper

CAOILTE CAME INTO THE DOORWAY, STOPPING THERE TO peer in past a group of men coming out.

There was a raucous crowd in the enormous room. Men were grouped all about at the scores of long plank tables, and more were coming and going constantly through broad, open doorways in each wall of the six-sided structure.

They were a widely varied group in composition. Men in the simple garb of farmers and herdsmen shared table and tankard with grandly robed men of the learned classes. Noblemen and warriors and artisans swapped tales, argued hotly, or played games of chance together. Amidst them, around the spits and cauldrons of the central fire, aproned cooks labored constantly to prepare vast quantities of food. Dozens of bustling stewards shuttled platters of mutton and beef and pork, hot round loaves of bread, vats of steaming broth, and pitchers of drink to the seemingly insatiable company.

Caoilte scanned the throng, then turned to look down at the two hounds standing behind him.

"Wait here, lads," he said.

Bran and Sceolan settled into positions on either side of the door as the dark warrior went through. He moved into the room slowly, his gaze roving searchingly over the faces in the shifting mass. Some few glanced with passing curiosity at this lean, worn, and grim-faced warrior who carried a second set of weapons upon his back. But most were too involved in their own activities to even take note of him.

One did take note, however, and detached himself from a laughing group to move toward the dark warrior. He was a rotund, red-cheeked, and bulbous-nosed individual clad in a steward's leather apron. His manner was brisk and cheerful.

"Well, good warrior," he said, giving Caoilte a shrewd lookover, "you've traveled a hard way, I'd guess. Can we serve you?"

"You can, Bruighaid," Caoilte returned, "but not with food. It's a man I'm seeking. The Little Nut he's called. A wandering harper. I've heard he has been travelling about from bruidhean to bruidhean, playing for his keep. He's a harper of great skill."

"He used to be, you mean," the man said, his cheery look souring somewhat with distaste. "Now his fingers shake too much to pluck the strings."

"You know him?" Caoilte said, a note of rising hope entering his voice.

"Aye," the man said unhappily. "It's my own misfortune to be playing the host to him. You know, I'm always to have on hand enough ale to satisfy a hundred men. But that one—tiny as he is—is greatly endangering my supply."

"Where is he?" Caoilte asked.

"There," the bruighaid said, jerking a thumb over his shoulder to the room's far side.

Caoilte saw a table close to the wall there. A lone figure was slumped over it.

"I thank you, Bruighaid," Caoilte said, and started toward it.

"If you're meaning to take him away, or even make an end of him for all that, I wouldn't be interfering," the man called after him. "It sounds hard, I know, but even a house of hospitality sometimes has its limits."

Caoilte moved on through the tables, edging through the crowd, past most of the men, into the outer area where the tables were empty. As he drew nearer the table with the lone man, he saw that it was, indeed, Cnu

Deireoil who sat there. He looked unconscious, face down on the ale-soaked planks. But one of his small, long-fingered hands was still clamped tightly about a tankard.

Caoilte sat down across from him.

"Cnu Deireoil," he said. Then, more loudly, "Cnu Deireoil, wake up."

There was no response. He reached an arm across to grip the man's slender shoulder and shook him roughly.

"Rouse yourself, little man. It's Caoilte. Wake up!"

With some spluttering and moaning, the harper stirred. Slowly, with great effort and apparently greater agony, he lifted his tousle-haired head far enough to rest it on the point of chin and look up at Caoilte with bleary eyes.

"What do you mean, disturbing a peaceful man?" he said in slurred indignation. "I've done no harm to you. Go away!"

"It's me, Cnu Deireoil. Caoilte!"

The little man looked more closely, broad forehead wrinkled in his concentration.

"So it is!" he said, then let his head topple sideways to the planks again. "It's even more reason for you to go away," he said dismissingly. "I've nothing more to do with the likes of you."

"You have to help me," Caoilte said urgently. "It's Finn."

"Finn?" Cnu Deireoil echoed, and gave a hollow laugh. "And what would I have to do with Finn, after what I've done? After what he said to me?"

Looking exasperated, Caoilte reached across the table again, this time to grab the man's hair and jerk his head up.

The eyes, pain-filled but fully awake now, met his as he leaned his face close, speaking with great ferocity.

"You listen to me, you ale-soaked ruin! I've searched through half the bruidheans in Ireland to find you. Finn is in trouble. He may even be dead. I need help and—the gods save me!—you're the only one left to give it. You can't deny me! You owe this to him!"

The drunken gaze cleared somewhat at these words, as

if the little harper's mind had grasped at least some of their significance.

"Finn . . . dead?"

"It could be. And it could be we might save him!"

Tears filled the red-rimmed eyes and ran down a face that sagged with despair.

"Finn hates me!" he wailed. "I've failed him!"

"That doesn't matter now," Caoilte said with growing impatience. "Sober up, man! Think! Everyone else has abandoned Finn. You can't do it, too. You can't crawl into that tankard and drown in your self-sorrow while he's in jeopardy!"

Cnu Deireoil waggled his head loosely from side to side.

"No. No. No," he said. "You don't need me. What can I do? I failed. I'm useless!"

"You surely are this way," Caoilte agreed, the last of his patience gone.

He rose and seized the little man, hoisting the limp and blubbering form under one arm and striding across the room.

"Bruighaid!" he shouted to the rotund man in passing. "Have you a washing place?"

"To the south," the man called back.

"And is the water cold?" Caoilte asked, moving to a door.

"Cold as the first spring streams off the winter snows," the man assured him.

"Good!" Caoilte snorted with savage satisfaction.

He walked around the south end of the bruidhean and past a stable where travelers were coming or preparing to leave, attracting a few wondering stares from them. To the south he found a large pool lined with stones, fed by a spring spouting up through a narrow cleft. Several men were busy washing off the grime of traveling, but Caoilte pushed through them to the water's edge.

"Excuse me a moment, good fellows," he said to them and then, unceremoniously, lifted the Little Nut high and flung him out into the middle of the pond.

*　　*　　*

"It was a bit harsh, don't you think?" the little man said, shivering beneath the thick wrapping of wool blanket.

"It worked," Caoilte said tersely.

The bruighaid set down a brimming bowl of steaming broth beside him. Caoilte pushed it over toward the harper.

"Here. Drink more of this," he ordered.

There was already a stack of empty bowls beside Cnu Deireoil. He lifted the new, full one, looked at it, and wrinkled up his nose in distaste.

"Ah, terrible stuff! I'd not be surprised if it did unpleasant things to you, as I've heard that water does."

"My mother said it would heal any ill," Caoilte returned. "Now drink."

"I find it hard to believe you actually had a mother," the little man said nastily, but he obediently drank.

They were seated at the table within the bruidhean again, the bruighaid very happily supplying all the broth they needed. It did seem to be having a most miraculous effect, at least coupled with the dunking. Cnu Deireoil seemed quite sober now, if a bit worse for wear. He listened intently as Caoilte continued to describe the recent events concerning Finn.

"Anyway, when I realized there was nothing I could do alone, I came back to Almhuin for help. Much good that did me!"

"So you're saying that he just vanished from this lake, without leaving any trace?"

"That's it," Caoilte agreed. "Not a soul around, his weapons left behind, along with his cloak, and not a sign of Finn."

"And the hounds found nothing?"

"We went all about the shore. There was no scent of him, at least that they could find."

Cnu Deireoil shook his head.

"I don't know, lad," he said darkly. "It does look very bad."

"I know it does," Caoilte admitted. "But I can't believe it's true. I'm certain that, somehow, I'd feel it if he were really dead. Maybe I'm wrong, but I can't rest until I know, whatever the truth is."

The little man studied the warrior closely for a long moment. There was no missing the determination, the desperate need that showed in Caoilte's eyes. Finally, Cnu Deireoil nodded.

"All right," he said, "I'll not say I share your faith, but I'll help you. Though I'm not certain yet just what you mean to do."

"Go back to the lake and search again," Caoilte said. "I've thought about it for days now. If Finn is alive, he either chose to sneak away and leave us, or he was somehow taken away against his will. I think that only seeing Sabd herself could have brought him to go off so suddenly, and if he was taken, it would need an enemy with great powers to do it."

"Like a great druid, maybe," Cnu Deireoil said, meeting the other's eyes knowingly.

Caoilte nodded and both said the dreaded name together: "Fear Doirche."

"But not so hasty," said the Little Nut. "It might have been some power he encountered by chance. Something that's nothing to do with the Dark Druid. We've met many such things before."

"There's still magic in it somewhere, and likely the Sidhe," Caoilte replied. "There's where I most need your help. Maybe you can find something that I can't." He smiled, adding in a bantering way, "Anyway, you're a better companion than no one at all, and even a bit better than the hounds."

"Your great praise won't sway me," the harper rejoined, smiling with some of his old spirit. "And I still don't know how much use I may be, but I'll go with you. I'll not let Finn down again."

"Good," Caoilte said, for the first time with some elation. "Now we have a chance. But we'll have to start at once."

He started to get to his feet, but Cnu Deireoil put out a restraining hand.

"Hold on, my friend. You're not meaning to walk to this far place?"

"I've no horses. But it's no more than four days' brisk marching."

"For a man with legs long as a colt's it is," he corrected. "But for myself it will be a bit more. No, if we're in a hurry, I think we'll be needing to ride."

"Fair enough. Do you think you can acquire a pair of mounts from our good host?"

"I might have been given them freely once, for a bit of playing," the harper said ruefully. "But I think the bruighaid is a little soured on me now. Still, I might barter them."

"Barter? With what?"

The Little Nut held up the leather case that held his prized harp.

"No!" Caoilte said, aghast. "You can't meant to part with that?"

Cnu Deireoil hugged it lovingly.

"It's been a fine companion," he said in a nostalgic way, but then added stolidly, "But Finn's been a better one. If it can't serve me one way, it'll still serve in another. I've had no feel for the playing of it anyway, since I left Finn."

"All right, then," Caoilte said regretfully. "Do what you must, but do it quickly. If Finn is alive, it's likely he's in great trouble."

A band of extremely determined men moved across the circular plain, wending their way through the scattered monuments on the way to the mound of the sons of Midhir.

The men were fearsome as well as determined in look. Though they were only a handful in numbers, their size made them seem like more. All were burly of build, with heads of long, coarse hair combed out stiffly or done in dozens of tiny plaits. Most sported flamboyantly curled or braided mustaches as well. Their clothing was simple and serviceable—leather tunics and trousers and harness fitted with plain iron. They wore little adornment, but one item was most striking in its gruesomeness, for many had several bleached skulls dangling from their belts.

They lumbered along, following a man of wide shoulders and barrel chest who stalked on legs as hard and gnarled of muscle as the trunk of an oak tree. His rough-hewn face was ruddy-cheeked, his eyes a steel gray, his hair a gray-white mass that streamed out behind him.

At his either hand strode two men even larger than himself, like two upright oxen in size and build more than men, broad of chest but narrow of shoulders, with heads that seemed like tiny boulders perched high upon the peak. Instead of the spears, swords, and shields carried by the rest, this pair carried double-bladed axes and massive clubs.

It was early morning. A fine, clear sunlight was slanting across the plain from the east, glinting on the dew-covered grass, striking the scattered stones to white, throwing lone shadows that neatly striped the smooth ground. The day was clear and fresh and fragrant and silent save for the pleasing sounds of birds. Quite an idyllic scene it might have been, all told, without the intrusion of the savage company.

Up on the mound, the sons of Midhir were coming out of the doorway of their home, donning sword harness and cloaks as they came. Behind them the sisters came to the door and nearby windows to look out, their expressions apprehensive.

As the young men gathered, muttering together in subdued tones, Finn appeared in the doorway. Moirrin was there and he paused to give her a smile before stepping past and striding into the group.

"Who are they?" he asked, moving up beside Donn and looking out toward the approaching men.

Donn turned toward him in surprise.

"What are you doing here? You shouldn't have been awakened."

"I wasn't. The sounds of your weapons rattling woke me. But who are those warriors?"

"Those are the warriors of Sid Fionnachaidh," the other said, "and that white-haired one is Lir, their chieftain."

"Ah!" said Finn, looking toward the man with interest. "The one who sent the bird?"

"The same. We were expecting that he might be coming to see about it when it didn't return. I understand that he was quite fond of it."

"What will he be wanting?" Finn asked. "He looks very grim."

"The bird, I'd imagine. Or revenge, once he discovers what happened to it."

"But that was my doing," Finn said. "If he means to talk with someone, it should be me!"

"It was in my house," Donn returned sharply. "It was my family the bird harassed, and his quarrel is with us. I'll see to this. If you must stay here, then stay behind us."

Finn dropped back, looking most unsatisfied, and the brothers closed ranks before him. Below, the company of Lir reached the bottom of the slope and stopped, looking up toward them.

"Yes?" Donn asked them in a haughty tone chill with indignation. "And what is it that brings you ruffians to disturb us so early in the morning? I much dislike having to rise with the sun."

"You know bloody well what I want, you arrogant whelp!" the gray-haired chieftain bellowed back. "What's happened to my bird?"

"How like you," Donn replied with a supercilious smile, "to send your horrid bird to harass us nightly, and then have the gall to complain to us when it doesn't come home to roost."

"It's you who've brought this upon yourselves," Lir stormed. "You and your fool pride. Now, you tell me quick, man: what's happened to my bird?"

Still smiling, Donn signaled. Two of his brothers went into the house, returning quickly with a jumble of feathers, bones, hanging wings, and dangling neck. This they took to the edge of the hill and simply dumped there. It rolled down the slope, fetching up in a pile at the chieftain's feet.

He stared down at the pitiful wreckage of the once magnificent bird: iron jaws open and twisted askew, wings shattered, feathers splayed, once fiery tail a burned-out stub. His face, first frozen by shock, now filled with sorrow. His gaze rose toward the brothers, who were looking down at him with broad smiles, and he cried out to them in anguish.

"You bloody, bloody assassins! How could you kill such a fine creature as this?" He looked as if he were about to cry. "Do you know what kind of skills, what kind of magic it took to create?" His tear-filled eyes dropped back to the ruins. His voice took on the petulant note of a child deprived of its favorite pet. "It's a score of generations it's been in my family. And now . . . now look at it!"

"It's only what you deserve for your unfair bullying, Lir," Donn told him unrepentantly. "The thing's been plaguing us for a year, damaging our house, scorching myself and my family."

"And whose fault is that?" the other shouted in return. "It might have burned your house about you. It might have killed you all, but it wasn't meant to. It was meant only to make you see reason, to make you give up this madness you began yourself! There was no reason to destroy it."

He moved around the bird, stepping up onto the mound, his voice threatening now.

"Donn, you and your brothers are even greater fools than I thought. This you will surely rue. I want payment for my bird. I demand log-an-echt."

Finn had listened to all this, shifting impatiently, his expression growing more irritated as the blustering of the aggressive Lir went on. But with this last demand, his restraint left him. Before the brothers could move to stop him, he pushed through them to the front, calling down to Lir.

"You've no right to be asking an honor-price for that creature. It was attacking these people in a most unsporting way, and it was killed in a fair fight."

The chieftain, a bit surprised by the sudden appearance of this audacious interloper, turned his gaze to Finn. He looked up and down the lean, ragged, shaggy-bearded figure questioningly.

"And just who are you?" he asked. "You're not of this clan."

"That's of no matter," Finn said. "I am a friend."

"A friend, are you?" the chieftain said, giving a snort of derisive laughter. "A madman I'd call you for taking their side. This has nothing to do with you, so stand out of it!"

"I will not," Finn stolidly returned. "I've chosen to

help them, and I'll not stand by and watch any people being unfairly treated!"

"You'll not stand by? Why, you filthy vagabond, what difference does that make to me? I'll have satisfaction for my bird, if I have to take it!"

"If you mean to make a challenge, Lir, it's me you should be speaking to," Donn said quickly, moving out in front of Finn.

But Finn sidestepped him, moving ahead again, calling out in a loud, clear, and defiant voice: "If you want satisfaction, you'll have to seek it from me! I'm the one who killed your bird!"

The chieftain's gaze went to him with amazement now. "You?" he said. And then he smiled. "You?" he said again, growing more amused at the idea. "You ragged, scrawny wretch?" He began to laugh heartily at that, looking around at his men. "Look at him," he said to them. "He's no warrior. He's a clown! That's what he is!"

The other rough warriors began to laugh as well, but Finn grew flushed with anger. His muscles grew tense and he stepped down the slope toward them, his voice coming hot with his outrage.

"Now you've given insult to me, Lir! And now it's for me to demand the satisfaction."

"Satisfaction?" said Lir, laughing all the more at this. "You surely do have a great wit, clown. None of us will be demeaning ourselves by meeting the challenge of the likes of you. And you couldn't be truly mad enough to meet one of my champions." He indicated the two enormous warriors who flanked him.

"I'll fight them both," Finn boldly proclaimed.

This brought fresh gales of laughter from Lir's men, and a look of consternation to the face of Donn, who had been watching Finn's performance as if he were viewing a lunatic.

"Both of them!" Lir got out after finally managing to overcome the choking effects of his laughter a bit. "You should be entertaining in the court of the High-King!"

"I still killed your bird, Lir," Finn told him coldly. "If you mean to have any satisfaction here, you will first have to deal with me." He paused, then added with careful emphasis: "Or is it afraid to do it that you are?"

The laughter shut abruptly off. Silence fell upon the men of Lir. The chieftain's smile switched to a look of rage and he grew florid.

"All right then, you misbegotten cur," he shouted, "you want to fight my champions? Then you will do so. Arm yourself, if you can lift a weapon with those scrawny arms. Prepare yourself to die!"

CHAPTER◇19

The
Search
Begins

FINN MOVED BACK AND TURNED TO DONN.

"Would you let me use some of your weapons?" he asked with an air of casual confidence.

"Have you lost your mind?" the son of Midhir retorted in disbelief. "Why are you doing this?"

A puzzled look crossed Finn's face.

"I . . . I don't know! The words came into my mouth without my thinking of them. It seemed as if"—he paused to consider—"as if I needed to say them. And I know that I have to fight."

"But do you even know *how* to fight?" Donn asked, glancing up and down him. "No insult meant, but you really don't look much the warrior."

Finn shrugged and smiled.

"I surely hope so," he said, glancing meaningfully toward the pair of hulking champions below.

"How can you be so unconcerned?" Donn asked in wonder. He shook his head, then turned to his brothers. "Well, if this fool wishes to kill himself, we've no right to interfere," he said resignedly, waving toward Finn. "Give him some weapons."

There was a brief discussion amongst them on the attributes of weapons, and a decision made. Soon various brothers were passing Finn different pieces of their own armament.

From one came a sword and harness, which Finn

slipped on without hesitation, drawing the blade from its
sheath. It was a fine weapon, with a long, slender, gracefully tapered blade of well-honed iron. The hilt was beautifully designed and worked, inset with curving lines of
gold and red enameling, its pommel decorated with two
ravens.

As it settled into his palm and his fingers closed upon
the grip, an even grater change came upon Finn. A new
certainty, a new determination seemed to actually fill out
the gauntness of his look. His face glowed, as from some
released inner energy. His body straightened and he took
on a prouder stance. They were very subtle alterations,
but they somehow made him seem to grow much larger,
taking on a prepossessing air.

"Yes," he said with assurance, balancing the weapon
and examining it critically, "this is a good sword."

He swung it back and forth to test the feel. As he did,
a brief vision flashed before him: a flickering montage of
many battles, of giants in glinting armor, massed warriors,
fearsome beasts, blood, chaos, and through it a sword
flashing in his hand, winning over all opponents. Another
sword flashed there too, always beside his, and he had a
glimpse of a stalwart dark-haired man at his right hand.
Then the vision, like the others, flitted away as it had
come.

Someone was handing him a shield. He shook his head
like a man awakened and took it, looking it over. It was a
rectangle of bronze with rounded corners, its front decorated with scrollwork inset with jewels. But it was a
sturdily constructed piece for all its fancy look.

He sheathed the sword and slipped his arm through
the shield's straps, then moved it about.

"This feels good as well," he announced. "But there is
something else." He considered, looking around. "Yes," he
said at last. "I need a spear. A stout, true casting spear."

"Then you will use my own," Donn said, offering Finn
the one he held. "We have none better."

Finn took it and examined it carefully. It had a slender,
pliant but sturdy shaft of yew. Fitted to it by copper rivets
was a silver head, long, narrow, keenly pointed, and with

two wickedly curving barbs on either side. He lifted it to check its balance.

"Very good," he declared. He slipped the leather thong attached to the haft's end over his wrist. "Now I'm ready."

"Good fortune go with you," Donn said. He looked down at the two champions and shook his head dubiously, adding, "You are certainly going to need it."

"Well, it's surely a great boost to me to know you're so confident," Finn replied lightheartedly. He then gave a broad smile to the watching Moirrin, turned, and strode purposefully downhill toward the waiting company of Lir.

"Which will you face first, clown?" Lir called to him.

Finn eyed the two men, then he said easily, "Why make a choice? I'll fight both at once!"

A murmur of disbelief went through the sons of Midhir. Lir shook his head.

"You are an audacious one, I give you that," he said. "Die as you wish."

He ordered the rest of his warriors back. They moved off, leaving the two champions on the level ground just below the base of the mound, with a generous area about them.

Finn reached the bottom, moved out to stand before the men. He took up a relaxed stance, grounding the spear beside him to lean on, looking careless and quite unprepared. He regarded the two critically. They loomed before him thick and solid as two of the monumental stones on the plain. Their return gazes were wary, sullen, hostile. They stood waiting, weapons gripped tightly. When Finn made no further move, their eyes narrowed in suspicion.

"Well, come on," Finn prodded. "What are you waiting for?"

The two exchanged a quizzical look. They were clearly thrown off guard by the presumption of this lean and ragged man.

"Won't you be coming at us?" one asked.

"I won't," Finn answered. "You come at me."

"But you're not even ready," the other champion pointed out.

"Ready enough for the likes of you," Finn told him. "What's wrong? Have I made it too difficult for you?"

Both of the pair grinned nastily.

"No, clown," one said. "You've made it too easy!"

With that he lifted his weapons and charged upon Finn, the other quickly following. Finn stood before them, still apparently unconcerned. The chieftain and his men watched with smiles of anticipation at what a fine end this fool would have. The brothers watched with apprehension, expecting a like result. Only Moirrin watched with confidence.

The pair came in, rumbling down upon Finn like charging bulls. Their weapons swung up to strike. They made a final bound that would bring them both upon their victim at once.

But even as they landed upon the spot where he should have been, it was emptied.

Scooting with the speed and agility of a hare, Finn leaped away, landing far to the side of one of the pair.

As the immense brutes registered this, they wheeled toward him. Neither was slow, but in contrast to the lightning moves of Finn, they seemed to wallow ponderously, like seacows in a heavy swell.

Finn landed and spun to face them. His move had put one champion behind the other, and Finn at once dove for the closest, raising his spear arm for a hard cast.

For all its present leanness, the sinewy arm of Finn still had great strength in it. It shot the spear straight and with tremendous force. The man barely had time to move. He began to shift his weapons up to fend off the blow, but much too slowly. The spear pierced his throat at the hollow, tearing through, the point slamming out the base of his skull in a shower of blood.

Lir's champion staggered and fell backward, thudding into his fellow. Finn kept hold of the spear thong, and the weapon was jerked free. The second champion, jolted by the falling man, sprayed with his blood, shocked by the suddenness of his demise, was momentarily caught off guard, staring at the collapsing form.

This gave Finn all the time he needed to act again, and he did so with great speed.

The second champion had less chance than the first. His gaze lifted from his dead companion to the attacking Finn. He lifted club and axe in a desperate defensive move. He lifted them too high. This time the spear shot under them, Finn's skill and power sending it unerringly to its mark. It struck into the middle of his broad belly, sinking deep.

The man grunted and bent forward. The weapons fell from his hands. He looked down at the spear projecting from him, and then his gaze, filled with pained surprise, lifted to Finn.

The eyes rolled upward and the man collapsed sideways, toppling like a felled tree, crashing to the earth.

There was a long, stunned silence. Both groups of onlookers stared in openmouthed amazement at the almost effortless way Finn had dispatched the two warriors.

Then, led by an elated Moirrin, a cheer rose from those upon the hill. The austere sons of Midhir—save for Donn, who maintained his dignity—cast aside their reserve to unabashedly proclaim their glee.

Lir, however, showed somewhat less enthusiasm, glowering in red-faced rage at Finn as he pulled the spear from the second corpse and stepped toward the chieftain.

"Now," Finn said, "will you take back your insult and let these people alone?"

"This . . . is . . . not . . . over," the other hammered out. "You'll pay yet for the destruction of my bird, and more for the killing of my champions." He looked up to those above, shouting to them: "And you, Donn—you have tricked me somehow with this man. He's not of your clan. He may not even be of the Men of Dea! You give him to me in restitution, or I'll have my satisfaction from you all!"

"You'll not have him from us, Lir," Donn said disdainfully. "We've no fear of your threats. Take your dead and be away now."

"There'll be no more playing after this, then," Lir called back. "You've thrown away your last chance. This time I mean to finish you. It's between our two clans, this is, and when we meet again, all of my warriors will be with me."

"You'll need them all, you blowhard, and more!" Donn answered.

Scowling, so angered he seemed incapable of further reply, Lir signaled his men toward the bodies. Several collected each of the two dead champions, heaving the massive bodies up with some difficulty, and staggered off under their burden. As they did, Finn went back up the hill to the gathered sons. He held out the bloodied spear to Donn.

"You were right," he said. "It is a very good spear."

"It is yours now," Donn told him, a note of respect in his tone. "Your feat has won it for you. Whoever you are, you are a warrior, and if you truly mean to stay with us, you'll have good need of it very soon."

As he said this, he looked past Finn to the departing men. Finn turned to look as well.

"It surely does sound as if he's determined to return," he said. "How large is his clan?"

"Not so large," the other answered with a wry smile. "There can't be more than five fighting men to every one of us."

Caoilte and Cnu Deireoil urged their horses out of the trees, following the two hounds down onto the shore of the lake.

Here they dismounted and looked around, Caoilte pointing out where he had first come in his search for Finn. From there they walked the horses along the water's edge to the little peninsula of rocks.

"There is where I found the cape and these weapons." He indicated the Storm Shield and the Mac an Luin, which were slung upon his mount.

The harper gazed out searchingly upon the lake. It seemed very peaceful and idyllic now, its surface ruffled by a light, fragrant breeze, sparkling under a bright sun.

"Surely not the kind of place where you might expect our Finn to fall into trouble," he said. "But then, the most comely face might hide the most devious heart."

"What do you mean?" Caoilte asked him. "Do you think there might be something in the lake? Some creature maybe?"

Cnu shook his head.

"No. Not that. You know it would take more than that. I've seen him battle a Master Otter larger than the hall of Tara and swim about it easily. Like a salmon he is in the water."

"I know," Caoilte agreed. "It was that made me think he couldn't have been drowned. At least . . . not against his will."

"True enough. And if it was the Dark Druid, or some other magic behind it, as you think, then we'll be seeking something more cunning, more treacherous, and more dangerous as well."

"A spell of some kind, then?" Caoilte said.

"It might be. On the way here, I've been thinking through all I know of the Sidhe lore for notions. There are many possibilities, but I believe this would have to be something unusual. Finn has encountered and survived some of the most powerful Sidhe magic. He'd not be easily taken in."

"Then what?" Caoilte asked, a touch impatiently now. "Come on now, little man! What do you think?"

"All right, then. If it was Fear Doirche and not some chance meeting with a supernatural force, then it had to be worked out carefully. That means someone was watching you."

"Watching us?"

"Certainly. To set a trap for Finn here would mean they had to know that you were coming here, and when."

Caoilte glanced around him at the woods with keener scrutiny this time.

"Watching us," he said in an uncomfortable way.

"The Dark Druid could do that easily," the harper assured him.

"But he couldn't know that Finn would go into the lake," Caoilte pointed out. "I'm afraid our poor lad had given over the Fian custom of an evening's wash in his brooding state."

"Then there would have to have been some lure . . . some ruse to get him here, and get him in. Of course, for that they'd have to know he was separated from you. For with you and the hounds, the chance of a trick succeeding would be very small."

"They'd know well enough, if they were watching us," Caoilte told him. "Hadn't it become Finn's habit to go off alone to do his brooding each day at evening time?"

"Then it would be easier. The trap would be set, and all that had to be done was to wait for him."

"Then what?" asked Caoilte.

"Well, the simplest thing would be to poison the lake," Cnu Deireoil said bluntly.

"Then . . . Finn could be dead after all?" Caoilte said in alarm. "He could be here now? His body drifted in the mud of the bottom?"

"I never said that wasn't a possibility," Cnu reminded him. "I'm a harper, not a seer. But we must start with the belief that he's alive, and that he did come out of this lake. We'll just have to search the whole shore."

"And what should we be looking for?"

"I don't know," Cnu Deireoil admitted. "The hounds won't be much use. Knowing they were with you, the druid would've likely used some magic to hide Finn's trail from them. And after so many days, there may just not be any other signs left." He paused, adding pointedly, "If there ever were any."

"Well, we'll just look," Caoilte said stubbornly. "We'll eye every pebble about this lake if we must. But we will find something!"

After tethering the horses, they began to move slowly around the edge of the lake, scouring every rock and every patch of earth from the water to the edge of the woods. They stopped to examine carefully each footprint, fallen tree, game trail, or disturbed bit of earth with great care, always hoping, but always disappointed.

"There are animal tracks aplenty," Caoilte said, beginning to sound a bit more frustrated, "and nothing else!"

"But there are no signs of animal carcasses or dead fish about the shore," Cnu Deireoil said in an attempt at optimism. "That would mean that at least the water wasn't poisoned."

"Look there," Caoilte said, pointing toward the tree

line just ahead. "The hounds seem to be interested in something."

Just within the border of woods, Bran and Sceolan were sniffing most intently about a spot. The two men ran up to them eagerly. Caoilte knelt to look, Cnu Deireoil peering over his shoulder.

"There is a print here," the warrior said, pointing to a faint mark close to the base of a fir tree. Then he shrugged dismissingly. "Ah, but it's only an animal."

"But what kind of animal?" Cnu Deireoil said, dropping down to peer more closely. "Have you ever seen one like it before?"

Caoilte made a closer inspection as well.

"No, now that you say it," he replied with greater interest. "It's not a bear or wolf. Why, it's like nothing so much as—" He looked up at Cnu Deireoil in disbelief. "Could it be a cat?"

"A very large one," the harper confirmed.

"Aye, large!" Caoilte said. "The size of a stag, at least, or maybe even a horse! But how could that be?"

"It couldn't. Not for any natural creature of Ireland." The Little Nut clutched Caoilte's arm excitedly, his face lighting with elation. "But don't you see, lad? That's the miracle of it for us! See? There are no other prints. A rain's washed them away. But this dear, lovely one here was sheltered by a tree root, preserved for us to find. Oh, good Danu's surely smiled on us!"

"Will you please just tell me what you've gone mad about?" Caoilte demanded impatiently.

"I know the creature that made this mark," the Little Nut replied. "I've seen them. I've even hidden from them once, when I was wandering alone on the empty moors. They're called pookas."

"Pookas?" repeated Caoilte. "I remember hearing some old tales of such, when I was a boy. People had seen them, and yet no one seemed to know what they really were."

"That's because they're not really anything," the other explained. "They're master shape-shifters who can take on any living form at will, save one: that of a man. Long ago they were Sidhe folk, but cursed for some treachery never to wear the human form again. They became solitary creatures, and many have turned into twisted, evil beings, out to do whatever mischief they can to mortal and Sidhe folk alike."

"You say they can take any form?" said Caoilte.

"Yes. A horse, a raven, or a hound are favorites. Anything they can use to sneak up on unwary victims. Some of them even favor grotesque combinations. I'm not surprised to find the likes of such creatures in league with the black druid!"

"Does this mean they have Finn, then?" Caoilte asked.

"It looks so. And though it gives me no happiness to think he's in the hands of Fear Doirche, at least it might be he was taken away alive."

"How, do you think?" Caoilte asked.

"Well, I'd say the pooka carried Finn away from here. That would surely keep you or the hounds from coming upon his trail!"

They stood and looked from the lake up into the trees.

"But what kind of force could they use to bring Finn across the lake to here and then away?" Caoilte wondered. "I can't believe that he'd go willingly."

"There's no way of knowing that," said the harper, adding in a cautioning tone: "And remember, we can't really even know for certain that he *did* go alive."

"Still, we have a means of seeking him," Caoilte said more optimistically, "and a direction to take."

He looked to the hounds.

"Bran, Sceolan, it's up to you now. The trail won't be easy to follow after so long, but if any hunters in all Ireland can do it, you can. Try to lead us."

The dogs at once moved in with their great noses to snuffle thoroughly at the single print. They divided, moving out in opposite, widening circles around the spot. Then Bran let out a yelp of triumph and ran a way up into the woods, stopping there to look back to them, tail wagging furiously.

"He's found it," said Caoilte to the Little Nut. "Stay here. I'll fetch the horses."

"Be quick," the harper called after him as he sprinted away. "There's no telling what great jeopardy he's in!"

CHAPTER◦20

Conflict

AT THAT PRECISE MOMENT, HOWEVER, FINN WAS NOT exactly in great jeopardy. He was lying on the grassy slope of the soft mound, below the house. He was gazing up to the sky, to the clouds drifting lazily above, and looking quite at ease. Though still bearded, he was at least washed now, wearing a clean white tunic and a brown wool cloak.

Beside him was the girl called Moirrin. She lay on her side so that she might keep her gaze upon him as she spoke.

". . . and for those long centuries, the Men of Dea came three times in every year to give battle to us on the green here. It's from those battles that all these dolmens have come, marking the graves of the slain, and the great oghams, marking the dying places of great champions." She gestured out at the broad plain and its plentiful scattering of monuments.

"Oh, it's been terrible and bloody battles that they've had here," she sorrowfully went on. "And all the hundreds of good warriors slain, and our own people worn away. But it was great slaughter my family did, refusing to submit even after my father was killed all those years ago.

"Then, one day, Lir of Sid Fionnachaidh, the great bullying chieftain you've met, came to us. He told us that many de Danaan leaders—ones that Lir, of course, considered weak—had declared themselves weary of the long war. It no longer made sense to host the Sidhe and waste de Danaan lives over our single clan, now so much reduced.

"But Bobd Derg, he that is the great High-King over

all the de Danaan, had argued that the pride of the de Danaans was at stake. We couldn't be allowed to succeed in our rebellion.

"Finally he'd agreed to seek a way of bringing us to heel that would risk no more lives, at least of his own people. Lir and his brutal clan were chosen to carry out this new plan. They've long had the task of enforcing de Danaan law among the Sids, few having the strength or courage to dare to challenge them.

"Lir said that he had accepted this task eagerly. He bragged to us that within a year he'd force us to submit. It was from that day his bird began coming nightly to harass us, to wear us down and force us to realize we'd never win. And though my brothers are too proud ever to admit it, the plan was near to succeeding when you came."

"And what caused this conflict?" Finn asked her, rolling onto his side toward her.

"The others wanted us to join them in the Sids," she said. "After the great battle for Ireland."

"These names," he said in puzzlement, shaking his head. "Bobd Derg, and the Sids, and the Tuatha de Danaan. I've a feeling I should know them, that there is so much I should remember."

"I'm sorry," she said, giving him a pitying look and shifting closer to place a hand upon his. "I wish we could help you, but we've none of the magic that might do some healing for you."

He shrugged and smiled.

"I thank you for your wish to help," he told her earnestly, "but, you know, it's really not such a discomfort to me. It's very strange. I should be anxious about my memories and who I am. Yet, these past days, I've felt . . . well, I suppose I felt free, somehow. It's as if I've found a relief from some burden, and I've nothing to think of but myself." He met her eyes searchingly. "Do you understand?"

"I'm not certain that I do, to tell the truth," she said, adding boldly, "But if you're content with us, I'll not say it makes me unhappy."

"That I'm most glad to hear," he told her with a grin.

"Still, I am curious to know more of you and your people. Please, would you tell me?"

"All right," she said. "It's a very old story, of course, and I'm certain that by now every mortal bard of Ireland has used his skills to build it into a most marvelous yarn. But at the heart of all their embellishing lies a very simple tale."

Finn settled back with his head upon her lap.

"Tell on," he said. "I'm certain no bard could do it any better than yourself."

"You're a most forward young man, and a terrible liar," she said, but with obvious pleasure, and making no effort to move him. In fact, one of her hands began to lightly stroke his temple as she went on.

"You see, many hundreds of years ago, the Tuatha de Danaan ruled Ireland, living upon its surface. When the mortal races invaded, there was a great war between the two forces for mastery of the land. Finally, it was the de Danaans who gave up the fight. They might have left Ireland, returning to the Land of Promise in the western sea. Instead they chose to stay in the land they loved, withdrawing beneath its surface, into the hidden places, the underground palaces called the Sids. To the mortals they then became the Sidhe—the folk of the Sids.

"It was Manannán MacLir, the god of the sea who understands all enchantments, who helped them. He found them places in the most beautiful glens and hills where they would be safest from their enemies. He gave them the power to create the great caverns that would become their homes, and the magic to protect the Sids with hidden walls."

"Hidden walls?" Finn said in puzzlement.

"You know of them yourself," she told him. "If any mortal tries to come unbidden to our mound, the protecting barrier stops them by sending them another way. It's called Astray."

"Of course!" Finn exclaimed with dawning understanding. "It nearly drove me mad!"

"But," she went on, "the most important thing Manannan did for the de Danaans was to make the Feast of Age for them. What they drank at it was the ale of Goibnu the

Smith, which kept whoever tasted it from sickness, and from death, and from growing old. And what they ate was Manannan's own swine, which could be killed and eaten one day, but still be alive and fit for eating the next, and so on forever.

"After a time, the kings of the many Sids decided that it would be better to have one leader over them all, than to be scattered through the whole of Ireland. It was the Dagda, who was their great champion, that they wanted, but he'd have no part of it. Nor would his son Angus Og, who wished to wander the world adventuring. So it fell upon his eldest son, Bobd Derg, who agreed to take the kingship for his father's sake."

"Now tell me how it is that your own family lives in a home above the ground and is at war with the rest of your people," Finn requested.

"It's a simple enough thing. When the other de Danaan leaders chose to withdraw, my father refused. He said that the surface was his, and no power could force him to retreat into some dank hole beneath the earth."

"That sounds like Donn speaking," Finn told her with a grin.

She laughed at that.

"Yes, they're much of a kind: proud and stubborn, and a bit foolish, too. But with the whole of the Sidhe against him, Father brought his clan here to set up our own home. They've been trying to make us give it up ever since."

"And you will not."

"We love Ireland. I love the surface world, to feel the wind and rain, to see the sky, to hear thunder and the calls of birds . . ." She looked up, basking in the sun, breathing in the freshness of the day. "To feel all that is worth the great price we've had to pay."

She paused, her gaze becoming wistful.

"If we could only be truly free," she finally went on. "Free to live in this world as the mortals do, to travel it, to meet others." She turned and fixed a gaze on him. "I have no one here," she said. "In a way, I'm still a prisoner."

At these words he frowned suddenly and sat up. His gaze went far away.

"What's wrong?" she asked him anxiously. "I didn't say something to disturb you?"

"I . . . I'm not certain," he answered. He shook his head, saying in a befuddled way, "It's just that when you were speaking, I saw an image of someone else . . ."

"A woman?"

"Yes. Fair, very young, most beautiful. I know I've seen her before. It's like the other visions I've had. I wish I knew what they mean."

She turned away from him, her expression glum.

"I think I know what this one means," she said. "Likely you have a woman, maybe a wife, waiting somewhere. And why not, with such a man as you are?"

"You think that I could forget a wife?" he asked. Then he smiled. He lifted a hand to touch her chin, lightly turning her head to him. "I don't believe that at all. If she were even half so comely as yourself, I could never forget her."

This brought a return of her own smile.

"Well, it's certain that, wife or not, you were quite a one with the ladies, wherever you came from."

"Wherever I come from," he echoed musingly. He moved to sit close beside her, looking out across the countryside. "You know, I can't even say whether I'm of those mortals you spoke about or of our own Sidhe."

"I've no feeling at all about it, myself," she said. "With most, you can feel it, almost sense an aura of mortal or Sidhe. But with you, there's nothing."

"Are the two still great enemies?"

"Not so much as wary sharers of the land. Though some Sidhe still hold a great hatred of mortals, as I suppose you could expect. But that's neither your problem nor our own right now. For you, it's all as new as if you were a babe. Why, you know," she said, looking to him with an expression of sudden realization, "you haven't even a name. I can't go on calling you the Stranger, as my brother does."

"Well, a man mustn't name himself," he said. "I give that honor to you, fine lady."

She nodded, accepting the honor most soberly, then considered.

"I know," she said at last, "we'll call you Anluan—great warrior. That fits you right enough."

"It's far too grand for the scuffly likes of me," he protested modestly.

"Still, it's my choice, and I will use it," she said determinedly. She rose onto her knees and faced him, putting a hand on each shoulder. "And so," she intoned with great solemnity, "I hereby name you my Anluan!"

And at this, she leaned toward him, lips parted, eyes bright. And he moved toward her, an arm lifting to encircle her waist as he joined in the kiss.

Miluchradh and Fear Doirche gazed down upon this scene through the curved wall of the glass sphere. The Dark Druid's expression was sardonic while the Seer's gaze was a brooding one.

"So Finn has managed to win himself a place in the family of Midhir," Fear said.

"More than that, it would seem," Miluchradh put in irritably.

"Now, now, my dear," he told her with a sarcastic smile, "you mustn't be vexed because this girl has wiles greater than your own."

"That shamelessness wench," the druidess shot back, fixing a blazing look upon Moirrin. "If I could find some way to destroy them both—"

"You'll do nothing," he said sharply. "Finn has assured his own destruction by joining with these rebels." He lifted his gaze from the couple of the scene beyond. "In fact, I believe that his end is coming upon him now."

From their vantage point, suspended just above the mound, they could see the entire plain. A large company was now visible moving across it directly toward them.

The Dark Druid settled himself more comfortably into the cushions and fixed an avid gaze upon this force.

"This," he said gleefully, "will be most enjoyable to watch!"

Meantime, just below, Donn had appeared on the hillside above Finn and Moirrin. As their attentions were still fully absorbed elsewhere, he coughed discreetly. Instantly they pulled apart, looking up toward him and flushing in embarrassment.

"Sorry to be...ah...disturbing you," he said in a clearly disapproving way. "But they're just coming now."

The two rose hurriedly and went up the hill with him, circling the house to the doorway. From here they could see the force advancing across the plain: some sevenscore men, all large, all heavily armed, Lir stalking along at their head.

The sons of Midhir were mostly out of the house already, donning their gear. Someone handed Finn the spear and shield that had been donated to him earlier.

"We will go down and meet them on the plain," said Donn. "Are you still with us, Stranger?"

"I am," said Finn.

The band of the sons of Midhir went down the slope, striding proudly to the base. Here they pulled up, waiting for the approaching clan to reach them. A spear's throw away, Lir halted his warriors, glaring across at the tiny band facing him so defiantly.

"All right, Donn," he shouted to them, "this is your final chance. Will you surrender to the will of the de Danaans and give that clown to me?"

"That I will not, Lir," Donn said grandly.

"Then we will end things," the other replied. "I've looked forward to doing it this way. And the de Danaans will be pleased that we've finished this forever."

"Better men than yourself have said they would do that," Donn said. "Come ahead now, Lir, for we've had enough of your blustering talk."

The warriors of Lir's clan began to advance, rumbling ominously forward, like a moving herd, as if they would simply trample anything that might come in their way. The sons of Midhir, so few and so frail in contrast, steeled themselves, standing up boldly, weapons raised.

"Be ready, brothers," Donn ordered. "Choose out their strongest champions first." He looked to Finn. "And, you, nameless one, I hope your last victory was no accident."

"So do I!" Finn answered with a grin.

And then the full force of Lir's clan struck like a wave coming upon twigs stuck in the sand. The torrent of men crashed in and the battle joined. Once more the sharp clattering of arms sounded across the plain, echoing amongst the monuments scattered like bleached bones.

The skull rolled over, plopping down upright to stare out with blank eye sockets.

The butt of the spear pole poked down into the wreckage again, levering up a length of charred timber that fell back, sending up a cloud of the soft, gray ash and revealing a jumble of other bones.

Caoilte MacRonan pulled back his spear and crouched to examine the remains curiously.

"What was it?" he asked with some repulsion.

Cnu Deireoil knelt by him, picking up the skull to examine. It was partially crushed and badly charred, but still intact enough. It was vaguely human, but far from completely so, its brows low, its jaws long and set with tearing fangs.

"It's some half-creature," the harper said. "Maybe wolf and man? I'm not certain. But I do know that it's the hideous kind of monster the Dark Druid would create."

Caoilte rose and turned slowly to survey the rest of the remains. The blackened circle of them filled the little hollow in the woods, but there was very little left. The effect of a fire on a structure of wattle and thatch was quite thorough. A few burned remnants of furniture and beams, some metal objects half buried in the ash, and the circle of the hearthstones were nearly all that remained as evidence of what had been there.

"Well, I've found no other signs of the dead," Caoilte said, poking his spear haft into another mound of wreckage. "If Finn was brought here alive, at least he didn't perish in the fire."

"No, and the fire could be a sign that he wasn't in their power."

"You mean, maybe he set it himself?" Caoilte asked hopefully. "Maybe he escaped?"

"Let's not move too quickly," the harper cautioned. "All we really know for certain is that the pooka's track leads here. But it could very well be that he was carried on it here to be hidden away." He glanced around him evaluatingly. "Before the fire burned back all the brush, this place must have been nicely concealed here."

"But why hide him here?" Caoilte asked. "And what happened?"

"Keep searching," Cnu Deireoil advised.

Both men took up their looking again, probing the ashes, turning over wreckage, until the Little Nut paused to look at something more closely.

"This may give us some answers," he said. "Come look at this!"

Caoilte moved to him and watched as the harper lifted a round object from a pile of scorched cloth. He wiped a coating of ash from it and held it up. The piece was warped by the intense heat and badly discolored, but it could still be recognized as a finely wrought brooch, decorated with enameling in curling, intricate designs.

"A cloak pin," Caoilte said. "And a rich piece."

"A woman's cloak pin," Cnu Deireoil corrected with a knowing smile at his friend.

"A woman," Caoilte repeated, shaking his head. "I might have known that there'd be one in this. Not Sabd?"

"I don't think so," the other said, examining the piece critically. "Such a piece as this was done by Sidhe craftsmen, and for a Ban-Sidhe of some rank—a druidess perhaps. At a guess, some friend of our Fear Doirche."

"Used to lure Finn into a trap, maybe?" Caoilte put in. "That might be the one thing that could fool our fool."

"Unless he came here willingly," the harper said.

"How did he leave here—that's what I'd like to know," Caoilte replied.

The excited baying of the two hounds came then, almost as an answer to his question. The men looked up to see the pair bounding through the trees toward them.

"What is it, lads?" Caoilte asked, moving to meet them. "Have you found something?"

They capered madly, charging back and forth before him, then turning to trot back the way they'd come a short distance. Here they stopped, looking back, clearly waiting for him to follow, tails wagging wildly, tongues hanging out.

"Is it a trail?" he asked.

Both animals gave vigorous nods.

"What kind of trail?"

Both animals leaped and turned, barking ecstatically.

Caoilte looked to Chu Deireoil, who gave him a broad grin.

"It's Finn!" he translated.

CHAPTER ◦ 21

The
Physician

A SCORE OF DEAD MEN WERE SCATTERED ABOUT THE field of standing stones below the hill. Some stained the monuments to earlier dead with their own fresh blood. Warriors of the clan of the chieftain Lir were at the task of carting the bodies away. It made a dismal scene, all painted in the lurid red-gold of a setting sun that struck across the plain.

In a newly erected camp on the edge of the plain, the rest of Lir's fighting men had built cooking fires and were seeing about the cooking of an evening meal. They were hardly in good spirits. They cast glowering looks across to the house upon the mound or sat sullenly, staring into the flames. Lir himself stalked back and forth through them, his face glowing as red as the coals with his rage, his voice scorching the men with his hot rebuke.

At once side of the camp, just across the small brook that ran there, some two dozen more men lay on beds of boughs covered with leaves and cloaks. Most were badly wounded, some few moaning with the pain, but most stoically silent.

Around them a young, long-faced and curly haired man briskly moved, administering to them in a careful but efficient manner, applying a salve here, feeding some liquid there, tying closed a gaping cut or binding a deep puncture wound.

But for all the grim look of the camp of Lir, it could not match the situation in the house of the children of Midhir.

Here, on pallets about the periphery of the circular room, nearly all of the brothers lay. The bodies of most of them were so thickly covered with wounds that sticks propped up their clothes to keep them from touching the sore flesh. Even the few who could still move about had been badly wounded, and often several times.

Moirrin and her sisters tended to the men, but their efforts seemed little, and their faces were clouded with great concern.

Donn, having only a deep gash in one thigh and a cut across his chest, was one of the least hurt. He moved around the room now, checking on each of his brothers. Finn sat by the fire watching him. His single wound, a slash across one upper arm, was being bound by Moirrin.

With his round of the house finished, Donn moved across to Finn, shaking his head.

"I can't believe you," he said. "Ten men you must have fought today, and bested every one like a man wrestling a babe, and not getting more than that scratch for it. The sons of Midhir are the finest warriors of the Sidhe, yet we're nearly hacked to pieces now."

"How bad is it?" asked Finn.

Donn shook his head.

"All but five of my brothers are sorely hurt."

"It's a great credit to their fighting skills that none are dead," Finn said. "You should be proud."

"But some are near death. And when Lir's men come against us again tomorrow, not even that deadly arm of yours will keep them off."

"Here, brother," Moirrin said to him, finishing with Finn. "Sit down here and let me see to your wounds now."

"I've no time for that," he said disdainfully. "I am the leader. I must keep charge of—"

"Sit down, brother," she ordered sternly.

Finn grinned as Donn sighed in resignation and obediently dropped down beside him on the hearth.

"Maybe Lir won't be coming again," Finn suggested. "Maybe he's had enough. You hurt him badly today. He might decide the cost of his vengeance has become a bit too dear."

"Not likely," Donn said unhappily, "for he'll have every

wounded man, even the ones near death, back in the fight tomorrow, while our own warriors still lie groaning on their pallets."

"How can that be?" Finn asked.

"There's a magic held by some of the Sidhe," Moirrin put in as she cleaned the wound in her brother's leg. "Lir has with him a physician named Luibra, famed even amongst the most powerful of the de Danaans. My brother Aedh knew him years ago." She indicated a brother sitting across the room. "He's told me often that Luibra can heal a man cut nearly in half if he can serve him quickly enough."

"Cutting off a head might be a bit too much for him," Donn added dryly.

"But if that's true, it's no wonder Lir keeps up his bullying!" Finn said.

"That might be so," agreed Donn. Then he shrugged. "Still, it makes little difference to us. It was a good fight we made against them, Stranger, but we all knew it would come to this in the end."

"I'm sorry to have brought it on you," Finn said.

"You brought nothing that wouldn't have come in time," Donn assured him. "And it's better to die in the fighting than cowering beneath our tables."

"Wait now!" Moirrin said angrily. "You're not just giving up? We've not fought so long to let them destroy us!"

"And what can we do?" her brother asked her in exasperation.

"I may have an idea," Finn said thoughtfully. "With his great numbers against you and his healer, Lir hasn't played you fairly in this fight." He gave Donn a cunning smile. "I'd say that things must be made a bit more even."

"Even?" Donn repeated, eyeing him quizzically. "How?"

"I mean to get a physician to heal your brothers," Finn announced boldly.

"Of course!" Moirrin said with elation.

"Now I know you're mad!" Donn said. "It will be too dangerous!"

"It may," Finn agreed, "but it's still the only chance

you have. If I'm to do it, though, I'll need the help of some of you."

Donn stared at the warrior for a moment evaluatingly. Then he shrugged.

"All right, Stranger. We'll help you. After what I've seen, I believe you can do anything you wish!"

The sky was still dark, the plain shadowed. The sun was still far behind the horizon, but throwing a fan of pale gold high into the eastern sky, and the gradually growing light had begun to make the stones show as pale, ghostly shapes in the gloom.

It also made faintly visible three figures stealthily making their way across the plain.

They slipped noiselessly, swiftly, from stone to stone. They cautiously and widely skirted the camp of Lir, heavily guarded by a cordon of warriors standing alert and wary by their blazing watchfires.

Beyond the camp, the trio entered the surrounding woods and turned to make their way back toward the rear of the camp. They found a sheltered vantage point from which to observe it and stretched out under cover, lying motionless, silent, keeping a close watch on it.

As the sun lifted closer to its first breasting of the horizon, its light grew bright enough to reveal the identities of the three figures as Finn, Donn, and the brother called Aedh.

"How soon?" Finn whispered.

"Very soon, I'd think," Aedh replied. "Luibra has told me that he must go out every dawn to seek the fresh herbs he needs to make his healing potions."

"If he does so today, we'll have him," Finn promised.

Not long after, the sun broke above the forest, spilling its sun onto the plain like honey-mead filling up a bowl. The camp began to stir to life, and a lone figure moved out from it into the trees.

"There he is," Aedh said. "That's Luibra."

"Good," Finn said. "Now we'll follow. Come on."

He led the way and they crept through the brush, staying parallel with the healer's course. As they went, the two brothers watched Finn moving ahead with such ease and silence that they exchanged wondering glances at his skill.

Finn kept them a safe distance from the healer, letting him work his way ever deeper into the woods and ever farther from camp. He paused often, plucking a leaf from this tree, scraping moss from that one, kneeling to pull up plants or dig in the earth for roots. He put all into what seemed a large bag of many bright colors.

At last, when he was kneeling in a small glade and busily excavating something that was apparently buried deeply, Finn whispered to his companions.

"All right. He's far enough out now. You two keep a watch for Lir's men. I'll approach him alone so as not to make him bolt."

The brothers moved to positions to keep watch back toward Lir's camp. Finn moved toward the glade, making not a sound of passage, slipping from the trees behind the physician and stealing up close behind him.

From so close, it could be seen that the man was very young in looks, fresh faced and long featured, with a great shock of unruly red-brown hair that gave him a rather carefree look. His figure was long and gangly, and he crouched with his knees thrust up on either side. He was humming a bright little air as he worked, as if greatly enjoying his early-morning expedition. His long fingers worked carefully at pulling a large, knotted root from the earth.

Beside him lay what had seemed a colored bag. In fact it was a patchwork cloak whose many cloth squares were of rich and varied textures. It now lay spread open on the ground, the materials he had already gathered piled in its center.

"A fine morning to be out," Finn commented pleasantly.

The surprised man shot to his feet, his hand jerking the root out as he came upright. He whirled toward Finn so quickly he nearly lost his balance, his expression a bewildered one.

But he seemed to recover quickly as he took in the relaxed and smiling Finn. He gave a broad and friendly return grin.

"Oh, hello," he said affably. "You startled me a bit

coming on me like that." He held up the root that dangled from his hand. "I've been out collecting."

"So I see," Finn said.

"I love being out in the morning this way," he went on casually, moving to the cloth and crouching to lay his prize carefully on the pile. "And I love getting away from those others for a time."

"That's a very nice cloth," Finn commented. "It seems a shame to be using it to bundle those things with all the earth and sap clinging to them."

"This is the cloak of wool of the Seven Sheep of the Land of Promise," the other told him, still in an easy, conversational way. "Its magic will enhance the powers of everything I fetch in it, and make the healing effect quite marvelous. It has many fine qualities, and it can never wear itself out."

"So you're a physician, then?" Finn asked innocently.

"I am," said the young man. He began to lovingly wrap the cloak about the pile. "But you know that as well as I."

"And why do you say that?"

He paused to smile up at Finn.

"Because, my friend, you're not one of Lir's men, and no other warrior would be stalking me through the dawn woods as you've been. Besides, I glimpsed a bearded, silver-haired warrior upon the plain. That was you, wasn't it?"

"It was," Finn admitted.

"You did a great damage to Lir's men. And, of course, that's something I'd know better than most."

"You know who I am, and you're not afraid?" Finn said with surprise. "Why not?"

"If you meant me dead, I'd be so now," the other replied simply. "I have much greater worth to you alive."

"You're a clever man."

"I am that," the healer agreed with a grin, "but it took little cleverness to know what you want. I suppose I'm to go with you now?"

"You are," Finn said. "And I promise no harm will be done to you."

Luibra stood up, slinging the bundle over his shoulder.

"I'm certain it won't," he said pleasantly. "The shame of it is, you know, that . . . I can't!"

At that he suddenly shot off, away from Finn, heading across the glade back toward the camp. He was very sprightly for one who seemed so ungainly, bounding across the ground like a deer on his long legs. In an instant he was nearing the trees, ready to plunge into their cover, a triumphant smile on his face, when a figure leaped from nowhere into his path.

He stumbled to a halt with a flabbergasted look at Finn, who now stood before him, quite at ease as before, not even seeming winded.

"Huh . . . how . . . did you manage . . . that?" the physician asked, panting.

A brief vision flickered through Finn's mind, of himself a quite young boy desperately scrambling after rabbits that scattered in all directions as he tried to keep them within the confines of a field.

"I can't be certain," he answered, "but I think I've had a great deal of practice."

"Well, it was quite effective," the other replied admiringly, regaining his affability with his wind. "I'm counted one of the fastest runners amongst the de Danaans. Nothing's ever caught me before, and I've had some mighty fast—and strange—things chasing after me, I can tell you."

"I'm sure you have," Finn said, grinning. "But you can't escape now. You know that."

"I know," Luibra cheerfully agreed. "As it appears I've no choice. I'll be pleased to accompany you, if that's what you wish."

"I do," Finn said, and pointed toward the woods. "That way. And you'll understand if I stay close behind you?"

"Oh, of course, of course!" the healer assured him, heading off in the direction Finn had indicated. "But you'll have no more trouble at all with me. To tell the truth of it, I'm not much heartbroken at being—stolen shall we say?—from that Lir. He's both a bully and a great boor. Helping him to carry on his outrages hasn't been at all to my liking."

"You're happy to leave him?" Finn said in surprise, following him into the trees. "But you just tried to escape!"

"Well, I had to do that, you know," Luibra explained. "It was my obligation. Now I've tried, and you've stopped me, so that's all ended. I'm free of it."

"If you dislike him, then why were you with him?" Finn asked.

"Oh, family oaths, bonds to the de Danaans, ancient rituals, my own dedication to healing," he rattled off carelessly, waving a hand. "All that sort of thing. Very complicated."

They had now returned to the spot where Finn had left Donn and Aedh on watch, and the two brothers appeared from cover to meet them.

"Aedh!" Luibra said with elation, moving up to clasp the son of Midhir affectionately. "It's been so many years!"

"Good to see you, Luibra," the other truthfully replied.

"I'm most sorry we've been on different sides in this," the healer said.

"Was he difficult to capture?" Donn asked. "Aedh said he was canny as a fox."

"He put up a great struggle," Finn said soberly. "He nearly escaped!"

"Thank you for that," Luibra said, grinning. "Well now, lads, where to? Back to your own home, is it?"

"You two stay close on either side," Finn told the brothers. "I'll be behind. Mind the fox well," he warned, adding to Luibra. "No offense to you."

"None at all," he replied. "It'll make me feel more secure."

They cautiously made their way through the woods, skirting the circular plain until they were on the side opposite the camp. Here the mound shielded them from the view of Lir's men as they moved across the open.

They arrived at the house without incident, the genial physician accompanying them with no resistance. As they came through the door, there was a chorus of warm greetings from the family, and Moirrin rushed forward to hug Finn in a spontaneous show of relief.

"My Anluan!" she said joyfully. "You did it!"

"I wish I could earn such a warm welcome," Luibra

said, eyeing the girl appreciatively. He looked at Aedh. "Is this your younger sister? My, she is quite something!"

She turned from Finn to fix a cool, appraising eye on him.

"I hope that *you* are something," she said warningly. "Even half what my brother says."

"Twice," he assured her with a grin. He stepped forward and looked about. "And you do seem to need my help badly."

"Will you treat my brothers, then?" Donn asked him. "Some of them are near death."

Not replying at once, Luibra moved about the room, briefly examining each of the hurt men. His expression was now a sober one, his movements precise and efficient. When he had circled the room, he returned to the others.

"Some are very badly wounded," he confirmed. "Still, they can be cured. But"—he fixed Donn with a calculating gaze—"what will be my own in return for doing this?"

"You hound," said Moirrin angrily. "I should have guessed the likes of you would need some payment."

"We will give you all our wealth for it," Donn told him.

"You both misunderstand me," he said, smiling soothingly. "It's no gold I want, for I'd never turn aside from hurt men, friends or enemies. But what will happen to me?"

"We promise that your life will be left to you," Donn said, "and you may return to Lir unharmed, once this is finished."

"I'd rather go somewhere else, if it's all the same to you," the healer answered. "And the freedom to do that is all the reward I could want." He set down his colored bag of medicines and began to undo his cloak.

"No more time must be wasted in beginning the healing," he went on, now adopting a brisk tone. "Have water boiled, and lots of it. And you"—he looked to Moirrin—"you will assist me." He flashed her a smile. "I'm certain you've the spirit for it."

This time she smiled back and bustled off to begin the preparations. Luibra tossed down his cloak and began to roll back the sleeves of his tunic. Finn stepped forward and laid a hand upon his arm as he did, leaning close to speak in a soft but meaningful voice.

"Be certain in all you do, healer. These people have come to mean a great deal to me. If you do them any treachery or harm, it's my own hand that will strike off your head for it."

Luibra looked down at Finn's hand, tightly gripping his sword hilts. Then his gaze, unflinching and unafraid, rose to the young warrior's determined face.

"I would never do anything purposely to harm them," he said earnestly. "I give you my word on that."

With this, he strode off to begin the work.

"Can he be trusted?" Donn said, gazing after him.

"Yes," said Finn. "I believe he can. I can see it in him, for all his odd manner. He is an honest man."

"I'd like to see the face of Lir when he realizes what's happened," Aedh said with glee.

"Yes," agreed Donn. "We'll see how much that bully likes things this way for a change."

"At least," added Finn, "if he still has a stomach for the fight, the terms of it may be just a little more equal."

CHAPTER◦22

Reunion

"OUCH! ARE YOU CERTAIN THIS IS THE WAY?" CAOILTE cried irritably as he pushed through some thorny underbrush, leading his none-too-eager horse.

"It's the way the dogs are going," Cnu Deireoil called back. "And stop complaining. It's not so bad as that."

Caoilte looked after the little man who was striding ahead, guiding his own horse and finding his way beneath the low branches and through the narrow gaps in the brush with little difficulty.

"It's fine for you to talk," Caoilte said critically, pushing aside a branch that had thwacked him smartly in the neck, "when you're no bigger than a hare yourself."

"We've got to keep close on Finn's trail," Cnu Deireoil reminded him, "and move as quickly as we can!"

"Well, Finn's trail has certainly been a wandering one," the dark warrior commented. "It's my feeling that he must have been hurt by that pooka creature we found."

"Or he might just be lost," suggested the harper.

"Lost? Not Finn. Ow!" Caoilte paused to pull a briar from his leg. "He would have found his way back to us."

"We should just be grateful he's alive. There's been quite a horde of the druid's creatures hunting him by the signs."

"Still," Caoilte said with continued pessimism, "if Finn were whole, he could have dealt with them."

"Maybe," the harper agreed unhappily. "Let's keep on."

They pressed doggedly forward through the dense

forest. It was a cool, overcast, humid day, and as the afternoon came on, it brought a fog with it, covering and filling the woods like a sodden blanket of gray wool. The vague shapes of the trees seemed to drift within this haze, and the weight of the damp air even muffled noise, so that the searchers moved in an eerie, silent world.

Then, abruptly, Bran and Sceolan came to a stop. In the fog the men and horses nearly trod upon them before pulling up. The two dogs stood a moment, heads cocked, ears lifted, before heading off again, this time at a run.

Harper and warrior exchanged a surprised glance.

"What's made them do that?" asked the Little Nut.

"I think I know," said Caoilte. "Listen!"

Both listened intently. Through the clinging fog, through the heavy silence, faint, far but still distinct, came a high, sharp clattering sound.

"What is that?"

"A sound I know well enough," said Caoilte. "The clash of arms! Come on!"

They ran forward, Caoilte now unmindful of the tearing underbrush as he pursued the hounds. The sounds of battle grew louder, the rattle of weapons joined by men's voices: shrill battle shouts and cries of agony.

"A large battle, I'd say," Caoilte remarked as he drew up with the harper. "Desperately fought, too!"

His long legs now carried him on ahead of the little man who, laboring to keep up, called after him complainingly.

"Wait, you great, loping fool! This is too fast!"

"Quit your complaining," Caoilte called back, giving him a vengeful smile. "We're in a hurry, remember?"

He pushed through a screen of hedge and vanished from the sight of the little man. Muttering a curse under his breath, Cnu Deireoil plunged through the same spot after him.

He found himself suddenly on the edge of an abrupt drop down a steep slope. He staggered forward, teetering on the brink, and would have fallen had not a hand gripped him by the collar of his cloak and hauled him back.

He recovered and whirled to find that the hand was

Caoilte's. He, his horse, and the two hounds were lined up on the edge.

"I'll not thank you for saving me after what you did," the harper began angrily. "Why, you're a—"

"Never mind!" Caoilte interrupted, pointing ahead. "Look there!"

They were on a ridge that overlooked a wide plain. The fog that had seemed to gather so thickly in the woods was much thinner there, revealing the circular shape of the area, the scattering of stones, and the central mound with its house. Also visible was the pitched battle that was taking place just below the mound.

A small group seemed to be surrounded by a much larger force. Bodies already thickly covered the ground about the fighters. There were only some dozen of the encircled men still on their feet, and they were fighting valiantly to hold their own against some fourscore warriors.

"That larger band seems quite determined," said Cnu Deireoil.

"But the smaller is doing them great damage," Caoilte replied, peering toward them. He grew suddenly excited. "And I think I know the reason for that! Look there, at the center, atop that dolmen! Do you know that fighting style?"

"I know that hair glowing like silver," the other said with like elation. "It's Finn! He's alive!"

"For the moment," said Caoilte. "But he needs help."

He turned to his horse and began to unstrap Finn's weapons from the saddle.

"Finn might be wanting these," he said, slipping them onto his back. He looked to Cnu Deireoil and the two hounds. "The three of you stay here with the horses."

And with that, he was bounding down the slope toward the battle.

Finn certainly was in sore need of help. The bulk of the remaining brothers were near to being overwhelmed, while one contingent of the largest and fiercest looking of the attackers, under the personal leadership of Lir, were directing their attentions solely to eliminating their most troublesome opponent.

To give himself greater advantage over such unfair

numbers, Finn had mounted to the flat stone that formed the tabletop roof of a dolmen. Here he kept a precarious perch as he hopped back and forth, parrying attacks from every side, leaping over swings at his feet, knocking back sword and spear thrusts with his blade, kicking back foes who tried to clamber up. But his spear was gone, his shield buckling, and his sword badly bent from the continuous, massive blows.

So hotly engaged were these opposing groups, that no one noted the warrior approaching until he had struck.

Caoilte, under the unequal circumstances, bypassed the normal combat nicety of choosing and challenging a warrior to single combat. Instead he just crashed into those massed about Finn, swinging out with sword and shield. He slammed one man from his way, hacked through the lifted spear of another, and kicked a third in the behind so hard the hefty fellow staggered forward, bringing down two more in a tangle.

This was enough to bring him to the attention of Lir's men. They turned, startled, as this unexpected force—whose ferocity made it seem much larger than it was—swept into them. The defense they put up was feeble at best. Striking to right and left, Caoilte quickly cut a pathway through them to the dolmen and leaped atop it.

Finn, who had watched his coming with some amazement, made no move to hamper this unexpected reinforcement, and Caoilte moved to his side.

Lir's men, thrown into confusion by the surprise attack and faced now with two fierce warriors upon the stone, hesitated in their assault.

"You can't know how glad I am to see you," the dark warrior said, beaming with his elation.

"Are you?" Finn said in a quizzical way.

"Of course!" Caoilte said, looking a bit surprised at this response. "But look, throw down those bits of iron. Here. Take these! I've carried them long enough for you."

He slipped off the Mac an Luin and the Storm Shield, handing them to Finn. Astonished, the fair warrior dropped his battered weapons to take the new ones.

"Why should you give me these?" he asked.

"Why not?" Caoilte replied, giving him a most peculiar

look this time. "They're yours, aren't they? And it's my guess you're going to have need of them."

This was far from understatement. For now Lir, outraged by the craven behavior of his men, was ranting at them to go on.

"Get at them, you cowards!" he cried. "Why are you delaying? They are only two."

Several of the warriors gave him looks which said clearly that "only" was not the word they would have applied. Still they went, trying to swarm up onto the stones from all sides at once, and the fight began again in earnest.

But the hapless warriors of Lir had no chance at all now. Finn and Caoilte moved back-to-back, shifting about to face any attack so swiftly and so agilely they might have been one being. The sword of Caoilte flashed out, striking down man after man. And in the hand of Finn, the Mac an Luin was a wielder of great carnage, while the Storm Shield boomed out like thunder when it was struck.

"This is a fight!" Caoilte said exuberantly. "Ah, but it's fine to be together like this again. Just like it used to be."

Finn cast a questioning glance toward him at that, but was too heavily engaged to make reply.

The pair battled on, apparently inexhaustible, devastating all those who came in around them. The warriors of Lir, for all their chieftain's exhortations, were growing reluctant to clamber up onto the stones.

Finally Lir himself, livid from rage and humiliation, stalked up below the dolmen and shouted up to Finn: "Insolent whelp! I'll take this no longer. See how you fare against the blade of Lir!"

"That beefy fellow seems a bit angry," Caoilte observed. "Is he challenging you?"

"He is," Finn answered. "And I'll be most happy to finally oblige him."

He hopped down from the dolmen before the chieftain. The other warriors drew back to give them a wide fighting space.

Lir did not delay, charging in at Finn like a maddened bull. Quickly it became clear how he had gained and held the leadership of his band of savage warriors. The massive chieftain was neither a scrupulous nor a subtle fighter, making up for his lesser agility with a direct, powerful, and ruthless attack.

He used his heavy body along with his weapons, slamming into Finn, knocking him back and pounding upon him, hammering at him with shield and sword as if he were a smith and the young captain an ingot of soft iron beneath his maul.

But it was only for an instant that this tactic worked upon Finn. He retreated until his back came against the hard stone edge of the dolmen's cap. There he recovered, altering his own tactics to match his opponent's, and the fight grew even.

For a time they battled toe-to-toe, exchanging massive blows, often locked together in brief contests of pure physical strength. But even the chieftain's superior bulk could now gain him no advantage over the sinewy and determined Finn.

Finally Lir's anger and frustration drove him to rashness. He launched himself straight forward, smashing Finn's sword and shield aside with his own and throwing his body against the young warrior. Finn rebounded from the outthrust boulder of Lir's chest, staggered, and dropped to one knee. Lir lifted his sword to strike at Finn's head, but Finn was quicker. The slender but deadly blade of the Mac an Luin shot out, thrusting into the chieftain's side.

Though not fatal, it was a serious wound, and quite enough to do for Lir. He grunted, staggered back, and fell heavily, crashing to the ground.

At the fall of their chieftain, the men of Lir stopped their fighting at once, having lost the only force that was still keeping them to it. They quickly pulled back from the remnant of the sons of Midhir and from Finn and Caoilte. Several of them, with great difficulty, scooped up the unconscious man and bore him away, staggering beneath his weight. Others gathered the rest of the fallen, and they retreated across the field.

As they hastily departed, a beaming Caoilte turned to his comrade.

"Well, we surely took proper care of that lot," he said, "whoever they were!"

"I thank you for the help and the weapons, stranger," Finn said graciously. He held the Mac an Luin out toward him. "But I should return these to you now."

Caoilte looked in bewilderment from the sword to Finn.

"Stranger?" he said. "What is it you're saying? What kind of game are you playing? You know me!"

Finn shook his head.

"I'm sorry," he said frankly, "but I don't remember ever meeting you before!"

Caoilte could only stare in disbelief.

The slender fingers strummed a light, soothing, and pleasant tune, its notes filling the place, seeming to impart an atmosphere—including the fragrance—of a soft spring morning.

Cnu Deireoil was the player. He sat on Moirrin's seat near the central fire of the house and strummed upon her harp in a casual, almost absent way. Beside him, on the hearth, sat a brooding Caoilte, while the dogs lay on the floor at their feet. The eyes of all four were fixed searchingly, curiously, upon their comrade.

Finn was moving about the room in company with Donn and the physician Luibra, seeing to the wounds of the brothers. Moirrin and her sisters were busy too in the administering. But the gaze of the red-haired girl kept straying to these strangers as she worked. She noted the direction of their gazes, and her face wore a troubled frown.

"And you say he had no memory of you at all?" Cnu Deireoil asked Caoilte as he played.

Caoilte shook his head irritably.

"No. He was pleasant, but he treated me like a stranger, and the hounds as well. His own hounds! Raised from pups! We that rescued him a hundred times!"

"Well, he does look much the leaner, as you do," the harper said thoughtfully. "And he seems a good bit older as well, although the beard's a part of that. Still, there's no denying it's him. Couldn't you find out anything else?"

"I really hadn't the time to talk more, had I?" Caoilte retorted impatiently. "Since the battle, he's been all abustle bringing the wounded here and seeing to them as if he were their own mother. Not a word to us. Not so much as a look at us!"

"Easy, Caoilte," Cnu Deireoil said. "They've had a hard time by the look of it. Let them see to their needs now. We're in no hurry. Relax. Listen to the music."

"Never mind that," Caoilte said sharply. "I only want to know what's wrong with Finn!"

With the examinations completed and the physician now dealing with the cures, Donn and Finn left the others and crossed the room to the new arrivals. The girl too left her work and followed along, clearly with some anxiety.

As Finn reached them, the two hounds rose and moved eagerly to him. He stopped to pat their heads and scratch their necks in a show of friendship that seemed quite unconscious.

It was Donn who first addressed the harper.

"Your music has a most soothing effect upon my brothers. It seems to ease their pain. Most are asleep."

"It's a fine harp," Cnu Deireoil said, caressing it lovingly and then setting it down beside the chair. "My talent is a modest one. I'm glad to be of help."

"It's a music with magic in it, certainly," the son of Midhir went on. "And yourself, you're of the Sidhe, are you not?"

"I was," the little man acknowledged. "Cnu Deireoil is my name."

"Of course!" the other said with the light of dawning understanding. "But it's more than a modest talent you're said to have. I've heard great tales of the Little Nut, whose music can charm the sun out on a stormy day."

"It may have been so once," he said, and shrugged. "But I fear much of the skill has been lost to me."

"You're most admired by my family," Donn told him sincerely. "You chose to leave the safety of a Sid and brave the wrath of the de Danaans to live in the outer world. You are most welcome here, for it's a spirit like our own that you have."

"Is it?" he said. "And just who are you?"

"Why, we're the children of Midhir!" Donn announced with a ringing note of pride.

"Are you now?" Cnu Deireoil said with interest. "Well, and I should have guessed as much. I've heard of you as well. But I thought that you had surely been destroyed by now."

"Not quite. Nearly, but for this one." Donn put a hand to Finn's shoulder. "He came from nowhere and gave new heart to us."

"I'm sorry not to talk to you before," Finn now put in. "Don't think that the desire hasn't been burning in me. It's just that my duty to these people was of the first importance. Indeed, it's been the only thing of importance to me lately. I have a responsibility here. No matter what my need to know about myself, that had to be seen to first."

"We understand, lad," Cnu Deireoil said, casting a meaningful look at the dark warrior. "Don't we, Caoilte?"

"That we do, I suppose," Caoilte grudgingly agreed. "But what do you mean, the only thing? Are you saying you have no memory of anything else? Not even of Sabd?"

There was a strange flicker, as of pain, that crossed the young warrior's face at that name. He frowned, concentrating. Then he shook his head violently.

"No," he said. "I . . . I don't think so. I have a faint image of a woman. I've had the same one before. But I've had many visions. Dreams more like." He looked closely at Caoilte, his expression clearing a little. "They have had you in them, I faintly recall. So I must know you. And there's no denying these hounds know me!" They were leaning against him now, heads back and eyes closed in utter rapture as he patted them.

"You must think harder," Caoilte said with force. "They are your own two hounds, Bran and Sceolan. The harper and I are your oldest friends. I am Caoilte!"

Finn looked from one to the other again more searchingly. Then he sighed in frustration.

"I'm sorry. I just don't know. You must tell me—who am I?"

Caoilte gave the little man a look askance. Cnu Deireoil shrugged.

"We may as well tell him."

"All right then," Caoilte said.

He moved up to Finn. He placed a hand on each of his comrade's shoulders, gripping it firmly. Holding Finn at arms' length, he met his eyes fixedly.

"Listen to me carefully," he said in a determined way. "Think! Remember! You are Finn, son of Cumhal, chieftain of the Baiscne clan, leader of the Fian clans of Linster, captain of the Fianna of all Ireland!"

The girl gave a gasp that blended astonishment with dismay. Her brother raised his eyebrows in a sign of his own rather more restrained surprise.

"Finn MacCumhal!" he exclaimed. Then he shrugged, adding in a casual tone, "Well, I knew he was no ordinary mortal."

But though the name was recognized by the others, Finn himself still looked quite blank.

"I am sorry," he told Caoilte sincerely, "but I've no memory of any of these things."

"You have to remember," Caoilte said, giving Finn a little shake in frustration, as if to jar him to it. "Remember Almhuin, your struggle against Tadg, the battle of the White Strand. Remember Sabd. Remember the Dark Druid. It was he put this spell upon you. You have to overcome it to rescue Sabd!"

Finn struggled, clearly in pain. But then he shook his head defeatedly. Caoilte turned away in frustration.

"I give up," he said. "Whatever magic is holding him surely has its grip upon him."

"What happened to me?" Finn asked. "Why have I forgotten my life?"

"That we don't really know," Cnu Deireoil explained. "But we're fairly certain it was a spell put upon you, and we think it was in a lake."

"I . . . I do remember another woman," Finn said. "A fair-haired woman who somehow became dark. She said she was helping me, but she tried to kill me. It's all confused in my mind, like a long nightmare."

"A woman, was it?" said Caoilte. "Well, we guessed as much."

"If this is some magic, shouldn't there be a way to counter it?" asked Donn. He looked to the physician. "Luibra, you'd be the best to know."

The young healer, who had been listening to this discussion as he worked, now came over to them.

"Well, that's a bit tricky," he said. "My own skills are with the body, not the mind. It's a more delicate thing that ointments and tonics can't reach. Still, there might be some way."

"It could be dangerous," Cnu Deireoil told him. "We think it was Fear Doirche did this enchantment."

"The Dark Druid?" Luibra breathed, clearly impressed. He looked at Finn. "My young fellow, you do manage to acquire some interesting enemies. Well, then, I agree that it would be dangerous indeed. Without knowing what magic he used, we might do more damage than good."

"There must be some way," Caoilte growled impatiently. "We can't leave Finn without his past!"

"Are you certain?" Cnu Deireoil said.

"Don't be a bloody fool," the dark warrior shot back.

Donn's brother Aedh came into the house then and rushed immediately to them.

"Donn," he said breathlessly, "a messenger's brought word from Lir!"

"So, he's survived?" Finn said.

"Worse luck for us," Donn said. "What does the blaggard want?"

"Revenge, it seems. He's more outraged than ever. Sorely wounded, but that only seems to have aggravated him more."

"I'm sure it has," said Luibra, clearly amused. "Especially without me to heal him!"

"He says this isn't ended," Aedh reported. "For these new insults to him, he will go to Bobd Derg himself. This time, he says, he will bring the whole of the de Danaans upon us to exact his due!"

Donn looked from Aedh around at the others, his gaze ending upon Finn.

"Well, my friend," he asked, "just what do we do now?"

CHAPTER ◇ 23

Remembrance

"I THINK I MAY JUST HAVE AN IDEA, FINN," CNU DEIREOIL said. He dropped down from the chair and moved up before the fair warrior. "It may not work, but then . . ."

"Anything," said Finn. "The agony of not knowing is maddening!"

"Well, it may seem a bit strange to you. But you have to put your thumb into your mouth."

"My . . . thumb?" Finn repeated as if he hadn't rightly heard.

"Of course!" Caoilte exclaimed. "The thumb! What fools we were not to think of it."

"One of us *did* think of it," Cnu Deireoil cattily pointed out.

Finn had lifted his hands and was staring at both his thumbs in a confused way.

"My thumbs?" he said again. "What power could they have?"

"Just your right one," the harper told him. "You see, Finn, there was an enchantment put upon it. You burned it upon a magic fish of knowledge."

"A fish of knowledge?" Finn said, giving the little man a most dubious look. "Get away! I think it's a tale you're telling me now!"

"It is not," Caoilte put in supportively. "When you burned your thumb, you plunged it into your mouth to cool it. Ever since then you've only had to put it in again when you need knowledge."

Tears in his eyes, Cnu Deireoil released Finn's hand and stepped back.

Finn slowly lifted the hand, fist tightly closed, thumb thrust out. He straightened, body tensing as he prepared himself for this. The men watched him expectantly. Moirrin's look was anxious.

He slipped the thumb into his mouth, holding it there in a contemplative way. Then his head dropped slowly back, his eyes closed, and he grew suddenly taut with strain as if something had seized him.

Within the darkness of his mind, images were beginning to develop. Flickering streamers of light began shooting out toward him from the void ahead. They grew steadier, stronger, brighter, widening into streams, into floods, taking on color, form, movement. Then he was within a geyser of images flowing together, enveloping him, catching him up and carrying him along. The events of his life rushed past: his lonely childhood in the glens, meeting the Little Nut and Caoilte, winning his father's place, battles and hunts and music and blood and women's faces, armored giants, strange creatures, haunted woods, mist-shrouded mountains and stormy seas and sunlit meadows blurring together in a torrent that surged over him.

His body was vibrating, jerking as if the stream of impressions were a physical one beating against him. He grew tauter, his body so strained it seemed near to collapse. The others watched, their looks growing more concerned with the obvious heightening of his torture.

Inside Finn's mind, the stream moved yet faster, the images shooting past like continuous lightning strokes, yet still all clear, each recognizable. The memories were recent now: the chasing of the fawn, the Dark Druid, his search, the winter, the spring, the forest and the lake, the woman and the water's closing over his head . . . the oblivion. The end came in a final burst of light that exploded about him, leaving him in a tingling blackness.

His body jerked a last time as the end came. Then he stood motionless for a long moment, head still thrown back. Finally, slowly, he pulled the thumb out, letting his arm drop limply to his side. The others leaned forward, breaths held, waiting, expressions fearful and hopeful at once.

His eyes opened. He looked at them, but his eyes didn't seem to see them. Instead they were fixed on something beyond them, and a vast despair, a vast sorrow came into his face. He opened his mouth and voiced a cry of great agony, all spoken in a single word.

"Sabd!"

Then, his energy drained by the ordeal, he staggered. Caoilte and Donn moved in and caught him before he fell, easing him down onto a bench. He looked up and saw the dark warrior. Grasping his arms, Finn leaned toward him, his voice broken, tears welling in his eyes.

"Caoilte! Caoilte, my friend! What's happened? Where have I been? And Sabd! What about Sabd?" He shook his head violently. "Oh, Danu, the pain! I can't bear it!"

Caoilte moved forward, cradling his friend's head as he would that of a stricken child.

"It's all right, Finn," he soothed. "It's come too fast. Be easy. It will be all right."

But his words seemed to do little to console the anguished man. He sat with head hung forward, body sagging, shoulders shaking with the emotions welling uncontrollably within him as if he had been overwhelmed and utterly shattered by the massive inrush of awful knowledge.

His eyes stared ahead of him, seeing nothing but the images of his past which still glowed there. Those standing about him watched him, their faces mirroring their own fears, clearly expressing a single question: had the shock of the revelations been too much for Finn? Moirrin, especially, watched with apprehension, her eyes brimming with tears in sympathy for him.

"Finn," Cnu Deireoil said with intensity, leaning toward the young man, "you must fight your feelings, lad. You must get control of them."

"It may be he can't," the physician put in darkly. "The magic he battles is very powerful. Maybe his mind—"

"No!" Caoilte said fiercely. "No magic can defeat him. That I'll not allow." He bent down, now speaking sharply, almost angrily, to his friend. "Finn, you have to come to your senses, and quickly. If Sabd is to be found, it's you who must do it!"

These words had an immediate effect upon Finn. His shuddering stopped. He drew himself upward and his gaze lifted again to the determined face of Caoilte. He seemed to draw even more new strength there, recovering further, visibly taking control of himself, pulling erect, his face setting into firm lines.

"Yes, yes!" he said with recovering vigor. "I have to find her, Caoilte. I have to!"

He jumped to his feet.

"We must go on, and quickly! All these days lost! All these days the druid has had her! We must hurry!"

Galvanized by the restored obsession, he stepped away, moving with a nervous energy as he took up the Storm Shield. He seemed totally oblivious to the others now.

"You brought me my weapons, too," he said to Caoilte. "Good friend. I thought I'd lost them."

No one else had spoken through any of this. But now, as Finn slipped the shield onto his arm, his gaze fell upon their watching faces. He looked around the room at the wounded men. He looked back to Donn, and then to Moirrin. Something seemed to strike him. His expression changed, as if a light of logic, of realization was striking through the blinding darkness of his obsession. The madness faded from his eyes, replaced by the clear look of understanding.

"No!" he said, dropping the shield. "I can't leave! Things are not finished here." He looked around at them again, this time contritely. "I'm sorry, all of you. I can see now that I've been . . . mad for a time. Too long a time. And I'm not meaning the loss of my memory. No. In a way, that's been my cure. Losing my past has made me see the truth. There are problems greater than my own."

"But Sabd—" Caoilte began.

"Of course I must try to find Sabd," Finn interrupted, "but I can't leave so many others to suffer, and she'd not want me to. Do you see, Caoilte? I thought that what made me want to serve others first was outside me. But it's not. It's in me. It *is* me. I can't walk away from these people now. They've become my family. I have to help them."

"There is nothing you can do to help us, Finn MacCumhal," Donn said stoically. "This is our fight, to be finished by us. You've never had a part in it. So leave us now and regain your own life."

"No!" Finn said with determination. "I will not see you destroyed. I will help you."

"Help us? How? Even you can't fight all the de Danaans. It will be thousands who come against us now."

"Then I will bring all the Fianna here to fight for you," he said.

"The Fianna?" said Donn. "Can you do that?"

"If I can't," he vowed, "then I'll return here alone to face the de Danaans with you. That I promise!"

He turned to Caoilte.

"We must go to Almhuin quickly," he said. "I must host the Fians."

"Well . . . ah . . . if that's what you wish," Caoilte said with a certain hesitation. "There might just be a few problems—"

"We'll talk about it on the way," Finn said briskly. "No time can be lost."

"Well, then, we have some good horses," the dark warrior said. "The Little Nut got them—"

"Ah, bless Cnu Deireoil!" Finn exclaimed. He looked about for the harper and realized that while the talk was going on, the little man had been quietly stealing toward the door.

"Wait!" Finn cried, moving after him. "My Little Nut! Where are you going?"

"I've done all I can for you," he replied, avoiding the other's eyes. "I told Caoilte I'd not let you down again, and maybe what I've done has made me feel better, but I know that it can't make up for the great wrong I've done you. You said you meant never to see me again, so I'll leave you now."

"My friend!" Finn said in distress, dropping down and pulling the little man to him in a great hug. "Please forgive me for what I said to you. The madness has gone from me and taken my hatred of you as well. I know now I can't blame you for what happened. I understand how the Dark Druid tricked Sabd. You couldn't have saved her. You've not failed me. It's you who have to forgive me." He held the man out and fixed him with a most earnest gaze. "Will you tell me that you do?"

Cnu Deireoil hugged him in return.

"And why would I not?" he said with great gladness. "Though it's more than I deserve."

Finn released him and rose, an arm still about the little man, turning to smile at Caoilte.

"So, we are three again," he said. "We'll ride for Almhuin at once." He looked to Donn. "How long do you think we have until the de Danaans come?"

"Lir must go to Brugh na Boinne to convince Bobd Derg and the leaders of the de Danaans to act against us," said Donn. "There may be some argument, but the High-King's resentment of us is strong. In the end, they will host. We have a few days, perhaps. No more."

"Long enough to return to Almhuin, raise the Fians, and march them here," Finn said with great spirit. "I'll match the speed of our fighting men against any in the world, even those of the Sidhe."

Caoilte and the Little Nut exchanged a troubled look.

"Ah . . . Finn," Caoilte ventured reluctantly. "Raising the Fians may not be quite so easy a task. I didn't like saying this before, with your recent . . . illness and all. But the clans may not be so eager to follow you now, after all that's happened."

"Then I'll convince them!" Finn proclaimed with confidence. "But we must start at once!"

He took up his shield and turned to Donn.

"I will come back," he said determinedly. "Never doubt it."

With that, he led his two comrades and the pair of hounds from the house. Donn, Luibra, and other of the Midhir family followed them out and watched them move swiftly down the slope to the horses tethered at its base.

"Do you think he'll come back, or will he be lost?" the healer asked.

"He will come back, I think," Donn answered. "He's proven himself a man true to his word. But if he brings no help, it will make no difference. We'll all die together here."

"Finn may come back," Moirrin said, looking after Finn with a great sadness, "but to me, my Anluan is already lost."

The litter bearers, straining more than a bit from their load, carried Lir through the opening into the immense cavern.

The interior of the Sid was a cheery and well-lighted place, bright with many tapestries, richly textured with metal and wood and glass appointments of all kinds. About a blazing central fire was a ring of tables. Here sat a number of slender, handsomely featured men, all quite fair, all with long hair and light, shining eyes.

They were watching with a great deal of amusement a pair of other men who were wrestling with a complex contraption involving some two dozen cauldrons and as many spits, tangled lengths of chain, scores of pulleys, levers, axles, wheels, ropes, and rods.

One of the two men was short and square of build but with unnaturally long arms as hard and sinewy as knotted roots of some ancient tree. He was leather-aproned, the bare flesh of his arms and legs soot-blackened, his face so dark his eyes were like hot coals blazing from a forge. The other was a huge bear of a man, with thick, bowed legs, muscled arms, and a barrel chest. His face was rugged and weathered to a ruddy hue. Though not as black as his working mate, he was still very grimy and sweaty from his labors.

Just now his massive body was set, straining with the effort, as he lifted a wooden wagonlike affair that held all the cauldrons. The load seemed greater than a dozen men should have been able to more than budge. But he held one end of it clear of the floor while the smaller man rolled a set of iron wheels joined by a thick axle underneath it.

"Be certain to keep it up while I set them!" the one beneath said. "I want no part of myself flattened in this!"

"Just be quick about it, Goibnu!" the other said through gritted teeth. "Can't you fit it in?"

"It was you designed the thing," shot back the other.

He forced the axle into grooves beneath the wagon with a smack of his huge mallet. Then he began a quick crawl out to safety.

"I think that between the pair of you, you'll manage to see that the thing never works, Dagda," said one of the young watchers, grinning. "You've been struggling at it for days now."

"Keep quiet, you," the large man he had called Dagda returned in a warning growl. "It's a very great thing I've done."

"If you knew what it was," teased another observer.

Angered, Dagda let the wagon drop—one of its new set of wheels nearly crushing the foot of Goibnu who yelped and jumped clear as it crashed down—and wheeled toward the offender.

"Three times nine cauldrons will this cooking oven have," he thundered, "and three times nine spits as well! The mechanism will turn them all about the fire with the quickness of a stream, and lift them from the cinders to the height of the roof to keep them always in the flame, and without more than a single man to be tending them!" He strode closer to loom over the other man. "And when have you ever had an idea in your own head, you useless parasite?"

"Be easy, Father," said a lean, grave-faced man with silver-blue eyes, lifting a calming hand. "We know what it is. But you have spent a great deal of time and effort on it."

"And just what else is there to do?" the big man said. "Stand about like the lot of you? That's not a life for me or for the smith." He looked to the black-faced man. "Right, Goibnu?"

"Right, I suppose," the other said with some doubt, examining his nearly squashed foot for damage.

"Well, let's not be larking about, then!" the Dagda said brusquely. "Back to it!"

The smith shot him a nasty look, grumbled, but fell to as the Dagda took hold of the wooden cart again.

"Now, if you'll just lift it here . . ." Goibnu suggested, taking up another set of axle and wheels.

As they resumed work, one of the watching men

glanced around to note Lir, who had now been carried up close behind their tables.

"Say, look here," he said, calling the attention of the other to the wounded chieftain.

"By Good Danu Herself," said the one called Bobd Derg. "What's happened to you, Lir?"

"The Sons of Midhir happened to me," stormed Lir. "And I want my revenge for it!" The bearers carried him around the tables and, with expressions of great relief, set him down between the group and the working pair.

Goibnu and Dagda were paying little attention to this. Finished with placing the wheels beneath the cart, they were now trying to attach chains to the cauldrons' handles.

"Calm yourself," Bobd Derg said soothingly. "What are you saying?"

"I've been outraged. Humiliated!" the chieftain roared. "Doubly outraged! Triply!"

"Hold on, Lir," the other replied. "You swore to me that you'd bring them to surrender, and without further loss of our own lives—not start your own war with them."

"And I would have. But they killed my bird! My finest bird—created by the magic of the Blessed Isles and the hand of our own smith, Goibnu there himself!"

"What!" said Goibnu, stopping his wrestling with a pair of metal levers to look toward them in outrage. "My bird of the flaming tail? It took me two full seasons for the crafting of that!"

"Well, it's gone now," Lir said ruefully. "And when I demanded satisfaction for the loss, they refused. They defied us. They dared to challenge us!"

"From the looks of you, they did more than challenge you," one of the company pointed out.

"And that's another thing!" Lir added. "They even stole Luibra from me! I had to go wounded while their wounds were healed, by my own physician!"

This drew some sniggering from the men, and an open guffaw from the Dagda. Lir glared around at them.

"So, they kicked you soundly in the backside, did they, Lir?" the Dagda put in, trying to force a cauldron into position in a harness. "Well, I'll not say you didn't need it.

A braggart like you, and after proclaiming you'd bring the Midhirs to heel."

"But they've used unfair means," Lir protested. "They've been joined by outsiders. Great warriors. One of them is like none I've ever seen. I think he uses some kind of magic. His skills are too unbelievable without it."

"They must surely be a powerful lot if they can make the difference between your host and the pitiful remnant of the sons of Midhir," commented Bobd Derg.

The Dagda, losing patience both with the complex tangle that had ensnared him and with the conversation, heaved the mass of chains down on the floor with a great clatter that reverberated through the room. He strode from the jumble of his vast machinery and stalked over to the wounded chieftain.

"For all these years you've been the arm of punishment for the de Danaans. And for all that same time I've watched you use the station to play the bully. It's always galled me, though I've said nothing about it. But now I'm glad to know you've gotten your proper comeuppance."

"That's a fine way to talk to me," Lir complained, "after what I've done to keep the de Danaan laws, after what I've suffered at the hands of these rebels."

"Rebels!" the Dagda repeated scornfully. "That's your name for them, not mine. I've always been against this war upon them. Let them go and live where they like— that's my feeling. And it's the feeling of others, too."

"You've no choice in this," Lir blustered defensively. "These are no pitiful remnant who can be ignored now. They are strong and defiant. And they might grow stronger. Outside warriors have joined them. Who knows how many might come? They may have put themselves in league with powerful forces. I can tell you, they'll never submit now. Their rebellion will become greater. That can't be allowed. I say, finish them quickly, before this becomes even more bloody."

Bobd Derg sighed, looking to the Dagda.

"I'm afraid he's right, Father. We can't tolerate this. It's not a matter of their freedom. Defiance like this cannot be allowed."

"My son, if you mean to call another hosting of the

Sidhe, and bring all the de Danaan might upon this one
small clan, you are a fool," the Dagda said with vehe-
mence. "I'll have nothing to do with it."

"I'm sorry for your feeling, Father," Bobd Derg told
him. "But if they're let to succeed in this, others may defy
our laws as well. They've had their final chance to surrender and they've refused. I tried to settle the feud without
more bloodshed, as you wished. The attempt failed. Now,
it must be finished in my way."

He looked around at the others.

"We will call a meeting of the kings of all the Sids. If
they are agreed, we will host."

"And then what will you do?" Lir asked him eagerly.

"Then," said Bobd Derg reluctantly, "they must submit or . . ."

"Or what?"

"Or be destroyed."

BOOK ◊ THREE

Into the Druid's Lair

◊

CHAPTER 24

A
Call
For
Help

"IT'S FINN! FINN HAS RETURNED!"

So went up the cry as Finn and his companions approached the fortress of Almhuin. When they trotted their weary mounts across the bridge and entered the yard, they found it already filled with a crowd of curious but subdued onlookers, whispering amongst themselves as they watched the still-bearded warrior ride in.

Finn and Cnu Deireoil climbed down from one horse and Caoilte from the other. In a tight group they started toward the main hall, Finn striding purposefully ahead, the harper and the dark warrior glancing about them with clear dislike for what they saw.

"A cheerful lot," Cnu Deireoil said sarcastically.

"Don't say I didn't give you warning," Caolite replied.

Goll MacMorna, already at the door of the main hall, now started forward to meet Finn. His greeting, characteristically for the dour man, was cordial, but brief and unemotional.

"My welcome to you, Finn MacCumhal. I am happy to see that you have returned alive."

"Are you?" Finn asked with a wry smile.

"That question is not a fair one, Captain," Goll responded in a matter-of-fact way. "You must know by now that I have no ambitions for myself. It is only my sworn duty to the laws of Ireland that moves me."

"I do know," Finn said with a certain contriteness. "Caoilte's told me why you came. I understand the need for it, and I know your reasons were only honorable ones. Forgive me for entertaining even the briefest notion of anything else."

"Think no more of it, Captain" Goll said briskly. "And I do welcome your return." He allowed himself the indulgence of a small smile. "The High-King, however, will be a bit less joyful."

"I'm certain he will," Finn agreed, smiling, too. Then he became more grave. "Though he may still have reason to rejoice. I know you've said that you would let me resume the leadership when I returned, but that I'll not be asking you to do."

Exclamations of surprise rose amongst those gathered. The brow of the chieftain's good eye arched to indicate his own great astonishment.

"What do you mean?" he asked.

"I mean that a great deal has happened, and that many things have changed," Finn told him. "I have to talk with the Fianna, Goll. They're the ones who'll be deciding the future now."

Goll's single, piercing eye fixed upon Finn's for a long moment. Then he nodded.

"I understand," he said solemnly. "I will have Fergus True-Lips see to their gathering." His gaze ran over the rather rough condition of Finn and his companions. "And what about yourselves? It seems you could use a bit of . . . ah . . . repairing?"

"We have become a rough-appearing lot," Finn agreed, looking over his companions.

"Well, you can make use of your own house," Goll told him. "It's been kept just as it was when you left here. I've seen to that."

He led the way around the main hall and to the smaller building Finn had built for Sabd.

"Go right ahead, Captain," Goll urged. "I'll see after getting the preparations underway."

He bustled off, and the rest of the gathering broke up as the people went back about their tasks. They left the little company standing, staring at the house.

"I . . . I think I'll just find my old place with the other warriors in the main hall," Caoilte said awkwardly. "I'll see you later, Finn." He turned and strode rather hurriedly away.

"Yes, well, I think I'll see to myself there, too," Cnu Deireoil said to Finn. "This . . . this is your place. I've a feeling you don't need any of us there with you. At least, not now."

He gave Finn's arm a squeeze of friendship and moved off toward the main hall, casting backward glances of great compassion toward his comrade.

Finn seemed not to notice the departure of his friends. He was still staring fixedly ahead of him at the home, his mind filled with an image of himself crossing its threshold with his bride. Then, slowly, his gaze lifted, rising up the whitewashed wall to the empty balcony of the sunroom he had built for Sabd. He saw another image of a slender figure there, staring out longingly over the bright countryside.

He shook his head in an irritated way as if to clear it of the maddening memories. He pulled himself up, set his face in a determined expression, and stepped up to the door. He raised its latch and pushed it open. Beyond, the interior of the room was a shadowed space.

He paused again, staring intently, expectantly, into the darkness, almost as if he hoped that, by some miracle, a familiar form might appear there.

Finally, somewhat reluctantly, he stepped forward. As he did, the two hounds moved at once to take up their familiar guardian positions on either side of the door.

He looked down at them pityingly.

"You feel it too, don't you, lads?" he said, giving each of the massive heads a gentle pat.

Then, after a last hesitation upon the threshold, he passed into the shadows of the room, swinging the door closed behind him.

The shutters swung back, letting the bright, clear morning light pour into the room.

Finn leaned out over the windowsill, taking a deep breath of the air. Then he turned and moved back into the room.

He was clean-shaven now, clad in a fresh tunic of white linen, his long fair hair washed and tied in a single, neat plait. He looked much like the Finn of earlier days once again, though still somewhat lean, and his body moved with its old vigor and unconscious grace.

He stepped to the bed and took up a cloak patterned in deep blue with tufts of white, slipping it about his shoulders. As he fastened the garment at his throat with a large, crescent-shaped brooch and pin, his eyes roved about the room.

It had been left as it was on Sabd's last day there. The dust of a year's neglect lay upon its furnishings, and this Finn had done little to disturb since his return, as if reluctant to violate the aura of a sacred shrine which hung about it. The once-bright tapestries were dimmed, the brass and silver objects were growing black with tarnish, the straw mats, bed clothes, rugs, and hangings had mildewed without a fire to keep them dry. A musty scent hung heavily in the air.

His gaze passed lightly across the small table near the bed, then paused and returned to it. He stared more fixedly for a moment, finishing the fastening of his cloak. Then he strode across to the table and stood looking down at the objects upon its top. The intricately decorated combs and brushes and mirror he had had Ireland's finest craftsmen fashion for his bride were neatly laid out there.

Likely they had been among the last objects in her hand that day. It might be that she had placed them there just before making her final climb to the granian.

He picked up the mirror and held it, gazing at its back. The complex swirls of the silver inlay were now black, the bright colors of the enamel dulled by a layer of dust.

He turned the mirror over. The reflecting surface, having been turned down against the tabletop, was still clean, still shining. He looked into it.

The face that stared back at him was no longer that of the Finn MacCumhal who had so joyfully handed Sabd this mirror on their wedding night. This face was leaner, harder, etched permanently now by lines of care about the mouth and eyes. The ravages of his hard and hopeless quest had marked him. They had aged him and made him grave. The carefree youth who had once gone boldly adventuring through Ireland was gone, and would not come again.

But his own reflection appeared to mean little to him as he stared into the mirror. The last face that the bright circle had held had been that of Sabd. And now, as he looked into its surface, it seemed as if his image faded, to be replaced by her own: wistful, eyes bright and trusting, beckoning him to her.

"My love, I am sorry," he said softly, sorrowfully, but with resolve. "But you have to understand what it is that I've got to do. I've not forgotten you. Somehow I will still find you, that I promise. But this thing has to be finished first."

With that he gently laid the mirror back upon the table. He drew himself up, his sorrow replaced by a look of great purpose. With the proud stride of the warrior, the chieftain, the Fian champion, he went to the doorway and threw open the door.

Outside, Caoilte and Cnu Deireoil awaited him. With the hounds trotting close behind, they accompanied him across the yard and through the doors of the main hall.

The vast room was now tightly packed with men. The chieftains and warriors of the gathered Fian clans filled the tables and stood shoulder to shoulder, crowding all the space from the tables to the outer partitions. They were muttering, their voices a deep and ominous rumbling, like the thunder of a distant but approaching storm. But a vast and even more ominous silence fell swiftly over the gathering on Finn's entrance.

He gestured for the hounds and his two companions to stop just within the door and went on alone, striding into the open area about the fire pit. As he moved, he was followed by hundreds of intent and solemn gazes. He returned none of them, only staring ahead as he circled the hearth.

His goal was the raised dais and its long table. Here sat the druids and bards of the Fian clans. Here also sat Goll MacMorna, who had left the seat of the captain pointedly empty, presiding from the seat at its right hand.

Finn climbed onto the dais, stopping before Goll.

"I thank you for this, Chieftain," he said graciously.

"It is only as you wished it," Goll answered in his frank way. "Say to us what you will, Finn MacCumhal."

Finn nodded. He turned, looking about him now, slowly scanning the grim faces as he spoke.

"Fighting men of the Fians, I understand what you feel on seeing my return. It was in anger that I left you. It was in madness that I abandoned you. I gave you insult, and I broke my oaths to you.

"I tell you now that I understand the obsession that held me. I had let my own desires, what I selfishly felt was my need to live my own life, come before the good of you and of all Ireland. I had given over my duty as your captain and denied the oath we all have taken. I've also come to know that my wandering quest for Sabd was a futile one.

"I've not lied to any man before, and I'll say the truth to you now: I still love Sabd, and I'll never cease to seek some way of finding where the Dark Druid has hidden her. But that search will no longer come before my duty as a warrior of the Fian, or before what I now know is my own life.

"Still, if I've always been a man of truth before, I've tried to be a man of justice, too. And for that reason, I'll not ask you to take me as your captain again."

This caused a sensation in the gathering. The sounds of amazement, of agreement, and, in a few cases, of protest filled the room. Finn raised his hands to silence them.

"No, my comrades," he said. "I will not. For the wrongs I've done you, I have forfeited the right to be your leader. I've not returned to Almhuin now to ask for that. I've come to ask for the help of the Fian warriors, for a single and maybe final time."

"Our help?" one of the chieftains called to him. "And just what is it you want from us?"

"I need your fighting skills to help me defend a family who may soon be destroyed," Finn answered. "The children of Midhir they are called. For many years they have been engaged in a bitter feud with others of the Sidhe. Now there are few of them left alive, and the whole of the Tuatha de Danaan will be coming against them."

There were mutterings of astonishment and dismay from many in the crowd, their meaning spoken aloud by Lughaid.

"Do you mean for us to go against the whole host of the Sidhe?"

"We can't do that!" Conan MacMorna loudly protested. "We've nothing to do with them."

"We do!" Finn argued. "The children of Midhir are still people of Ireland, like ourselves, and they need our help. All they want is freedom, and for this they've been unfairly attacked. Still they've fought on, through all the years, their numbers worn away, but stubbornly refusing to submit. All they want is what we ourselves have won, what we believe in and have given our oaths to defend. How can we let such people be destroyed?"

"It's a great deal you're asking of us, Finn MacCumhal," said another chieftain. "You berate us and abandon us, and now you return to ask that we follow you against a force whose power we can't even begin to guess!"

"He's right!" another said, looking around at the company. "We all saw the host of the Sidhe at the White Strand, sweeping through the great army of Daire Donn like a wind blowing loose straw from a path! Why, no men of Ireland have dared to challenge them since the last battle at Tailltin."

"They were defeated then," Finn countered.

"Were they?" one of the bards put in. "Some of the tales say that it was the de Danaans who chose to quit the fight and withdraw to the Hidden Places, from which they might plague the mortals at their ease. And others say that their powers have grown ever greater with the passing years."

"He may be right," added the gray-haired druid named Cainnelscaith. "Do we dare risk having the wrath of all the Sidhe falling upon ourselves? If we were destroyed, wouldn't that leave all Ireland lying helpless before them?"

There were many voices of agreement raised at that. Finn looked around him in open disbelief.

"Can I believe what I'm hearing?" he said. "Is this the men of the Fianna who sound so fearful? Why, it's the very size and the danger of this challenge that should bring you to accept! When I came here, I thought every man would leap to it, eager to have a chance at the greatest fight he has ever known."

He had their attention now. All listened intently to his words.

"Think of it," he went on in impassioned tones. "You're fighting men of the Fianna. Your whole life is seeking a challenge—especially a fight. You've defeated every mortal who has come against you. What worthy opponent have you left to try your swords against? Isn't this the great challenge you've all dreamed of? Can you call yourselves Fian warriors and not accept it?"

There was a murmuring of interest, of excited talk, of rising emotions, as the speech of Finn had its effect. Clearly he was appealing to many. Heads were nodding. Arguments were developing. A rumbling of talk grew swiftly louder.

Finn looked to Goll, impassive through all of this.

"And what about you, Chieftain of the MacMornas?" he asked. "Your clan is one of the fiercest in all Ireland. Will you join me in facing the hosts of the Sidhe?"

"I'll say nothing for my clansmen," Goll answered in his frank, reasoning way. "Though the cause may be a just one, what you're asking is not for the good of those we're bound to serve. The chieftains of the Fians have no right to lead their warriors into a choice. Each man must make it for himself, freely, and it's for us to accept whatever they decide to do."

"Your logic, as always, shows you the truth, my old friend," Finn told him.

He turned and looked around him at the gathering again. He saw the mixed expressions upon the arguing men. He saw the doubts and concerns and even fears in the stalwart faces.

"Men of the Fianna," he told them, "I said I'd not force you to this. Goll is right. This is not for Ireland's defense, or for the lords who pay us. This is for ourselves. It is for a chance to face an adversary more powerful than any we have ever known. It is for the chance to find out, finally, whether we can overcome the power we have so long wondered about, to face it as we face the nightmare terrors of our sleep, and, by defying them, banish them for good. It is our chance to prove ourselves the equal of any force. And it is our chance to help those who seek the freedom we've pledged our lives to protect."

The room was absolutely silent now, all hanging on his words. They rang out with great power in the vast room, true and clear and eloquent as the song of a high-bard.

"I'm telling no man that he must help me. But I have given my own word to help these people in their fight, and I'll die to keep that word if I must. When I leave here, with a host of fighting men or alone, it will be to face the Sidhe. I have betrayed you, but I am still your comrade. Whether you come with me or not, I'll understand."

He turned and strode from the room, leaving the others looking after him in silence. When he passed through the doors, it was only Caoilte, Cnu Deireoil, and the two hounds who followed.

"Well, warriors of Ireland," Goll said, looking around him at the assembly searchingly, "what will it be?"

The host of the Sidhe poured from the forest onto the circular plain and advanced upon the mound.

There were great companies of men afoot, each clad in flowing cloaks of its own brilliant color. And there were troops of horsemen on bright prancing steeds, silver rings brightly jingling on the hafts of their spears. Together they formed a most handsome army—slim, tall, fair warriors with gleaming weapons—but a formidable and grimly determined one as well.

Above them flew the children of the dark Morrigan, the raven goddess. Against the gray background of a heavy overcast, their squadrons seemed like tattered canopies of black cloth that drifted ominously over the future battle-field. They filled the air with shrill caws of anticipation, and their glinting eyes fixed greedily on the plain, eager for the first sign of the hot blood they thirsted after.

Toward the house of the children of Midhir the great force moved, their numbers filling all one side of the circular plain as they closed in about the mound, forming a sea of shifting, glittering men, so that the scattered monuments seemed like islands thrusting above the choppy waves.

Atop the mound, Donn's family and the physician named Luibra watched the coming tidal wave of men, the young warriors all armed and standing proudly, without a sign of fear. But against such a vast host, their paltry number seemed almost a joke, a hare planning to withstand a wolf's attack.

"I'm afraid even skills as great as mine couldn't save you from this!" Luibra commented.

"Thank Danu you have those skills," Donn said. "There will be many who'll have need of you today."

"I never thought I'd be saying this aloud," Moirrin told them, "but I feel afraid."

The healer put an arm about her shoulder in a comforting way.

"Be steady, my girl," he said. "It's out of our hands now."

When all the forces of the Tuatha de Danaan had been drawn up, Bobd Derg rode forward. With him were other kings of the many Sids, each one resplendent in his rich dress.

They pulled up their horses at the base of the mound, and Bobd Derg called to those above.

"Well, sons of Midhir, you have forced us to bring the whole host of the Sidhe against you once more. It is a sad thing for me. I had hoped we might be saved more bloodshed. I hoped that you might come to give up your foolish rebellion. Now, that cannot be."

"Where is your mortal?" Lir demanded, riding up beside the king. "He is the one I have come to face. Let us see him!"

A figure that had up to this point been concealed behind Donn's brothers now moved to the front, revealing himself as Finn MacCumhal. But the warrior who now stepped into the open was a far different looking man from the one who had faced Lir before. Now he was clean-shaven, his fair hair washed and bound and shining brightly even in the gloom. The Storm Shield hung upon his arm and the Mac an Luin was at his hip.

"Is that the one?" Bobd Derg said in surprise, looking to Lir. "Is that your ragged stranger?"

Lir was clearly nonplussed. He considered Finn carefully, then he nodded.

"Aye, that's the one. He was leaner and bearded before. But that's him."

"Then you are a fool, Lir," the king of the Sidhe said caustically. "The man who stands there is no simple mortal. He is Finn MacCumhal, Captain of the Fianna!"

"What?" said Lir in shock. And there were murmurs of surprise from those around him.

"He is," Bobd Derg said. "He has the de Danaan blood from his mother, Muirne, granddaughter to our own past king! The weapons he carries now he took from our King of the Country of Fair Men when none of our own champions could win them."

"Well, it's of no matter who he is," Lir said, managing to recover his blustering way. "If he's as powerful as you say, then his joining these rebels only makes things the more serious. I want my satisfaction."

"Very well," Bobd Derg said unhappily. He looked up to the captain. "Finn MacCumhal, will you pay log-anecht to Lir and withdraw your help from the sons of Midhir?"

"Will my doing so mean that they will be left in peace?" Finn asked.

"It will not," Bobd Derg told him with regret. "One way or another, their rebellion must be ended now."

"Then I will not give honor-price to Lir, for all my actions against him were fair ones"—he fixed the chieftain with a hard stare—"as he well knows. It is his dealings and your own with the Midhirs that have been unjust."

"We have only done what was needed to end their rebellion," the Sidhe chieftain protested.

"I had heard that the leader of the Tuatha de Danaan was a man of fairness and honor," Finn said. "Do you really mean to use all of your might to crush this tiny band of valiant people?"

"They've given me no other choice," Bobd Derg said heavily.

"Then I must stop you," Finn grimly replied.

"You are a brave man, Finn MacCumhal," the High-King said. "But can you think to withstand the Sidhe alone?"

"Not quite," Finn said.

He turned as Caoilte moved from behind the sons to hand him a long, curved horn made of beaten bronze. He put it to his lips.

It gave forth a long, low, single note that carried over the plain, echoing away. And then, from beyond the forest to the south, there came a rumbling. A surging mass spilled out onto the plain. It was the warriors of the Fian companies moving forward behind the Baiscne and MacMorna warriors, the silken banners of the many clans fluttering above.

They pulled up only a long spear's throw from the de Danaan force, filling all the other half of the plain. And so the two hosts of nearly equal size, Sidhe and Fian, took the measure of one another grimly.

"Has it come to this, then?" Bobd Derg asked Finn. "Do you mean to bring your warriors into this fight to help these people?"

"We do," Finn said. "They have been wronged and unfairly treated. They want only freedom, and you denied it. It is for us to defend freedom."

"You're interfering with our rights," said Lir angrily. "It's a great insult for your mortals even to defy us!"

"We would defy anyone who acts as you have," Finn retorted. "Even the winds and seas themselves!"

"Not since the final battles between the Gael and ourselves have mortal fighting men of Ireland dared to meet us in combat," Lir told him ominously.

"And since then you've become too full of power," said Finn, "too arrogant, too proud of yourselves and contemptuous of us. Most mortals have come to fear you or to worship you as gods. But we do neither. We are the Fianna!"

"You risk much here, Finn MacCumhal," warned Bobd Derg.

"So do you," Finn answered. "Back away now, for we will not."

"You know that we cannot back away," the High-King

of the Sidhe replied. "This is now more than the freedom of the sons of Midhir. It is the honor of us both at stake here."

"Do what you must," said Finn, "but don't think we'll be disheartened or beaten by your magic. The swords and spears and spirits of our good fighting men will withstand it."

"We will not use our powers against you," Bobd Derg said in indignation. "We are a fair people, no matter what you feel, and our fighting men are a match for your own without magic helping them."

He turned toward a shining company of silver-cloaked men massed close behind him.

"Withdraw, druids," he told them. "Raise no spell of rain or darkness or blood or wind to confound the warriors of the Fianna." He looked about him at his assembled kings. "This will be a test only of ourselves." He gave Lir an especially hard glare. "Is that understood?"

"I . . . It is, my king," Lir said, but with somewhat less enthusiasm than he'd evidenced before.

"Very well, then," Bobd Derg said to Finn. "Perhaps the time has come to see who holds the greatest power in Ireland."

"Likely the fates would have brought it upon us one day," Finn agreed.

"Then make ready," the king told him. "For when our forces meet, Ireland will likely never see a bloodier day!"

CHAPTER 25

Treaty

THE FIGHT WAS BRUTAL. THE TWO FORCES CLASHED together on the plain and their battle raged all about the hill. To the bloodthirsty ravens soaring overhead, it looked like a wild sea in a great storm, its surface surging and glittering with the violent movements of men and weapons.

Neither side showed any signs of giving way. The Fianna, used to driving back numbers many times theirs, now found themselves hard-pressed to hold their own against a host of nearly equal size. And the warriors of the de Danaan, themselves accustomed to sweeping aside mortal adversaries, were clearly astonished to have these keep up a stolid front before them.

Still, neither side showed any hesitation or any weakness in the fight. The slender, beautifully lethal de Danaan spears, their glinting points fashioned in the forges of the magic smith called Goibnu, were blunted against the stout, iron-bound Fian shields. The lovingly honed swords of the Fian fighting men, tested in scores of battles, bent and twisted against the elegant, frail-seeming blades of the Sidhe. Warriors of equal courage, strength, and skill fought toe-to-toe, locked together in thousands of single combats that seemed to have no easy victor.

Upon the mound stood the only observers of this savage spectacle: the healer Luibra and the daughters of Midhir, joined by the druids of the de Danaans, adversaries joined as one audience in this calm spot amidst the raging violence. Nearly deafened by the noise of rattling weapons and shouting men, they watched closely, horrified and fascinated at once by the conflict, eyes searching for those they knew in the milling mass.

Moirrin's eyes were fixed always on Finn, easily following his shining silver hair as he moved. He had led his own clansmen and the sons of Midhir in an attack directly against the de Danaan leadership.

They were face-to-face with them now, and Finn strode forward to confront the stout chieftain of Sid Fionnachaidh.

"Well, Lir," Finn said, "it's you who've brought this about, and all to repay the wrongs you claim I've done you. Go back before me now, or we must finish the fight that you and I began."

Lir looked from Finn to Bobd Derg, his expression uncertain. The High-King of the Sidhe gazed back with a resolute eye.

"It's the truth he's speaking," he said. "We've not come here to gain your own revenge for you. Accept his challenge now, if you've the will."

Lir's face reflected the complex emotions that filled him now. His fear of fighting Finn once more gave way to despair at the meaning of Derg's words, and then to a look of stoical resolve. Clearly, willing or not, the blustering man had no other choice if any honor were to be salvaged from the debacle.

He drew himself up into a fighting stance and, this time with no bragging word, moved upon his foe.

It was no easy fight for Finn. The huge chieftain's desperation generated an enormous power within him. He battered at Finn with sword and shield, dealing swift, massive blows that drove the younger warrior back.

Those fighting around them paused in their own combats to watch, none with more interest than Bobd Derg himself.

Finn retreated slowly, fending off the blows, not striking back at first. Soon the chieftain's initial surge of energy began to wane. The blows came more slowly. Lir began to pant with the exertion.

It was then Finn acted. He moved to one side, dropping his sword, leaving his chest exposed. Lir, seeing the opening, lunged forward, all his weight behind the thrust. But Finn sidestepped it. With a *humph* of expelled breath,

Lir sailed by. Finn swung around, slamming the Storm Shield against the chieftain. Lir staggered back, lost his footing, and crashed to the ground.

Finn bounded forward to stand above him, bringing up his sword to point at Lir's unprotected chest.

"If I strike this time, you will die, Lir," Finn told him. "It's ended now. But you can have your life. Surrender and forget your revenge."

The chieftain looked up to him, the anger of his defeat showing in his crimson face.

"I will not forgive your insults," he said. "And I will never yield. You've won, so kill me now!"

"I'll kill no defenseless man," Finn said, stepping back and lowering his blade point.

"You arrogant whelp!" Lir growled. With a surprising eruption of power, he lifted up, swinging his sword back for a cut at Finn. But Finn was swifter, his own weapon rising again, the point shooting forward to drive through the chieftain's heart.

Lir grunted and grew stiff. His arm stopped in mid-swing, the weapon falling from his hand. He shuddered, and then he toppled backward to the sod, sightless eyes staring upward to the iron skies.

Finn looked up to see Bobd Derg nearby, watching him from a circle of warriors, Sidhe and Fian alike, that had formed about the field of this contest. Finn stepped away from Lir's body and strode toward the High-King, stopping close before him to eye him challengingly.

"Well, High-King, is it you and I who must fight now?"

There, in the midst of the battle, the two leaders—the young captain and the ageless ruler of the Sidhe—took the measure of each other for a long moment while their warriors watched expectantly. Then Bobd Derg looked around at the battlefield where the two forces were still locked in a grim struggle, strangle holds upon one another.

"It will make no difference," he said slowly, earnestly, and regretfully. "If I kill you, or you me, or we kill one another, it will be the same. Look about, Finn. Our two forces are equal in this. No one can win. If the fight continues, it can only end with all of us measuring our lengths upon the bloody ground."

"It could be so," Finn acknowledged. "And I've no love for seeing my warriors or your own wasted."

"Lir has received his satisfaction," Bobd Derg said, "and he has paid for his mistakes. We are all men of Ireland here. To destroy one another would be a great wrong."

"But you wanted to destroy the sons of Midhir, your own people, only because they meant to have their freedom," Finn pointed out.

"Because they defied our rules," the Sidhe ruler corrected. "I thought that to allow it might have meant others could choose to do the same."

"And if they do?" Finn said. "What difference? This one, tiny group—"

"Say no more," Bobd Derg said with a smile. "You're sounding like my own father now. And your willingness to defend these proud rebels has made me see that he was right. Midhir is long dead, as are most of his clan. These few that are left have earned the right to freedom with their bravery. More shedding of blood would make no sense. So, Finn MacCumhal, if you will agree to a truce, we will talk of a final peace with them."

"I will agree, and gladly," Finn told him, sheathing his sword.

Bobd Derg did likewise. The two moved together, each man's sword hand stretching forth, clasping the other's wrist in a gesture of peace.

Each hand took a goblet and lifted it from the table.

Finn and Bobd Derg turned, lifting the goblets high, and looked around them with broad smiles.

The house of the children of Midhir was crowded with men, both the chieftains of the Fian clans and the kings of the many Sids mixed there, along with Donn and his own family, Cnu Deireoil, Caoilte, and the physician Luibra. All of them raised their goblets in reply.

"We salute the fighting men of the Tuatha de Danaan," Finn said. "Never have we faced warriors bolder or more skilled. From this day on, we'll consider them not as strange beings or sheoguey creatures from the hidden places, but as worthy adversaries and fellow men of Ireland as well. And should they wish to walk the surface of the earth, they'll have no resistance from us, but will be welcomed, for they've a right to it as much as we."

"We thank you for that, Finn MacCumhal," said the High-King of the Sidhe graciously. "But there are few of us who would choose to do so. We've become people of another world now and, alas, perhaps something besides men. Our powers would soon disappear if we were to leave the Sids which protect us, and not many would wish to give up what we have grown so used to over these centuries."

This brought smiles and murmurs of assent from many of his people.

"Yes," he went on, smiling himself, "the truth of it is that we've come to accept and even enjoy the way most of your mortals see us. They've forgotten that we were mortals ourselves long ago. The dim tales of us have been transformed to legends by your own bards. And since the men of Ireland now fear or respect or even worship what they think we are, I've a feeling they'd find it a bit uncomfortable, and maybe disappointing, to have us walking amongst them again."

He looked to Finn, a certain nostalgic tone entering his voice now. "No, my friend, the world has become a place only for your mortals. The real magic is fading, and maybe we'll fade with it one day. But I'm certain that it's larger and brighter the memory of you and the Fianna will become. What you are will keep living in the spirit of Ireland, even when your kind of man is gone from the world."

He looked around him once again, raising his voice to address all in the room.

"Our bond is made," he proclaimed. "From this day, the children of Midhir are free to live upon the earth. And from this day, the Fianna will deal as openly and equally with the Tuatha de Danaan as they do with the other men of Ireland. May the bards long relate the tales of the warriors who were not only champions over all the other mortals in the world"—he smiled in an ironic way—"but walked with the gods as well."

He touched his goblet to Finn's, and both men drank.

A cheer went up amongst the surrounding group, and the assembly fell to a general celebration. They mingled and talked, mortal and immortal telling tales, comparing weapons, exchanging great lies, laughing and drinking. And for that time they were as one great company, a sight never seen before in Ireland, or, indeed, ever seen since.

For Cnu Deireoil it was quite a reunion, with him greeting many old friends. For Caoilte and the others it was clearly a most exhilarating event. But Finn soon seemed to grow moody. After a time he left the celebration and slipped outside.

Below the mound and far across the plain the two hosts were absorbed in a celebration of their own, blending in a massive, single crowd where Fian and de Danaan fighting men became indistinguishable, sharing food and drink and fires. Finn watched them for a time, but the sight did little more to cheer him. Finally he moved around the house to a quieter spot and sat down on the hillside, staring toward the horizon thoughtfully.

"There you are," said a voice, and he looked up to see Moirrin standing beside him, looking down with an expression of concern.

"I . . . just felt a need to be away from the others for a little time," he said. He managed a faint smile. "After so long alone, I feel a bit strange in such a company. That must be it."

"Is it?" she asked. "Or is it that your own sorrow has come back on you, now that this is over?"

"Well, Cnu Deireoil did warn me that it would happen," he admitted.

"And so," she said, dropping down beside him, "what will you do?"

"I don't know," he said. "I vowed to myself that I'd not waste my life in useless wandering again. I know now that is madness."

"But if you never find your wife again," she ventured carefully, "will you ever forget? I mean . . . could you ever—"

He turned to her, taking her hand.

"I know your meaning," he told her. "If she had never been, then it would be you. I want you to believe that,

Moirrin." He shook his head regretfully. "But now, there's no way that can ever be."

She looked deeply, searchingly, into his eyes, and then she nodded.

"Yes," she said in a controlled and forthright way. "I understand. I had to talk to you. Before, just after you had remembered, you left here so quickly. I couldn't know how you felt. Now I know that you truly love her, and you'll not be happy until she has been found."

"But that may never come," Finn said in frustration. "I've searched the corners of Ireland for nothing. I have no way to find her."

"But you have," she said. "I have heard the whole story from Cnu Deireoil. I've told it to Bobd Derg. He has said that he could help you!"

"What?" Finn said excitedly. "When?"

"Just now," she told him. "But, Finn," she went on more hesitantly, looking away from him as if suddenly ashamed to meet his eye. "You must know this: I . . . I thought of not telling you. I thought that maybe you really didn't care for her. That maybe you had given up. I hoped that you might be . . ." She paused and shrugged. "Well, I just had to know." She fixed him with an anxious gaze. "Can you forgive me for my selfishness?"

"Moirrin, I understand," he told her earnestly. "I'm only sorry that—"

"No more of that," she said sternly. "I need no pity from you, Anlu—I mean, Finn MacCumhal. Be off with you now. You must be anxious to speak to the High-King."

He looked at her for a moment as if wanting to speak but not knowing what more to say. Finally he leaned forward and kissed her gently upon the lips. Then he arose and strode regretfully away.

She made no move to follow him. She only murmured, "Good-bye, Anluan," and sat staring out over the countryside.

As Finn rounded the building, he brushed past Luibra who was just coming around the other way. The physician paused to look after Finn, noting his eager expression. Then he went on to her.

"Well, that must have been good news for him," he said.

When there was no reply, he lowered his lanky form beside her. He put out a hand to her chin and gently but firmly turned her face to him. There were tears in her eyes.

"Let go," she said irritably, shaking her head to cast off his hand. "You've no healing for me."

"You might let me try," he said with a smile, putting a comforting hand upon her own.

That she let stay.

Meantime, Finn entered the hall and quickly sought out Bobd Derg.

"Moirrin said you might help me to find Fear Doirche," he said.

The talk around them stopped. At the sound of the dreadful name, Fian and de Danaan men alike turned to look at the two. Caoilte exchanged a look of consternation with Cnu Deireoil.

"I have heard your story," Bobd Derg said. "I feel deeply for you. The laws of the Tuatha de Danaan forbid anyone to reveal the location of another's Sid. But because of our new bond, and because of the great wrong he has done to you, I will help you."

"Do you mean you can tell me where he is?" Finn asked with eagerness.

"I can," the king answered. "But first, understand this, Finn: it is very dangerous. Few among us have his powers, and you will be facing him upon his own ground. You'll have very little chance against him."

Finn met his gaze with a grimly determined eye.

"Tell me!" he said.

six were still breathing.

Then gradient had sounds stopped abruptly. The town

CHAPTER◇26

The
Amulet

THE INFANT SLEPT PEACEFULLY, CURLED WITHIN ITS nest of twigs and leaves. For the rudeness of its bed, it seemed at ease and quite comfortable. More importantly, it seemed secure in the presence of the fawn that slept beside it, the animal's soft body curved around it for additional warmth in the tiny grotto.

Then something, something so faint it might have been more sense than sound, a disturbance of the aura of peacefulness or a scent of evil, snapped the fawn awake. It lifted its sleek head, its brown eyes fixed upon the opening of the burrow, its ears cocked, looking out to where a watery sunlight filtered in.

It held its position that way for a long moment, listening. Then, slowly, it unwound itself from around the sleeping child and climbed to its stalky legs. The baby stirred a bit, uneasily, and the fawn looked down toward it with a very human expression of concern. But it curled itself deeper into its nest and relaxed again and stayed asleep.

The fawn moved silently, carefully, out of the burrow, pausing just outside to look around. It was early. Morning light fell sluggishly through a heavy morning fog, turning it to swirling milky haze that filled up the small, steep-sided valley.

It was very still, even the sounds of morning birds were muffled in the fog. The fawn took a few tentative steps into the glade, looking around sharply, in a suspicious way, still listening.

Then the faint bird sounds stopped abruptly. The fawn stiffened, directing its attention straight ahead. The scraping sounds of footsteps were now audible, coming closer through the fog, and accompanying them, a sharp, rhythmic tapping. And then there was a shadow, a faint outline far away but moving swiftly nearer through the fog, taking on form and shape until its outline was clearly visible. It was a tall figure, wrapped and hooded in a long, dark robe against the chill. In one hand it clasped a rod of gnarled wood, polished to black and shining softly, using it as a staff as it strode forward with the long, arrogant stride of a master of its domain.

On coming in sight of the fawn, it stopped, a good distance away. It lifted its free hand to the hood and pulled it back, exposing the scarred countenance of the Dark Druid.

"Well, my little fawn, here I am again," he said in a grim way. "You have had more days of your lonely life here. And I have come to put my question to you once more. Will you agree to accept me? Will you give me your love and save both yourself and your child?"

The fawn's only response was to lift its head higher and fix its brown eyes firmly on him in a defiant glare.

His face grew darker in anger.

"You fool!" he said with venom, taking a step forward. "How long will you defy me? How long can you tolerate this?"

As if he had violated some invisible boundary in his forward step, the deer retreated, taking up a defensive position before the cave's mouth, body sideways to block him.

He made a gesture of disgust and stepped back.

"Phaugh! I'll not violate your precious safety. I'll come no closer. You have nothing to fear. But you cannot forever stay here. No"—his voice became insinuating—"no, you care for the child too much. Your own need to protect it will betray you. Soon it will crawl, and then walk. It will wish to leave, but it will have no place to go. It will wish to talk, but you will not speak to it. You will cry out for the ability to speak. You will not be able to explain to it. You will not be able to teach it to be human. You will watch it develop, helpless to act. You will watch it not learn to walk but to crawl, its legs and arms stunted, knobbed and bent. It will mewl and whine and snort. It will become a beast, a deformed creature as awful as the creations within my Sid, if it survives. And how long can you stand that, Sabd?"

In response she lifted her head a little more stubbornly.

"You are still defiant," he said. "Or you try bravely to seem so. But sooner or later you will realize that there is no other chance for you. No one will come to save you this time. No friend will help you to escape, and no one will ever find you here. I will keep trying. One day, Sabd, one day you will submit!"

He turned and stalked away into the mist. His footsteps, interspersed with the tap-tap of the stick on the rocky ground, faded away.

Once he was gone, the fawn turned and went back into the cave. It looked down at the sleeping infant, which, too long deprived of the familiar warmth and comforting presence and security of the fawn's body, was stirring restlessly, near to waking, its face wrinkled.

The fawn settled in softly around him again, its body surrounding him. It looked down at the face, and concern was in its eyes. All it could do was to nuzzle the baby softly and rock gently, moving the tiny form.

The infant relaxed, again sleeping contentedly. But the fawn did not go back to sleep. It stayed looking down at the child, a distinctly human helplessness and sorrow glowing in its dark eyes.

Bands of warriors marched away from the hill of the sons of Midhir, Fian clans with their chiefs, and Sidhe bands with their kings, dispersing to return to their own territories.

Just below the mound, the rest of the warriors were still gathered, making their own preparations to depart. Above them, Finn stood before the house with his comrades, Moirrin and Luibra, and others of the children of Midhir, watching the departures.

"Well, it looks as if the time's come for me to be starting off myself," Finn announced.

"Not alone," said Caoilte.

"This is something that only I must do," Finn told him firmly.

"You'll never succeed alone," Caoilte shot back. "You still need a guardian every moment of the day. Why, look what happened the last time you got out of my sight. No, Finn, if you're going, then so am I."

"I'm going as well," proclaimed the Little Nut.

"But it's even more dangerous for you than for Caoilte," Finn argued. "You're of the Sidhe. He'll have special reason for wanting to kill you."

"Don't waste your words, Finn MacCumhal," the harper told him stubbornly. "I may have won forgiveness from you, but not from myself. Until Sabd has been returned to you, and that black monster destroyed, I won't be content again."

Finn nodded.

"I understand," he said resignedly. "Though I wish it could be otherwise, I'll not stop you."

He turned to look at Moirrin.

"It'll be the hardest saying good-bye to you," he told her with great feeling. "I'll think of you."

"And I of you," she told him. She threw her arms about him in a great hug. "I wish good fortune to you, Finn MacCumhal. I thank you for the freedom you've given us. And I'll pray to Danu that you discover what you're seeking."

She stepped back, and he turned toward the physician, putting a hand on his shoulder in a last gesture of friendship.

"And what about you, Luibra?" he asked. "You're free now as well. What will you do?"

"Oh, I don't know," he said in a casual way. "This is a pleasant sort of place. I thought I might just hang about for a time." He looked at Moirrin with a broad grin. "I've gotten quite used to the people here."

She smiled in return, and Finn smiled too, nodding in an understanding way.

So, with their farewells complete, Finn and his companions moved down the hillside to where his own warriors and those of the Morna clan were gathered.

"Before we leave, Finn," Goll MacMorna said to him, "I wanted you to know that the chieftains of the clans have spoken to me. There's not a one of them that feels you shouldn't remain captain of all the Fians, including myself."

"It's a great honor you all do me," Finn answered, "but until this has been finished, I'll ask no Fian warrior to accept my leadership again. It's my request that you return to Almhuin and see to the running of the clans. If I don't return, then there's no better man to take the captaincy. If I do"—he shrugged—"well, then we'll see."

"Very well, Captain," Goll said, pointedly putting an emphasis upon the title. "I'll do as you've asked. But your chair at the feasting table will be empty until you return, as I know you will."

Lughaid now moved up beside them, facing Finn with a determined look.

"Finn," he said, "the others of our clan and I ask you to let us go with you."

Finn fixed a stern and scrutinizing gaze on the young warrior.

"Lughaid, you told me once that if I continued with my quest, it was as a madman and not your chieftain that I did it. I can't ask you to follow me now, and I don't expect any of my clansmen to risk themselves."

"I'll not apologize for those words," Lughaid said reasoningly. "Your quest then *was* a mad one. Still, there is some sorrow in us that we abandoned you. And now it's no aimless search you're going on. You mean to battle against the Dark Druid. It's much help you could be needing to succeed, and we—your clansmen, your sworn warriors, and your friends—we mean to go with you."

Finn smiled and clapped a hand to his shoulder.

"It's an honest man you are, Lughaid, and I'd be truly a madman to deny your help. Any warrior of the Baiscne who is willing can come and be welcomed."

"Finn!" called a voice then, and they turned to see Bobd Derg moving down the hill from the house of the Midhirs in company with Donn.

"Before you leave, I must speak once more with you,

and privately," the de Danaan king said as he reached the waiting men.

Finn moved away from the others, walking off a few paces with Donn and Bobd Derg as the others watched with curiosity. The king addressed the captain in a conspiratorial voice, his words grave.

"Fear Doirche, vile as he is, has broken no de Danaan laws, and I can ask none of my people to act against him."

"I didn't expect it," Finn said. "You've done enough in giving me the location of his Sid."

"Still," the king persisted, "I can't have you thinking that I condone what he's done to you. I've long wished for some excuse to destroy that creature and his evil lot myself. If you're intending to try to do so, then I feel bound to give you what help I can."

"What kind of help?" Finn asked.

"Very limited, I'm afraid," Bobd Derg said frankly. "First of all, you may find the Sid of the druid without much difficulty, but without de Danaan guidance, you will never be able to reach it. So, I've found a volunteer to go along with you." He gestured toward Donn.

"Donn?" said Finn, looking toward him.

"That's right," the young man agreed. "Bobd Derg can ask none of his own people, but I'm not bound by those constraints. I can take you through the druid's barriers and into his hidden place."

"But why should you risk yourself?" Finn asked.

"Because we owe a great debt to you, and I wish to pay it," Donn answered proudly. "It's a small enough return."

"But there is something else," said the Sidhe leader. "You may not even survive long enough to reach the druid's lair without some other help. You see, he has been watching you."

"Watching me?" Finn said and began to turn his head to look around.

"Careful," the king warned. "We can't let him know what I'm saying to you. Cnu Deireoil told me that he suspected this, and I'm convinced he is right. Fear Doirche has been spying upon you and knows your every move. When he realizes you are starting toward him once again, he will use every kind of magic and treachery against you. You've already had a taste of his powers."

"But what can we do against them?"

"Well, I can't give you a magic to counter his, but I can at least give you a chance to reach him unharmed. I think I have a means to blind him. He'll have no way to know when you are coming against him, or from where, or in what numbers, at least until you are very near to him. From there, you will be on your own."

"Of course, I'll gladly accept your help," Finn told him. "But what do you mean to do?"

From a leather pouch, Bobd Derg pulled a round amulet of glowing red stone, holding it palmed so that only Finn could see.

"This should counter Fear Doirche's magic. At least, I hope so. We can only see."

"How?" Finn asked.

"Just walk back to your men. Continue your preparations to depart," Bobd Derg advised. "I'll see to the rest."

Meanwhile, from a vantage point high above the plain, the Dark Druid and his seer stood looking down upon the departing hosts.

"You see?" she said, sweeping a hand over the scene. From their height, the streams of warriors flowing out in all directions from the central mound looked like wheel spokes radiating from a hub. "They are all dispersing. Their great war is ended."

"And leaving MacCumhal alive," the druid said angrily. "Where is he?"

She swept a hand forward and the bubble swooped down closer to the group.

"Here he is," she said, suspending it close above the Baiscne group.

"Back with his warriors again, and quite as fit as ever he looked," Fear said unhappily. "Oh, Miluchradh, you have truly failed me. Now he has his memory again, he has been reunited with his warriors, and he has gained the friendship of Bobd Derg. He is more powerful than ever!"

"Look here," she retorted. "In what I did, I succeeded. None of this is my fault. Anyway, he's no greater threat to you now than he ever was."

"No threat? And where do you think he'll be coming now?"

"You mean here?" she asked him in surprise. "But how? You don't believe Bobd Derg might tell him? Betray the oath and reveal another Sid to mortals?"

"I do. There's no love between our good High-King and myself. He's long been jealous of my power. If there is any chance Finn has learned of my whereabouts, I need to know it. So, my dear, keep a close watch upon your captain." He tapped her arm lightly but meaningfully with the knob of his druid rod. "And don't fail me this time. Stay close. Stay very close."

Down on the plain, the last of the groups were preparing to start out. Bobd Derg stood at one side of the Baiscne men with Finn, apparently watching them, but surreptitiously casting searching glances up at the skies about him.

Finally, he seemed to note something. His eyes fixed upon one point for an instant, then shifted quickly away.

"What is it?" Finn asked, noting his odd move.

He started to lift his head to look as well, but the king stopped him.

"No, Finn. Don't look yet. I think I've discovered what I was seeking. There is something floating above us now. Glance up and to your left, but do it carefully. Don't make a big show of it."

Finn casually glanced up. He almost missed it, but then, against the edge of a drifting cloud, he noted it: a faint spot of distortion, like the wavering caused by heat.

"I see something," Finn said. "A pale circle of shimmering light?"

"That's it," said the king. "I'm certain that it's the way the druid is watching you. It's a magical force of some kind, projected by a woman of the Sidhe, a druidess and seer called Miluchradh. She left us to join him years ago as a result of her rather bizarre practices and unusual appetites."

"A dark woman?" Finn asked with curiosity. "Very beautiful?"

"Ah, I see you've met her," the king said, eyeing him meaningfully.

"He has that," Cnu Deireoil put in with a leering smile.

"It really wasn't me," Finn protested quickly. "But what happens now?"

"Now, you simply watch," Bodb Derg replied. "We'll have to wait and see if this light comes closer. I may only have one chance, and I want to be certain it's a success."

Back in the druidess's lair, the two were still observing the preparations.

"It looks to me as if they're nearly ready to start away from here," she said. "Most likely they'll go to the south, back toward his home."

"I don't trust him," Fear said. "You keep watching. And stay closer. Closer, I said!"

"Yes, yes!" she responded with annoyance. "Closer!"

Then, with obvious intent and a malicious smile, she waved downward sharply. This caused the bubble to drop with stomach-wrenching abruptness to within a spear's throw of the ground. The druid's face tightened with a spasm of nausea.

"I'll stand no more of this place," he said irritably. "Inform me at once when you've discovered where they're bound," he ordered, and turned to stride out of the room.

Below, noting that the faint shimmer had dropped very low, Bodb Derg lifted the amulet up, the jewel dangling from his hand.

"All right," he said to Finn. "Be ready. I'm not certain just what will happen now."

Then, in a swift move, he swept the jewel high, holding it up toward the round, shimmering patch.

The druidess saw his move and her gaze went to the amulet. She froze, her eyes widening with shock as they registered what it was he held.

"No!" she screamed in terror, leaping to her feet. "No!"

Below her, the amulet flared suddenly with an intense ruby light.

CHAPTER ◊ 27

Blinding
the
Druid

THE LIGHT SPOUTED FROM THE ROUND AMULET IN A stream, growing broader as it shot upward.

From inside the crystal sphere of Miluchradh, it seemed as if it were a ball of energy that was rising toward her with incredible speed. The druidess desperately waved her hands upward in an attempt to lift the sphere to safety, but her reaction was too slow. The beam struck. There was an explosion that shattered the fiery stream into a thousand tendrils of blue-white lightning that spread out around the sphere with an intense crackling of power.

From below, the Seer's bubble became suddenly visible as a solid, red-tinged sphere, encircled, entrapped, by the flickering network of lines.

Within, the curved glass walls were turned a shimmering, blinding white. Miluchradh screamed in agony; a long, shrill sound, met and matched and drowned by a sharp sizzling as energy flaring around the sphere's circumference began to flash inward. Bolts of light from every side shot in like spears, all toward Miluchradh, drawn to the source of the sphere's existence, seeking the magic heart of its power.

They attached to her, actually seeming to sink into her flesh like barbed points. She froze, stiffening as they caught her, enmeshed her, pulled her up taut and held her rigid but vibrating from the energy coursing through her, over her, pulsing about her, filling up the ball. They formed another writhing web of lights with her, the captive fly, at its center.

Her eyes, dazzlingly aglow with the blue light that filled them, fixed on Fear Doirche.

"Help . . . me!" she managed to cry out.

The Dark Druid was for a moment held fascinated, horrified at the sight. But as the light swiftly intensified, he turned away, leaping into the corridor.

She tried again to scream after him, but was now too imprisoned by the enveloping power, her open mouth filled with coiling serpents of light.

The Dark Druid started up the corridor at a run as the light flared behind him. But he took only two steps before there came an enormous explosion.

A wind blasted up the tunnel, knocking him down, washing a torrent of wind, light, and debris over him.

In the main cavern, the creatures of the Dark Druid looked up as the sound of the explosion reached them. They saw the torrent it created shoot from the tunnel mouth, knocking the ram-headed guards aside and jetting far out into the air of the vast space, ends curling back like a flicking tongue, before it faded.

At the same time, but some distance away, the party of Finn MacCumhal watched the fingers of lightning flicker around the reddish sphere, grow for an instant brighter, like a meteor in its final plunge, then die away, leaving an empty sky.

"Well, that's gone, anyway," Bobd Derg said with satisfaction. "If I was right, the Dark Druid won't be using that method to spy on you again."

"Aye, but he might have other ways," Cnu Deireoil said.

"Once you're beneath the umbrella of forest about the man's lair, you should be able to approach him," the king replied. "It'll be more difficult for him to set traps."

"Then it's time for us to be going," Caoilte put in. "The more swiftly we come against him, the more chance we will have to keep him off guard."

So, making their final farewells to the others, Finn's company left the plain of Midhir's children, heading toward the north and west. The warriors and the hounds moved at such a rapid pace that the horse of Cnu Deireoil nearly galloped to keep up.

Meantime, in the druid's lair, the crumpled form of Fear Doirche slowly stirred. Debris matting his back fell away as he sat up and then, with an effort, levered himself to his feet.

He was unhurt, but much ruffled and clearly shaken. He looked around dazedly. It was dark in the corridor. The torches had been blown out, and there was only a faint glow coming from the opening to the chamber of the glass sphere. The only sound was the rising voices of commotion from the astonished inhabitants in the outer cavern.

Fear stepped back to the opening into the sphere. Here he stopped, staring ahead, eyes wide with shock. The curved walls had lost all but the faintest glow. Their polished surfaces were crazed or scorched dark, like a glass bead suspended in a fire, from the enormous power that had been directed back through the sphere by the amulet of Bobd Derg.

And, in the center of the floor, upon the scorched and still smoldering remains of once plush cushions, lay crumpled a tattered, blackened form.

He stepped toward it. Impossibly, it shifted. Agonizingly, it moved. Slowly, slowly, a head rose up, lifting a face toward his.

It could barely be called a face. All its wealth of hair, its lashes and eyebrows had been burned away. The flesh of the face had been withered, its fullness sucked from it, its nose whittled to a sharp beak, its teeth protruding, leaving it little more than a skull. Indeed, the whole body, revealed by the shredded gown, had been horribly wasted, the skeletal remains of the once lush form covered by a dry, wrinkled skin like crumpled parchment. It was as if, when the life force she used to power the sphere had been reversed upon her, it had drained her vitality, leaving her a mummy, but a living one.

She lifted a bony hand toward him in a gesture of supplication. Her lipless mouth moved as if she were trying to speak. Then she fell back, breathing loudly through the wasted remnant of her once elegant nose. But her eyes, like polished marbles glinting in the dark pits of her sockets, stayed fixed upon him.

He stared at her a moment, the shock his face had first registered changing to intense revulsion. Then, abruptly, he turned his back on the pitiful wreck and strode out of the room. Propelled by a great urgency, face set, he rushed down the tunnel and out onto the landing. Some of the druid's people were swarming up the stairs in response to the blast. A large crowd of others were milling excitedly about below. He leaned over the rail, shouting out to them in a voice that echoed in the vast space: "Send out the warriors! Send out the bears and the pookas!"

They looked up to him. He was a wild and desperate-seeming figure there, his long form bent far out over the open space, his torn robe and his tangled hair fluttering about him.

"Double the guards about the mount!" he ordered. "Watch all the perimeters of my domains. Keep careful watch. I must know of anyone approaching us! Be on guard! All of you, be . . . on . . . guard! Finn MacCumhal must be coming here!"

He turned and saw the two ram's-headed guardians of the seer struggling to their feet, still bewildered by the blast.

"And, you two," he said brusquely, gesturing up the corridor, "go in there, and take care of that!"

"There!" Donn at last said, pointing ahead. "There is the place Bobd Derg told me of. There is Ben Guailbain."

Finn stared curiously ahead. On the horizon, thrusting up from the forests, was a ridge of purple-gray mountains, its southern end rising into a knobbed peak.

"But I've seen that place before!" Finn exclaimed. He looked to Caoilte. "Haven't we?"

"Aye, we have," the dark warrior agreed. "And it was just before we were waylaid at that lake, there, in those woods farther to the south."

"No wonder, then," said Donn. "He knew that you were getting close. That's why he acted against you. Well, this time he won't see you. Still," he added cautiously, "he's bound to be on guard, and it'll be a dangerous journey for us once we reach the outer boundary of his domains. From there, we will go most carefully."

They moved on, still sweeping along at a swift pace, the sturdy Fian warriors showing no signs of fatigue.

They entered the forested lands that lay just before the mount, pushing on through the more rugged country of hills and lakes, into ever denser growth. They went more slowly now, more warily, mindful of watchers or traps.

Then, suddenly, ahead of them, a shape reared up in the bushes. Before any of them could react, it dove out, rushing between them and knocking them aside, then darting away. It looked to the casual eye like a great stag, but the quick-eyed Cnu Deireoil spotted the strange, catlike feet of it as it leaped across a bush, and he knew the truth.

"Look there!" he shouted. "A pooka! Stop it! It'll warn the druid!"

Finn and his party were after it at once.

It bounded through the trees, but so large was it that it had heavy going, the dense underbrush slowing it down. In the open, it might even have outrun them all. As it was, all of the others of Finn's party dropped behind, leaving only Finn, Caoilte, and the hounds to keep on, slowly catching up with it.

It crashed along, straining to get ahead, but they continued closing. Then it gave a shout, in a coarse but distinctly human voice that brought looks of surprise to Finn and Caoilte.

"Oy oy! Aengus! Take off! Take off! It's them!"

Just ahead another beast, this one like a great wolf, lifted from the brush, turned a startled face toward them, then turned and ran.

"Caoilte, you and Sceolan get that one," Finn shouted, pointing toward the stag. "Bran, with me!"

He and one hound veered off after the second creature while the other pair kept on after the first.

The staglike pooka, seeing its pursuit cut in half, now turned on Caoilte. It reared up. The form of it began to change right before him, bulding in a grotesque way, legs thickening, lengthening, forelegs filling out to brawny arms, stag's face thrusting outward into a long snout, fangs erupting from the lengthening lower jaw.

"My Danu!" Caoilte breathed, looking up at the growing thing. Then, prudently deciding not to wait for it to become whatever monstrous creature it was changing to, he simply heaved his spear at it with all his force.

Its point slashed deep into the belly of the pooka, seeming to rend it. The whole being convulsed and, as if it were a punctured wineskin, began to sag down. As it did, it began to go through a rapid series of shape shifts, a plethora of animal parts altering, mixing, jerking the animal about so violently it seemed as if it would be torn apart. It ended, suddenly and finally, in a horrible mixture not even recognizable. The pooka shuddered one last time and then, mercifully, was still.

Meantime, Finn and Bran were pursuing the other creature. As a wolf, it was lither and speedier in the brush. Only by their greatest efforts did Finn and the hound keep it from gaining on them.

It dodged and turned for some while, trying to lose the pursuit, but without luck. Finally, when the thing realized it couldn't shake them off, it desperately tried something else. When it reached the next opening, with a good patch of open sky showing above, it began to transform.

It was far enough ahead to effect this change before Finn and Bran came up, and it was clear why it needed open space. It swiftly sprouted enormous wings and tail and, not even taking time to alter the wolf's body shape, leaped upward, flapping madly to pull itself from the ground.

Finn and Bran came into the open just as it started to rise. Finn cast his spear, but the pooka was far enough up already to maneuver, swooping around in a tight bank to dodge the spear. This lost it altitude, however, and it began to flap again, straining to lift itself out of their reach.

Bran, moving ahead of Finn, leaped for a dangling leg and missed. Finn dropped the Storm Shield, crouched and made a leap of his own as it came over his head, grabbing on to a leg with one hand. But the creature, by an immense effort, still managed to flap higher, lifting him up with it.

It rose slowly, fighting to get above the trees, but Finn's weight was too much. Suddenly exhausted, one of its wings folded and it went over, sweeping down to crash into the upper branches of a large oak.

In a tangle of branches and wings and flailing limbs Finn and the pooka fought. The creature struck out with claws and teeth. Finn tried to swing away from its reach long enough to draw his sword. It snapped out and he pulled back, nearly falling, clutching a branch to dangle by only his right hand.

He looked up to see the creature altering to the shape of a great cat. Claws shot out to grip the tree firmly, and it began slinking out toward him, grinning evilly.

He felt for his sword hilt with his left hand. The cat prepared to leap. His hand closed on the weapon as it sprang. It hurtled toward him as he, in a single move, pulled out the sword, swinging it up. The pooka crashed against him, its own weight driving his blade through its breast to erupt from its backbone. Locked together, the two tumbled from the tree, crashing to the ground.

Finn lay still a moment beneath the creature, his breath knocked from him. Bran came up to nose at him anxiously.

"I . . . I'm all right, lad," he finally gasped out. And with a grunt of effort, he rolled the heavy carcass off him.

Caoilte came into the clearing with Sceolan, and they rushed to him.

"Are you all right?" the dark warrior asked, helping Finn up.

"When all my breath comes back to me," Finn answered, panting. "What about the other one?"

"Dead," Caoilte said tersely.

"Let's hope there are no more," Finn said. He looked up and pointed. "There's still a way to go."

Above the trees, to the west, the rounded crest of the mount loomed ominously.

This time the fawn did not hear the noise until it was close outside the cave.

It looked up in alarm as a shadow fell across the

entrance. Rising from the resting infant hurriedly, it rushed outside, stopping just before the opening.

There stood the Dark Druid, closer to the cave this time, watching. He was grimmer than before, his look still a bit harried, a bit more desperate. He fixed a firm gaze upon her and his voice was hard.

"I've come to give a final choice to you, Sabd. Give up your stubbornness. Come to me now, of your own will." He put out a hand palm up, fingers extended. "Just touch this hand that I hold out to you in love, in worship. Do it and I will give you your own form, and you can live in comfort with your child."

She stepped back before the doorway as before and stood proudly erect, head lifted, dark eyes blazing in defiance.

His look grew dark. A sudden fury blazed in his eyes.

"Then enough!" he said. "I will play no more games with you. I have no more patience and no more time!"

He swept forward, thrusting out his stick. She might have leaped away, but she stayed protectively before the cave, seemingly more concerned for the infant than herself.

The stick touched her. It seemed to freeze her.

"Now!" he said in triumph, "I have you, and if no other way, then in my own! You'll come with me. You have no will to refuse me, Sabd. As before, you cannot escape." He gestured behind him with the staff. "Come!"

As if an invisible leash about her neck was hauling upon her, the fawn went with dragging, reluctant steps, following the point of the rod.

But as the poor creature moved away from the opening of the cave, there came a sound from within it. The infant, perhaps sensing its loss, feeling loneliness or fear or the cold, stirred uneasily and began to whimper. They were soft, faint sounds of discomfort at first, but they built quickly as they went unanswered.

The fawn, with what was clearly an immense effort of will, began to turn her head. Either the cry was stronger than the spell, countering some of the effect, or the spirit of the mother gave her the power. But, either way, her head came around by agonizing degrees, the dark eyes fixing with great anguish on the cave.

"Forget the child, Sabd," the druid said with cruelty. "It won't be coming. If you mean to refuse me, then I'll leave you nothing to remind you of your Finn. If you force me to take you, I'll see every part of him destroyed, including his child. I'll see that all you will have left to you is me!"

At that, he gave a hard jerk forward with the rod, forcing the fawn more rapidly along.

The cries became a wail now as the baby realized it was not to feel any comfort. The fawn continued to look back as it was drawn on, on, inexorably on . . .

The pair moved out of the glade, up the steep hillside, leaving the child crying in its nest, alone, as its mother disappeared.

CHAPTER ◊ 28

Ben Guailbain

"AH, WELL, IT DOESN'T SEEM TOO MUCH FARTHER NOW," the young warrior Lughaid said flippantly.

Indeed, the grim mountain was now largely visible ahead as the party moved onto the uplands right about its base.

"Don't ever be too certain when it's the Tuatha de Danaan you're dealing with," Donn cautioned. "In fact, I'd say that we'd best start being more caref—"

His voice cut off abruptly. A strange blurring of the countryside occurred, suddenly, in a wrenching move, as if they had been violently whirled around.

The sensation stopped with another, shocking wrench, leaving them all staggering.

"By the great gods," said Lughaid, "what happened?"

"The earth itself shifted about on us, so it did," said another warrior.

"But . . . what happened to the mountain?" said a third, pointing ahead of them in shock.

Where it should have been, looming up before them, there was now only a line of trees and empty sky.

"By Danu, we can't have lost it?" Lughaid said.

"And so you haven't!" Cnu Deireoil said with a laugh. "Look over there."

He pointed behind them. They all turned to see the mountain rising there, and seemingly a bit farther away than it had been.

"But that can't be!" Lughaid said in a bewildered way. "It was just ahead of us!"

"We've been sent Astray," Donn told them.

"Astray?" asked a young warrior. "What's that?"

Donn sighed over the man's incompetence and looked to Cnu Deireoil.

"Would you explain it?" he said impatiently.

The little man genially complied.

"It's a magical protection all the Sids have," he explained. "Only those of the de Danaans know how to pass through it without the owner's permission."

"Yes, but this took even me by surprise," said Donn, eyeing the mount thoughtfully. "I didn't expect the druid's aura to extend out quite so far. He surely must be very powerful."

He looked around at the group with a severe eye. His voice took on a sternly lecturing tone.

"Now, listen carefully—everyone must stay very close to me. I can get us through this, but I must concentrate all my attention on that mount. You will not look around you but only at me. If you fail to do so, even for a moment, you may be separated from us and lost!"

It was in a very tight group that they proceeded then. They went slowly, man and hound all staring at the young son of Midhir. He walked stolidly on, keeping his eyes fixed firmly on the mountain of the druid, face tensed in a frown of concentration. They closed upon their goal without further incident.

At last they came to the end of the forest. Close upon the base of the cliffs, the trees petered out, leaving a wide band of open, rocky slope about the mount. The company stopped well within cover.

"Stay hidden," Finn advised his companions. "The Dark Druid may have watchers on the mountain. We don't want him knowing we're here just yet."

"This Dark Druid lives in there?" Lughaid asked, peering out from cover at the brooding pile of stone.

"He does," Donn answered. "Somewhere within that hill lies his Sid. But that's all Bodb Derg could tell me. No other of the de Danaans, save the outcast ones, has been within it."

"Do you think that Sabd is in there, Finn?" Cnu
Deireoil asked.

"If she's not, he'll tell me where she is," Finn told him
grimly.

"But just how are we supposed to get at him?" Caoilte
wondered.

"There must be an entrance somewhere," Donn said.

They scrutinized the face before them carefully. It
sloped steeply upward, some of it rocky, some sparsely
covered with grass and brush. Donn shook his head.

"It doesn't look promising at all here," he said. "Follow
me."

They moved on about the mount, slowly, staying well
within the cover of the trees, pausing here and there so
the son of Midhir might make further examinations of the
slopes. They stared out at section after section, his attention fixing most closely on the portions which were steeper
and more bare. And the longer this process dragged on,
the more often did Caoilte exchange looks of impatience
with Finn.

Finally Donn stopped for a long while to stare out at a
large, smooth, nearly vertical area of cliff face. After a
thorough inspection, he nodded.

"There," he said, "I think that's it."

"You think?" said Caoilte.

"I can't say for certain," the son of Midhir replied
defensively. "The druid has it well hidden."

"Then just how is it we're supposed to get in?" Caoilte
asked again.

"I don't know," Donn tersely replied.

"Well, a great help you are," Caoilte said irritably. "I
thought you were supposed to know!"

"Only if Fear wants me to," he replied as if he were
speaking to a particularly stupid child. "Most de Danaans
don't hide Sid entrances from one another. He does. And
even if I could find it, I couldn't open it without his letting
me."

"Well, that's just grand, that is," said Caoilte in frustration. "A lot of good it did us to creep here so stealthily. We
can't get in, and even if we move into the open, he'll know
where we are."

Donn gave him a most disapproving glare.

"You certainly have one of the most gloomy outlooks I have ever encountered," he said.

"At least I'm not useless to us."

"Useless?" Donn repeated indignantly. "Why you—"

"Never mind," Finn said sharply. "If we can't open the entrance, then we'll just have to get Fear Doirche to do it for us."

"What?" said Caoilte in surprise, looking to him. "Do you think he's going to open up, knowing you're out here?"

"He might," said Finn, "if he doesn't know how many of us there are."

"What do you mean?" Caoilte asked suspiciously. "You haven't had another of your reckless notions, have you, Finn?"

"It might be I have," he said thoughtfully. He looked to the son of Midhir. "Donn, how hard would it be for me to open the entrance from the inside?"

"Oh, no," Caoilte said, shaking his head, "It's worse than I thought."

"For you it might be impossible," Donn said. "But I'm certain I could manage it once I saw its workings."

"I can't ask you to risk yourself," Finn said.

"You're not. It's my own choice. Besides," he added, "If you want to have your best chance at success in this, you'll have to take me."

"You're meaning to get that druid to let the two of you in and then try to open the door for us?" Caoilte said. "Maybe they were right to call you mad, Finn."

"No, Caoilte," said his friend earnestly. "This must work. He doesn't know how many of us there are. Maybe he will let me in, if he thinks I'm no danger to him."

"He'll just kill you."

"Maybe not before we can let the rest of you in."

"You'd be taking far too great a risk," Caoilte protested. "Why go inside alone? If you can trick him into opening the Sid, we could rush from cover and charge through behind you."

"You've too far to run," Finn countered. "It might give

him time to slam his door closed in your faces, and that would be our finish. Besides, Sabd could well be in there with him. If he's threatened by an attack, he might harm her. But if I'm inside, I might have a chance of getting to her . . . of protecting her."

"No you wouldn't," Caoilte said forcefully. "Not a chance at all . . . alone."

"What do you mean?" said Finn.

"I mean that you've got no idea what kind of force you'll be facing in there. We know that he at least has a company of warrior creatures. You and Donn can't battle them, rescue Sabd, and open the door to us. You need more help."

"But if we take too many with us, it's not likely the druid will be letting us in," Donn pointed out.

"Caoilte doesn't mean a company," Finn told him with a grin. "He means just one"—he looked to the dark warrior—"don't you, Caoilte?"

"I do," he agreed, and gave a heavy sigh. "And who else is fool enough to be forever leaping into the flames beside you?"

The two hounds moved in closer then, sitting up and drawing Finn's eye to them. They whimpered urgently.

"Good thinking, lads," Caoilte said to them. "We can take the hounds as well," he told Finn. "If the druid doesn't know how intelligent they are, he'll not think them dangerous."

"I don't know," Finn said with misgiving.

"But they can help to protect Sabd if there's a chance," Caoilte argued.

That seemed enough to sway Finn. He nodded.

"All right," he said. "You four, then. But that's all. The rest will stay out here."

"And what about me, Finn?" said Cnu Deireoil. "I might be able to give help to you."

"You, Cnu Deireoil? But why should you risk yourself?"

"I have to, Finn, don't you see?" he said. "I was of the Sidhe. I might be able to help you fight the druid . . . somehow. You've got to let me do something!"

Finn put a hand upon his arm.

"My friend, I appreciate this, but it's too dangerous. Donn can give me all the help to fight him. Stay here."

"But Finn—"

"I said, stay here," Finn said firmly, and the little man sat back, looking sullen.

"Now, Lughaid," Finn said briskly, turning to the young warrior, "you keep the men here until you see that entrance open—"

"*If* it opens," added Caoilte darkly.

"I agree with Donn about your gloominess," Finn replied. "But, as I say, Lughaid, *when* the Sid opens, you must lead our warriors in."

"Aye, Finn," the other said earnestly, striking a gallant pose and gripping his sword hilt. "We'll be ready."

"I know you will," said Finn. He looked to the ones who would accompany him. "Let's go, then."

The five left the group and moved through the trees until they were well away from the others. Then they moved boldly out from cover and up the hillside toward the cliff face.

"Just how is it we're going to convince him to let us in?" Caoilte asked.

"He has more than one score to settle with me," said Finn. "I mean to give him his chance to do it."

"What's stopping him from just blasting us with a thunderbolt right before his cliff?" the warrior asked.

"Nothing," Finn answered frankly. "But if I judge him rightly, his own pride would never permit it. He's been humiliated more than once. He's tried to kill me and failed. He'll not pass a chance to have me close, to make me squirm before his people, as I did to him."

"I hope you're right," said Caoilte with some doubt.

"So do I," Finn answered fervently.

They reached the base of the cliff, looked up at the ominous, frowning face of it uncertainly.

"I don't see anyone," said Caoilte.

"They're there," said Donn. "Go ahead, Finn. He'll hear you."

Finn lifted his voice and shouted.

"Fear Doirche, let us in!"

* * *

Sabd cowered back into the cushions as the Dark Druid advanced upon her threateningly.

"Get back from me," she cried in desperation.

"Oh no, my love," he said. "None of your pleading will keep me away this time. I've put the human form upon you again for only one reason. If I can have you no other way, then it will be this one!"

He dropped down beside her. A hand shot out to grip her arm and he pulled her toward him. She bent back as far as she could in an effort to escape.

"You'll have nothing!" she told him. "I'll die first."

"My touch won't kill you," he replied, seizing her other arm. "And your struggling will only bring you more pain. I don't want that, but nothing will stop me now."

He pulled her closer, his face moving toward hers.

She fought to break his hold, but it was in vain. She could not break loose. She was weakening. There was no escape.

"Wait . . . wait!" she gasped out. "My . . . my baby!"

He pulled back a little, his shrewd gaze on her.

"Your baby? What about it?"

"If . . . if you are right, that I am abandoned," she said reluctantly, "if there is no other hope left to me, then . . . then I cannot let him die."

"So, your pride is finally softening?" he said with hope.

"I can't bear to let him die alone there," she admitted despairingly. "He's all that I have left. If you promise to truly care for him, then if I must surrender to you, I will. I'll buy my baby's life any way I must."

"Very well," he said, smiling greedily. "But you must prove that willingness to me!"

"I'll do as you wish," she said in agony. "You have my promise. Only, bring my baby to me."

"It will survive a while longer," he said callously. "First you must prove what you have said. You must prove it now."

She dropped her head, her body sagging limply in surrender. "Very well," she said brokenly. "If that's what I must do. I give myself to you, Fear Doirche."

He smiled, rising to his feet. He looked down gloatingly at her, his lustful gaze roving across her as he began to unfasten his robe.

"I've waited a very long time for this," he said slowly, savoringly.

"Master! My master!" cried a cat-headed guard, rushing into the chamber.

Fear wheeled on him angrily.

"Fool! What do you mean, disturbing me in here?"

"But it is Finn MacCumhal!"

"What?" he cried, stepping toward the man.

"Finn?" she said with astonishment, sitting up.

"He's outside our entrance now, master," the guard went on. "Calling for yourself he is."

The druid shoved past him, out of the room. The guard followed, and so did an eager Sabd. They went around and up the stairs to a corridor on the cavern's farther side. It led to a niche where a narrow opening allowed a view down the hillside.

Just below stood Finn and his companions.

"Fear Doirche!" Finn was calling. "I have come to see you. Let me in!"

Sabd moved to the slit and looked down. Her face lit up with her ecstasy. She tried to call out.

"Finn!"

But at a gesture from the druid, the guard seized her and pulled her back from the opening.

"So, he is not dead," she said triumphantly. "He has found you."

"It will do him no good," Fear said. "He was a fool to come. Now I can crush him." He lifted his druid rod.

"What?" she said fearfully. "You mean to do it so?"

"I have taken enough chances with him," the druid growled in reply.

"After your bragging to me? After your claims of your superiority over him?" she said. "After he humiliated you, you'll not face him?"

The druid looked down toward Finn again. A series of images ran through his mind: his defeat in Finn's hall, the warnings of Miluchradh, the destruction of the seer's sphere.

"He is dangerous," Fear said, the point of the rod lifting higher. "Too dangerous."

"You are afraid," she said harshly.

It was like an arrow shot. He was jolted and wheeled toward her, replying in an outraged, defensive way, "I am afraid of no one."

"Then show me," she said challengingly. "If you would gain any admiration from me, face him. Prove what kind of a man you are!"

"I will, then!" he said with force. He turned to the balcony, shouting down to the cavern's floor: "Open the entrance. And have a guard ready to give escort to Finn MacCumhal and his company." He turned to her, extending an arm. "Come, my dear fawn," he said. "Let us go down and greet our guests."

Down before the entrance, the echo of Finn's last call was dying away. There was only silence in response.

"I don't think there's anyone home," said Caoilte.

As if in reply, the ground began to shake.

"Yes there is," said Donn.

A crack began to run up through the cliff face.

"What do we do now?" Caoilte asked, watching the crack slowly widen.

"This game will be the druid's," Finn said. "We'll have to play it out the way it comes to us. Once inside, we need to create a row some way, make a diversion that will give Donn a chance to open the door." He looked to the dogs. "If Sabd is there, you lads must try to get to her. Protect her. I'll see to the druid."

"And me?" said Caoilte.

Finn gave him a little smile.

"You can see to the rest."

"Oh, thank you very much," he answered. He looked up at the opening. The halves of the cliff had now pulled aside with a rumbling, like vast portals sliding back, revealing an enormous tunnel leading into the shadowed depths.

The movement stopped. The tunnel waited.

"Well," Caoilte said resignedly, "shall we be going?"

They started in. But they were barely past the opening when it began to rumble closed, quite swiftly, behind them. They looked around to see the view outside rapidly narrowing. As it was nearly to a crack, a small figure darted through, stopping to face them.

"Cnu Deireoil!" Finn cried. "I told you not to come!"

"Too late," the harper said with a victorious grin.

Behind him, the cliff face boomed closed.

CHAPTER 29

A
Desperate
Try

"GOOD. LET HIM DIE WITH US," CAOILTE SAID WITH satisfaction. "It's what he deserves."

So the party, its numbers swelled by one diminutive harper, went boldly on into the druid's lair.

When Finn and his comrades came out of the end of the corridor and entered the enormous cavern, they stopped to look around them curiously.

"By all the gods, this is a place of horrors," Caoilte said with revulsion, ducking a batlike creature that swooped low overhead.

"It's even worse than I'd imagined," Cnu Deireoil added, sidestepping a slithering creature with a human head. "Why, that monster's used his powers to enslave hundreds of mortals here!"

Just outside the mouth of the tunnel, Donn pointed out a strange knob of shiny black rock protruding from the stone wall.

"There," he murmured to Finn. "That's what opens the cliff face. If I can get to it, I can work it easily."

But there was little they could do about it then. For from either side, a horde of the druid's armed creatures swarmed forward, forming a ring around the tiny band.

Caoilte's hand went to his sword hilts as the bristling wall of weapons closed about him, but Finn put a restraining hand upon his arm.

"We can't start something yet," Finn reminded his comrade urgently. "We must know where Sabd is first."

Caoilte nodded and, very reluctantly, relinquished his hold upon his weapon. They allowed the surrounding mob to hustle them forward across the vast floor of the Sid, toward the central stones, the fire, and the ring of tables.

As they passed through the circle of stones and neared the tables, most of the horde stopped, spreading out to form a cordon around the outside, filling the spaces between the obscene monoliths. Only a score escorted the band through a gap in the tables and into the area about the great fire. The dissolute Sidhe seated at the tables paused in their eternal debauchery to stare bleary-eyed at this band of newcomers. The wretched, half-bestial serving creatures stopped their incessant labors to gaze in wonder and in fear.

The party came to a halt near the hearth, the hybrid warriors closely surrounding the visitors.

"It's incredible that people of the de Danaan race can sink to this," Donn said with disgust, staring around him at the circle of fallen Sidhe.

"Even the Children of Danu aren't beyond being corrupted by their own powers," Cnu Deireoil told him.

"Careful now, everyone," Caoilte warned. "There he is."

For the Dark Druid himself had now come into view, moving grandly down one of the sweeping curves of staircase. But Finn had no eyes for him. They were fixed upon the young woman moving down beside him.

"Sabd!" Finn breathed, his face lighting with joy.

And as the girl saw him, a like glow of happiness flushed her pale skin.

When they reached the base of the stairway, the two hulking bears moved in swiftly, flanking Fear Doirche and the girl as they walked out into the central ring.

Once past the tables, Sabd started to rush forward eagerly, arms up in greeting.

"Oh, Finn," she cried, "I knew that you would come."

"Not just yet, my dear," the druid said sharply, and one of the bears bounded forward to block her way.

Dismayed, she was forced to retreat to his side, where

she stood, closely hemmed in by both bears. Fear nodded in satisfaction.

"Much better. We don't want to be getting too close to your . . . husband"—he spat out the word like something foul—"until we draw his claws." He looked to Finn, his expression smug and contemptuous. "So, I ask you to surrender to me now, 'Captain.' Give up your weapons to my warriors."

"And why should I do that?" Finn said. "I came to face you. Meet me on equal terms."

"On equal terms?" the druid repeated, laughing. "Oh, no. Not so long as the Storm Shield and the Mac an Luin are in your hands. Give them up, MacCumhal."

"I will not," Finn replied.

In answer to this, the Dark Druid lifted his rod in a swift move and touched Sabd with its silver tip.

Finn cried out in anger, but there was nothing to be done. In moments the silver aura had transformed her back to the familiar shape of the fawn.

"Now, MacCumhal, refuse me again, and it's a shape much more terrible than this that she'll wear next. I'm certain you've seen some of my other creations about the room. Act quickly!"

The silver tip moved closer to the fawn.

"All right, druid," Finn agreed reluctantly.

He passed the Storm Shield to a wolf-headed guard and began to unstrap his sword harness.

"We have no other choice," he told his companions unhappily.

Donn and Caoilte complied, passing their weapons to the surrounding guards, but the dark warrior was muttering, "I knew it. I knew it," to himself the whole time.

Now the Dark Druid, leaving the fawn between the two bears, walked forward confidently to confront his prisoners.

"You took your final risk in daring to come here, MacCumhal," he said. "This is my domain. Here I have my power. You thought to challenge it? How foolish." He gestured upward at the cavern's red sun. "It's my power which keeps that globe burning." He swept a hand about him at the hybrid beings. "It's my power which enthralls these slaves."

"If you are so mighty," Finn said, unimpressed, "why did you have to take my weapons?"

Fear stepped up close before him, lifting the rod to point.

"Because you stripped me of all my weapons with the trickery of your little dun," he said. "And then you humiliated me before your company. A company of mortals!"

He swept the rod sharply around on the last word, cracking it across the side of Finn's face, raising a welt there. Finn gave no sign of pain, continuing to fix the druid with a stony glare.

The rod swung back, the silver tip pointed at Finn's throat this time.

"Now," Fear said slowly, savoring each word. "I will make you crawl. I will make you dance. I will make you fly. This time *you* will entertain *my* company."

The degenerate Sidhe about the tables shouted their approval and laughed with perverse glee at the prospect.

Cnu Deireoil moved forward to Finn's side, peering up under the rod to the druid, his face fearful, his voice piping and timorous.

"Wait, now, great druid," he said. "Before you deal with him, wh—what about us?"

The druid gazed down at him, first looking irritated by the interruption, then more intrigued as he saw the harper's face.

"Ah, little man! I remember you." He lowered the stick from Finn and tapped him lightly on the head. "I have some unfinished business with you as well."

"Not so hasty, great druid," the Little Nut said, trembling in a terror-stricken way. "I've a sorrow for what I did to you, so I have. Finn's yours now. You don't need to be harming us."

"What is this?" The druid seemed surprised. "Where is your loyalty to your great captain?"

"Loyalty?" Cnu Deireoil repeated with scorn. "Why, he nearly killed me when you took the girl from me. And he forced me to come here."

"You traitorous dwarf," Caoilte snarled. He tried to get at the harper, but two guards pulled him back.

"Please," the little man pleaded, "please let me prove it to you. I can prove my worth to you. I...I could entertain."

"Entertain? You?" the druid said, giving a laugh that was joined by the reveling company. "And what could you do?"

"Well, it has been said that I'm a fair musician," he modestly replied.

As he said this he glanced up at Finn. Unseen by the druid he gave just the slightest, quickest wink.

Finn looked from him to Caoilte. The dark warrior inclined his head a fraction in a gesture of understanding, though no faint shifting of his glowering expression revealed a change in him.

"All right, little one," the druid agreed, "let's hear you, then. I'm in no hurry to have my revenge upon MacCumhal. And if you don't please us with your playing"—he smiled sadistically—"well, there are other things we can have you do. But what will you play?"

"A harp is best, I think," he said.

"Then, musicians, give him a harp," the druid commanded.

A harp was passed to him. The druid moved back, taking his place at the tables. The fawn, still flanked by the bears, stood close by. Cnu Deireoil moved out in front of the others. He stood a moment, examining the harp, his fingers resting lightly on its strings. A frown of uncertainty wrinkled his wide brow and pursed his small mouth.

"Well, get on with it," Fear ordered brusquely.

"I will, then," the harper assured him. He cast a last look, filled with hope and fear alike, toward Caoilte. Then he began.

The tune, a soft, sorrowful, and lilting one, came falteringly at first. The little man's slender fingers, which used to fly upon the strings, seemed clumsy. Caoilte squeezed his eyes shut despairingly.

"Well, there's a last hope gone," he murmured darkly to himself.

"If that is your best playing, you would entertain us

better as a dancing hare," Fear said, looking around at his company with a cruel grin.

They laughed maliciously in response.

Cnu Deireoil glanced around at the circle of depraved faces. He looked at the grinning druid, then toward his comrades. His gaze went finally to the fawn, watching him so anxiously with its dark eyes. He steeled himself and tried again.

And now the notes began to come flowingly. The strings began to sing, spinning out not music alone, but a bright aura that fell upon the crowd. They began to listen, slave and master alike. The faces of the degenerate company grew rapt. Even the Dark Druid seemed absorbed, fascinated by the sudden skill of the little man.

Finn caught Donn's eye and gestured with a glance toward the door. Donn began to ease back through the ring of spellbound guards. Finn caught Caoilte's eye and passed a wordless message. The two sidled slowly, cautiously, toward the ones who held their weapons.

Donn worked his way unnoticed out of the ring, slipped through the circle of tables, and eased between two of the warriors in the outer cordon around the standing stones. He began to move stealthily toward the tunnel mouth and the stone knob that would open the outer door.

But as he passed into the open area beyond the stones, his movement seemed to catch the eye of the Dark Druid. Clearly not so much held by the music's enchantment as the others, he stared in puzzlement, then shook his head as if to clear it of the bright web the harp had spun. He looked again, and his face grew darker with his sudden rage.

"Stop that man!" he shouted, jumping to his feet to point after Donn. "It's a trick!" At the same time his other hand thrust out the druid rod to point at Cnu Deireoil.

From the silver tip there shot a stream of silver light. It slammed through the harp, shattering the strings, and burst against the little man's chest. He was lifted and thrown backward, tumbling across the floor to crash into the hearthstones and fall in a crumpled pile.

"Kill them all now!" the druid bellowed.

Donn turned and ran. But with the end of the music,

the guards came back to life. A weasel-headed one turned and cast a spear. It struck Donn in the back and he staggered, falling to the ground some distance from his goal.

But in the confusion Caoilte and Finn were still able to act. They leaped upon the guards, knocking them aside, seizing their weapons. They drove the startled few around them back.

"At them, all of you!" Fear ordered in his towering, overwhelming rage. "No more delay. No more trickery. Just finish them now!"

The Fian champions and their two hounds were immediately deluged by attackers. They formed a square, fighting back the waves of savage, beastlike warriors who now poured in from outside the tables to come at them.

"So much for that plan," said Caoilte, sweeping out to drive three warriors back. "We're in it this time . . . again."

"No worse than usual," said Finn. He knocked aside an axe blow with his shield, parried a sword cut, kicked a ram-headed giant in the groin, and added, "Well, maybe a bit worse."

The battle raged on, all Fear's warriors now crowded in around the four, filling the space between the tables and the fire. The debased and dissolute Sidhe, frightened by the violence so close, hid cowering beneath their tables.

Meanwhile, across the cavern floor, outside the circle of the fight, Donn stirred.

Slowly one of his arms moved back. With an effort he managed to grasp the haft of the spear with his hand. It had struck just below his shoulder blade, the point piercing the sinewy muscle there and not penetrating deeply. He gave a great tug, grunting with pain as the point came free. Tossing the spear away, he crawled forward, heading for the tunnel. He went unnoticed by all the others, whose attentions were now focused on the melee.

In the center of it, Finn and his companions fought on savagely and swiftly, using all their power, skills, and courage to keep off the milling pack. Bodies began to pile in a rampart about their feet. Blood ran in streams across the stone floor, glinting in the red glare of the fire and the

crimson globe. The animal-headed warriors began to hesitate before their untiring violence.

"Kill them," the druid shouted. "The man who hesi-
tates will crawl on his belly for eternity!"

They reluctantly moved in again.

Donn reached the tunnel mouth. He crawled to the
base of the wall just below the protruding bit of stone.
There was no guard about him, as all the warriors were
engaged in the fight. He lifted his head, gazing up toward
the black knob. It seemed to be very far away.

Finn and the others were more hard-pressed now. The
threats of the ranting Dark Druid were enough to overcome his warriors' fear of the two men and their hounds.
The poor creatures sacrificed themselves bravely in their
desperate attempts to strike their trapped foes. The four
were finally beginning to wear down.

At the cost of his fingernails, Donn managed to drag
himself up the wall of rough stone. He hung there,
exhausted, panting heavily. Then he gathered himself
determinedly and thrust out a hand. It struck the dark
stone, shoving it in.

As a grinding sound arose within the wall behind it, he
slid limply to the floor, unconscious.

The grinding sound became a rumbling that grew
swiftly louder, the noise echoing even above the sounds of
the fight.

"The outer doors!" shouted the druid. "See to it, some
of you! Quickly!"

A number of Fear's bestial warriors left the fight and
rushed toward the tunnel mouth. But they were not quick
enough. As a ram-headed one reached out to grab the
black knob of stone, a sword cut took away his arm. It
came from Lughaid, who now moved forward, leading the
Baiscne men out of the tunnel.

They surged into the main cavern with shrill battle
cries and engaged the startled warriors of Fear, driving
them back. As they did, the densely packed ring of
fighters about Finn and his comrades broke apart, the
druid's creatures turning and moving out to face their new
opponents.

In moments the floor of the Sid was the scene of scores

of separate combats. The flickering, blood-hued light of the raging fire cast giant, madly writhing shadows of the combatants all about on the cavern's floors and walls. The battle was savage, the beast-headed men of Fear desperately trying to hold back the onslaught of Finn's men. But even the fierce-looking creatures, with numbers more than twice those of their opponents, could not match the ferocity of the Fian warriors in their full battle rage. They slashed through the druid's host like scythe-bearing farmers harvesting fall wheat, quickly taking the fight into the inner circle, fighting about the grotesque stones and upon the tabletops.

In moments it was clear that the battle was turning upon Fear Doirche.

"Follow me!" he told the bears. "And bring the fawn!"

Swiftly they moved back from the tables, passing through the ring of stones and crossing the floor toward the nearest stairway.

"He's taking her!" Finn cried, pointing out their departure to Caoilte.

They were engaged with only a handful of Fear's warriors now, and the Baiscne men had nearly reached them.

"Go after her!" Caoilte said. "Take the hounds. We can deal with the rest!"

Finn made no argument.

"Bran, Sceolan, with me," he said and, leaving the battle to his comrades, hacked a way through his opponents into the clear and sprinted away, the hounds at either hand. Ahead of them, the fawn was moving reluctantly along, being driven ahead by the two hulking beasts. By the time they reached the base of the stairway, Finn and the lads were closing rapidly.

Fear looked back and saw their approach with alarm.

"Stay here," he commanded the bears. "Kill anyone who tries to follow me!" Then he swept out his druid rod to touch the fawn, using its power as before to force her ahead of him, up the stairs.

The bears turned and set themselves to meet the attack of the charging three. But Finn and his hounds did not hesitate. Finn dove upon one of the beasts while Bran and Sceolan leaped for the other. Finn's bear rose up and struck out with its forepaws, but he slammed the blows aside with a sweep of the Storm Shield and swung a powerful sideways cut that took away the crown of the animal's head.

It toppled backward, already dead. Bran and Sceolan, meantime, had fastened themselves to the other bear, dragging it aside. With the way clear, Finn vaulted over the fallen beast and leaped on up the stairs. Behind him, the hounds fought a snarling, rending battle with the Dark Druid's remaining pet.

Out on the floor, the battle was continuing, the warriors of Fear Doirche fighting doggedly on, but with no real heart, as if they had no choice but to sacrifice themselves for their master.

Caoilte was having no trouble dispatching any who still dared to challenge him. But as he heaved a lanky, weasel-headed attacker into the fire, his foot struck something. He looked down upon the limp and huddled form of Cnu Deireoil.

He crouched down to examine the little man. He was very still, his clothing, face, and hands scorched from the energy of the druid's rod, the shattered remains of the harp upon his chest.

"Cnu Deireoil," Caoilte said sorrowfully, putting out a hand to touch him. "Is it really dead that you are?"

"Of course not," came the reply as the harper opened his eyes, grinning up at him. "But I thank you for your keening over me."

"Why, you rogue!" the dark warrior angrily exclaimed. "What do you mean, playing the dead man that way?"

"With the swords flashing all about me, I thought that it was the safest way to be," he answered.

"Well, you're right enough in that," Caoilte agreed. "Stay here until it's finished."

He started to get up, but the little man grabbed his arm to restrain him.

"Wait," he said urgently. "Where is Finn?"

"Up there," Caoilte said, pointing upward toward the spiraling stairway far above them.

There, with the circle of the cavern floor dwindling

beneath him, Finn climbed on in his pursuit of Sabd and the Dark Druid.

The fight with the bears had delayed him long enough to let Fear Doirche gain some distance upon him. But the druid was moving much more slowly, forced to drive the balking fawn ahead of him. As they passed above the midway point and climbed toward the narrowing peak of the cavern, Finn was again closing in very rapidly.

They reached a landing outside a row of small tunnels. It was crowded with red-capped men, none more than waist high, who had left their tinkering within the warren to look down with curiosity upon the fight.

As the Dark Druid swept through them, they scattered in terror before him. They closed ranks behind him, babbling excitedly, only to be scattered again as Finn charged onto the landing.

He pushed through the milling flock of them, reached the base of the next flight, and gazed upward. No more than a score of steps above was the druid, who looked back to see him, then, with a snarl of rage, swung the rod back to point down at him.

The silver tip flared. Finn threw the Storm Shield up before him in defense as a stream of light shot from the rod. It struck the curved surface of the shield and caromed away, only to explode against the inner wall just beside him in a blossom of sparks.

The force of the blast so near him knocked Finn sideways. He slammed against the rail and teetered there a moment, then began to topple forward, over the edge.

CHAPTER◇30

Vengeance
and
Salvation

FINN WAS STARING DOWNWARD AT THE CAVERN FLOOR
with its fire and its milling combatants as he began to fall
toward it.

Then, dozens of tiny hands were clutching him, hauling
him back to safety. He turned and looked around him at a
surrounding group of the little men.

"I thank you for that," he told them gratefully.

"It's our pleasure," a bearded one told him. "You just
be after the Dark Druid, lad. Five hundred years we've
labored for him here. He's our own enemy as well!"

Fear Doirche, seeing Finn recover from his attack, had
continued his climb. Finn started after him again, but this
time more slowly and with much more caution. For the
druid now continued to pause at intervals and fire another
burst of the energy at him. And though the strange metal
of the shield turned the shots away, Finn had to stop and
cover himself each time, giving Fear a chance to keep
ahead of him.

They spiraled upward, upward toward the cavern's
peak. They climbed past the level where the incandescent
globe was suspended. The crimson light radiating from it
was intense here, the heat nearly searing, the air filled
with an acrid scent like that of white-hot iron. Both men
were bathed in sweat now as they labored on, and the
fawn dragged itself wearily from step to step on wobbling
legs.

Finally their journey reached its end. The stairway came onto a final landing, a narrow, railed gallery that circled the cavern just beneath the peak. Above arched the rough-hewn rock surface of the cavern's roof. Below hung the druid's glowing sun, blocking all view of the cavern floor.

The druid stopped there and turned to face his pursuer. He fired another energy bolt from his rod, but Finn's shield turned it away to explode against the opposite wall. Finn moved toward him and he backed away, pushing the fawn behind him, directing bolt after bolt of his power toward Finn.

The warrior strode on, shifting the Storm Shield to deflect each shot, his determined gaze fixed on Fear Doirche.

They circled the peak that way, reaching the top of the stairway once again. Fear glanced down, then back to Finn.

"You've nowhere left to run," Finn said. "If you go down, my warriors will have you."

"I'm not afraid of them," the druid said with continued arrogance, drawing himself up proudly.

"But you should be afraid of me, druid," Finn told him coldly. He took another step toward him. "Release her now, and I will still let you keep your life."

The druid cast a desperate look around him. Finn took another step, the Mac an Luin lifting in his hand.

"Release her now, Fear," he ordered, "or you will die."

"No!" the druid shouted. He jumped backward and the rod swung around, its lethal point touching the fawn's neck. "So long as I have her, you can't harm me. Put down your weapons, or *she'll* be the one to die here!"

"Not this time," Finn said. "You'll only kill us anyway."

"I will surely kill you," he callously admitted, "but your Sabd would not be harmed. Refuse, and you will watch her be destroyed. You may take your vengeance upon me then, but it will do her no good. Think, Finn. You can exchange your life for hers."

"It's more than that," Finn said. "If you destroy me, it'll leave my comrades in jeopardy and hundreds of others still slaves to your power."

"What do they matter?" Fear harshly replied. "Nothing matters now but the woman. The woman that you love! I know that love holds you. Oh, yes, I know! In that terrible obsession we are one, my enemy!" The silver tip of the rod began to glow. "So decide quickly, MacCumhal. Very quickly!"

Finn looked from the trembling fawn to the druid, hesitating, his face filled with uncertainty.

But the fawn, listening, seeing the agony in Finn, drew herself up in a determined way, her body tensing, her slender legs growing taut. Then, in a sudden, courageous move, she dove from beneath the rod's tip and ran toward Finn.

The druid reacted swiftly, swinging the rod about to point after the fleeing Sabd. The tip flared brightly.

"No!" cried Finn, stepping toward her.

The beam shot out. It struck the floor of the landing just beneath her, bursting in a shower of lights. The fawn was thrown forward, tumbling headlong to land before Finn's feet, sprawled motionless.

In shock, Finn moved toward her, starting to lean down. But the druid's voice stopped him.

"Hold there, MacCumhal!" it said, grating out the words.

He looked up to see the glowing tip pointed at his own face.

"Why did you do that?" Finn asked him in anguish.

"I had no wish to," the man said, a sorrow in his own words. "Believe that. I loved her."

"Then why didn't you let her go?" Finn asked. "She only wanted freedom!"

Fear's dark countenance convulsed with sudden rage.

"No," he growled. "She wanted you! It was you who killed her. You who had to come for her, who forced me to this! And for that, I will destroy you now!"

The rod lifted again, the silver tip rising to point at the warrior's face. Once more the tip began to glow.

But as the beam shot out, a form hurtled from the stair top onto the druid's back, knocking him forward. The rod was knocked aside, its bolt of light diverted to crack against the stone above.

Fear Doirche now swiveled to try to grapple with the thing upon his back. Its long, spindly legs wrapped about him like a spider's and it clawed at him with bony, taloned hands.

As the two swung around, an astonished Finn caught a glimpse of the skull-like head of Miluchradh. Fear managed to break free, turning to face her, but it was only for an instant. Before he could lift his rod in defense, she was upon him again, hurtling herself against his chest.

He staggered backward with her upon him, colliding with the rail. Her hands went to his throat and she leaned forward, forcing him back. He fought desperately, one hand trying to yank her away, the other striking at her with the rod. But the rage and madness that now twisted her wasted face seemed also to have generated an immense power to her shriveled limbs. She hung on, pressing forward, until his back was arched out over the rail.

"You see what I am?" she shrieked, her face close to his. "You did this to me. Now . . . now you are mine, my love!"

She leaned forward, crawling onto his chest. He flailed out wildly, but her weight finally overbalanced them. They rolled backward over the rail, tumbling down, still locked in their embrace, landing upon the globe.

There was an explosion and a flare of light, sparks rising up in a high arch to touch the roof and then fluttering back. Finn threw up an arm to shelter his eyes against it. But it died in an instant, leaving no trace of druid or druidess.

Finn stood for a moment, staring down in astonishment. Then a low moan brought him around.

The fawn was stirring.

Quickly he moved to kneel by her, lifting the sleek head gently to cradle in his lap. As he did so, he realized with a look of wonder that the slender form was beginning to shimmer with a silver light.

Far below him, on the cavern's floor, the explosion had drawn all eyes upward. The fighting stopped. Then the combatants looked about them in wonder as shimmering halos of silver light enveloped all of the druid's creatures. Before the astonished gazes of Finn's men, the forms within the translucent cocoons transformed, and the lights faded, leaving hundreds of fully human men and women stretching and looking about them with delight.

"We're free!" a woman cried. "The druid must be dead! We're all set free!"

Most of the warriors of Fear threw down their weapons, raising arms in surrender to the Fian men.

"We're no longer your enemies," one told Caoilte. "We're free of the Dark Druid. Please let us leave this place!"

"What should we do, Caoilte?" Lughaid asked.

"Let them go," he answered. "We've no more quarrel with them."

"And what of them?" the young warrior wondered, pointing to the degenerate de Danaans still cowering beneath the tables.

Caoilte pointed to a number of the one-time slaves who had retained their weapons and were now advancing upon their former masters, faces grim with obvious intent.

"Let them deal with that vermin," he said pitilessly. "They've years of torture to repay."

"Look there," said a warrior, pointing upward. "That light's failing."

Indeed, the red glow of the massive globe was fading, like a superheated ball of metal removed from the smith's forge.

"If the Dark Druid is dead, the magic that powers it is gone, too," said Caoilte. "Lughaid, see that everyone gets out of this place. See to our wounded. Help these poor wretches, too. I'm going to see what happened to Finn."

As he crossed the floor and started up the stairway, Bran and Sceolan rose from the body of the second bear. They were a bit ruffled and sported a few scratches as evidence of their fight, but the second creature lay dead beside the first.

"Good lads!" Caoilte told them. "Come with me. Finn may need help!"

As they climbed upward, the freed slaves of Fear Doirche began to stream from the cavern, up the corridor, out into the daylight many had not seen in years. The light of the globe was fading swiftly, but the great fire, stoked higher by the Fian men, was sending out enough ruddy, flickering light to illuminate the vast room.

Above, Finn was still cradling the head of Sabd, but now restored, like the others, to human form again. She moaned, shifted uneasily, and then her eyes opened.

"Finn," she said weakly, "you have come." Then there came a look of surprise at her own voice. "And I . . . I am a woman?"

"The druid is dead," he told her. "The spell that was on you is broken forever."

"That doesn't matter anymore," she told him urgently. "It's only important that I can tell you of your son!"

"My son?" he said, shocked.

"Yes, yes. He is ours. I've given him a name—Oisin. But please listen now. There's little time." She was breathing in a labored way, forcing the words out. "He is hidden. There is a little vale not far from here, deep and steep sided. At its bottom a small cave. He is there. You might never have known. But now you can find him. Find him."

"First I must see to you," he said.

"There is nothing to do for me," she said more weakly. "I can feel it."

"No," he said fiercely. "I won't believe that. I've freed you. We'll be together now. We can go anywhere. Sabd, the world is yours again!"

"I am glad to be a woman a final time with you," she said. She lifted up and pressed her lips to his. Then, drained by the effort, she let her head fall back against his cradling arm. Her voice came faintly, the words touched with regret: "I only wish . . . I might have held my baby . . . one more time."

When Caoilte and the hounds reached the top of the stairway, they found Finn still sitting, the form of his wife still cradled in his arms, his head bent over her.

"Finn," the dark warrior called.

Finn's head lifted to him.

"Sabd," Caoilte began, "is she—"

He stopped. For the look in his friend's eyes had given him his answer.

The band of men halted at the base of the mist-shrouded vale. Cnu Deireoil astride his horse, Donn, bandaged and pale but proudly on his feet, Caoilte, Lughaid, and the others of the Baiscne clan all halted as Finn moved forward.

He advanced slowly, almost fearfully, toward a small cave mouth. The two hounds sat on either side of it as if on guard.

As he reached them, he patted the massive heads.

"Good lads for finding this," he said.

He crouched down, peering into the shadows of the cave. There was no sound and no movement from within.

He hesitated, glancing back toward his comrades. Then he put on a determined look and, crouching down, entered the hole.

The others waited, watching expectantly, hopefully, fearfully. For what seemed long moments there was no sign. Then there came a whimper, and then a more forceful cry.

Finn reappeared, crawling backward. He raised himself up and turned to them, a squirming object in his hands.

They surged forward to meet him, surrounding him, staring down at the object with fascination. It was squalling lustily now, its face red and puckered.

"Is it all right?" Caoilte asked, staring in wonder at the tiny being.

"From its fine yelling it surely sounds well enough," Cnu Deireoil said, grinning. "A grand bard it ought to be!"

The infant, now appearing to recognize the presence of this circle of staring men, ceased its crying, gazing curiously up at them with eyes of a brilliant green.

"It has the eyes of Sabd," Caoilte remarked.

"This is no 'it,'" Finn told them sharply. Then he smiled proudly down upon the child. "This is my son! *Our* son, Oisin!"

He bundled the infant warmly, tenderly, in his own cloak, and then the party moved away, out of the vale, out from the shadow of the mountain of the Dark Druid, back toward home.

Glossary

Here is the approximate pronounciation of some of the
more difficult names:

Baiscne	Bask-na
Caoilte	Kweel-ta
Cnu Deireoil	Nu Der-ee-oil
Cumhal	Koo-al
Cainnelscaith	Kennel-skath
Daighre	Dair-y
Fear Doirche	Fear Dwar-ka
Fionnachaidh	Finn-ak-eye
Garbhcronan	Garv-kronan
Lughaid	Lew-y
Miluchradh	Mil-uk-ra
Sabd	Sa-va
Sceolan	Sko-laun
Suanach	Swan-ak

The following are terms about which the reader might
appreciate having some further information:

Almhuin (All-oon) The name of the home fortress of Finn
MacCumhal. It was previously land owned by Nuada
Silver Hand, a past High-King of the Tuatha de Danaan
and grandfather to Muirne, mother of Finn. It is today
known as the Hill of Allen and is located near Kildare.

Ban-Sidhe (Ban-Shee) Simply translated as "Woman of the Hidden Folk," the term has today come to be a label for a hideous apparition which wails mournfully to announce the coming death of a true Irishman. Like the leprecaun, it is a much degenerated remnant of the old beliefs, its sources unknown to most in the modern world.

Ben Guailbain (Ben Gul-ben) This brooding mountain, now known as Benbulben, is located near the present-day city of Sligo, near the west coast of Ireland. It was a favorite landmark of the poet William Butler Yeats.

Bruighaid (Brew-y) The official entrusted with the running of public houses of hospitality in Ireland. A most honored profession.

Bruidhean (Breen) A public house of hospitality, usually set up on the junction of several roads. It was intended to serve the needs of any traveler without charge and is an excellent example of the characteristic hospitality for which the Irish are known.

Dagda One of the greatest champions and oldest members of the Tuatha de Danaan. He figured prominently in the destruction of the Fomor hold on Ireland, hundreds of years earlier, afterward refusing the kingship of his people. In later mythology, he becomes a sort of earth-father figure to the mortal races.

Daire Donn (Dar-y Don) A descendant of the monstrous Fomor, he gathered an enormous force from many lands, dubbing himself High-King of the Great World. His attempt to invade and conquer Ireland was thwarted by Finn and the Fianna in the famous Battle of the White Strand, near Bantry, on present-day Dingle Peninsula.

Danu The queen of the magical isle known as Tir-na-nog (Land of the Ever Young). She aided an outcast and wandering tribe of mortals, giving them magic powers. In gratitude they took the name Tuatha de Danaan (Children of Danu). She became the supreme goddess in the pantheon of the mortal races.

Dord Fionn This great horn of Finn MacCumhal was used to call all the Fian bands together in a hosting. Legend says that one day, when Ireland is in great danger, it will sound again, calling Finn and his warriors from the hidden cavern where they now sleep.

Fidchell (Fid-kell) A board game, somewhat like the modern game of chess. It was a favorite pastime for Irish warriors, after war and hunting. Its mystical qualities figure prominently in various legends, including an early one concerning King Arthur.

Lochlanners Bands of ruthless sea raiders who constantly plagued Ireland, it is likely they are what we now know as Vikings. The legends often associate them with the Fomor, a race of monstrously deformed pirates who date back to some of the oldest tales.

Mac an Luin Meaning "Son of the Waves," this sword and a shield dubbed the Storm Shield are the fabled weapons of Finn. Legend links their creation to mystical forces of the Sidhe, and to the magic properties of Balor One-Eye, the giant leader of the Fomor.

Manannan MacLir Known as a god of the sea, this strange character appears often in the legends, usually as a mentor of the Tuatha de Danaan, sometimes as a prankster to the mortal races.

Muirne (Mur-na) As mother to Finn, she protected him from death after the High-King of Ireland and her own father, the druid Tadg, conspired to kill his father, Cumhal MacTredhorn. She had Finn hidden safely away until he reached manhood and was able to battle for his rightful place.

Nuada Once the High-King of the Tuatha de Danaan,

he was called Silver Hand because of a metal hand that had replaced one lost in battle. He died in the final battle to free his people from their long enslavement by the Fomor.

Ollamh (Oh-la) The title of an Irish bard. The bards held a special position in Celtic society, being entertainers, journalists, and historians at once. The training was grueling, involving years of study and the memorization of many books of poetry. Of the many ranks of bard, Ollamh was the highest, with a prestige often nearly equal that of a king.

Sidhe (Shee) Meaning "People of the Hidden Places," this is another name for the Tuatha de Danaan.

Silver Strand The site of the great battle with the aforementioned Daire Donn, located on present-day Dingle Peninsula.

Tadg (Teig) The grandfather of Finn, a member of the Tuatha de Danaan, and a powerful druid as well.

Tara The political and religious center of the Celtic period in Ireland, this beautiful site can be found not far to the northwest of Dublin. The rings and mounds of the ancient fortifications are still identifiable and are well worth visiting.

Teach mi-cuarta (Chok mi-karta) This refers to the main structure of the Celtic fortress, a large, usually circular hall where the warriors gathered.

Tir-na-nog This translates as "Land of the Ever Young" although it is also known by many other names, including "The Land of Promise." Experts disagree on its exact location, but many place it somewhere in the western sea (the Atlantic).

Tuatha de Danaan (To-aha day Don-an) The mystical Children of the Goddess Danu, this race was original-

ly a mortal one. After coming to Ireland and wresting
control of it from the savage Fomor, they in turn lost it
to new mortal invaders. With the help of Manannan
MacLir they retreated to hidden palaces and became
the Sidhe, a once honored and powerful group who
have degenerated over the intervening years. In some
portions of Ireland the superstitions about the "Others" still persist. (The mounds that are said to mark
their dwelling places dot the countryside!) For most of
us, however, only a few, quaint creatures of folklore—
like the banshee and leprechaun—are all that's known.

ABOUT THE AUTHOR

KENNETH C. FLINT became interested in Celtic mythology in graduate school, where he saw a great source of material in this long neglected area of western literature. Since then he has spent much time researching (in the library and abroad in England and Ireland) those legends and incorporating them into works of fantasy that would interest modern readers.

Riders of the Sidhe, Champions of The Sidhe, and *Master of the Sidhe* tell of the Fomor invasion of ancient Ireland. *Challenge of the Clans, Storm Shield,* and *The Dark Druid* recount the saga of Irish hero Finn MacCumhal.

Mr. Flint is a graduate of the University of Nebraska with a Masters Degree in English Literature. For several years he taught in the Department of Humanities at the University of Nebraska at Omaha. Presently he is Chairman of English for the Plattsmouth Community Schools (a system in a suburban community of Omaha). In addition to teaching, he has worked as a freelance writer, producing articles, short stories, and screenplays for some Omaha-based film companies.

He currently lives in Omaha with his wife Judy (whose family has roots in Ireland) and his sons Devin and Gavin, and he is hard at work on his next novel.

Eighteen years ago, Dr. Kenneth Cooper started America running with the landmark publication of his first book, AEROBICS. Since then, millions of Americans have participated in an exercise explosion—not only running, but cycling, swimming and skiing.

Now, Dr. Cooper presents *new* and definitive guidelines for the safe approach to exercise in

RUNNING WITHOUT FEAR
(25546-0 • $3.95)

Dr. Cooper confronts the crucial question of what constitutes healthful exercise. He provides the runner with clear guidelines that will help you determine if you are pushing too much and putting your health in danger.

Bantam also has all these other ground-breaking titles by Dr. Kenneth Cooper to offer:

☐ 23546	AEROBICS	$3.95
☐ 24788	AEROBICS FOR WOMEN	$3.95
☐ 26083	AEROBICS WAY	$4.50
☐ 34422	AEROBICS FOR TOTAL WELL-BEING (A Large Format Book)	$11.95

Bantam Books, Inc., Dept. KC3, 414 East Golf Road, Des Plaines, Ill. 60016

Please send me the books I have checked above. I am enclosing $_____ (please add $1.50 to cover postage and handling). Send check or money order—no cash or C.O.D.s please.

Mr/Ms _____

Address_____

City/State _____ Zip _____

KC3—8/87

Please allow four to six weeks for delivery. This offer expires 2/88. Price and availability subject to change without notice.

THE UNFORGETTABLE *WEST OF EDEN* SAGA
CONTINUES

WINTER
IN
EDEN
BY HARRY HARRISON

The extraordinary novel *West of Eden* began the rich, dramatic
saga of a world where the descendants of the dinosaurs struggled
with humans like ourselves in a tragic battle for the future of
Earth. Now the saga continues. A new ice age threatens Earth.
Facing extinction, the dinosaurs must employ their mastery of
biology to swiftly reconquer human territory. Desperately, a
young hunter named Kerrick launches an arduous quest to rally a
final defense for humankind. With his beloved wife and young
son, he heads north to the land of the whale hunters, east into the
enemy's stronghold, and south to a fateful reckoning with destiny.

Buy both *West of Eden* and *Winter in Eden* (on sale August,
1987) wherever Bantam Spectra Books are sold, or use the handy
coupon below for ordering:

☐ **WEST OF EDEN** (26551-2 • $4.50 • $4.95 in Canada)
☐ **WINTER IN EDEN** (26628-4 • $4.50)

Bantam Books, Inc., Dept. HH3, 414 East Golf Road, Des Plaines, Ill. 60016

Please send me the books I have checked above. I am enclosing $_____
(please add $1.50 to cover postage and handling). Send check or money
order—no cash or C.O.D.s please.

Mr/Ms _____

Address _____

City/State _____ Zip _____
                                                    HH3—8/87
Please allow four to six weeks for delivery. This offer expires 2/88.
Prices and availability subject to change without notice.

VARAGOZA   UROLOGIST
RAFAEL
MAXMU
MAXIMO
MAXIMO

BANTAM
SHOP-AT-HOME
C·A·T·A·L·O·G

Special Offer
Buy a Bantam Book
for only 50¢.

Now you can have Bantam's catalog filled with hundreds of titles plus take advantage of our unique and exciting bonus book offer. A special offer which gives you the opportunity to purchase a Bantam book for only 50¢. Here's how!

By ordering any five books at the regular price per order, you can also choose any other single book listed (up to a $4.95 value) for just 50¢. Some restrictions do apply, but for further details why not send for Bantam's catalog of titles today!

Just send us your name and address and we will send you a catalog!

BANTAM BOOKS, INC.
P.O. Box 1006, South Holland, Ill. 60473

Mr./Mrs./Miss/Ms. _____
                        (please print)

Address _____

City _____ State _____ Zip _____
                                              FC(A)—11/86
Please allow four to six weeks for delivery.